THE FORGOTTEN FAMILY

Recent Titles by Beryl Matthews from Severn House

THE OPEN DOOR
A TIME OF PEACE
WINGS OF THE MORNING

THE FORGOTTEN FAMILY

Beryl Matthews

This first world edition published in Great Britain 2006 by
SEVERN HOUSE PUBLISHERS LTD of
9–15 High Street, Sutton, Surrey SM1 1DF.
This first world edition published in the USA 2006 by
SEVERN HOUSE PUBLISHERS INC of
595 Madison Avenue, New York, N.Y. 10022.

British Library Cataloguing in Publication Data

Matthews, Beryl
   The forgotten family
   1.   Adopted children - Fiction
   2.   London (England) - Social life and customs - 19th century - Fiction
   3.   Domestic fiction
   I.   Title
   823.9'14 [F]

ISBN-13: 978-0-7278-6427-7 (cased)
ISBN-10: 0-7278-6427-0   (cased)
ISBN-13: 978-0-7278-9175-4 (paper)
ISBN 10: 0-7278-9175-8   (paper)

All Severn House titles are printed on acid-free paper.

Typeset by Palimpsest Book Production Ltd.,
Polmont, Stirlingshire, Scotland.
Printed and bound in Great Britain by
MPG Books Ltd., Bodmin, Cornwall.

One

The tangle of children in the middle of the road were shouting, screaming and laughing. Queenie bounced about on the pavement, making as much noise as her many brothers and sisters. With a gurgle of delight, she launched herself into the middle of them.

'Get off, Queenie,' they shouted.

She kicked and fought with all her might. Although she was the youngest of ten, and tiny compared to the rest of them, she was a force to be reckoned with. There was nothing she liked more than a good scrap.

The fight broke up, leaving her giggling on the road with her favourite brother, pounding away with her little fists to show how much she loved him.

'Pack it in!' Harry roared as he tried to fend her off. 'I've had enough.'

'You're a coward, 'Arry.' She jumped on him for good measure, refusing to let him get up.

Grabbing his sister round the waist, he surged to his feet, tossing her over his shoulder. At twelve years old, he was growing into a strapping lad, and a two and a half year old girl couldn't do him much harm, as long as he kept out of the way of her flailing hands and feet.

'Watch her, Harry.' The eldest boy, Ted, was doubled over, out of breath. 'She'll catch you where it hurts if you're not careful.'

Harry grinned, looking down at his sister's bare feet as they thrashed about. 'I think she should have been a boy.'

They were all sitting on the curb; Harry had dumped his burden down and now sat beside her. The entire Bonner brood were in a row – dirty, ragged, and happy, oblivious to the filth

1

and squalor they lived in. Only the eldest had shoes, under-clothes were unheard of and, anyway, as it was summer, no one worried about things like that.

'Queenie,' a familiar voice called.

Ted gave her a push. 'Mum's shouting for you, urchin.'

Scrambling to her feet, she ran into the small slum house. It only had two rooms up and two rooms down, with a wash-house at the end of the yard, shared by four families. There were beds everywhere, and Queenie shared one with her sisters; two of them sleeping at the top and two at the bottom. There were only four girls in the family, the rest were boys, and Queenie preferred them. They were more fun.

'Look at the mess you're in.' Her mother swore as she stripped off the filthy frock, and dumped Queenie in the old tin bath full of water.

Squealing in protest, she tried to climb out, but this only earned her a sharp clip around the ear.

'Ouch!' With a growl of rage, she lashed out, but her mother was too strong for her, holding her in the water with ease. And to add to the torture, even her hair was washed.

'Why you cleaning up Queenie, Mum?' Harry wandered in. 'She'll be filthy again in five minutes.'

'Oh no she won't.' She tipped a jug of water on her daughter's hair, making her shut her eyes tight and splutter. 'Look at that. Get the dirt off her and she's got nice fair hair, and, with her bright blue eyes, she don't look half bad.'

Harry stood watching, his smirk changing to a frown when he saw a clean frock being slipped over his sister's head. It had even been ironed! 'What you doing this for?'

'Tell him, Fred,' Hilda ordered her husband. 'And you'd better tell the rest of them, as well. Don't want no trouble later.'

Queenie was glad she was out of the water and dry again. She didn't care for water. As her mother tried to get the tangles out of her hair, she watched her dad talking to Harry. She set her mouth in a firm line, trying not to yell as her hair was pulled so much it hurt.

Suddenly, Harry turned, his face like thunder. 'You can't do this!'

'Shut your mouth,' their mother shouted. 'It's none of your

2

bleeding business. We can do what we like. They're paying good money, and we need it.'

'If it's money you want I'll pack up school and get a job. You can't do what you're planning. It's cruel. She's one of us.'

'You try skipping out of school and you'll get the thrashing of your life. You're never gonna get out of this hell hole without proper learning. You can't do nothing about it. It's all settled.' She glared at her husband, wanting support, but he was keeping quiet.

Harry looked fit to explode and it frightened Queenie. He was always laughing and happy. She'd never seen him angry before. She ran over to him, throwing her arms around his waist and gazing up. 'What you angry for, 'Arry?'

Swinging her up into his arms, he hugged her tightly, then put her down and stormed out of the house.

She went to follow him, but was caught by her mother and dragged back. 'You'll stay here, my girl. You got people coming to see you soon, and I want you clean.'

She scuffed her toe over a hole in the oilcloth. 'Don't like being clean. I want to see 'Arry.'

'You'll do as you're told.' Her mother dumped her on one of the beds. 'Stay there and don't you dare move. I don't want so much as a speck of dirt on you.'

Picking at the frayed edge of the blanket, Queenie kept her mouth shut. Her mum never usually took much notice of her, but today she'd washed her and changed her frock. She was very worried now. Harry was mad about something, and all the others had gone quiet, looking in at her from time to time, their faces serious.

'You told them, then?' her mother snapped when her father returned.

'They know, and I've threatened to knock them all into next week if they cause any trouble.'

'Fine bloody mess we're in when we've got to do something like this.'

'Stop moaning, woman. Do you want to end up in the bleedin' workhouse? 'Cos that's where we're heading.'

Hilda's hands were shaking. 'You know I don't. Now, isn't it time they was here? They said ten o'clock this morning, didn't they? You sure they're coming?'

3

'Course I am. The man what asked me gave me a guinea as soon as I told him you'd agreed. And didn't he come and look at her himself?'

Seeing her mum and dad weren't watching, Queenie slipped off the bed and crept towards the door, only to be caught by the scruff of the neck, and hauled back.

'I told you to stay where you were,' her mother shouted and gave her a fierce shake.

'I wanna play with the others.' Her bottom lip stuck out in defiance.

'Well, you can't.'

Queenie's lip trembled, but she never cried. It never did any good.

The unusual sound of a carriage coming up their street, made her dad rush to the door. 'They're here.'

'Bout bleedin' time!' Her mother scooped Queenie from the bed. 'You behave yourself, you hear?'

The smart carriage and horses had caused quite a stir, bringing everyone out to have a look.

'Cor, look at that.' Queenie strained to get away from her mother's grip. She'd never seen anything like it before, not up close anyway.

A man got out and told Queenie, 'Stand by the door and let the lady see you.'

She was pushed forward, and she stared wide-eyed at the woman inside. The lady was wearing a very large hat, and Queenie thought it must be heavy to have that on top of your head. She wouldn't like it.

After a moment of studying her intently, the woman nodded to the man standing with her dad.

'All right,' he said. 'She'll do. Five pounds, we agreed.'

'Five guineas.' Her mother held on to her daughter tightly. 'We won't take less.'

After counting out the money and handing it to her dad, the stranger picked her up and put her in the carriage. Getting in after her to control her struggles.

What was going on? She didn't like this. Panic flooded through Queenie and she fought like a demon. 'What you doing? I don't want to go away. Let me go!'

'Behave yourself, and don't you cause the nice lady no trouble.' Her mother leaned in and glowered at her.

The carriage began to move and, in sheer terror, Queenie fought her way to the window, leaning through the opening and holding out her little hands. 'Mum, stop them! 'Arry, stop them. Help me, help me . . .'

They were moving quickly now, and Queenie watched helplessly as her brothers and sisters waved. Harry was crying. Why was he crying?

The man spoke; his voice was deep and stern. 'Sit still.'

'I don't wanna go with you.' Her voice trembled. 'Where we going?'

'I told you to sit still.'

At the authoritative tone of the man's voice, Queenie scrambled to the corner of the seat and huddled in a tight ball, confused and very frightened. They were going very fast and leaving her family behind.

The man glared at her, then seeing she was quiet, turned to the woman who hadn't uttered a word so far. 'I think you're crazy, Mary. Look at her.'

'She's beautiful.' The woman smiled at Queenie, and the man snorted in disgust.

'I should never have gone along with this crazy scheme of yours. Albert was making arrangements for you to adopt a baby.'

'I know, but it is taking too long, and I'm tired of waiting.'

'You can't take a child out of the slums and expect her to adjust to life in our class. She's probably never worn shoes, and all she has on is that old dress.'

When he reached out to lift up her dress, Queenie bit him, drawing blood. With a smothered curse, he pulled out a white cloth from his pocket and wrapped it around his hand. 'She's not even civilized.'

'Would you be if you had been born into those conditions?' Mary looked sad. 'They have one child after another, and I can't even have one. At least we can give her a better life. Thank you for finding her for me, Henry.'

'That's what brothers are for.' He reached across and patted her hand. 'I know how unhappy you've been not having children of your own, but I'm not sure this is a wise thing to do. We could have found you an unwanted baby.'

'No, I wanted a child who had little chance of a good life, and change that for her. They clearly didn't want her, but I do.'

Henry pulled a face when he remembered how easily his brother-in-law could erupt. 'I don't know what Albert is going to say when he sees her.'

'We'll have her nicely dressed before he comes home.' She smiled at Queenie again. 'Don't be frightened, child. You're quite safe with us. What is your name?'

'Queenie.' The woman looked quite nice when she smiled. Her mum never smiled.

'Oh dear, we shall have to change that. I think we'll call you Eleanor.'

Queenie began to shake. They were taking her away somewhere, and the woman was calling her a daft name. They were going to kill her! 'I wanna go home,' she shouted in terror. Her brothers and sisters had always surrounded her, and she wanted them here now.

'That is where you are going, Eleanor. To your new home. You'll have a room all to yourself, and a large garden to play in.'

But Queenie could not be comforted with promises. And the thought of having a whole room to herself wasn't right. She had spent her short life crowded into the small house, surrounded by her brothers and sisters. Would she ever see them again? Loneliness gripped her, making her curl into a tighter ball whimpering. As soon as she got out of this thing she'd run away.

It was a long journey and they'd stopped a couple of times, but the man had made her stay in the coach, watching her carefully. Eventually, the carriage passed through high gates, and all Queenie could see was trees and green grass. Being used to concrete and grey roads, the colour was so bright it hurt her eyes.

'Are you coming in, Henry?' his sister asked, when they stopped outside the house.

'No, thank you, Mary. I've done my part in finding you a child, now the rest is up to you. I would rather not be around when Albert returns.'

Mary laughed, a pleasant musical sound. 'You make him sound like an ogre.'

'I think I'll stay out of his way for a while.' Henry got back into the carriage, and handed Queenie out to a man wearing a green suit.

6

When the man put her down, she turned in a slow circle, looking for a way to escape. There wasn't one. The gates were shut, and there was a high wall for as far as she could see. Bursting for a wee, she ran over to a tree, squatted down and relieved herself.

A large woman wearing a black dress and a white pinny, rushed over to her. 'No, no, my girl, we have a proper place to do that.'

'I couldn't hold it no longer.' Her bottom lip stuck out. They were lucky she hadn't done it in the carriage.

The woman shook her head in dismay. 'Dear me, Madam, we are going to have a difficult time with this one.'

'She's a spirited little thing, Nanny,' Mary said happily. 'But isn't she pretty?'

Queenie stared at the woman who'd been called Nanny. She didn't seem too pleased about her being here, so perhaps she'd help her escape. Standing on tiptoe, she tugged at the pinny. 'I wanna go home. Will you open the gate for me?'

The only answer was another shake of the head.

'Bring Eleanor in, Nanny. We must make her presentable before my husband comes home.'

'Why she keep calling me that?' Queenie protested, as Nanny swept her up into her arms. As they went through a great big door, panic swamped her and she struggled fiercely. 'My name's Queenie an' I don't wanna be here. I want 'Arry,' she shouted. 'He'll come for me and set the coppers on you.'

'What is she talking about, Nanny?'

'The police, Madam.' Nanny put her down.

'Ah, I see.' Mary looked at the small, glowering child, and fought back a chuckle of delight. 'She bit Henry.'

Nanny kept a perfectly straight face. 'She's been brought up rough and used to defending herself, I expect. But she appears to be bright enough. Mature beyond her years.'

'Indeed. They have to grow up quickly where she comes from.'

The cold on her feet caught Queenie's attention, and she gazed down at the coloured tiles. They were very pretty. As frightened as she was, she couldn't help gazing in wonder at her surroundings, then padded around inspecting everything. It was all very clean, and so much space! Her whole street could sleep in here. Spotting an open door, she shot through it. This room was even bigger. She'd never seen anything like it.

'Eleanor.'

She wasn't going to answer to that soppy name, so she continued her investigation. There were shelves all around the walls, up to the ceiling, with coloured things in neat rows. The woman in the pinny was beside her. She reached out and touched one. 'What's these?'

'Books, and you'll be able to read them one day.'

'Blimey.' She looked up. 'You rich?'

'No, I'm employed by the family, and I'm going to look after you.'

'Don't need no looking after. I see to myself.' Her lip stuck out again but there was fear and confusion in her eyes.

'We must go up to the nursery and get you ready to meet your new father.' Nanny took her by the hand, and nodded to the mistress.

Queenie felt the soft carpet on the stairs tickle her feet. Halfway up, the stairway curved, and once she reached the top she could look down and see where she had been. Giving a nervous glance through the banister, she edged towards the wall. It was very high up here. The room they took her to made her gasp in astonishment. There was only one bed, and loads of room left over.

'I'll send Molly to help you. The new clothes are in the dressing room. I have ordered various sizes, so something should fit. I'll be back in a short time.'

When Nanny urged her through another door, Queenie tried to run when she saw what waited for her. 'Ooh, no! Water.'

She was caught easily by the woman who stripped off the dress and put her in the bath.

'I've bin washed,' she shouted, starting to struggle. Then she stilled when something caught her attention, and she began sniffing the water, soap, and anything near her. What was that smell?

'That's lavender.' Nanny looked amused as she soaped Queenie. 'It's nice, isn't it?'

She wasn't too sure about that. She continued to sniff loudly. She'd never smelt anything like it.

A younger girl came in. 'Madam said I was to give you a hand.'

'Dry Eleanor, please, and then we'll dress her in the new clothes.'

The girl smiled at Queenie. 'Hello, my name's Molly.'

'I'm Queenie,' she said, fed up. The vigorous drying made her teeth rattle. 'I bin washed already today.' She glared at the girl, hurt that she had to suffer this *twice*.

Molly just laughed, and took her back into the bedroom, where the girl began to dress her.

'Ugh!' Queenie tried to take off the knickers they'd just put on her. Even though they were nice and soft, she didn't want them on her.

'No, Eleanor.' The large woman spoke firmly. 'Little girls mustn't go around without undergarments on.'

This whole business was frightening her. Next something was put over her head and a dress on top of that. She squirmed uncomfortably with so many clothes on. When they put socks on her feet that was too much. She wanted to cry, but she wouldn't, because that always got her a cuff round the ear.

'There are shoes of different sizes, Molly, so find her something that fits.'

Seeing they weren't taking any notice of her, Queenie had the knickers and socks off in a second, throwing them on the floor.

'Oh, dear, Nanny.' Molly picked them up. 'I don't think she's used to wearing these.'

'She isn't.' Nanny put them back on, sighing. 'Poor little thing is going to hate shoes.'

'This pair fit. Stand up and see how they feel, Eleanor,' said Molly kindly.

They felt awful. How could she run in these? The dam burst, allowing the pent up tears to flow down her face. She wailed, 'My name's Queenie, and I want to go home. I want 'Arry.'

'There, there.' Molly gathered the distressed child to her. 'This ain't right, Nanny. The mistress should've got a baby, not a little child who's gonna miss her family.'

'My . . . name's . . . Queenie.' She was sobbing in earnest now, and felt she had to keep telling them this, because they didn't seem to listen.

'I tell you what – ' Nanny sat on a chair and settled her on her lap – 'we'll call you Queenie when the mistress isn't around, but when she's here we'll have to call you Eleanor. Will that be all right?'

Queenie allowed Molly to mop up her tears, and make her blow her nose.

'Why – ' she hiccupped – 'can't I go home?'

'Because you live here now.' Nanny smoothed a hand over Queenie's hair. 'You must promise me to be a good girl, or it will be hard for you. Your parents don't want you back, and if the master and mistress feel they can't keep you, then you might be sent to a home. You'll be much better off here. Do you understand?'

Something stirred in Queenie's mind; a vague memory of something that was spoken of with fear in their street. Workhouse. That was bad. Even her mum was afraid of that.

'Do you understand?' Nanny repeated.

She nodded, terrified, and clung to the woman who was showing her kindness. 'Don't let them do that to me.' Looking up, her eyes wide with hurt, she asked, 'Why don't my mum want me?'

'There are too many of you, and she can't feed you all.'

'I don't eat much,' she whispered, as the tears flowed again.

Two

'Wake up!'

Queenie was being shaken gently, making her eyes snap open as she tumbled off Nanny's lap, landing with a thud in her unaccustomed shoes. She gazed up at the woman who had brought her here, her teeth chattering with fear.

'She was worn out.' Nanny stood up. 'So I let her sleep for a while.'

'My, don't you look pretty.' The woman bent down and straightened the bow in Queenie's hair. 'I've brought you a present. It was mine when I was a little girl.'

Queenie took the dolly from her. It had blonde ringlets, a bonnet, dress, shoes . . . Queenie lifted the skirt . . . and those things. It was pretty, but she didn't want it. All she wanted to do was go home and be with her brothers and sisters. It was too quiet here. Saying nothing, she put it on the bed.

'I don't think she's used to having toys to play with.' Nanny turned to Queenie. 'When someone gives you something, you must say thank you.'

'Thank you.' She didn't know why she had to say that, but the woman with the pinny was being kind to her. Suddenly, she began to fidget, crossing her legs and looking round in panic.

'Ah.' Nanny scooped her up and hurried to a room along the corridor where there was a privy. Queenie thought it was funny having it inside the house.

After she'd finished her clothes were tidied again. She jumped, spinning round in alarm, at the sound of gushing water. She looked in the toilet bowl and saw it was clean, and it had little blue flowers all over it. Where did the water go? This was strange and must be thoroughly investigated. Harry wouldn't half laugh if he could see this. She wished her favourite brother was here with her.

'I don't suppose you've seen one like this, have you?'

'Ours is at the bottom of the yard and stinks rotten.' She sniffed. 'This don't.'

'The master is very keen on having proper water closets. Now, you must be hungry. We'll have lunch in the school-room, and then you'll be taken to see the master.' Holding Queenie by the hand, she led her to another room.

'What shall I do with this?' Molly held up Queenie's old frock for her mistress to see.

'Throw it away.'

With a yelp of alarm, Queenie lunged, grabbing it out of the maid's hand and clutching it protectively. 'That's mine!'

'But you don't need it any more,' the woman said to the glowering child. 'You have nice clothes now.'

'Don't want rotten clothes.' Burying her face in the frock, she took a deep breath of the familiar smells of home.

'I suggest we let her keep it for a while,' the nanny said. 'This must be very frightening for her, and it is something she's familiar with.'

'Very well, you know best about these things. Have your lunch and then try to persuade her to leave it up here while she comes downstairs to meet her new father.'

Queenie sat on the frock at the table so she could leave her hands free to eat. First, Molly served them with soup, but when she picked up the dish to drink it, she was stopped.

'No, you must use this.' Nanny put a shining spoon in her hand.

It was a messy business as Queenie struggled with the unusual implements. She didn't know what was wrong with fingers; that's all they used at home. But the grub wasn't bad.

Her frock had to be changed, even though they'd put a bib round her neck, and her face washed – again! All the time she held on tightly to her old frock, not daring to let it go.

The woman came back. 'Ready to go downstairs, Eleanor?'

Nanny stooped down in front of her. 'Leave your frock here. It will be quite safe.'

Queenie clutched it desperately. 'No, you'll take it away.'

'I promise you it will still be here when you come back.' Nanny eased the garment out of her hands, then she said very softly, 'You can trust me, Queenie.'

Reluctantly, she put the frock on the bed next to the dolly,

12

and then glared fiercely at everyone. 'Don't touch!'

'We won't,' Molly assured her.

'There's a good girl.' The woman held out her hand. 'Come on, Eleanor.'

Sticking her hands behind her back, she clumped down the stairs, scowling. 'Can I go home soon? I don't like it here.'

'You'll soon get used to it.' The woman helped her down the last couple of steps.

Queenie beat her off. 'Don't touch!' She turned to the woman everyone was calling Nanny to make sure she was following them. 'You tell her to let me alone.'

Nanny just laid a hand on her head to guide her through the door in front of them.

'This is Eleanor, my dear.' The woman pushed her towards a man standing by the fireplace.

When he gazed down at her, Queenie knew she was in trouble. She had learned very early to tell when someone was angry and could lash out. But she had also learned not to show fear. She glowered back in self-defence. 'Don't you hit me. My brother 'Arry will come and bleedin' well bash you up.'

He spun round to face the woman. 'What have you and Henry done, Mary? I told you I was arranging for us to adopt a baby. How old is this child?'

'Two and a half.' She was unperturbed by her husband's wrath. 'Don't worry, dear, she will soon settle down.'

He shook his head, turning to study Queenie again. 'Are you sure that's her age? She sounds older.'

'They have to grow up quickly in the slums or they don't survive.'

The look he gave his wife was one of disbelief. 'Do you really believe you can take a child of this age from that environment and bring her up as our daughter?'

'I'm certain we can do it.' Mary laid a hand on her husband's arm. 'She seems a bright child, and will soon adapt to her new life.'

Albert looked very doubtful as he studied the small child in front of him. 'This is highly irregular, Mary, you know that, don't you?'

'Yes, but Henry has been thorough and her parents have signed a document saying they give up all claim to her. He's a lawyer and knows what he's doing.' She gave her husband a pleading look. 'We can give her a much better chance in life. They didn't want her, Albert, but I do.'

Albert gasped when Queenie kicked him on the shin with her new shoes to gain his attention. 'You take me home.'

Nanny caught hold of her. 'You mustn't do that, Eleanor. The master isn't going to hurt you.'

'My name's Queenie,' she shouted, stamping her foot in frustration, fear making her lash out at everyone near.

'That's a pretty name.' The man didn't look quite so angry now; he seemed sad.

'It's my proper name.' She swiped quickly across her eyes to stop the tears falling.

'I wanna go home. Go tell 'Arry. He'll come for me.'

'Don't you think you would rather live here in this nice house?' He bent down reaching out to steady her as she shook her head so fiercely she nearly toppled over. 'Well, before you decide, why don't you come and have a look at the garden? It's very large, and there's a pond with fish in it. Want to see it?'

Now he was at her level he didn't seem so frightening. Her natural curiosity took over. The fish sounded fun . . . perhaps a little look. 'Suppose.'

'Good, come on then.' He straightened up and held out his hand.

'Don't need help. I walk on my own.'

'Independent little thing, isn't she?' he remarked to his wife.

Queenie clumped along beside him, relieved to see Nanny was coming with them. Once outside, she gasped in wonder. It was a blooming park! 'Crumbs, where's all the houses?'

'This is our garden,' the man told her.

Her mouth dropped open. 'This is all yours?'

He nodded, then winced when she loudly said, 'Bloody 'ell!'

She stomped on to the grass, looking back at him. 'Where's the fish, then?'

'I'll show you in a minute.' He frowned at Nanny. 'Why is she walking flatfooted like that? Is there something wrong with her feet?'

'No, sir, she isn't used to wearing shoes, or . . . ahem . . . undergarments.'

14

His attempt to stifle a groan wasn't successful, making Queenie take a couple of steps back. Just to be on the safe side. He had big hands.

'Come here, child.' When she hesitated, he bent to her level again, holding out his hand. 'I'm not going to hurt you, I want to look at your shoes.'

Edging cautiously towards him, she stuck out one foot. 'They're 'orrible.'

'Hmm, I can see that.' He removed the shoe. 'Now the other one.'

Sticking out the other foot, she breathed a sigh of relief when they were both off. Then she sat down on the grass and whipped off the socks. Standing up again, she did a little jig, loving the feel of the grass under her bare feet.

'That's better, is it?'

She nodded, taking a closer look at him. 'You got funny coloured eyes.'

'Hmm, so I've been told.' His mouth turned up in amusement at her direct remark. 'I believe they are called amber.'

'Oh.' She had to have another look at those. 'Mine are blue.'

'Yes, I can see that, and they're very pretty.'

No one had ever told her that before. She shuffled a bit closer. He didn't seem too bad because he'd taken off her shoes. Perhaps . . . She pointed towards her knickers. 'I don't like these rotten things, neither.'

'You must keep those on.'

From the tone of his voice, she knew it would be daft to disobey. Shame. Still, she'd got rid of the shoes.

'Mary.' Albert straightened up. 'Buy her some lighter and softer shoes. And, Nanny, put shoes on her for only a short time each day until she gets used to them.'

'Yes, sir.'

'Does that mean you approve and we can keep her, my dear?' Mary asked hopefully.

'I don't think we have any choice. Her family obviously don't want her, and if she's returned to them, they will most likely try to sell her again.' He studied the little girl waiting impatiently for him to show her the pond. 'She's an appealing child, and I dread to imagine what might happen to her if we don't keep her here.'

15

His wife couldn't hide her delight. 'She won't be any trouble. You will hardly know she's here.'

'I have agreed that we keep her, but I am most upset. You should have consulted me first, but it is done now.'

'I thought you would be pleased, Albert. You are always concerned about the plight of children like her, and urging Parliament for better education rights for the poor.' Her mouth turned up at the corners. 'You are very vocal on the subject, I am told.'

Queenie was getting fed up with waiting and began to wander off. She'd find the fish herself, and maybe a gate. It would be easy to run now she had nothing on her feet. A large shadow loomed beside her.

'The pond is this way, child.'

She followed as they walked round bushes taller than her, and then she let out a gasp. It was big, and there was a stone thing in the middle, running with water. She took off towards it as fast as her legs would carry her.

The man caught her. 'Careful, water can be dangerous if you fall in.'

He kept a firm hold on her while she knelt down and peered into the pond. The fish swimming around were a pretty colour. She cast a glance at the man beside her. 'You eat these?'

'No, they live here. This is their home.' He watched her face intently. 'Just as this is now your home.'

Sitting back on her heels, the pleasure drained from her face, her eyes pleading. 'It's nice here, but I wanna go home. I want my brothers and sisters. I want 'Arry. He looks out for me.'

His face turned to thunder. 'I'll kill Henry for allowing you to do this, Mary.' Then he stormed off.

Albert Warrender couldn't remember when he'd been so angry. His wife was a kindly soul and he understood her anguish at remaining childless. It was also a great sadness to him, as well, and he had agreed that they adopt an unwanted baby – and goodness knows, there were plenty of them – but plucking a child of this age away from her family was cruel. Henry was a damned fool, but he had never been able to deny his sister anything she wanted.

When he looked back on the ten years of marriage to Mary,

he was filled with sorrow. After losing three babies, it had become clear that his wife would never be able to carry a child full term. Her health was fragile, and she suffered from long bouts of depression. Theirs was a barren marriage, but he loved her dearly and hadn't been able to hurt her by seeking his freedom and marrying again.

On reaching the stables he saddled the huge stallion, knowing that he needed the challenge of controlling the fractious animal. He had been a Member of Parliament for the last eight years, and he loved the work. After the loss of the third baby, Mary had been desperately ill and they had moved out of London. He'd agreed to an adoption, hoping that, and the country air, would bring the laughter back into Mary's life, and his own, but he had never expected her to do something this outrageous.

It was dark when he finally returned home, dusty, spent, and not much calmer. The house was quiet as he made his way up to the nursery. He hadn't been able to banish that distressed little face from his mind. He was deeply concerned for the child and shouldn't have taken off like that, but he trusted Nanny to take good care of the girl. She had been his nanny and was no longer young, but he had kept her as a permanent member of his household, to live her declining years in peace and security. He knew there would be little chance of that now. He must see that she had all the help she needed.

Opening the door quietly, he stepped into the room. The bed was empty. Concern swept through him, until a slight snuffling sound made his gaze dart towards the corner of the room. Huddled on the floor was the tiny child, clutching something to her.

'She doesn't like the empty bed, sir.'

He spun round at the sound of the voice behind him.

'She's used to sleeping with her three sisters.' Nanny spoke softly. 'I've put her back in bed four times, but she won't stay there.'

'What's she holding?'

'The frock she arrived in. She won't let it out of her sight. It's the only thing she's got to remind her of home.'

He controlled his temper, remaining outwardly calm. 'Get two extra pillows, please.'

17

While he waited for those, he picked up the sleeping child, noting that her face was wet with tears. When she whimpered, he spoke gently, his deep voice seeming to soothe her. 'All right, little one, we aren't going to hurt you.'

Placing her in the bed he then tucked the two pillows either side of her. Queenie immediately turned and snuggled up to one of them.

'She might stay there now.'

'I never thought of that, sir. Now the bed doesn't seem so empty to her.'

They both remained, staring down at the little girl.

'What a mess!' Albert ran a hand through his hair. 'I've got to sort this out, and see that everything is done legally.'

'Yes, sir, she will have to stay now.'

He nodded grimly. 'How is my wife, Nanny?'

'Happier than I've seen her for a long time. She came to read her a bedtime story, then kissed her, and went away smiling.'

'Mary is not strong, and the burden is going to fall on you.' He looked down fondly at the woman who had been like a mother to him. 'I'll see you have more help. If it gets too much, you must let me know at once.'

'Thank you, sir. If you could release Molly from her other duties, that would be appreciated. She has a nice way with children.'

'I'll arrange that.' Closing his eyes for a brief moment, overcome with fatigue, his mind ran through the things he had to take care of. Then he opened his eyes again. 'Poor little devil.'

'Now, don't you get upset.' Nanny gave him a confident smile. 'She's only a baby and will soon forget her other family.'

'I hope you're right. But I'm going to tear Henry limb from limb!'

Queenie watched them leave the room, and then buried her nose in the frock. I won't forget, she raged silently. Mum and Dad didn't want me, so I'll forget them, but I won't forget Ted, Harry, Jack, Tommy, Bert, Charlie, June, Pearl or Maggie. I won't forget them. Never!

* * *

Henry Jenson's house was only two miles away, so Albert took a fresh mount and headed for his brother-in-law's. It was nearly midnight when he arrived. The door was opened as soon as he thumped on it, and he swept aside the flustered servant, storming into the library, knowing that was where he would find Henry.

'I ought to give you the thrashing of your life,' he growled, as Henry leapt to his feet in alarm.

'Now, Albert.' He backed away, hands up in defence. 'Mary will take good care of the child.'

'Mary can't take care of herself, let alone a troubled child who has been taken away from her family and dumped with strangers. The little girl's terrified!'

'That bad, is it?' Henry visibly blanched as his brother-in-law took a menacing step towards him.

'Now, I'll tell you what you're going to do. From this moment on, that child is mine! You are to see that the adoption is legal. I don't want *anyone* else to have a claim on her.'

'I'll see to it—'

'You make sure you do. You make this legal – and with the utmost speed. If anyone comes near me trying to take her away, then I'll break your bloody neck. Is that understood?'

'I'll get straight on to it, Albert.' Henry swallowed and cleared his throat.

'Make sure you do, or your life won't be worth living. And as soon as it's done I want a notice put in the papers announcing the adoption.'

Henry nodded and held up the decanter. 'Er . . . would you like a drink?'

'No, I wouldn't!' Albert stormed out of the house, and galloped away.

Henry collapsed into a leather armchair, pulled the stopper out of the decanter with his teeth, and filled a glass with brandy, his hand shaking. Albert Warrender was a powerful man with hair as black as night, and eyes that glowed like burning coals when in a rage.

He emptied the glass in one gulp. Facing his sister's husband when he was in that kind of a mood was not something he would recommend to anyone.

Three

October 1905

Her father, standing in his usual spot by the fireplace, glowered at her, but Ellie wasn't fooled for a moment by his stern expression. She loved him and knew his every mood, and his mouth had twitched when she'd walked into the room. Even so, although he had always been extremely indulgent and forgiving of her boisterous moods, she knew he was near the end of his patience.

'Your explanation had better be good, Eleanor. This is the second school to send you home in disgrace.' He held up the letter she had given him from the school. 'Fighting again!'

'I'm sorry, Father.' She cast a quick glance at her mother, but she was sitting with her hands in her lap, clearly content to leave this matter with her husband. Ellie drew in a deep breath. 'They started it first.'

'They? There was more than one this time?'

'Um . . . three, actually.'

He looked up at the ceiling for a moment, then back to her, his amber eyes smouldering. 'I can see they gave you a black eye. I was hoping that the exclusive finishing school would teach you to control your temper. Why were you expelled when it was three girls who attacked you?'

Shuffling carefully, she slipped out of her shoes. For some strange reason she always wanted to get rid of her shoes when she was in trouble. 'I think I broke one girl's nose, and the other two—'

He held up his hand to stop her. 'There's no need to go into details as I shall, no doubt, be receiving letters from the outraged parents.'

'They deserved it, Father. They called us – me names, and I wasn't going to put up with that. Just because they come from titled families they think they're better than anyone else.' She held his gaze boldly. 'I told them you were richer and more noble than all of them.'

'You were defending *me*?' He shook his head in disbelief.

Ellie squinted at her father with one eye – the other one was fast closing – and tried a little smile. 'They said their fathers were in the House of Lords, but you were only in the Lower House. I told them that all the intelligent men were there, and it was where all the hard work was done. Their fathers only took their seats to sleep off a heavy lunch.'

'Oh, my.' Albert turned away, his shoulders shaking.

'It was quite a scrap.' There was pride in her voice. 'And I won, but they went crying like babies to the Head.'

Her father faced her again, in control. 'You should not have reacted in such a violent way. I'm quite capable of defending my own reputation.'

'I know.' Ellie studied the floor, trying in vain to hide her smile. 'They said I took after you. Perhaps one day women will be allowed in Parliament.'

Albert turned to his wife. 'What do you suggest we do with her, Mary? Do you know of another school who would take her, or has her reputation spread to the length and breadth of the land?'

'But Father – ' Ellie didn't give her mother a chance to answer – 'I shall be eighteen in January. Must I still go to school? I would much rather stay here with you and Mother.'

'She does have a point, Albert.' Her mother's tone was gentle, as always. 'A private tutor for a short time might be the answer. I don't believe Eleanor is at fault here. The other girls started the argument, so she should not have been expelled.'

'It does appear to be that way, but the argument should not have turned into a fight. However, your suggestion of a private tutor is a sound one. I shall advertise at once.'

'Does this mean I can stay at home?' Ellie asked, relieved. She hated being away from home.

'I believe it is the only answer.' Her father shook his head in mock dismay. 'We have run out of suitable establishments for you.'

'Oh, thank you.' She threw her arms around him and hugged him tightly, then did the same to her mother, only gently this time. Ellie couldn't remember her ever being very strong, but she had become rather pale and listless of late. It was distressing to see her deep auburn hair prematurely sprinkled with grey, and her green eyes clouded with pain. 'I'm sorry to have worried you again, Mother. I don't mean to get into trouble, but I just can't seem to avoid it.'

'You have been a joy to us from the moment you arrived, Eleanor.' She kissed her daughter's cheek with undisguised affection. 'Now you must go and explain to Nanny, but don't stay too long. She is rather frail.'

'I won't tire her.' Ellie had always loved Nanny, and it was sad to see her so weak, but she must be a good age, as she had also been her father's nanny.

She ran towards the door, eager to see the woman who had practically brought her up, and skidded to a halt at the sound of her father's voice. She turned.

'Shoes,' was all he said.

'Oops, sorry.' Scooping them up and not bothering to put them on, she made for Nanny's rooms. Her father had provided her with a private place of her own, containing everything she could need for her comfort. The elderly woman was being well looked after, which was only right.

Knocking on the door, she waited until she heard the call to come in, and then opened the door enough to be able to peer in. 'Hello, Nanny. I've come to confess my sins.'

'Thrown you out again, have they?'

'It wasn't my fault.'

'No, it never is.' She waved a hand. 'Come in and let me see you.'

Ellie was delighted to be home again and to see the woman she thought the world of.

Nanny allowed her cheek to be kissed. 'I don't know why your father sends you to boarding school. It would never work, and I've told him many times.'

'Well, I'm staying home now, and he's going to get me a tutor for a while.'

'Whoever he employs will not stay long.' Nanny shook her head as she gazed at her former charge.

'Why am I such a trial to everyone, Nanny?' Ellie sat on the floor, sighing deeply, tossing her shoes under a small table. 'I can't seem to keep out of trouble.'

'You've always had an independent streak, speaking your mind without a thought that you may upset someone. It's your nature, and we've never been able to change you, though we've tried very hard to make a lady of you.'

Ellie grimaced.

'Don't worry; we all love you the way you are. Now, you can make me a cup of tea while you're here.'

'I've been told I mustn't stay too long and tire you.' Ellie scrambled to her feet and headed for the small stove in the corner of the room. Nanny was served the same food as everyone else, so she didn't need to do any cooking.

'And that's another thing we've never been able to break you of.' Nanny gestured to Ellie's bare feet. 'You've never liked shoes, have you, Queenie?'

Ellie stopped dead as the name ran through her mind, sounding familiar, and for some odd reason, making her feel sad. She turned, a deep frown on her face. 'What did you call me?'

'Eleanor.'

'No, you didn't. You called me Queenie.'

'Did I?' Nanny laughed. 'My silly old mind. I must have been thinking about someone else. Hurry up and make the tea. I'm gasping.'

While Ellie busied herself, she couldn't get the name out of her head. Why had it given her such a start when she heard it? They didn't know anyone of that name. With a shrug, she concentrated on what she was doing. Must be someone from Nanny's past. When people got old they often dwelt on days gone by, but she couldn't help feeling there was something she should remember.

'What are you doing, Eleanor? It doesn't take all day to make a pot of tea, surely?'

'Just coming.' Ellie laughed. That sounded more like Nanny. She took the tea and placed it on the table.

She only stayed long enough to drink the tea and explain what had happened at school. Then, seeing that Nanny was getting tired, she left.

Her father was no longer in the library, and her mother had retired for her afternoon rest so, putting on her shoes, Ellie made for the stables, knowing her father would most likely be there with his beloved horses.

She was right. He was running his hands over a beautiful dappled grey mare, and talking to one of the grooms. She charged up to them. 'She's beautiful. I haven't seen her before.'

'I only bought her three days ago.' He watched the horse nuzzle Eleanor. 'Looks like you're friends already.'

Ellie laughed when the mare gave her a playful shove. 'I think she likes me.'

'That's good, because I bought her for you.'

She nearly knocked her father off his feet in her eagerness to thank him. 'Can I ride her now?'

'Go and get changed and I'll come with you, just to make sure the animal behaves herself.'

Ellie tore back to the house, excitement bubbling away. This was a good day. She had got off lightly for being expelled, and she wouldn't have to go away to school again. She now had a horse of her own and, best of all, her father was coming riding with her. She loved that. He was such fun.

The horse was lively, but Ellie had no trouble controlling her. Her father had always insisted that she ride astride, as it was safer than side saddle. She had been riding for as long as she could remember, and like her father, she adored horses. There was no greater pleasure than a gallop through the countryside, whatever the weather.

After half an hour, they stopped on a rise to admire the view.

'You suit each other,' her father said. 'So, what are you going to call her? Her bloodline is good.'

'I don't know. She's a regal looking animal.' Her mind ran over suitable names for her, but one jumped immediately to thought. 'I know, I'll call her Queenie.'

There was silence for a while as her father studied her intently. 'What made you choose that name?'

'Nanny called me that while I was making tea for her.' Ellie frowned as she remembered. 'Is she all right, Father? She said her mind was wandering, but the name seemed familiar. Do we know of anyone by that name?'

'No, not now.'

The tone of her father's voice made her look up sharply. He sounded hesitant, which wasn't at all like him. Her curiosity got the better of her and she asked, 'But we did in the past?'

'It was a long time ago. You were only a baby.'

24

'Oh, was she a servant?'

'No, she was just someone we knew for a while. Now, back to the name. I think you should call her Silver Princess.'

Ellie studied the animal's coat as the sun caught it, making it shimmer. 'That's a perfect name for her.'

'Good.' Her father remounted. 'We must return now because I have to be in London this evening.'

Sorry that their short time together was over, she got back in the saddle, and they cantered towards the house. She was bursting with questions about the person they had known when she'd been tiny, but her father had changed the subject, and she knew more questions would not be answered. Still, it explained why the name had sounded familiar. And Nanny's lapse of memory. Perhaps she could get her to tell her about the girl sometime. That was something else she had never been able to control – her curiosity. She knew she had nearly driven her parents and Nanny mad when she was little with her unceasing questions. Dismissing it from her mind, she laughed at her father and urged Silver into a gallop, leaving him to catch up.

Nanny's slip was causing Albert concern. The name Queenie had been dropped after only two weeks of her arriving. The first few months had been difficult. Eleanor had never mentioned her parents, but had constantly asked for her brothers and sisters. The one she had missed the most was called Harry, and it had torn the heart out of Albert to see her forlorn little face as she had asked repeatedly for him. It had been a relief when that had stopped and, fortunately, she had been young enough for the memories to fade as she'd settled into her new life. They had invited lots of their friends' children to play with her. By the time she was ready for school, she appeared to have no recollection of her former life.

They had all been careful to show her love, and to let her know they were happy she was with them. And that had been the truth. Mary adored her, and his wife's bouts of depression became a thing of the past. Nanny had loved and protected her, and he had been, and still was, captivated by her lively intelligence and independent nature. It hadn't always been easy, of course, as she seemed to attract trouble, but he could never be angry with her for long. She had a beguiling way, and an openness that was, at times, disconcerting. His Eleanor did not tolerate rudeness from anyone, no matter what their station in life. There was still an element in her of the battling little girl they had brought into their home, and he was pleased it hadn't been entirely educated out of her. When he thought back to the time he had first seen her, and then looked at her now, he loved and admired her unconditionally. She was a happy girl, but was that happiness now in danger?

There was a worried look on his face when he knocked on his wife's door, then he strode in. Mary was propped up in bed reading a book.

'How are you feeling, Mary?'

'I'm fine, Albert.' She smiled. 'Did you enjoy your ride?'

'Very much.' Settling in a chair beside the bed, he told her how delighted Eleanor had been with the mare.

'I knew she would be, but why do you look so worried, my dear?'

'Nanny called her Queenie today, but quickly recovered by saying that she had been thinking about someone else.'

Mary closed the book, and sat forward. 'Did Eleanor recognize the name?'

He shook his head. 'No, but she wanted to call the mare Queenie. I talked her out of it, though.'

'That's a relief.' Mary settled back on the pillows again. 'If she hears the name too often, she may begin to remember things. My first memories are from about the age of four. I certainly cannot recall anything when I was younger than that, but being removed from her family was traumatic for her, and you never know if memories might surface.'

'That's what worries me. We are going to have to tell her one day—'

'It is only right that she knows, Albert.' Mary reached out for his hand. 'She has been happy with us, and still is, and as far as she is concerned, she is our daughter. But I'm going to ask you to wait until she's older and more able to cope with the revelation.'

He sighed. Like his wife, he was reluctant to do anything to make Eleanor unhappy, and finding out that she was not their natural child would most certainly upset her. And he was quite happy to leave it for a while longer. He was a coward when it came to telling her. 'Very well, but I will have a word with Nanny to make sure she doesn't make the same slip again.'

'That would be wise.' Mary closed her eyes for a moment, and then opened them again, looking directly at her husband. 'As you are aware, the doctors have given me only a few months to live, so by asking you to wait, I am leaving this burden with you.'

'Doctors have been wrong, Mary. If you take life easy . . .'

'No, my dear, we must face this. I have already stayed alive for longer than I thought possible, but I did so want to see our daughter grow into a woman, and she is almost there. In my bureau there is a box with all the details of Eleanor's past family. You may give it to her when you feel the time is right, or burn it.' She gave a tired smile. 'I know you love our daughter, and will always do what is right for her. But I would like your promise that when the time comes, you will not leave her to face this alone. Stand by her side, Albert, and support her, whatever she decides to do.'

'I promise.' Albert stood up. 'Now you must rest, Mary. I'm sure you are worrying unnecessarily. We will *both* be here to look after her.'

Four

Over the next week Ellie enjoyed the freedom of roaming the estate, riding Silver and visiting Uncle Henry. He had one child, a son two years younger than her, who was away at school.

She gave the horse over to the care of one of her uncle's grooms after her ride, and bounced into the library to find him.

'Hello, Eleanor.' He glanced up from the letter he was writing. 'Are you bored with nothing to do? This is the third visit this week.'

'I never get bored.' She sat down and grinned. 'I've come with a message from Mother. She would like you to join us for dinner tonight. Father's coming home.'

'You may tell her that I would be delighted to come.'

'Good. Have you heard from Philip this week?'

'He's returning tomorrow. He has been unhappy at that school and your father has suggested that the tutor he is engaging should teach both of you.'

'What a splendid idea! Father is so sensible.' Ellie giggled when her uncle pulled a face. 'I don't know what you have against him. I do believe you are afraid of him, Uncle Henry.'

'You've never seen him in a rage. It is a frightening sight. I did something once he was furious about, and it's not an experience I would wish to repeat.'

Settling back in the chair, Ellie rubbed her hands together in glee. 'Do tell.'

He sighed, gazed at her intently for a while, and then gave a crooked smile. 'It was a long time ago, and everything turned out well in the end.'

Disappointed, but not prepared to let the subject drop, she leaned forward again. The past had been mentioned again, and she was beginning to get curious – more than curious really. 'Have we got family skeletons, Uncle Henry?'

The look he gave her was wary. 'No more than any other family. Why do you ask?'

'Well, the other day, Nanny called me Queenie—' She leapt to her feet as her uncle choked on a mouthful of whisky, and thumped him on the back. When he had recovered, she continued. 'I asked Father who she had been talking about, and he said it was someone they'd known a long time ago, when I was a baby. Do you know who it was?'

'I'm afraid I can't help you there.' He took a cautious sip of his drink, dismissing the subject.

But Ellie never gave up easily when she wanted to know something. There was a mystery here, and she found it intriguing. 'Do you mean you can't help, or that you won't?'

'Both.'

'Uncle Henry,' she said laughing, 'all any of you are doing is making me more curious.'

'Ah, and we know that's a dangerous thing to do, don't we?'

'You'll have to tell me one day.'

'It isn't anything important.' He waved her away. 'Now, be off with you, and thank your mother for the invitation.'

She stood up. 'Don't be late. Father likes to dine on the dot of eight thirty.'

'I wouldn't dare.' He visibly shuddered.

She left the house, amusement showing on her face. The way her uncle had spoken about her father made him sound like a monster, but he wasn't like that. He could be stern when it was needed, and with her that was often, but the rest of the time he was kind and understanding. He was patient with her, and gentle with her mother. She couldn't wish for a better father.

As soon as she was in open country, she urged Silver into a gallop. Of course, she should have a groom with her, but that wasn't necessary when she was so close to home. At least, she didn't think so, but her father would have other ideas if he found out she had left the estate on her own. Still, Philip would soon be home, so she would have a companion for riding and lessons. It would be more fun with the two of them, and they got on well together. Philip's mother had died when he had been born, and they were more like brother and sister, than cousins.

29

Bending low in the saddle, she urged, 'Go girl.' She hoped the tutor liked riding because she didn't want to spend all her time indoors studying. Neither would Philip. He was a good rider, as well. Though not as good as her.

Albert was muttering irritably as he strode along the corridor towards his office in the Palace of Westminster. They had just wasted precious time on something of no importance, and it had left no time for his speech on improved education for the poor. This subject had been his passion long before Eleanor had arrived in his life; since then it had been an obsession. Some progress had been made over the last fifteen years, but not enough. One way to alleviate poverty was to give children, whatever their background, a decent education, thus equipping them to help themselves. Next on his campaign list was housing.

When he threw open the door and marched in, a young man leapt to his feet so violently that his spectacles slipped sideways. He straightened them at once.

'And you are?' Albert barked, still seething.

'Stanley Rogers, sir. You asked me to meet you here at two o'clock. About the position of tutor to your daughter.'

'Ah, yes, of course. I apologize for keeping you waiting. Please be seated.'

For the next hour, Albert questioned Mr Rogers with great care. His references were excellent, but did he have the temperament to deal with Eleanor? If the young man showed any weakness, she would have him running for cover. His mouth twitched when he thought about his daughter. He couldn't love her more if she had been his natural child.

He decided to see if Mr Rogers was easily frightened. 'My daughter is strong-minded and has been expelled from two schools – the last one a finishing school of high repute – and she refuses to be turned into a lady. She is not tolerant of fools and will defend what she feels is right – with some force.'

Stanley Rogers didn't even blink. 'Then it would seem wise to continue her education at home, sir.'

'I am of that opinion as well.' Albert scrutinized the proposed tutor. He had interviewed five applicants so far, but he rather liked the look of this one. He was only twenty-five, but age was irrelevant in this case, character was the important factor in a tutor for Eleanor. He was tall, and rather too thin, and first impression was of an ordinary looking man, until you saw his grey eyes, magnified slightly by the spectacles. They shone with determination and intelligence. Albert was aware that he had also been assessed during the interview. Mr Rogers wasn't going to take any chances, either. He admired that in the young man.

'Are you married, Mr Rogers?'

'No, sir. I would not contemplate marriage unless I was in a position to provide adequately for a wife and family.'

Sensible, as well. Albert had made up his mind. He wanted to engage him. 'My daughter is seventeen and bright, showing great interest in the changes happening in this country. I also have a nephew who is two years younger than her. He is unhappy away at school. Would you be prepared to teach them both?'

'Yes, sir.'

No hesitation. 'I must warn you that this might not be an easy task.'

'I enjoy a challenge, sir.' His grey eyes glittered at the prospect.

'I shall, of course, pay you extra for the additional pupil.' Albert stood up. 'The position is yours if you think it would suit you. There is a small, but comfortable gatehouse you may live in while you are with us. If things work out, we shall need you for two years or more. My daughter will not require a tutor for long, but my nephew must have a good education so he can eventually take over the reins from his father.'

Stanley Rogers also rose to his feet. 'That is very satisfactory. I look forward to working for you, Mr Warrender. I have your address in Kent, so when would you like me to start?'

'As soon as you can. My daughter has, no doubt, been running wild this last week whilst I have been in London.'

Stanley smiled for the first time. 'Would tomorrow afternoon be suitable?'

'Perfect.' Albert watched the new tutor walk out of the room, and felt sure he had made the right decision. Appearances could be deceptive, but he had a strong feeling that Eleanor would have to watch her manners around that young man.

His deep chuckle echoed around the empty room as he remembered the little girl from the slums, whose vocabulary had been limited but colourful. It had taken them some time to stop her swearing. Eventually the past had been put behind her and forgotten. She had settled down to a happy life with them. He hoped it stayed that way and her past remained buried, but he knew that when she reached eighteen she should be told. There now seemed to be a danger of her finding out from some chance remark, and that would be intolerable. He had to be the one to break the news to her, but how he dreaded it.

'You look lovely.' Ellie's mother nodded in approval. 'That pale cream is perfect and brings out the golden tint of your hair.'

Ellie wriggled, pulling a face. 'I dislike dressing up like this. Why do we have to wear so many clothes?'

Her mother's smile was indulgent. 'At least you have no need of stays. Your youthful figure is slender enough.'

'I'm never going to lace myself into those abominations.' Ellie lifted her hands in disgust. 'When are women going to be sensible and wear clothes that are comfortable and easy to move around in? Did you hear that Mrs Dunsford was riding a bicycle and her skirt got caught in the wheel? She came off and broke her arm.'

'I did hear, but what was our neighbour doing on one of those contraptions? With motorcars and bicycles it appears that the horse and carriage is not good enough. And some foolish men are even trying to fly!'

'Oh, Mother.' Ellie laughed at her bewilderment. 'These are all exciting inventions.'

'You may think so, Eleanor, but I much prefer to use the carriage.' Mary walked over to the window. 'Our guests are arriving. Come, we must not leave your father to greet them alone.'

Hurrying downstairs they managed to take their places just as the guests were announced. It was to be a small dinner party this evening with only three guests. One of them, Henry, had already arrived. The other two were Lord and Lady Douglas.

'Allow me to introduce our daughter, Eleanor.'

Ellie stepped forward, curtsying as gracefully as she was

able. It was not a skill she had ever mastered properly. She had never met the Douglas's before, but they appeared pleasant enough. She spoke when spoken to, and never put a foot wrong to embarrass her parents. She was well aware that these were often occasions of political expediency for her father.

'Are you not at school?' Lady Douglas asked.

Before she could reply, her father said, 'We have decided that Eleanor would benefit more from a private tutor. I have engaged a suitable man and he will be arriving tomorrow.'

Ellie made the mistake of glancing at her uncle, who gave her a wicked grin. With the utmost difficulty she managed to remain composed. He knew that her father had just saved her from having to admit that she had been expelled for fighting. Not that she cared what anyone thought of her, but she did care what people thought of her parents.

To her relief the dinner gong sounded and, as she turned to her father, she saw his mouth was twitching in amusement. That was nearly her undoing. He didn't care, either, but neither of them would upset her mother. Uncle Henry, holding out his arm to escort her to the dining room, saved her from a fit of the giggles.

During the meal her mother was talking to Lady Douglas about clothes, servants and things like that, but that was of no interest to Ellie, she was listening intently to the men airing their views on politics.

Noting her avid interest, Lord Douglas gave her a condescending smile. 'And what do you think of this woman, Pankhurst, and her Women's Social and Political Union?'

'The WSPU.' Ellie sat forward eagerly, but, before saying anything else, cast her father an enquiring look. When he inclined his head, giving her permission to speak freely, she continued. 'I believe it's a brave thing to do, and much needed. Times are changing fast. Women can no longer be confined to the home. They have brains and want more from life, and a say in the laws of the land. They would be an invaluable asset in politics, but I fear they have a long and hard battle in front of them.'

Lord Douglas looked surprised by her vehemence. 'You have a daughter with strong opinions, Albert.'

'I have always encouraged Eleanor to express her views. She has a lively interest in how our country is run.'

'And run very efficiently by men. Can you imagine the mayhem if we allowed women to have the vote, and even stand for Parliament?'

'Do you believe it would be detrimental to the good of the country, Eleanor?' her father asked.

'No, I don't. Women live in the real world. They bring children up and deal with the hundred and one things that crop up daily. And it isn't only the wealthy classes you need. It's the ordinary women struggling to feed their families. They're the ones who know the harsh realities of life, and what changes are needed. I believe it's madness to exclude a whole section of society on the excuse that they are women.'

'And are you intending to become one of these militant women?'

'Oh, no, Lord Douglas, I leave politics to my father. He has liberal views.'

'Indeed he has,' Lord Douglas said wryly. 'He would like to curb the power of the Lords.'

Albert sipped his wine, eyes shining with amusement. 'And we shall succeed one day.'

'And women will get the vote one day,' Ellie stated confidently.

'Ah, your daughter is just like you, Albert, but you will both have a fight on your hands.'

'We love a good fight.' They spoke at the same time, father and daughter smiling at each other.

Five

'What do you think he'll be like?' Philip fidgeted nervously. 'Hope he's not too handy with a cane.'

'Oh, Philip.' Ellie laughed. 'Father wouldn't choose someone like that.'

'Of course he would. He must be in despair with you. You've been thrown out of three schools.'

'Two.' She pulled a face. 'Don't make it sound worse than it is.'

'It couldn't be much worse. How did you manage it? I couldn't even get sent home *once*, and I tried hard enough. That school was beastly. Do you know that we had to wash in freezing water, and then run around the field five times before we could have breakfast.' Philip shuddered. 'They said it was good for building character. It would be just my luck to find this tutor was of the same mind.'

'He won't be anything like that.'

'I hope you're right.' Philip stared gloomily out of the window. 'Now it's raining.'

'For goodness sake, cheer up.' Ellie marched across the room towards her cousin. 'Come on, I'll teach you how to fight, then if you have to go to another school, you can get yourself expelled.'

'Stop it, Ellie.' He fended her off, slipping behind a chair for protection.

She stalked him as he tried to avoid her, laughing with glee. 'You're a coward, Harry.'

Philip frowned, keeping her at arms length. 'What did you call me that for?'

'Call you what?' Ellie asked.

'Harry. You called me Harry.'

'Of course I didn't . . .'

'What are you two up to?'

35

'Nothing, Uncle Albert.' Philip ducked out of Ellie's way.

'Come now. We could hear you in the library. Eleanor?'

'Sorry Father.' Ellie straightened her skirt until it was hanging straight to the floor. 'I was offering to teach Philip how to fight, but he ran away from me.'

'Very wise of you, Philip.'

'She's too strong for me, sir. And she's being silly by calling me Harry.'

A stillness descended upon the room as Albert stared intently at his daughter. 'Why did you do that?'

'I didn't, he's imagining things.'

'I was not!'

'That's enough! Mr Rogers is waiting to meet you, so behave yourselves or he will resign before he has even begun the lessons. And that will mean boarding school for both of you again.'

That threat sobered them, and they dutifully followed her father into the library. They stopped suddenly when they saw the young man standing by the bookcase, reading, with spectacles on the end of his nose.

She nudged Philip, and whispered in his ear, 'I told you father wouldn't engage an old man, didn't I?'

Uncle Henry was also there, and gave them a stern look, warning them to be quiet.

'This is Eleanor and Philip.' Albert motioned them forward. 'It may be prudent to keep them apart during lessons, as they have a tendency to argue, as you no doubt heard.'

The tutor replaced the book on the shelf in an unhurried fashion, pushed his spectacles up on his nose, and studied the two in front of him.

Ellie felt distinctly uncomfortable under the scrutiny of his alert grey eyes, and that was something she was not used to. Her hand came up to pat her hair, wondering if it was in place after her tussle with Philip. If she had thought it would be possible to manipulate him, then she had been wrong. There was a quiet air of strength about him.

'And what do you argue about?' His gaze encompassed them both.

It was Philip who spoke first. 'Everything, sir. Ellie has strong opinions – for a girl.'

'And do you dislike her for that?'

'Oh, no, we're good friends.'

Mr Rogers nodded, turning his attention to Ellie. 'I understand that you have been asked to leave your school for fighting. Will you tell me why that happened?'

'Three girls said something I didn't like, so I hit them.' Ellie was rather taken aback by this conversation, casting a puzzled glance at her father. He was standing by the fireplace, his expression one of passive interest.

'Did the show of aggression solve anything?'

'Solve anything?' Ellie had to think about that. The girls said even worse things about her afterwards, and she had been sent home in disgrace. 'Well, I suppose not.'

'I am pleased you recognize that.' The tutor gave a nod of satisfaction. 'There are other ways of dealing with such things, and we shall learn how to turn these situations to our advantage, by controlled and reasoned debate. Your father is very skilled in the art.'

'I know,' Ellie said proudly. 'I would be very happy if you could teach me to be as wise.'

Mr Rogers turned to her father. 'With your permission, sir, we shall begin lessons tomorrow at nine o'clock.'

'Of course. My wife is resting at the moment, but you will join us for dinner this evening and meet her then,' Albert told him. 'Now, Eleanor and Philip, you will show Mr Rogers the school room, and then help him to settle in the gatehouse.'

'Yes, Father.'

Albert watched them leave the room, and as soon as the door closed behind them, he gave a worried sigh.

'Why the frown, Albert?' Henry asked. 'He appears to be a wise choice for tutor.'

'You heard the altercation in the other room?'

'Yes, but that's nothing unusual when they're together. They don't mean anything by it. Our children are fond of each other.'

'I agree. However, when they were playing around Eleanor called Philip, Harry.'

Henry stopped in the act of reaching for the decanter. 'Oh, Lord, that's worrying. Has she remembered?'

'No, she didn't seem to know she had even done it, and said Philip was imagining things.'

'Only we know he wasn't.' Henry sat down heavily. 'She was only a little thing when she came here – far too young to remember her life before, so why should that name come out now?'

'I can only think that Nanny may have triggered something in her mind when she called her Queenie.'

'Eleanor told me about that. What are you going to do, Albert? She's growing up, and it would be cruel if she did remember something of her past life. Will you tell her one day?'

'I hate to admit it, but that may well be my unpleasant duty sooner than I had hoped. I am most uneasy about the appearance of these names from the past.' Albert began to pace the room. 'As you are aware, the doctors have given Mary a short time to live, and she has asked me not to say anything while she is still with us.'

'My poor sister.' Henry stared sadly at the fire. 'But that leaves you with a heavy burden.'

'Indeed it does.' Albert poured them both a drink.

Later that day, Henry was dozing in one of the library chairs as Albert envied his brother-in-law's ability to relax wherever he was. It was something he had never been able to do, and this afternoon he was too wound up even to sit still. It had shaken him badly to hear that Eleanor had called her cousin, Harry. He had thought her past was buried deep but it seemed that the memories might surface.

His insides clenched painfully as he tried to decide what to do. It would be desperate if she remembered on her own. He could just imagine the confusion and upset that it would cause her. If this had to come out into the open, then he wanted to be the one to tell her, and be with her to help her through the shock. But what if she didn't remember – what then? He would surely do more harm than good by telling her. He had always prayed that that part of her life would remain hidden, but he was very much afraid that wasn't going to happen now. And Mary was quite right, Eleanor had a right to know.

Oh God, what should he do?

Spinning on his heels away from the window he strode out of the library, along the passage and up the stairs to his wife's bedroom.

Opening the door quietly, he walked towards the bed. Mary was sound asleep, the deep purple under her eyes stark against the waxen skin. He knew she was suffering, but he never heard her complain. He had consulted every physician he could find, but they all said the same thing – there was nothing that could be done. The miscarriages she had endured had done great damage to her health, and now disease had set in. He felt guilty about that, but she had so longed for a child. After the second loss he should have insisted they adopt and forgot about having a child of their own, but she had begged him.

Running a hand through his hair, he took a deep breath. All the doctors could do now was keep increasing the medication to keep her as comfortable as possible, but he had been warned that it was only a matter of weeks – months at the most.

He walked softly out of the room. He couldn't tell her about Eleanor calling Philip, Harry. He couldn't do anything to upset the short time she had left with the daughter she loved so much – the daughter they both loved.

Utterly disconsolate, he went downstairs and knocked on Nanny's door.

'Come in.'

'Hello, Nanny.' He sat next to her. 'How are you today? Do you have everything you need?'

'I'm in better spirit than you, by the look on your face.'

His smile was wry. She always went straight to the point. 'I need to talk to you.'

'I'm listening.'

He then told her what had happened, wiping his hand over his eyes when he had finished. 'For the first time in my life I don't know what to do.'

'This is my fault.' Nanny slapped the arm of her chair in annoyance. 'When I called her Queenie, I had been remembering her as a little girl. It was a stupid slip of the tongue. I'm so sorry.'

'You mustn't feel like that,' Albert said fondly. 'When she came here, it was a traumatic time for her, and those memories, although forgotten over the years, must still be there.'

Nanny nodded. 'I think you'll have to watch her carefully, and if anything else like this happens, then you must tell her the whole story.'

Albert dipped his head, and then looked up again, anguish etched on his face. 'I'm terrified of losing her.'

'That's a chance you will have to take, but I don't believe that will happen. She will certainly be shocked and upset, but she loves you both very much, and I'd be surprised if the bond between you was broken.'

'Do you think she will want to find her other family?'

'Maybe, maybe not.'

'That isn't much help, Nanny. You know her better than anyone else.'

'I still can't tell you what she will do. Eleanor has a strong will, and may well want to see the people who sold her, even if it's only to tell them what she thinks of them.'

Albert flinched.

Nanny watched him. 'Yes, that still hurts, doesn't it? How do you think Eleanor will feel when she finds out?'

'It will tear her apart.' Albert was on his feet, unable to remain in the chair. 'She's going to hate us when she finds out we bought her, and she mustn't find out while Mary is still alive. I know I'm going to lose Mary soon, but if I also lose Eleanor, it will destroy me.'

'Come and sit down again.' Nanny waited until he had perched on the edge of the chair, tension radiating from him. 'Do you remember the first time you saw her?'

He nodded, a slight smile touching his lips.

'You took her out to see the fish in the pond, and when you found out she wasn't used to wearing shoes, you removed them, allowing her to run around in bare feet.'

A deep chuckle rumbled through him. 'And she wanted to remove her undergarments as well.'

'Yes, she was a bit disappointed when you refused that request.'

They both laughed then, remembering.

'But you had taken off her hated shoes, and at that moment I believe she fell in love with you.' Nanny leaned forward and squeezed his arm. 'When you came home after spending time in London, she would rush up to you, climb on your knees, and demand to be told what you had been doing. She giggled in delight when she heard about the fierce arguments that took place in Parliament. She was too young to understand what it was all about, but you were a good storyteller.

40

She has always asked you to take her to London so she could see where you work, but you never have.'

'I've always been afraid to in case she found it familiar and remembered.'

'You won't lose her. She adores you.' Nanny spoke gently. 'If you have to tell her, there will be difficult times ahead as she tries to come to terms with the revelation, but stay by her side, and you will both come through it. She hasn't been the easiest child to bring up, but she has a good nature, and that is because of the love and affection you and the mistress have always shown her. When her boisterous side got her into trouble, which has been often, you've reprimanded her, and then forgiven her. She knows she is lucky to have understanding parents. If she does set out to find her other family, she will soon discover that she's had a much better life with you than in the slums of London.'

'I hope you're right, Nanny.' Albert stood up. 'Thank you for talking this through with me.'

'I'm always here if you need me. Have you told Eleanor how sick her mother is?'

'No, Mary doesn't want her to know.' Albert shrugged helplessly. 'But Eleanor's not a fool. She knows how serious her mother's health is.'

'The mistress is entitled to conceal her illness as much as possible, if that is the way she wants it.'

Albert sighed again. 'I don't know how she keeps going, but she fairly sparkles at the dinner table, and no one would guess the severity of her suffering.'

'She has a great deal of courage. Now –' Nanny changed the subject – 'don't forget to send the new tutor to see me. I need to check that he is suitable.'

Albert tipped back his head and laughed freely for the first time that day. 'I'll bring him to see you this evening. I believe you will find him very suitable.'

'He had better be, or Eleanor will have him running in circles.'

Six

When Mr Rogers entered the schoolroom the next morning, Ellie and Philip stood up. 'Good morning, sir,' they chorused.

'I hope you were comfortable in the gatehouse, sir.' Ellie had taken an instant liking to the tutor when she had met him yesterday, and that was more than she could say about most of the teachers she had encountered.

A glint of amusement showed in Mr Roger's eyes. 'Very comfortable, thank you, Miss Warrender. And I do believe Nanny approves of me. Please sit down.'

Philip dug Ellie in the ribs when the tutor turned away from them, staring out at the garden, hands behind his back. 'What's he doing?' he mouthed silently.

Ellie shrugged, and waited, easing her feet out of her shoes.

He remained in that position for a minute or two, and then faced them again. 'It's a pleasant day, so get your coats and we shall walk in the garden while you tell me what you have been learning. I want to know what you like and don't like, and any subjects you would like included in your lessons. I shall then be able to set out a schedule for each of you.'

Philip was already on his feet, a smile of pleasure on his face, as Ellie struggled to get back into her shoes.

'I'll meet you by the lovely pond I can see from here, in five minutes.'

Neither of them liked being indoors for any length of time, whatever the weather, and in their haste to get out they collided in the doorway, each one fighting to get through first.

'My goodness,' Philip gasped, as he scrambled into his coat. 'I think I'm going to like him. Is he really going to give us a choice of what we want to learn?'

'Sounds like it, within reason, I expect.' Ellie was ready and heading for the garden as fast as she could. The tutor had said five minutes, and she wasn't going to take a second longer. This was an unexpected treat. She hadn't been looking forward to spending hours in the schoolroom.

Lifting her skirt she ran, with Philip right behind her, she wondered if Mr Rogers could ride. Lessons on horseback would be fun.

As they skidded to a halt in front of him, he glanced at his watch and nodded in approval. 'This is a pleasant spot.'

'Oh, yes.' Ellie watched the brightly coloured fish swimming around. 'It's my favourite, along with the stables, of course. We have six horses. Do you ride, sir?'

'I do, but I am not an expert. My mount has to be of a docile nature. Now, let us walk around the garden while you tell me all about yourselves. Before lunch we shall concentrate on getting to know each other, then this afternoon we will settle to the lessons.'

That was such good news that even Philip couldn't stop smiling.

'What are they doing in the garden, Albert?' Mary asked.

'I suspect young Rogers is getting them to talk about themselves in a more relaxed atmosphere than the schoolroom. I was told by his last employers – the Beresfords – that his methods are unconventional but effective.'

Mary slipped her hand through his arm. 'He's certainly caught their interest. Look at their animated faces.'

When she swayed slightly he caught her around the waist. 'Sit down, my dear.'

Shaking her head, she leaned against him, giving her usual reply. 'I'm all right. A little spell of dizziness, but it has passed now.'

He knew it was more than that. This morning the physician had increased the medication again, and warned him that time was short. His wife would not be able to keep going for much longer. It was only her sheer determination keeping her on her feet. He supported her, allowing her the pleasure of watching Eleanor laughing happily in the pale autumn sunshine.

'You must marry again, Albert. You are still young enough to father children, and perhaps have a male heir.'

He shook his head firmly. 'I am forty-five now and have

no wish for a young family. I have Eleanor, and she is the only heir I need.'

'You were so angry when Henry and I brought her home. Do you remember?'

'I was furious.' Laughter rumbled through him. 'Henry thought I was going to kill him.'

'But it has all turned out well, hasn't it?' She gazed up at him, her eyes misted with tears. 'She has brought us great joy.'

'Indeed she has, and she's growing into a fine young woman – when she isn't brawling.'

His dry tone made Mary smile. 'But it is always in a good cause. She finds injustice of any kind abhorrent.'

'So do I, but I don't roll up my sleeves and start throwing punches.'

'And a very good thing that you don't, Albert, or you would soon be thrown out of Parliament.'

'True.'

'Ah, they are moving away now, heading for the stables, no doubt.' Mary sighed when they disappeared from sight. 'How pretty she is. I'm sad that I shall not be around to arrange her coming-out, or have the joy of seeing her marry and have children of her own.'

'If you take life at a steady pace and do as the doctor advises—'

'No, Albert, I am not a fool. The pain is becoming harder and harder to control, and I am increasingly fatigued.'

Albert had never felt so helpless. What could he say? Mary knew what was happening to her.

'I am aware that I must leave you and Eleanor soon. No woman could have asked for a finer husband. I was not able to bear the children you so badly wanted. You could have cast me aside and married someone else, but you never did. I have been blessed to have your love. I have left you the burden of telling Eleanor that we adopted her, but I'm sure it will not make any difference to the love she feels for you. Don't stay in mourning too long; a month is quite long enough, for you know how I dislike sombre clothes and faces. I shall not be here for Eleanor's eighteenth birthday, but I ask you to see that the occasion is celebrated with friends, music and laughter.'

'I'll do all you say, Mary, but you will be able to make the arrangements yourself.' Albert tried to look confident, but it was hard. The doctor's prognosis this morning had been grim.

'Perhaps. Now, I'll go and rest before lunch.'

'I'll help you to your room.'

'There's no need, Molly is waiting upstairs for me.' She reached up and kissed his cheek. 'I'll let you know when walking is too much for me.'

He watched her leave the room, head high, and step sure. He marvelled yet again at her cheerful fortitude, and her immense courage. He was very concerned about the conversation they'd just had. It was almost as if she were putting her affairs in order. He hated to see her suffering like this, but he also dreaded the thought of losing her. It was coming though. She knew it, and, if he was honest, so did he.

Turning away from the window he went to his study to write a speech, and possibly an important letter. He was seriously considering resigning his seat in the House of Commons. It wasn't a decision to be taken lightly as he had gained a lot of satisfaction in his years in Parliament, and there was still much he wanted to achieve, but he was needed here. Mary's illness was now severe and he had to stay near her. He would never forgive himself if she died while he was away. And when that day came, Eleanor was going to need him. The future was uncertain, making it hard for him to concentrate on his work.

Sitting behind the huge oak desk, he rotated his shoulders, trying to ease the tension, and then closed his eyes, bowing his head. He was a wealthy man and could find plenty to occupy him around the estate. Also, Henry was urging that they go into business together and buy a swath of forest a few miles away. It was full of good timber and if they replanted new trees to replace those being felled, it could be a profitable venture for some time to come. And land was always a good investment.

With his mind made up, he lifted his head and reached for paper and pen. It was time to make the change.

Albert had been working for about two hours when the door burst open, and the maid, Molly, rushed in. One glance at her stricken face and he was immediately on his feet.

'Oh, sir, come quick. It's the mistress . . .'

45

He didn't wait to hear any more, but ran to his wife's room as fast as he could, with Molly right behind him.

One look at Mary was enough. 'Send one of the grooms for the physician. And don't delay! And get a message to her brother, as well!'

The maid ran out, tears of fright running down her face. Albert could hear her thumping down the stairs, already calling for help. He prayed that Doctor Brewster would hurry. He sat on the bed, cradling his wife in his arms.

'I've sent for the doctor, my dear. He'll soon be here to give you something for the pain. Hold on to me.'

She was soaking wet with perspiration and curled into a tight ball as she fought the pain. Her hands gripped his arm, and if he hadn't been wearing a jacket her fingers would have pierced his flesh. She was in agony.

It seemed a lifetime before the doctor arrived, but in fact it could not have been more than twenty minutes. 'Give her something,' he ground out between clenched teeth.

Albert stayed exactly where he was, watching the doctor work. In a mercifully short time he felt Mary relax, and he settled her back on the pillows. She was conscious, just about, but she was still in pain, albeit more bearable.

'Can't you put her right out?' Albert's hand was shaking as he ran it over his wife's hair. Mary shouldn't have to suffer like this. She was, and always had been, a good woman.

Doctor Brewster led him to the other side of the room, and spoke softly. 'I have given her as much medication as I dare at this moment. Any more and it will end her life.'

'How much time has she got?'

'Twenty-four hours at the most.'

'Then I ask you to stay and see that she does not have to endure such pain again.' Albert looked across the room at his wife. 'You must do whatever needs to be done to keep her free from pain. I will not have her last hours a torment. Do you hear?'

When the doctor nodded in agreement, Albert returned to his wife. Her eyes were open.

'Ask Molly to wash and change me.' Her speech was slurred, but she was aware of her dishevelled appearance. 'Then I want to see Eleanor.'

'Of course, my dear.' He bent and kissed her forehead.

'Doctor Brewster is going to stay for a while and make sure you are comfortable.'

She nodded weakly. 'Eleanor.'

'I'll fetch her as soon as Molly has finished.'

The maid was hovering outside the door, so Albert told her what was needed, and then made his way up to the schoolroom.

Taking a deep, steadying breath, he opened the door and walked in. 'I apologize for interrupting you, Mr Rogers, but Eleanor's mother is unwell and is asking for her.'

Ellie leapt to her feet, rushing over to her father. 'Is she bad, Father? Is the doctor with her?'

When she turned to leave the room he caught hold of her arm. 'Don't rush. Molly is making her comfortable before you see her, and yes, the doctor is with her.'

'You look awful, Father.' Ellie was trembling now, fully aware just how sick her mother had become over the last year.

'I was talking to her but a short time ago, and her collapse has come as a shock. We knew this was going to happen, Eleanor, but I had refused to admit that it could be so soon.'

Ellie gulped. 'Can we go to her now?'

He nodded. 'My apologies again, Mr Rogers.'

'I understand, sir.'

Albert had to keep a firm grip on his daughter to stop her running to her mother. As ill as she was, Mary would be upset if she was seen in anything but a clean and tidy state. When Ellie saw her mother she nearly cried out in dismay. She had seen her at breakfast, and although pale, she had talked to them quite normally. The change was terrible.

As her father squeezed her shoulder in support, she gazed up at him, shocked. 'She was all right this morning.'

'No, she wasn't. The Doctor had increased her medication again, giving her enough relief to join us. Your mother has made a valiant effort to keep going, but the end is near, and we must prepare ourselves for that.' He slipped an arm around her. 'Come, she has been asking for you.'

They went over to the bed and Ellie knelt down, taking her mother's hand in both of hers, struggling to keep the tears at bay.

'Eleanor.' Mary opened her eyes, although it was clearly an effort, then she smiled. 'I shall be leaving you soon . . .'

47

'No, Mother!' Ellie cried in dismay.

'Sush, do not upset yourself. It is best, for I can endure no more of this.'

Ellie bowed her head and kissed her mother's hand. 'What am I to do without you?'

'You will have your father. Look after him, darling. He is a good man. Promise me.'

'I promise.'

'There is one more thing I would ask of you.'

'Anything, Mother.'

'If you hear anything about something your father and I did some years ago, I want you to remember that we love you dearly. We could not have had a daughter we were more proud of. From the moment you arrived we adored you. You have brought great joy into our lives. Remember we have always loved and wanted you.'

Mary shuddered, absolutely spent, and Albert leant over the bed. 'No more talking, my dear, try to sleep now. We'll be right here when you awake.'

As her mother slipped into a drugged sleep, Ellie glanced at her father, distressed and confused. 'What was she trying to say? It didn't make sense. I know you both love me, so why does Mother want me to remember that? Nothing would ever make me forget.'

'I pray that you don't.' Her father closed his eyes for a moment, tired and drawn.

Ellie smoothed a lock of hair away from her mother's face. 'Will you tell me what it was you did that is worrying her so much?'

'If you really want to know then I'll tell you one day.' Albert drew up two chairs for them to sit on. 'But this is not the time, Eleanor.'

'No, of course not.' Ellie was too distressed to pursue the subject. And, with all the medication the doctor had given her, Mother was probably not talking complete sense anyway.

It was a long night's vigil. Ellie, her father and Uncle Henry stayed by the bed, refusing to move for anything. The entire household was awake, knowing this night could only end in one way – the death of the gentle mistress they all admired and respected.

The dawn was just beginning to lighten the sky when Mary opened her eyes, her face etched with pain. 'Queenie!' she called out. 'See, Albert, how lovely she is. See how beautiful our little girl has grown . . .'

Ellie jumped to her feet in alarm. There was that name again.

'Doctor!' Albert shouted, gathering his wife in his arms as Doctor Brewster hurried into the room. 'She's in pain again. Give her something.'

But there was no need. It was over.

Seven

The funeral arrangements were all in place; mourners invited, with food and accommodation settled for the many people attending. Mary had been greatly loved, and Albert was determined that the service should be a memorial to her life – cut short far too soon.

Resting his head back on the chair he closed his eyes, trying to snatch a little rest. The last five days had been a nightmare. He missed the gentle presence of his wife. They had been happy together, and there had been a feeling of completeness after Eleanor became their daughter.

With that thought he opened his eyes, sitting up straight. Eleanor was inconsolable at the loss of her mother, so he had insisted that she join Philip in the schoolroom to continue her lessons. She had not yet mentioned Mary's last call to Queenie, but he knew the questions would come and he would have to deal with them. The funeral was in two days, and he doubted she would wait long once it was over. That was why he had now resigned his seat in Parliament, for when she heard the truth his darling girl was going to need him. He prayed she turned to him, and not away from him.

Hauling himself to his feet he left the study and went to see if Nanny was happy with the bath chair.

'Hello, Nanny, how are you feeling today?'

'I've felt better, but nothing will keep me away from the funeral. That bath chair is an uncomfortable contraption, but it will do.'

'Good. Our butler, Dobson, has offered to look after you during the service.' Albert smiled at the elderly woman. 'You will only have to endure the discomfort for a short while.'

'I know, but it will be a sad occasion.' Nanny sighed. 'Are all the arrangements in place?'

Albert nodded, his expression sorrowful. 'Once the funeral

is over I believe Eleanor will start asking questions. I'm going to need your help if she does.'

'I'll do what I can. Eleanor comes in every day after lessons to see me. She talks about her mother, cries a little, and laughs at the happy memories. You keep your feelings under tight control, but she doesn't. Her recovery will be quicker than yours, I believe.' Nanny studied him carefully. 'She will come to me if she is upset; she always has done from the moment she arrived.'

'That gives me some measure of comfort.' Albert stood up, suddenly restless. 'I'll ride over to see Henry. I feel the need for fresh air and exercise.'

The loss was almost too much for Ellie as she struggled to pay attention to the lesson. Mr Rogers was teaching them French, and in normal times she would have found it great fun, but she couldn't seem to get interested in anything at the moment. Father had explained that until the funeral was over it would be hard, but after that they would be able to start living again. It wasn't going to be easy without her mother though, and things would never be the same. There would be a large empty hole in their lives. It hurt so much to know they would never see her again. Her father was under great strain. He seemed to have aged ten years over the last few days. She was trying hard to be brave and not add to his burden.

The words on the page in front of her were just a blur and she gave up trying to read them. Mr Rogers was being very kind and understanding.

'Ellie.' Philip was also subdued. 'It's luncheon time.'

'Oh, is it?' She looked up at the tutor. 'I'm sorry, Mr Rogers, I have not been very attentive.'

'It's a difficult time for you, but you have tried, and I do not ask for more than that at the moment,' he said. 'We shall get back to some hard work once the mourning period is over. I suggest that you forget about studies for the next three days. The weather is dry and you might like to go for a ride. But make sure you eat first.'

'Thank you, sir.'

The day of the funeral was overcast. Ellie, dressed all in black, gazed out of the window at the garden. 'I wish the sun would shine.'

Her father joined her, also dressed in deep mourning. 'We must go, Eleanor.'

Slipping her hand through his arm they walked together through the hall to the front door. Waiting for them was a carriage with a team of four matched black horses, with black plumes dancing in the slight breeze. It was a magnificent sight, but Ellie couldn't appreciate it, and was relieved to see the wreaths of bright flowers covering the coffin. Her mother had always loved nice colours.

Her father led her to another carriage and they climbed in. Uncle Henry and Philip were already inside, waiting for them.

No one spoke on the ride to the church, each one coping with the grief in their own way. The procession caused a lot of interest, with men doffing their hats in respect as they passed. There were a great many people attending the funeral, and Ellie knew that her emotions would have to be controlled. Her mother would have expected them to act with dignity, and she was determined not to let her down. She trembled. It was going to be an ordeal though.

The church was full to overflowing when they arrived. Ellie stayed close to her father's side, praying for some of his strength to see her through this. Uncle Henry was struggling to remain composed, for he had loved his sister dearly, and Philip kept his head bent, not looking at anyone. Nanny was pale and strained, but the glint in her eyes said that she was determined to say a proper goodbye to her mistress. Ellie admired her for her courage, for she was quite frail.

The service was a blur to Ellie, though the music and singing by the choir was uplifting. Her father had chosen the music well, keeping away from anything sounding too dreary.

After the service they made their way to the graveside, and seeing the hole in the ground was nearly Ellie's undoing. But just before the coffin was lowered, the sun burst through the clouds, making her feel as if her mother was smiling down at them. It brought a measure of comfort.

They had no time for themselves for the rest of the day as they received family and friends wanting to offer their condolences. Ellie had never seen a lot of them before, and couldn't help wondering where they had all come from. The funeral had been at eleven o'clock, and it was five o'clock before the last of the mourners had left.

Then it was the reading of the will, and Ellie was amazed to find that her mother had left the huge sum of five thousand pounds in trust for her until she was twenty-one. Also, her jewellery was to come to her. There were bequests for all the servants, and the rest of the considerable fortune had been left to her husband and brother. Philip hadn't been forgotten either, also being left a sum in trust for when he was older.

'There is just one more item.' The solicitor looked at Albert. 'Mrs Warrender wishes me to remind you that there is a box which I believe you already know about?'

Albert nodded.

'Your wife states in her will that she leaves this in your care to do with as you think best.'

Ellie was surprised at her father's grim expression at the mention of this box, and couldn't help wondering what was in it. There seemed to be mysteries popping up all over the place, but she must hold her curiosity in check for a while. Her father was clearly exhausted and troubled.

Two weeks passed before Ellie felt able to approach her father, but then she could contain herself no longer. After knocking on his study door, she waited until he called for her to enter. He was at his desk and it was covered with books and papers. She hesitated. Perhaps this wasn't a good time as he appeared to be extremely busy.

'Come in, Eleanor, don't hover in the doorway.'

'I apologize for interrupting your work, Father, and I can come back another time if this isn't convenient.'

He stood up. 'I am never too busy to see you. Have you finished your lessons for the day?'

'We have. Mr Rogers makes everything very interesting and we do not mind staying a little later if necessary.' She gave an impish smile. 'That shows what a good teacher he is.'

'Indeed it does. I was fortunate to employ him.'

'He's fun in his quiet way.' Ellie grinned. 'But he is most uneasy on horseback.'

'I have seen him, and it surprises me that you and Philip manage to persuade him into the saddle as often as you do.' Her father laughed, and then became serious again. 'If your mother were still with us she would be arranging your coming-out season. Once our mourning period is over I shall see about it.'

'Oh, Father, I don't want all that fuss. I think the whole business of "a season" is too silly. And I certainly don't wish to be presented at court.' She pulled a face. 'If I tried a deep curtsy I would fall flat on my face. I have never been able to master the move with grace.'

'I'm sure you are too harsh on your abilities . . . But you didn't come here to talk about your studies.'

'No.' She took a deep breath, going straight to the point. 'Will you tell me who Queenie was?'

'I didn't expect you to wait this long before asking.'

'You have had so much to do and I didn't want to disturb you, for I am aware that you don't wish to talk about this or you would have brought up the subject yourself. After Nanny and Mother called me by that name, I am more than a little curious.' Ellie shrugged. 'But it is more than that. I have gained the impression that this person has something to do with me. Who was she, Father?'

'Before I tell you, please remember your mother's dying request not to forget that we love you very much.'

'I'll remember.' Now Ellie was alarmed. Her father looked frightened; that was the only way she could describe it, and she had never seen him like this before. 'If this has nothing to do with me, and you don't wish to talk about it, then just say so, Father, and I'll not broach the subject again.'

'It is time you knew, and it does concern you.' He hesitated as if steeling himself. '*You* are Queenie.'

She gasped and gave a disbelieving laugh. 'My name is Eleanor, and it's only recently I've heard the other name. I don't understand.'

'I'll explain.' He perched on the edge of the desk as if his legs would no longer hold him. 'Fifteen years ago Mary and Henry brought a little two and a half year old child into this house . . .'

Ellie listened in absolute horror as the story unfolded, and her safe happy world shattered around her. She wasn't their child! She was some girl from the slums. It was hard to breathe as she rocked back and forth in the chair she had slumped into.

'You bought me? My real family sold me to strangers?' The hurt was indescribable. 'I'm not your daughter?'

'You are!' Albert crouched down in front of her, taking a firm hold on her hands, his eyes pleading. 'We legally adopted you. You *are* our daughter.'

Ellie never liked to cry, but now the tears were running down her face. 'How much did I cost you?'

'That doesn't matter—'

'It does. How much?'

'Five guineas—'

She surged to her feet, shaking off his hands, then ran full pelt out of the room and out of the house. She had to be alone. It was too much to discover that the parents she loved were not her real mother and father. She felt utterly bereft as she reached the pond. Sinking down, she buried her head in her hands and sobbed like a baby. Her comfortable world had just disintegrated into a million pieces.

It took every ounce of Albert's self-control to stop himself running after her. But he knew he had to give her time to adjust and think things through. He prayed that as the shock receded, she would understand that she'd had a much better life with them.

His heart was thumping uncomfortably, making him rub his hand over his chest as he tried to control the panic. 'Think it through, my precious girl,' he murmured. 'Don't turn away from me.'

Tears gathered, blurring his vision. It was going to tear him apart if he lost her now, but if she wanted no more to do with him, then he would have to find the courage to deal with it. How bleak his life was going to be without Eleanor and Mary's love. If this had been left to him, he would never have told her, but Nanny and Mary had opened the door by saying too much in her presence, leaving him little choice. Eleanor's curiosity had always been insatiable.

Pouring himself a large brandy with shaking hands, he wandered over to the window. The pond was her favourite spot, and was where he had taken her as a frightened little girl when she had just arrived. After she had been plucked from the only life and people she had known. His heart still ached when he thought about that little face gazing up at him in fear and confusion.

'I'm here for you, Eleanor, just as I was that first day, and have been ever since. Come to me.'

It was almost dark. Ellie shivered, not only from the cold, but also in disbelief. The family she'd been born to had sold her. How could they have done that? Were they monsters?

She scrambled to her feet, anxious now to find out more about her real family, and about herself when she had been brought here. The person to ask would be Nanny.

Without knocking, she rushed into the elderly woman's room. 'Tell me about Queenie. What was she like? Where did her family live; how many of them were there? Why was I sold? Why did they buy me?'

Nanny managed to stand up, holding out her arms to the distraught girl. 'He's told you then?'

'Oh, Nanny.' Ellie sobbed on her shoulder. 'I don't know who I am any more.'

'Come and sit down.' Nanny hobbled over to a settee where they could sit together. 'I'll tell you everything.'

Ellie listened to the story about the little girl her mistress had brought home one day and placed in her care. Slowly, the tears dried and her mouth opened in amazement. 'All I had on was a frock?' she gasped. 'Father didn't tell me that.'

'Oh, yes, and when you swore at him, he fell in love with you.'

'I used bad language?'

'Terrible, and it took us a long time to break you of the habit.' Nanny held on to Ellie's hand. 'He adores you, and so did the mistress. You are their daughter, and have been from the moment you arrived.'

Nanny then went on to explain as much as she knew about the other family. 'There was one brother you kept asking for. His name was Harry, or 'Arry, as you called him. I can tell you no more than that.'

'I'm finding it hard to accept all of this, Nanny. And I'm ashamed to say I ran away from father before he had a chance to explain fully.'

'I know what a shock it must be, but they've given you a good life – much better than you would have had as a slum child. Don't turn away from him, Eleanor. You couldn't have had more devoted parents, and he needs you.'

After hearing about Queenie, she could see how lucky she had been. As devastating as the news was to her, that stricken looking man she had left in the study was her father. The only father she had ever known. Nothing would ever change that.

'Go to him.'

Giving Nanny a quick hug, Ellie ran from the room and to her father's study. Opening the door quietly she saw he was standing by the window, head bowed.

'Father.'

He spun round.

Walking slowly towards him, she put her arms around him and held on tightly.

Words were unnecessary.

Eight

Father and daughter remained like that for several minutes, neither speaking, both relieved that the bond between them was unbroken. If they could survive this, then they could survive anything. Ellie had loved her gentle mother dearly, but her father had always been extra special to her. Now she understood why.

After a while Ellie looked up, a wistful expression on her face. 'Nanny said I swore at you.'

'Indeed you did. It was amazing to hear such language coming from a young child, but it was probably normal speech where you came from. I was determined to have you for my daughter from that moment on. I stormed round to Henry and demanded that he made the adoption legal. I didn't want anyone else to have a claim on you, ever.'

'I'm sorry I ran away from you, but I was so very shocked and hurt. I needed time alone to clear my mind and have a talk with Nanny.'

'I understand.' He led her over to the chairs and they sat opposite each other, as they had done countless times while they had deep discussions about all sorts of things. 'Will you tell me how you feel?'

Ellie closed her eyes for a moment. She was still reeling from shock, but her logical mind was telling her that she had been lucky. Opening her eyes again, she took a deep breath. 'It will take me time to come to terms with this news. In one way I wish you had never told me, but it's right I should know, even if it is painful. But in my heart it changes nothing. You have been the best parents a girl could wish for. We have, sadly, lost Mother, but you are my father, and always will be.'

Albert breathed an audible sigh of relief, visibly overcome. 'I was so afraid I would lose you.'

'Not a chance.' She reached across for his hand, watching

his long fingers curl around in a firm grip. 'But I have to find out what Queenie's family were like. It's the only way I am going to be able to put this behind me and get on with my life. Do you understand?'

'I do.' Albert stood up. 'Now it's time to open your mother's box. Come with me.'

They went to Mary's room, the first time either of them had been in there since the night she had died. It was clean and tidy, without a trace of that awful time.

Albert removed a small wooden box from Mary's bureau and placed it on the dressing table, handing Ellie the key. 'Your mother said I was to give you this if I felt it was right to do so. If you hadn't wanted to know about your other family, then I wouldn't have shown you this, but as you do, then you need to see what Mary has saved all these years.'

With shaking hands she took the key from him and opened the box. On the top was a small scruffy frock. Ellie held it up.

'Mary's first thought was to burn that, but you wouldn't let it out of your sight. When they did eventually get it away from you, she decided to keep it. That was all you were wearing; no shoes or undergarments.' His voice was full of emotion.

Speech was beyond her as she examined the small item from her past. Lifting up the frill around the hem she could see that it had once been pink, but now it was badly faded. Laying it carefully aside, she picked up a sheet of paper with a list of names written in her mother's tidy hand. Frowning, she held it out to her father.

'They are the names of your brothers and sisters. You were determined not to forget, so you kept repeating them over and over. You were little more than a baby, so Mary made a note of them, just in case you needed it in the future.'

She counted the names and gasped in astonishment. 'There were nine?'

'Yes, you were the youngest, making ten children in the family.'

Trying hard to bring some memory to the surface, she read down the list, repeating the names out loud. Ted, Harry, Jack, Tommy, Bert, Charlie, June, Pearl, Maggie. She ought to know them, but she didn't. It was distressing to think that she came from a large family and couldn't remember any of them.

Putting the list aside, she removed the rest of the items, all papers. It was on the adoption correspondence that she discovered her name – she had been Queenie Bonner, from Whitechapel. Right at the bottom was a photograph of a small girl staring at the fish in the pond.

'That was taken the day after you arrived.'

At the sight of the small girl, Ellie began to sob. 'How could they have sold me?'

Albert gathered her in his arms. 'They had too many children. They didn't want you – but we did.'

When she had stopped crying, he looked into her eyes, his face etched with strain. 'What do you want to do now you've seen this, Eleanor? If you want to leave it, that will make me happy, but whatever you decide, I'll help and support you all the way.'

The last thing she wanted to do was make him unhappy, but she knew herself well enough to know that she couldn't ignore this as if she had never been told. The news had shattered her comfortable world, and she needed to put it to rights again. It was the only way she could think of doing that. 'I want to find every one of them; see them face-to-face. Find out what kind of a life I would have had if I'd stayed in the slums with them.'

'That will be quite a task. I expect they are scattered around by now, but we know where you lived, so that will be the place to start. After that I could employ a man to track down the rest of them for us. When each one is found, we shall go and see them together.' He grimaced slightly. 'Unless you wish to meet them on your own, of course.'

'No, Father, I would like you to be with me.' She gave a watery smile. 'I want them to see how lucky I've been.'

The intensity of the emotion he was feeling was written across his face – relief, love and joy at her words. 'I take it that you would like to see Mr and Mrs Bonner first.'

Ellie's mouth set in a firm line. 'Yes. They are the ones who sold me. Then the others in any order we can find them.'

Albert's expression was serious. 'Be very sure this is what you want to do, Eleanor. It could be painful for you.'

'I know that.' She lifted her head, a determined glint in her eyes. 'But it's something I must do.'

'Very well, we shall begin our search tomorrow. Do you wish to keep this between ourselves, or shall we involve others?'

'Uncle Henry should certainly be dragged in to help, and Philip must be told.'

'That's sensible. It would be difficult to keep this from him, especially if we keep disappearing to check out leads.'

'Oh, yes.' Ellie pulled a face. 'What about Mr Rogers? He isn't going to like me skipping classes.'

'He's London born and bred, so he might prove useful if we have several places to investigate at the same time. If you don't mind him knowing, then he might be able to help.'

'I don't see there is anything to be ashamed of, Father. I may have started life as Queenie Bonner, but I am legally Eleanor Warrender, and proud of that.'

'And I'm proud that you are my daughter.' Albert bent and kissed her cheek. 'I knew you were a sensible girl when you asked me if we eat the fish in the pond.'

'What?' Ellie's eyes opened wide. 'Why would I have thought that?'

'Because food was short where you came from. You were tiny and undernourished, but I saw intelligence in your bright blue eyes, and I knew at that moment that I wanted you for my daughter.'

'I'm so pleased you chose me.' Ellie's mind began to clear. This darling man had had no part in taking her away from her family. He had been presented with a child they could not possibly return to the slums. What a dilemma that must have been, but he had immediately set about putting things right. She had always loved him, but now her heart swelled with respect and pride for what he had done.

'We chose each other, and you brought us great joy. Your mother suffered from bouts of depression over the fact that she couldn't have children, but once you were ours, she was happy.' He stood up. 'Come now, we must both get some sleep. Tomorrow morning, we shall all gather in Nanny's room to discuss our strategy.'

* * *

Sleep was out of the question for Ellie as she tossed and turned, her mind in turmoil. No amount of effort made her recall the time before she came here. She had always believed she was an only child, but now she had nine brothers and sisters. It was hard to grasp that fact. One of them, Harry, was supposed to have been her favourite, and she couldn't help wondering what he was like. Her earliest memory was when she had been around four and her parents had taken her to the seaside. And yet there must be something buried deep in her mind, because Philip said she'd called him Harry when they'd been messing about. It was frustrating, but perhaps things would come back when she saw where she had come from.

Climbing out of bed, she put on her robe, pulled back the curtains and stared up at the sky. It was a clear night with stars twinkling in the darkness.

'Are you one of the stars now, Mother?' she whispered. 'Are you looking down on us? Am I doing the right thing? I'm so worried. Would it be better to leave it alone? I know Father would prefer that. And does it really matter? Will I be making things worse and cause us unnecessary pain?'

Ellie rested her head on the cold window, trying to stem the flow of doubts surging through her.

She didn't know how long she'd been standing there, but gradually the cold made her move. However, her mind was made up. Right or wrong, she had to find the Bonners, and somehow put that past life to rest in her thought, or she would never find any peace. It would haunt her, and the only way to deal with something frightening, was to face it.

With one last look at the stars to say a silent thank you for helping her to sort out the jumble of her thoughts and fears, she jumped back into bed, pulling the covers around her ears. Dawn wasn't far off, but she fell asleep at last.

Uncle Henry, Philip and Mr Rogers had been summoned to Nanny's room at nine o'clock that morning. One of the maids had brought in a large tray of tea, and while Ellie poured, Philip collected two more chairs from the hall. It was rather crowded in the room, but everyone was far too curious to mind.

Ellie handed round the tea, and then when everyone was sitting, she went and stood beside her father.

62

'I apologize for disturbing your class times again, Mr Rogers, but there is a chance we shall be doing this quite often for a while, and we would appreciate your cooperation. My daughter wants this news out in the open, and I agree with her.'

Stanley Rogers nodded, looking as puzzled as Philip.

'Fifteen years ago a little girl of only two and a half was brought into this house by my wife and her brother. Her name was Queenie Bonner, and her home had been in the slums of Whitechapel. We adopted her and renamed her Eleanor.'

Philip gasped in astonishment.

Mr Rogers said nothing, listening intently as the story unfolded.

Placing an arm around his daughter, Albert continued. 'Eleanor wishes to trace the Bonners.'

'All of them?' Henry was aghast at the suggestion. 'Queenie was the youngest of ten.'

'We know it might be impossible to find all of them, Uncle Henry, but we should be able to trace some of them.' Ellie spoke firmly, seeing her uncle was going to protest.

'Oh this is madness!' Henry stood up, glowering. 'And what are you going to do if you do succeed?'

'I really don't know.'

'They'll take one look at you and beg for money. That's all they were interested in, and if you turn up looking like the fine lady you are, they'll expect more.'

'Then they will be disappointed.' Ellie shook her head.

Henry still protested, but gently now. 'Why do this, Eleanor? It will cause a lot of pain, and most likely, trouble. The Bonners were a rough lot, and if they find out who you are and where you live, you will never be free of them. This is a dangerous course to take. Leave it where it belongs – in the past.'

'They won't be told my name, and Father will be with me all the time,' Ellie said. 'We have discussed this and know the risks.'

Albert nodded in agreement at his daughter's words. 'Have no fear, Henry, we'll be careful. This is something Eleanor feels she must do.'

'You have no idea what trouble this could unleash, Albert.' Henry still wasn't convinced. 'But if your mind is set, then we must all do what we can to help.'

'I know London well, sir.' Mr Rogers got to his feet. 'I would be happy to assist you in any way. I also was adopted, and therefore have some understanding of the situation your daughter finds herself in.'

'Really? Would you share your experiences with us?' Albert studied the young man in front of him, surprised. This had not shown up on any of the information he had received before employing him. 'Unless, of course, you prefer not to talk about it?'

'I don't mind at all.' Mr Rogers smiled encouragingly at Ellie. 'My situation is difference from yours. I was left at a workhouse when no more than a week old. A young couple soon adopted me, and like you, I have been very fortunate to find kind parents. There is no way to trace my natural mother.'

'Oh, I'm so sorry.' Ellie was finding it difficult to understand why anyone could abandon their child. 'Would you find them if you could?'

Mr Rogers nodded. 'I would do the same as you. Not because I have any desire for permanent contact with them. I have had a happy life, but I would like to face them and ask why they abandoned me.'

'Exactly. That is what I want to do. Mr Rogers understands, Father.'

'Indeed he does,' Albert said. 'Your help would be much appreciated.'

'We'll all help.' Philip's face was alive with excitement. 'What can we do, Uncle Albert?'

'Nothing for the moment. Eleanor and I just wished you all to know what was going on.'

'Very wise.' Nanny spoke for the first time. 'Ever since Eleanor reached the age of fourteen I have been urging the mistress to tell her the truth, but I understood her reasons for not doing so. She was becoming too ill to deal with the trauma the revelation would cause.' Nanny looked around the room. 'There is nothing to be ashamed of here. That little girl was brought here in an unconventional way, but the master soon put that right. Eleanor has grown into a sensible girl, and I'm positive she will handle this with care.'

Ellie went over and kissed her cheek. 'Thank you, Nanny.'

Henry sighed. 'Well, if you are determined on this crazy

scheme, then I'll check to see if they are still living at the same address.'

'Good, that is a start. You will do that today, Henry?' Albert urged. 'We wish to get on with this without delay.'

'Yes, yes, of course,' he muttered irritably as he walked towards the door. 'Damned madness, that's what it is.'

'Can I come with you, Father?' Philip called.

'No, you can't. It's no fit place to take anyone.'

'I believe it's time we started our lessons.' Mr Rogers ushered them out of the room.

Ellie caught hold of Philip's arm. 'Stop looking so grumpy.'

'How can we concentrate on lessons with all this excitement going on?' Philip eyed her with renewed interest. 'You're not my cousin after all.'

'I most certainly am, and you'll be asking for trouble if you say anything like that again.'

As they left the room she heard her father chuckle, and she turned round to wink at him.

Only when they'd all gone did Albert sit down next to Nanny. 'Eleanor is making a valiant effort to deal with this and remain cheerful. She has courage, as we have always known, but this has caused her great distress.'

'It was bound to, but she has found someone who understands how she feels. Employing that young man is turning out to be a blessing. Fortune was smiling on you that day.'

'You could be right.' Albert drained his second cup of tea and put it back on the table. 'But there are going to be difficult times ahead.'

'You will both come through this, scarred, no doubt, but stronger.

'I hope you're right, Nanny.'

Nine

Dinner was an informal affair on the evening Henry returned
from London. Albert had insisted that Mr Rogers and
Nanny join them to hear what he had discovered on his trip.

However, much to Ellie's frustration, the Bonners were not
discussed until the meal was over and they had retired to the
drawing room. She could hardly contain herself, but knew
better than to broach the subject until her father was ready to
do so.

When everyone was settled with a drink, her father looked
at Henry. 'What did you find out?'

'I didn't go to the house, of course, not wishing to arouse
the Bonners' curiosity, but the area is just as disgusting as I
remembered. The landlord of the local hostelry told me that
the Bonners are still at the same address, but the children have
all left home.'

Ellie's insides clenched in apprehension. So, she would be
able to see them.

'I'm not surprised the children have gone. They will be
quite grown up after fifteen years.' Albert turned to Ellie. 'We
shall pay them a visit tomorrow.'

'Just a minute.' Henry was on his feet in alarm. 'You can't
just walk up to them and ask why they sold Queenie. It's a
damned rough street, Albert, and no place for a young lady.'

'I am sure you exaggerate.' Albert glowered irritably. 'How
are we to see them if we don't go there? What do you suggest,
that we summon them here?'

'You know you can't do that.' Henry was clearly annoyed
with Albert's tone. 'But it isn't safe to take Eleanor there.'

'There is a way, sir.'

All eyes turned to Mr Rogers.

'If you go there pretending to be on official business, it
should be safe enough. Tell them that the government is

looking into the possibility of improving housing for the poor, and they will treat you with respect.'

'That's a splendid idea, Father.' Ellie was enthusiastic. For a moment she had believed it wouldn't be possible to go to Whitechapel. 'I could pretend to be your secretary, or something.'

'Hmm, it might work.' Albert dipped his head, deep in thought, and then he looked up again. 'I have no wish to have my daughter frightened. Mr Rogers, would you come with us just in case there is trouble? You could pass as my assistant, while Eleanor pretends to make notes.'

'I would be happy to accompany you.'

'Can I come too?' Philip was fidgeting with excitement.

'Not this time,' Albert said kindly to soften the refusal. 'But we may well need you when we trace some of the children.'

'All right.' Philip had a gleam in his eye. 'Does this mean there won't be any lessons tomorrow?'

'I'll leave work for you to do,' the tutor told him. 'You will be on your honour to study while I am away.'

'Yes, sir.' Philip pulled a face, disappointed. 'It won't be much fun stuck in the schoolroom on my own.'

'You may bring your lessons to my room and keep me company for the day.'

'Thank you, Nanny.' He brightened at once.

'Now that's all settled, I suggest we make an early start in the morning. There is a train at nine o'clock.'

'There's one more thing, sir, it would be unwise to use your own name.'

Albert pursed his lips. 'You are right. Now, what shall I call myself?'

'Mr Higginbottom.' Philip rocked with laughter.

'Something a little less memorable, I think.' Albert's voice showed his amusement. 'What about Smythe?'

'That should do nicely.' Henry nodded. 'Is there anyone in Parliament by that name?'

'At least two.'

'Ah well, that should cause enough confusion if anyone makes enquiries about the government interest in the area.' Henry actually laughed, more at ease about the scheme now. 'I wish I could come with you, but the Bonners might have long memories.'

'You can't take the risk of being recognized.' Albert helped Nanny out of the chair. 'It is way past your bedtime.'

When Ellie came to the other side of Nanny, she smiled at both of them. 'Thank you for including me in the discussions. I may be infirm, but my mind is still sharp. The young man has come up with a sound plan, but you all make sure you take care of my girl.'

'We will, Nanny.' Mr Rogers opened the door for them. 'She will come to no harm, I promise.'

'I shall expect a report as soon as you return home.'

'I'll come and see you at once,' Ellie assured her.

With a nod and a grimace of pain, she allowed them to take her back to her room, where the maid, Molly, was waiting to help her to bed.

Surprisingly, Ellie slept well that night, but had difficulty eating her breakfast. Her nervous stomach would not take the array of cooked foods on the sideboard. The thought of what this day held was making her feel sick, and yet she *had* to know what the Bonners were like. She just had to.

'Are you all right, Eleanor? You are not eating.'

'I'm not hungry, Father.' She glanced hesitantly at him. 'I'm putting you to a great deal of trouble.'

Folding his napkin, he reached for her hand. 'Are you having doubts?'

'I'm full of doubts, but I must see where I came from. I feel incomplete, and it will plague me for the rest of my life if I don't do this. But I am so very frightened.'

'Don't be.' He squeezed her hand. 'Mr Rogers and I will be with you the entire time. They won't know who you are unless you decide to tell them. Now, we must go or we shall miss our train.'

The tutor was already outside with the carriage to take them to the railway station. Out of respect for the family he was also in mourning clothes and Ellie thought the sombre dress would not cause too much attention in the poorer parts of London. Not that she could remember what that was like, of course, but she had read accounts of the hardship and poverty. And the fact that a frock was the only garment Queenie had been wearing drew its own picture. She still couldn't imagine herself as that little girl. In her mind, Queenie and Eleanor were separate people, but perhaps that would change after today.

The weather was cold but dry when they arrived in London. Her mother had disliked the city, never wishing to visit, and so Ellie had never been here before. Even though she was extremely nervous, there was also excitement about the day ahead. Her father had arranged for a Hansom cab to be at their disposal for the day.

'River Street, Whitechapel,' he told the driver as they got in. 'Let's get this done first, and then have lunch. Would you like to visit the Palace of Westminster before returning home?'

'Yes, please.' Ellie had longed to do this for a long time, and once the visit to Whitechapel was over it would be something to look forward to.

'Is that also agreeable to you, Mr Rogers?'

'I would enjoy that very much, sir.'

The men continued talking, but Ellie took no part, she was watching the passing scenery: there were people everywhere, carriages, horse drawn buses and delivery carts, and even a few motorcars. They were rather noisy. In fact everything was noisy after the tranquillity of the countryside. She was beginning to understand her mother's aversion to London. She had loved peace and quiet, and there seemed to be very little of that here.

Suddenly they came to a halt, and Ellie hung out of the window in wonderment. 'Look, Father, women with banners are blocking the way. One says, "Votes for Mother". It's the WSPU. I wonder if Mrs Pankhurst's there.'

'Right in the front, I expect.' He looked wryly at his daughter's animated face.

'Do you think they will succeed?'

'One day, maybe, but it will not come quickly. Radical change never does, and there is a great deal of opposition to giving women the vote. Many men consider they haven't the intellect and should continue doing what they do best – looking after their husbands and raising the children.'

Ellie spun back in her seat, indignant. 'Women are just as intelligent as men, and in some cases more intelligent.'

Albert held up his hands. 'I agree with you, but I am considered to have outlandish views on many subjects – for a man.'

'Oh, you should not have given up your seat in Parliament. The government has need of men with vision.'

'Thank you, Eleanor.' He bowed his head in acknowledgement of the compliment. 'There may come a time when I shall return to politics, but for the moment I need to be free.'

'Of course.' Ellie knew the decision must have been hard for him, and once they were through this period of mourning, and their search for the Bonners was over, she would encourage him to return to parliament. She turned to Mr Rogers. He had fitted into their lives so quickly that it would be hard to imagine him not being with them now. He was so interesting to talk to, as well. 'Do you believe that women should be allowed the vote?'

'I am sure it will happen one day, but your father's right, those women have a long, hard struggle ahead of them. But, to answer your question, I do believe they have the right to a say in things that touch their lives.'

Ellie smiled in satisfaction, then jumped up again. 'Oh, we're moving again. The constables have cleared the road.' She settled back to watch the passing scenery again, her nervousness forgotten in the excitement. But it crept back as the views changed from fine houses and well-dressed people, to small dwellings, and ragged children playing in dirty streets. Was this how she had lived? It was shocking.

'We're almost there, Eleanor.' Her father spoke gently. 'Do you have your notebook at the ready?'

She nodded and whispered, 'Is this really where I came from?'

'Yes, but try not to let it upset you too much. Your time here was short.'

At that moment the cab stopped. Mr Rogers got out first, then her father, and finally Ellie stepped on to the street she must have known well as a small child. She lifted her skirt to avoid the worst of the dirty road. Everything looked grimy, even the people who were watching their arrival with suspicion.

''Ere, giss a penny.' A small boy of about six held out his hand.

Ellie was about to open her purse when her father stopped her. 'No, we shall be besieged if you do.'

She gazed regretfully at the urchin, who hadn't missed the exchange.

'Does you always do what he says?'

70

'I most certainly do.' She slipped into her role. 'I work for him, you see. He's an important man in the government.'

'What's a toff like him doing down here?' The boy eyed him up and down, then wiped his nose on his sleeve. 'What you all dressed in black for? The old Queen died ages ago.'

'We have had a family bereavement.' This scruffy little boy certainly wasn't frightened of them.

'Alfie, come away.' A woman rushed out of a house, clipped him round the ear and dragged him inside.

A few men and women were standing by their front doors. They didn't appear to be very friendly, and Ellie moved closer to her father, wondering if any of them were the Bonners.

Seeing they had an audience, her father began to explain why they were there, making the story sound plausible. He was, after all, a politician, and used to speaking to the public.

He caught their interest and the residents gathered round, eager to air their views. Ellie scribbled industriously in her book, and Mr Rogers walked around, talking to others who were keeping their distance. The subterfuge seemed to be working.

After about twenty minutes, Albert said, 'You have been very helpful. Would you be kind enough to tell me your names?'

Ellie made a list of the names, waiting all the while for one name. When it came she actually jumped, looking up sharply to study the man and woman talking to her father.

'Would you mind if we had a look inside your house, Mr Bonner? It would help my report if I could actually describe the living conditions.'

'If you wants to.' Mr Bonner led the way with his wife close behind him.

The place was very small and Ellie wondered how they had managed to cram ten children into this tiny dwelling. Nanny had told her that she hadn't liked sleeping in a bed on her own, so they must have all been crammed together. She drank in the scene, her heart hammering, but nothing was familiar.

'Do you have any children?' her father asked.

'We had ten, but three died, and the rest have gone their own ways.' Mrs Bonner scowled. 'Don't never bother with us now. Ungrateful lot after the struggle we had to bring them up.'

Albert ignored her outburst. 'I'm sorry to hear that three of your children died. What were their names?'

'It was Charlie, June and Queenie.'

Liar, was the word that ran through Ellie's head as she looked at Hilda Bonner, but she made a note of the other two names, wondering if they had sold them as well. If they were dead then it made her sad to realize she had a brother and sister she would never meet.

'And where do your other children live, Mrs Bonner?' Mr Rogers asked.

'A couple in Wandsworth and one in Hammersmith, but we don't know where the rest are.'

'I know Wandsworth well.' Mr Rogers looked suitably interested. 'Whereabouts do they live?'

'Pearl is in Crondall Street. Married a bloke by the name of Greenway, and Jack's in the same street. Doing all right for themselves.'

'I'm pleased to hear that.' The tutor nodded to Ellie to let her know he knew where it was.

They moved outside again, where an even larger crowd had gathered.

'You ought'ave charged them an entrance fee, Fred.' One of the neighbours grinned, a cigarette hanging out of his mouth. 'Surprised you didn't think of that, Hilda.'

'Shut your mouth, Joe,' Fred Bonner snarled. 'Or I'll shut it for you.'

Seeing there was danger of a fight breaking out, Albert and Mr Rogers urged Ellie towards the cab.

'What do you want to do, Eleanor?' Her father placed a protective arm around his daughter. 'Do you want to leave without saying anything?'

Taking a deep breath, she turned to face the Bonners. She couldn't think of them as her parents, that was very clear to her. 'You said three of your children had died and one of them was Queenie.'

'S'right.' Fred Bonner lit a cigarette.

'Then you are not telling the truth. Queenie didn't die. You sold her to strangers for a few pounds.'

'You don't know nothing about it,' Hilda said, clearly agitated.

'But I do.' Ellie carefully removed the pins from her hat,

72

took it off and shook her fair hair free. 'You see *I* am Queenie.'

There was a stunned silence as everyone stared at Ellie. Then Hilda Bonner whispered something to her husband.

'Course she ain't, you daft old woman.'

'She could be, the hair's right, so's the eyes.' Hilda came closer. 'You really my Queenie?'

'Yes, but I'm not *yours*.' Ellie slipped her hand through her father's arm. 'You gave up the right to call me that fifteen years ago.'

Hilda turned on her husband. 'How's she know that if she isn't Queenie?'

Fred looked doubtful now, glaring at Albert. 'I ain't never seen you before. What you say your name was?'

'I didn't, but it's Smythe.'

Fred laughed. 'Who you trying to kid, mate? That's only a posh name for Smith, ain't it?'

'Is it? I really wouldn't know,' Albert lied with aplomb.

'Never mind about that!' Hilda slapped her husband to gain his attention. 'I wanna know what she's doing here.'

'Perhaps she's come to give her old mum and dad a helping hand.' Fred swaggered up to Albert, a calculating gleam in his eyes. 'You're the one who wanted her, are you? What's it worth for us to keep out of your way?'

Ellie was sickened by the callous behaviour, and spoke before her father could reply. 'You'll get nothing from us.'

'What you here for then?'

Facing the woman, Ellie held her gaze unflinchingly. 'I want to know why you sold me to strangers for the paltry sum of five guineas.'

'Paltry!' Fred shouted. 'That was a bleedin' fortune to us.'

Ellie ignored him and didn't look away from Hilda. 'You haven't answered my question.'

'We had ten of you to feed, and when some gent offered us money for you, we took it.'

'Didn't you have any regrets when they took me away?'

'We was too bloody poor to have regrets.' Fred studied Albert, who was stopping them from getting too close. 'You took her on, did you?'

'I did, and I'm proud to have her for my daughter.'

Hilda said nothing, but her husband snorted. 'Looks like we did you a good turn, girl.'

73

'Oh, you did. I've had the most wonderful, loving parents.' She looked up at her father. 'We have finished here, Father, let us leave.'

She was lifted into the cab, quickly followed by Albert and Mr Rogers, all eager to get away from this place. As the cab pulled away, they could hear a row going on.

'Find out where he lives. We've got his name.'

'Don't be daft, woman, you don't think that's his real name, do you? And he certainly ain't from the government. The whole thing was a bloody lie . . .'

They were soon out of earshot and Ellie relaxed, closing her eyes for a moment. That had been an ordeal, and she'd been tempted to leave without telling them who she was, but in the end she'd wanted them to know.

'Eleanor.'

Opening her eyes, she saw her father watching her anxiously. 'Are you all right?'

'Yes, yes I am.' She sat up straight. 'I didn't know how I would feel when I saw them – if I would be drawn to them, or angry with what they had done? Would I hate them, or perhaps feel the blood tie and want to get to know them better?'

'And how do you feel?' her father prompted when she stopped speaking.

'It was strange. I wasn't afraid to be standing in that squalid street, perhaps it was some latent memory, but I didn't feel any connection to the Bonners.' She shook her head, not being able to believe her reaction to seeing the woman who had given birth to her. 'They meant nothing to me, in fact I felt sorry for them. Trying to bring up ten children in that hovel must have been awful. I'm grateful they sold me to you, for they saved me from a squalid existence. I'm glad I've met them, but I have no wish to see them again.'

Albert smiled in relief. 'I don't believe you were ever fond of them. When you came to us you wanted your brothers and sisters, especially Harry, but you never asked for your parents.'

'It was right to come here, Father, and thank you for bringing me.' Taking the list out of her purse, she crossed off the names of Hilda and Fred Bonner. 'And thank you also, Mr Rogers, for finding out where two of the others are living.'

'If we can find one, then that will probably lead on to others,' Mr Rogers said. 'They don't appear to have much to

74

do with their parents, but they are bound to have kept in touch with each other.'

'We'll arrange a visit to Wandsworth soon, but now let us enjoy the rest of the day.' Albert gave the cab driver fresh instructions, and then sat down again. 'Lunch first, then a visit to the Palace of Westminster.'

'Oh, I am looking forward to that. Are you, Mr Rogers?'

'It will be an exciting afternoon, and I shall expect you to write an essay about it tomorrow.'

Ellie grinned when she heard her father laugh. He was looking happier and more relaxed than she had seen him for a long time. And it felt as if a weight had been lifted from her mind after seeing the Bonners. There was nothing there for her. She was free, and she was pleased she'd had the courage to come. The next task was to try and find as many of her brothers and sisters as possible. She was sure that would be more emotional.

Ten

Without even stopping to take off her hat and coat, Ellie went straight in to see Nanny when they arrived back home, knowing she would be waiting impatiently for news.

'Sit, sit,' the elderly woman ordered eagerly. 'Tell me what happened, and I want every word, mind you.'

Ellie spent the next hour explaining about the Bonners, with Nanny nodding in approval every now and again.

'I'm glad I saw them, Nanny, because now I know that they meant nothing to me. I could never think of them as my parents, and it was clear that they had no affection for me.'

'I guessed that might be so, for you never spoke of them. But you loved your brothers and sisters. Meeting them could be upsetting for you, Eleanor.'

'I realize that. Mr Rogers was very clever and found out where two of them are living. Father said we shall visit soon, and I'm hoping to persuade him to go tomorrow.'

The maid entered to find out what Nanny wanted for her evening meal, and the first dinner gong sounded, Ellie leapt to her feet. 'Oh, I haven't changed yet!'

'You'd better run. Don't keep your father waiting.'

Lifting her skirt she ran into the hall, nearly colliding with the tutor. 'I do beg your pardon,' she gasped. 'I've been talking too long and shall be late for dinner. Are you joining us?'

'I have been invited to dine with Nanny.'

Ellie gurgled in delight. 'That means you are still under scrutiny.'

'It would appear so.' He didn't try to hide his amusement as he headed for Nanny's room.

Ellie just had time to change into a dark purple mourning dress as the final gong sounded. Only after a mad dash did she manage to join her father just in time, and out of breath. She felt as if she were seeing him in a fresh light. He was so tall and handsome, elegantly dressed, and as unruffled as usual, even after the kind of day they'd had. Was this how the little, frightened girl had first seen him? Was she drawn to the kindness in his eyes? Was the trust between them formed the moment he had removed the shoes she'd hated so much? Her eyes swam with tears. It must have been, but that child had seen a younger man. Now his black hair was laced with grey, and his face lined with worry and fatigue. Losing the woman he'd loved, and now the worry of looking for the Bonners, was taking its toll. She didn't want to cause him more grief, but she just had to do this. With a determined look in her eyes, she stood beside him. 'When can we go to Wandsworth, Father?'

'Tomorrow is Sunday and that might be a good time to find them in. What do you think? Is that too soon for you?'

'Oh, no, that would be perfect. Thank you.' Seeing there was no one else with them, she asked, 'Is Uncle Henry joining us tonight?

'He's coming later with Philip.' He threaded her hand through his arm and led her to the dining room. 'We shall be dinning alone.'

It was nine o'clock before Uncle Henry and her cousin arrived. Philip rushed up to Ellie, one question after another tumbling out.

'There's a fire in the small sitting room, Eleanor. Why don't you take Philip in there and tell him all about today?'

'It looks as if I'll have to, Father, or he will burst with curiosity.' Ellie laughed as her cousin dragged her to the other room.

They sat on the floor in front of the fire, and for once, Philip was silent while she told him about the Bonners and the way they lived.

He shuddered when she had finished. 'Sounds terrible. I bet you're pleased you live here and not there.'

'I am.' She drew up her knees, resting her chin on them and staring at the dancing flames. The things she had always taken for granted, like good food, cleanliness, warmth, comfort and love, now came into sharp focus. No longer would she thoughtlessly accept them. Her life was privileged. She wondered how many thousands like those they had seen today had enough to eat and a good fire to keep them warm on this cold early November evening. Very few, she suspected. Her father had campaigned tirelessly for better education and living conditions for the poor, and now she understood his passion. Someone ought to care . . .

'Don't look so sad, Ellie.' Philip was frowning with concern. 'I don't care that you were adopted. You're still my cousin. Nothing's changed.'

'Thank you Philip.' She was touched by his little speech, but he was wrong about one thing. Something had changed. She had changed. She would never be quite the same person she had been before finding out the truth about herself.

'What are you going to do when you see your brothers and sisters?'

'I don't know.' She sighed. 'It depends what they are like, and if they're pleased to see me. If they have the same attitude as the Bonners, then I'll just walk away and try to forget about them.'

'That won't be easy.'

'No, it won't, but after today I believe I'm stronger and more able to cope with whatever happens. I pray so, anyway.'

Philip smirked. 'You were already strong enough.'

Pushing away her worry, she surged to her feet, determination in her eyes. 'Let's see, shall we? I bet I can pick you up.'

Philip shrieked, crawling out of her way on hands and knees.

'Sounds like our children are up to their boisterous games again.' Henry shook his head listening to their play fighting. 'They should be acting like a young lady and gentleman by now.'

'Let them stay children for as long as possible. They will have the responsibilities of adulthood soon enough.' Albert poured them both a generous brandy. 'Though Eleanor was very mature today, behaving impeccably. I was very proud of her.'

'Tell me what happened.' Henry sat in a comfortable leather armchair and savoured his drink.

He listened to Albert's detailed account of their meeting with the Bonners. 'Ah, Eleanor kept her thinking straight, and didn't get emotional or panic.'

'It went well, but I was damned glad to get her away from there.' Albert gave a faint smile. 'Quite a crowd had gathered and they didn't look too friendly when they realized that we weren't there on official business. I almost threw her into the cab. I had the impression that she was the calmer of the two of us.'

'That's because you were more aware of the danger, Albert. Things could have turned nasty very quickly. Eleanor has led a sheltered life, and is quite innocent of the ways of the world.'

'I know, and that is causing me some concern. We've met the Bonners, and Eleanor has realized that there was never any affection between them. They didn't want her, and felt no remorse over what they'd done. I saw the determined set of her mouth when she crossed off their names from her list, but their attitude must have hurt her. However, I am confident that that part of her life has been laid to rest. The difficulty will be when she comes face to face with her brothers and sisters. What is she going to do then, Henry? They won't be so easy to dismiss.'

'You could be right about that.' Henry held out his glass for a refill, a wry twist to his mouth. 'You could end up with a huge family. I wish you had never told her. Why did you do it?'

Hauling himself to his feet, he poured Henry another drink, leaving his own glass empty. 'I was left with very little choice in the matter. First Nanny let the name of Queenie slip, and then Mary called her that just before she died. And I know Mary thought she should be told soon.'

'Yes, that's true. But this could turn out to be damned tricky. Talk to her, Albert, tell her that you can't take the entire Bonner brood under your wing.'

'We only know where two of them are at the moment. I'll see how those meetings go. I have agreed to take Eleanor tomorrow. She is eager to see them.'

'Would you like me to come with you?'

'No thanks, Henry. We'll go on our own.'

The next morning Ellie was too pent up to take any notice of inclement weather. She paced up and down the hallway, waiting for her father to finish his business with Uncle Henry. They were buying a forest, or something. Ordinarily, she would

79

have been interested in the new business venture, but today she just wished they would hurry.

'Eleanor.'

She spun round to see her father standing behind her. 'Are you ready?'

'Yes, the carriage is being brought round now.'

'Oh, good.' All of a sudden she felt paralysed and her feet wouldn't move. Doubts assailed her and she stood helplessly before her father. 'Suppose they don't want to see me?'

'You won't know that unless you go to them.' He watched his daughter warring with emotions. 'The choice is yours, Eleanor. We won't pursue this matter further if that is your wish.'

'If only I could remember them.' She stripped off her gloves, straightened them out, and then put them back on, easing them over her fingers, showing her agitation. 'I'm frightened. Suppose my brothers and sisters don't want anything to do with me?' Her hands shook.

'Ah, it has just hit her.' Henry was now standing next to Albert. 'Sometimes a shock has the habit of creeping up on you after the event.'

'I don't know what happened in that house all those years ago.' Albert made her sit on one of the hall chairs and crouched down in front of her. 'But I can tell you that you have only ever been a joy to us. Even when you first arrived and couldn't understand why you had been taken away from your family, you were obedient. You even tried to wear the shoes you hated, just to please us. You were a delightful little girl and no trouble at all. Once we'd managed to stop you swearing, of course.'

Her laugh came out on a sob as she leaned forward to throw her arms around his neck, nearly toppling him over. 'How did I come to be so lucky?'

'That's what we thought when you used to run around the garden barefoot chasing anything that moved, and squealing with laughter. He stood up, pulling her to her feet. 'I'm not going to tell you what to do, my dear, this is something you must decide for yourself.'

The panic had receded. 'If I don't do this then I shall wonder about them for the rest of my life, and regret not having had the courage to face them. But, I promise you, Father, that should the reception be hostile, then that will be the end of it. We won't look for any more of them.'

'Let us go, then.'

By the time they reached Wandsworth, Ellie had managed to gain some control over her nerves. She had to remain calm. It was at her insistence that the Bonners be found, and she would have to deal with the consequences of that decision – whatever they might be.

The Hansom cab stopped at the end of Crondall Street.

'Wait here for us,' her father instructed.

'Yes, sir.' The driver tipped his hat, looking pleased to have such a lucrative fare.

Ellie gazed up and down the long street, and although it was still a poor area, it was much better than Whitechapel. The houses were in good repair, and the gleaming steps showed that the residents cared about cleanliness. 'This is a nicer area, but how shall we find out where Pearl lives?'

'Simple. We just ask.' Albert knocked in the nearest door, and when a middle-aged woman opened it, he smiled. 'I beg your pardon for troubling you, Madam, but my daughter and I are looking for Mrs Greenway.'

She seemed startled to find such elegant people on her doorstep, but returned the smile. 'She lives at number twenty-eight, sir.'

'Thank you very much.' He bowed slightly, his manners impeccable no matter who he was dealing with.

Ellie watched him with pride. He had always told her that all should be treated with respect, regardless of their station in life, providing they did harm to no one. She added her own thanks.

'Come, Eleanor, let's see if Pearl is at home.'

As they walked up the street, Ellie couldn't help glancing back. The woman was still watching them with curiosity.

The house was like every other one in the street, the curtains were clean and there was a small vase of yellow chrysanthemums on the windowsill, making a lovely splash of colour on this dreary November day. Ellie liked that touch, and took a deep breath as her father knocked on the door. She was trembling in anticipation. What could she say when she saw her sister? Her mind was a complete blank.

When the door opened she gasped. Standing there was a young woman with a child perched on her hip. But it was her appearance that was the biggest shock. There was no doubting that this was one of her family. It was like looking at an older version of herself; the hair was the same colour, eyes a paler blue, but the features were almost identical. There was no need to ask if this was Pearl. They stared at each other, mesmerized.

'Forgive us for calling unannounced, but my daughter would like to speak with you.' Albert turned to Ellie, and then stepped back. 'You must talk to Pearl on your own, my dear. I'll wait by the cab for you.'

He was leaving her on her own? She wanted to call him back, but realized what he was doing. This first meeting with her sister should be between the two of them, and he wouldn't interfere.

'Who are you?' Pearl was puzzled.

Ellie gulped, and managed to whisper, 'I'm Queenie . . . your sister.'

There was a stunned silence, and then Pearl beamed. 'My God, that's why you look familiar. Come in.'

The front door led straight into a small room; cheaply furnished, but spotlessly clean. The baby was put on the floor where it could crawl and play with a rubber ball.

'Let's have a look at you.' Pearl grabbed hold of her arms, turning her to face the light from the window. 'Take your hat off.'

When Ellie had done this, her sister nodded and kissed her cheek. She had tears in her eyes. 'Oh, yes, you are Queenie. You always were the prettiest of us all, even as a baby. I've got so many questions to ask you, but I must go an' get Jack and my husband Dave. Sit down while I nip next door.'

Ellie waited, overwhelmed by the excited greeting. For the first time she was really happy that her father had told her about the adoption. It couldn't have been more than a couple of minutes before she heard the tread of heavy feet and a man burst into the room. His colouring was darker, but there was no mistaking the family likeness.

'Queenie!' Jack hugged her. 'How bloody marvellous. We never expected to see you again. Tell us where you've been, what has happened to you?' Then he frowned. 'Why are you wearing mourning?'

'My mother died recently, and it was only then my father told me that they had adopted me.'

Another man came into the room, watching the scene with interest.

'Dave, come and meet my long lost sister, Queenie.'

'Pleased to meet you. Pearl's often talked about you.'

She shook hands with him shyly. She had been hoping they would be pleased, but after yesterday she'd been bracing herself for rejection. But they all looked delighted she was here.

'Well, well, our little Queenie.' Jack shook his head. 'Who'd have thought it. Tell us what happened to you.'

'My name's Eleanor now. When I went to my new home my mother renamed me, but my friends call me Ellie.'

Jack grinned. 'You sound posh. Have you been happy, Ellie?'

'Yes, I've been very lucky.' She then gave them a brief outline of her life and what a shock it had been to discover that she had a large family somewhere. When she told them about her visit to Whitechapel, Pearl snorted in disgust.

'We ain't never forgiven them for selling you like that, and we all got out of there as soon as we could.'

'Do you know where any of the others are?' Ellie took the list out of her purse. 'Only I would like to find everyone, if I can.'

'Well, June died of whoopin' cough and Charlie got run over by a cart when the horses bolted.' Jack sighed. 'And when they took you away, Harry left. We ain't seen nor heard from him since. Ted's in Hammersmith, but we've lost touch with Maggie, Bert and Tommy.'

'We'll see if we can find out anything, Queenie. Oops, sorry, Ellie.' Pearl laughed, standing up. 'I'll make a nice pot of tea. What about that man who was with you? Would he like a cuppa?'

'He's my Father, and I'm sure he would. He waiting for me down the road by the cab.'

'I'll go and get him.' Jack headed for the door.

The young man striding towards him was clearly one of the Bonners. Albert watched his purposeful step, and waited, wondering what kind of a reception Eleanor had received from her forgotten family. It hadn't been easy for him to walk away, leaving her to face them alone, but he'd felt it was right that did. He had always been protective towards his daughter – too protective perhaps, but he had never been able to remove the picture of a confused little girl from his thought. The pleading in her clear blue eyes still haunted him. However, if he'd stayed they might have been uneasy in his presence. He knew how much this meant to Eleanor and he didn't want to do anything to make it more difficult than it already was.

'Sir, I'm Jack Bonner.' He held out his hand. 'My sister's about to make a pot of tea and we would be pleased if you would join us.'

Albert shook his hand, noting the easy smile and firm grip. 'Thank you, I would like that.'

They walked up the road together, Jack talking excitedly. 'It's smashing to see our little sister again, and such a relief. We've worried about her over the years, wondering if she was all right. It tore our family apart when she was taken away, for we all loved the little devil.'

'You can rest assured that she has had a good life and been much loved.'

'That's obvious.' Jack cast him a speculative glance. 'But she shouldn't have been taken away from us like that.'

'I agree.' Albert stopped walking and faced Jack. 'It was not of my doing, but when I discovered what had happened, I did what I could to put things right for the little girl. My fear was that if we didn't keep her she might be given to someone else who would not treat her well. I made the adoption legal so she could not be taken away. I have never regretted my decision. She brought my wife and I a great deal of happiness.'

Jack nodded, seeming satisfied with that explanation, and they began walking again. 'I understand you have recently lost your wife, sir.'

'Yes, it has been a sad time.' Albert changed the subject, as Mary's death was still an open wound. 'We visited your parents yesterday.'

'So Queenie told us. Sorry, I should call her Eleanor now.'

'I have no objection to you calling her by the name she was first given.' They stopped at the front door. 'After seeing the way your parents live, life must have been incredibly hard for you.'

'It was.' Jack shrugged. 'But we didn't know nothing else. Come in, sir.'

Eleven

When her father walked in, Ellie jumped excitedly to her feet. 'Father, this is my sister Pearl and her husband, Dave.'

Pearl appeared slightly flustered at having the distinguished man in her front room, almost curtsying when she greeted him. 'Thank you for bringing Queenie to see us, sir. She hasn't been out of our minds all these years.'

'I'm sure she hasn't.' He shook hands with both of them, and then looked at the baby on the floor, who was studying his highly polished shoes with fascination. 'And who is this?' He swept the baby up high, making it gurgle in surprise.

'That's our Jimmy. He's just over a year old, sir.' Pearl reached out for the dribbling baby. 'I'll take him, shall I?'

'He's all right with me, aren't you little fellow?' The baby blew bubbles when he gurgled this time, but Albert wasn't at all concerned, and sat down holding him on his knees.

Pearl lurched forward to wipe the baby's mouth and nose. 'He'll dribble all over you if he isn't kept well mopped up.'

Albert smiled. 'It won't be the first time.'

Dave laughed. 'You look as if you're used to kids.'

'I have a nephew I used to look after when he was a baby.' He glanced at Ellie, amusement in his eyes. 'Eleanor was too old to dribble on me when she came to us, but her language was colourful.'

That had everyone in the room laughing. Ellie felt for her father. He loved children and should have had hoards of them running around him.

'I'll bet it was.' Jack chuckled. 'She spent too much time with Harry, and he could cuss with the best of them.'

At the mention of this brother, Ellie sat forward. 'Do you know where Harry is?'

'No, we're sorry.' Pearl shook her head. 'After you'd gone,

Harry demanded to know where you were being taken. When Mum and Dad said they didn't know, that was more than he could take and he exploded. He received a thrashing from Dad and then walked out and we've never seen or heard from him again.'

The disappointment was crushing. Ellie had been told that she'd cried repeatedly for Harry, more than anyone else. 'But how old was he?'

'Twelve.'

'That is appalling.' The baby was struggling to get down, so Albert put him back on the floor. 'How would a child of that age survive on his own?'

'We don't know.' Jack's mouth set in a grim line. 'God knows where he went. We searched high and low for him, but he'd just vanished. He'd loved little Queenie an' couldn't take what had happened.'

'Oh.' She looked at her father, eyes pleading.

'I'll get a man on to the search right away. Don't upset yourself, my dear, we'll find him if at all possible.' Albert turned his attention back to Jack. 'What about the others?'

'Ted's in Hammersmith an' we see him from time to time. Maggie went into service an' has moved around so much that we've lost contact with her. She always was a bit of an outsider and couldn't wait to get away. Lord knows where Bert is, and the last we heard of Tommy he was runnin' with a rough crowd. Charlie an' June died.' Jack nodded to his sister. 'What about that tea?'

As Pearl left the room, Ellie sighed. 'It doesn't look as if we'll be able to find everyone, does it?'

'It might not be possible, Eleanor, but we'll do our best. Jack, will you tell me how old you all are now?'

'Well, let me see . . . Ted's the oldest at thirty, I'm next at twenty-eight. Harry twenty-seven. Maggie twenty-five. Pearl twenty-four. Bert twenty-three. Tommy twenty-two, and then there was June and Charlie who died a couple of years after Queenie left. So, that would make our little sister nearly eighteen.'

Ellie nodded. 'Yes, in January.'

Pearl returned carrying a tray of tea and a homemade fruit-cake. This was all laid carefully on the small table by the window. The best china had obviously been brought out for the occasion.

Standing up, Ellie went over to help serve the tea. 'Your cake smells delicious, Pearl, and what a lovely tea service. The decoration of purple pansies is very pretty.'

'Do you like it?' She smiled broadly. 'Dave bought it for me as a present after Jimmy was born. Do you think your . . . er . . . dad would like a piece of cake?' she asked quietly.

'I'm sure he would, but do go and ask him.' She touched her sister's arm. 'Don't be afraid of him. He's the kindest man you could ever wish to meet.'

Pearl shuffled uncomfortably. 'You both look and talk posh. We ain't used to mixing with such folk. He's a real gent.'

Ellie didn't want them to feel uneasy. It was right that her father was shown respect because of his station in life, but she wanted to be accepted. 'And I'm your sister. For the first two and a half years of my life I lived with all of you in Whitechapel. Underneath the finery and upper class accent I'm still Queenie Bonner. I'm not ashamed of that, and neither is my father.'

'No, I don't think you are, or you wouldn't be here.' Pearl relaxed a little.

Ellie leaned forward and whispered in her ear. 'I got expelled from two schools for fighting.'

With a shriek of glee, Pearl spun round to face her brother. 'Jack, Queenie got slung out of two schools for fighting. Do you remember how she always jumped into the middle of us when we was having a scrap?'

He roared, slapping his thigh. 'We couldn't stop her. Harry got the worst of it every time. She did love to lay into him, calling him a coward when he wouldn't fight back.'

Albert was amused by their memories. 'She has never tolerated injustice of any kind, and has not hesitated to defend her beliefs, and my reputation, with her fists.'

'She was a right little tearaway, and it don't sound like she's changed much.' Pearl was now completely at ease. 'Would you like a piece of cake with your tea, sir? I made it this morning.'

'I would indeed.'

Once they were all served, Ellie sat down again, eager to find out more about her family. 'Jack, I understand that I was very attached to Harry. Would you tell me what he was like?'

'He was a nice kid. Probably the best of the lot of us, and

everyone liked him. He was always cheerful with never a bad word to say about anyone, until you were sent away.' He shook his head, his expression sad as he remembered. 'He couldn't abide cruelty, and you being taken away like that was too much.'

'Dad nearly killed him.' Pearl's voice was husky. 'We searched for months, but there was no sign of him. We don't know if he's dead or alive. He'd burst with joy if he could see you now.'

'I wish I could remember you all, but I can't.' Ellie hurt to imagine the suffering one young boy had experienced in wanting to protect her.

'You was little more than a baby when you were taken away, and you had a new life. The memories of the old one were bound to fade in time.' Jack squeezed her hand. 'But we're very pleased to see you all grown up and looking well.'

'Would you like more tea, sir?' Dave took Albert's cup. 'And another piece of cake?'

'That would be most acceptable. Pearl is a fine cook.'

'Ah, she's a wonder in the kitchen.' He gave his wife an affectionate glance as he poured the tea and sliced the cake.

'You have a comfortable home,' Albert said to Pearl, before turning his attention to the two men. 'How do you earn a living?'

'Me and Jack have got our own business,' Dave told him with a touch of pride. 'It's a small ironmongers and cobblers shop. Nothing grand, but we earn enough to pay the rent and buy food. We're good at mending shoes. Learnt the trade from one of the best cobblers in the business, and when he died we decided to go it alone.'

'Best move we ever made.' Jack joined the conversation. 'We're getting a reputation for good work.'

'Well done.' Albert was impressed. 'That's the way to build up a loyal cliental. Are you married, Jack?'

'I could now the business is doing all right.' He grinned. 'But I haven't met anyone I want to settle down with yet.'

Pearl laughed. 'Tell the truth, Jack. You don't want a wife; you're too content on your own.'

'I admit it suits me fine. The shop is enough for me at the moment.'

Ellie was delighted to know that at least two of her family were working to improve their lives.

Albert removed a small black leather case from his pocket. Flipping the lid open he handed Jack a calling card. 'That's where we live, and we would appreciate knowing if you hear any news about your other brothers and sisters.'

This action startled Ellie. Her father had been adamant that they should not know where they lived, but he was obviously happy for Jack to have the information, or he wouldn't have given it to him. Her father was a good judge of character though, and Ellie was more than a little relieved that her forgotten family appeared to be hardworking, respectable people. It was a comfort because after yesterday she'd had grave doubts about the Bonners.

'Thank you, sir.' Jack tapped the card. 'This is very trusting of you, and we won't make a nuisance of ourselves, but it will be nice to know where our little sister is now.'

'I'm sure it will.' Albert stood up. 'Would you give us the address of your brother in Hammersmith. We'll have time to call on him before catching our train.'

'You're going now?' Pearl looked alarmed. 'Jack?'

'I'd better come with you.' He gave his sister a reassuring glance.

'Is there a problem?' Albert frowned.

'I'd better explain. Ted's in a bit of a mess. His wife died in childbirth eighteen months ago and he started drinking heavy, so much so that he lost his job. He ain't got over losing Annie. We've done all we can to help him, but he don't want to know.'

'Is he violent?'

'I wouldn't put it as strong as that, sir. He gets fighting mad at times, but he holds himself in check around us.' Jack sighed. 'It ain't like him, but he adored his missus.'

'She was very nice,' Pearl said sadly. 'We ain't been able to shake him out of the grief an' he drinks to try an' forget, but we all know that don't help any. Once you sober up the problems are still there, only worse. That's what's happened to Ted. If you see him, don't judge him too harshly, sir. He's really a good man.'

'I understand. What do you want to do, Eleanor?'

'If Jack is willing to come with us then I'd like to see him. That's if you don't mind, Father? We might be able to help.' She was dismayed by the news, but it had been naive of her to believe that they would all be like Pearl and Jack. Ted had obviously suffered a great loss and she could empathize with that. 'We must see him.'

'I agree.' Albert turned to Jack. 'We'll go now, if that is convenient for you? The cab is waiting for us at the end of the road. We shall, of course, bring you back.'

'I'll just get my coat.'

Pearl hugged Ellie. 'This has been the most lovely surprise. Please come and see us again.'

'I will. Often.'

'Thank you for bringing her, sir.' This time Pearl didn't look as if she wanted to curtsy when addressing Albert. 'This can't have been easy for you.'

He smiled wryly. 'I admit to being dismayed when my daughter wanted to find her family, but now I've met you, she was quite right to do so. It has been a pleasure to meet you, Pearl, and thank you for your hospitality.'

Jimmy, who had been very well behaved while they had been there, began pulling on Albert's trousers, telling him a tale in his own baby language. Albert bent down and swept him up. 'That's very interesting, young man. It's been a pleasure meeting you, as well.'

Pearl laughed at the exchange, and then took her baby from Albert, resting him on her hip for comfort.

'Right, I'm ready.' Jack came back, stopped in front of his sister and squeezed her shoulder. 'Don't worry, we'll be able to handle Ted between us.'

After Ellie and her father had shaken hands with Dave, they left the house. And as they made their way to the cab, she couldn't help worrying about what they were going to find in Hammersmith.

Twelve

'Will you wait here, sir?' Jack jumped out of the cab. 'Let me see what state he's in first.'

The house they had pulled up outside was dilapidated and dingy, making Ellie grimace at the contrast with the house they had just left. But they had come this far and she was determined to see Ted. 'Father, if Jack goes in alone, he might refuse to see us.'

'I was thinking the same. We'll come with you, Jack. Don't tell your brother who we are, merely say that there is someone here who wants to see him.'

'All right.' Jack looked rather doubtful, but didn't argue. Albert Warrender seemed a strong man and well able to handle himself if Ted proved difficult.

The stairs didn't look, or sound, too safe, as they made their way up to Ted's room. They made alarming cracking noises.

'This is awful.' Ellie held up her skirt to prevent it from sweeping along the stairs. They were rickety, covered in dust and litter.

'Ted, it's me, Jack,' his brother called when they stopped outside a door at the end of the landing. 'You in? There's someone here to see you.'

The door crashed open, making Ellie gasp in horror. The man standing – no swaying – in front of them was haggard, unshaven and filthy. The smoke and smells coming from inside the room were appalling.

'What do you want, and who the bleeding hell have you got with you?'

'Watch your language!' Albert pushed him aside, strode in and stood in the middle of the room, surveying the utter chaos. The bed was unmade, dirty linen and clothes were tossed everywhere, and several empty bottles lay on the floor.

Ellie edged in, coughed and put her hand over her mouth to prevent the cigarette smoke from choking her, relieved when her father threw open the window.

Ted snarled and turned on Albert. 'What you bloody well doing? Get out of here or I'll throw you out, and take that fancy bit with you.'

'Don't make threats you can't carry out, young man. I may be years older, but I'm in better health than you. I assure you that you will come out the worse in any fight.'

'Oh, listen to the big man.' Ted clenched his fists, taking a step forward. 'But I'll bet your easy living has made you soft.'

Albert stood his ground. When Ted threw a punch it wasn't very accurate, missing completely. Albert only had to move his head slightly. 'You'll have to do better than that.'

'Don't fight, please!' Ellie was nearly in tears. They shouldn't have come.

Jack caught her arm to stop her from moving towards the two men. 'Leave them, your dad knows what he's doing.'

'I don't understand.' She searched in her purse for a handkerchief to wipe her eyes.

Jack grinned. 'If anyone can knock some sense into Ted, then your father's the man. I should have done this myself before now, but it's hard to see your big brother suffering so much.'

She watched in horror as her father lifted Ted right off his feet and tossed him into the only chair in the room.

'Sit there and don't move. There's someone who wants to meet you.' Albert held out his hand to Ellie. 'Come on, my dear, tell this drunken fool who you are.'

The belligerence had drained out of Ted for the moment and he was now subdued, knowing he had met his match.

Edging towards her brother, she said quietly, 'I'm your sister, Queenie.'

When he didn't speak, just stared at her open mouthed in disbelief, she held out her hand in a gesture of friendliness. 'I really am Queenie.'

'What the hell you playing at, Jack?' he asked, turning to his brother. 'Why'd you bring them here to see me like this? I don't want their pity.'

Ellie's head came up, she'd had enough of this. 'And you won't get it. Can we leave now, Father?'

'Aren't you pleased to know your sister has been well looked after? Don't you even have a kind word to say to her after all these years?' Albert spoke softly, but there was no disguising the anger running through him.

'I'm sorry, sir.' Jack shook his head when his brother remained silent. 'I shouldn't have brought you here. Ted's beyond help. He won't even make the effort to pull himself out of this mess.'

'Then we shall have to make him.' Albert reached out and caught Ted by the shoulders. 'Stop wallowing in self pity.'

'You don't know what you're talking about,' Ted shouted. 'I lost my wife and baby. We had a nice home, then I lost my job, and it's all gone.'

Albert pulled the protesting man upright until they were face to face. 'It's gone because you drank too much, and you let everything you had worked for slip through your fingers – even your dignity. It is a very foolish man who allows that to happen. And I do know what I'm talking about. My wife and I lost three babies, and she died a short time ago.'

'What's going on here?' A scruffy man came in, stinking of beer and a cigarette hanging out of his mouth. 'Don't want no fighting in my house.'

Pushing Ted towards Jack, Albert said, 'Get his things together. We're taking him away from here.'

''Ere, you can't do that. He owes me four sodding weeks' rent.'

'How much?' Albert towered over the man.

'Thirty bob.'

'You're a liar.' Taking a ten-shilling note out of his pocket, Albert held it out. 'That's all you're getting, and it's more than this disgusting place is worth.'

The note was snatched and deposited in a trouser pocket. 'I'll be glad to get rid of him.' Then the landlord shuffled out and disappeared down the stairs.

Jack was supporting his brother, who had a bewildered look about him.

'Father, what are you doing? He doesn't want our help.' Ellie was clenching her hands in agitation.

'We can't leave him here.' He smiled comfortingly at her. 'He needs help, whether he wants it or not, and I won't have my daughter treated with such disregard.'

'Your daughter?' Ted came to life again. 'Are you the bastard who bought her?'

'Your parents sold her to my wife and her brother, and yes, I am the bastard who adopted her.' He swept a disgusted glance around the room. 'Now, collect everything you want to take with you. We're leaving.'

'You can't bloody well do this.' Ted struggled to stand by himself.

Albert ignored him, speaking to Jack. 'Are the public baths open today?'

'We needn't go to all that trouble. I have a bath in my house, and I can find him some fresh clothes.'

'Good, we'll return to your place then, get him cleaned up, then I'll take him home with us.'

'Come on, Ted,' Jack urged. 'This man's giving you a chance to make a fresh start. What do you want to take with you?'

Swaying alarmingly as he reached for the bed, Ted fell to his knees and pulled out a small attaché case. 'This. It's got my picture of Annie in it, and the only things I want to keep.'

'Right.' Jack picked it up with one hand, using the other to support Ted as he struggled to his feet. 'Let's get you out of this dump.'

It took the two men to get Ted down the stairs and into the cab. It had exhausted him, and it was apparent that, not only was he terribly drunk, but he was a sick man as well. He was asleep as soon as he slumped in the seat.

'He can stay with me for a while.' Jack spoke quietly, not wanting to wake his brother. 'It's very kind of you to offer to take him home with you, but you don't have to do this. Now we've managed to get him away from that place, we might stand a chance of getting him well again.'

Albert was doubtful. 'If he stays here he will continue drinking, but if he comes with us he'll have more chance of recovery. I have a brother-in-law living close by, and between us we might be able to give him the help he needs.'

Jack sighed. 'You could be right. Fresh surrounding will help, I expect. He was so happy with Annie, and he's right clever. Got more brains than the rest of us put together.'

'Really?' Albert sat up straight, interested in that piece of news. 'What was his work?'

'He's a real wizard with figures. As a kid he did anything

he could to earn enough money for special lessons. He had a good job in an office, but when he couldn't stay off the drink, they sacked him.'

'Who was he working for?'

'A firm called Spencer and Spencer. They're in the City somewhere. We was all so proud of him. Fancy one of us working in an office!'

Albert gasped in amazement. 'I know of them; they are accountants of high repute. Your brother must be good.'

'He is, and it broke our hearts to see him sink to this state. He's a kind man and don't deserve to suffer like this. He's needed a strong hand to make him pull himself together, but I just haven't been able to bully him.'

'That's why he must come with us.' Albert gave Jack a slight smile. 'Henry and I are quite expert at – bullying – when necessary.'

The cab pulled up at Pearl's house and she came out with her husband.

'Give us a hand here, Dave,' Jack called. 'We've got to get Ted into my place and clean him up.'

Ted was still out cold, and a dead weight, but the three men managed to carry him into the house, then Albert came out again to see to the cab. 'I will be another hour, I'm afraid. Would you still wait for us, or send another cab along for us?'

'I'll go to the Coach and Horses, sir, to get food for the horse and myself. But I'll be back by the time you want to leave.'

'Thank you.' Albert slipped him a generous tip, then turned to Ellie. 'Go and stay with Pearl while we sort out Ted. He must be in a more sober condition before we can travel.'

'Come on.' Pearl took hold of Ellie's arm. 'I'll make you a nice cuppa. You look as if you can do with it.'

Albert smiled encouragingly at his daughter. 'Don't look so upset, my dear. Everything will be all right, and I do believe he's worth saving.'

'I expect that's so, but I don't like him very much, Father.' Ellie's voice trembled.

'He isn't very likeable at the moment, but – ' Albert grinned, enjoying himself – 'you wait and see the difference after Henry and I have worked on him for a while.'

Her father's amused expression made her gloom fade a little. 'Ah, he doesn't stand a chance, but where is he to stay? The gatehouse is already occupied and you can't put him in there with Mr Rogers.'

'No, of course not. Ted must have some privacy while he tries to deal with his inner demons. Henry has accommodation above the carriage house. Ted will be comfortable there.'

'And what is Uncle Henry going to say about that?' she asked.

'Quite a lot, I expect.' Albert turned and strode back into the house, chuckling quietly to himself. They didn't have long to get Ted ready.

It was chaos in the scullery. A large tin bath had been pulled up to the fire, and water was boiling in every possible receptacle. Ted was sprawled in a chair, taking no interest in the proceedings. Albert studied him with compassion. The man was in a bad way, but there was something about this brother of Eleanor's that had stopped him from walking away and leaving him to his fate. He had been harsh with him, knowing it was the only way to reach through the stupefying haze of drink.

As soon as the bath was filled with steaming water, Albert said to the others, 'Right, let's have him out of those clothes.

With the three of them stripping him, all Ted could do was snarl in protest. He was soon dumped in the bath, and Jack and Dave began scrubbing him and lathering his hair. Seeing they were coping very well, Albert picked up the old clothes and tossed them out the back door.

'I'll give those to the rag and bone man tomorrow.' Jack ducked just in time as his brother threw a punch and tried to get out of the bath. But months of too much drink and not enough food had taken its toll, and he was too weak to put up much of a fight.

Jack had found him a set of clothes, and after drying him it took all three of them to dress the uncooperative man.

'That's better.' Albert mopped his brow. 'Put the kettle on, Dave, and let's get some tea into him.'

'I'd better come on the train with you.' Jack had stopped calling him sir now Albert was as dishevelled as the rest of them with his jacket off and sleeves rolled up.

'He looks quiet enough now.' Albert rolled down his sleeves and slipped on his jacket. 'Eleanor is strong and will be able to help support him if he still finds it difficult to stand.'

'She was shocking upset when she saw him.' Jack explained to Dave how Ted had just ignored her.

'That was rotten for her,' Dave agreed.

'It was.' Albert checked the time on his pocket watch. 'But she knew this wasn't going to be easy. She is determined to see every one we can find, and she won't back out now, no matter how unpleasant or distressing the search may be. We had no idea what we were going to discover when we started out on this quest, but Eleanor has a determined nature, and her mind is set on this.'

'Get me a drink, Jack.'

All eyes turned to the man in the chair.

'Is the tea made?' Albert asked Dave, who nodded. 'Good, then give Ted a cup, and something to eat.'

'I don't want tea or food.' He sounded quite rational now, only mildly irritated.

'That's exactly what you *do* need. And all you are going to get.'

Ted's hand was shaking badly as he ran it over his eyes. 'I don't know who the hell you are – and do you always get your own way?'

'Invariably.' Albert smiled. 'As you have no recollection of what happened in your room, I'll introduce myself. My name is Warrender. I have an adopted daughter who happens to be your sister, Queenie, but I don't think you believed her when she told you.'

'Queenie? Is this true, Jack?' He looked round wildly. 'Where is she? Is she here?'

'She's next door with Pearl.'

'I got to see her.' With a tremendous effort he managed to stand. 'Our little Queenie's all right?'

'Not so little now.' Albert pushed him gently back into the chair. Good, he was coming round slowly, and there was already a faint indication of the real man. 'You'll be able to see a lot of her because I'm taking you with us to Kent. Fresh air and good food will help your return to full health.'

Frowning, Ted shook his head as if trying to clear it; his breathing becoming more and more laboured. 'Why are you doing this?'

'Because you are Eleanor's brother and need help.'

97

'Who the blazes is Eleanor?' Ted was thoroughly confused again. 'What's he talking about, Jack?'

'When they adopted Queenie they gave her another name.' He handed his brother a large cheese sandwich. 'Eat this.'

After eating that and drinking three cups of tea, he seemed to sink back into a confused state again, promptly falling asleep just as the cab arrived back to take them to the station.

'You sure you're gonna be all right?' Jack looked very concerned. 'This is more than too much drink. Ted's ill as well.'

'I am aware of that and we'll see he has a physician to look at him, but first we must take him to Kent. We have only to manage the train journey, and there will be a carriage waiting for us at the other end.'

Between them they managed to haul the now unconscious man into the cab, as Ellie and Pearl joined them.

'Oh, sir,' Pearl was agitated. 'He's real sick. We ain't never seen him this bad.'

'Don't worry, he will have the best attention.' Albert helped his daughter into the cab, shook hands with everyone else, then said, 'You have our address, Jack, and if you would like to visit us next Sunday, you would all be welcome. You can then see how your brother is faring.'

'Thank you very much. We'd like that.'

'Splendid, we shall expect you for lunch.'

Eyeing the sleeping man opposite her, Ellie yawned. She was exhausted, and completely at a loss to understand what her father was up to. Not only had he invited Pearl, her family, and Jack to visit, but he was taking Ted home with him – or at least – to Uncle Henry's. Although she was terribly worried and churned up inside, she stifled a giggle. Oh, her uncle was going to be furious.

Closing her eyes, she listened to the chug of the train, finding it soothing. If the rest of the journey was as peaceful as this, then it would be all right. She hoped Ted would stay asleep. She wanted to ask her father why he was doing this, but she was much too tired to talk. The joy of finding Jack and Pearl had turned to dismay when she had seen Ted.

Opening her eyes, she smiled when her father winked at her. Whatever this was all about, he wasn't saying. But she knew her father was a kind man and never did anything without a good reason.

Thirteen

The days were short at this time of year and it was dark when they reached her Uncle Henry's. The journey had been accomplished without incident as Ted couldn't seem to stay awake, and he hadn't said a word the entire time. Her father had remarked that he probably hadn't slept properly for a long time, and by the look of the exhausted man sitting across from her that was obvious. Ellie couldn't decide how she felt about this brother. The shock of seeing him in such a poor state had made her want to turn away from him, and she was ashamed of that. Her father had shown more compassion than she had, and this man was her brother. She should have felt more for him than revulsion.

As soon as they pulled up outside the house, the grooms rushed to hold the horses. Ellie and her father were helped out of the coach just as Henry and Philip appeared.

'I wasn't expecting you. Is everything all right?'

'I need your help, Henry.' Albert reached into the carriage to help Ted out. He was awake, but still very weak, and clearly far from well.

Philip rushed in to help support Ted.

'Good God! Who's that? He needs a doctor by the look of him.' Henry moved forward to assist.

'It's one of Eleanor's brothers, the eldest.' Albert slipped his arm around Ted to steady him. 'You have rooms above your carriage house, so would you let him stay there for a while?'

Henry barked out orders, making his servants rush off to do his bidding. Then he glared at Albert. 'Bring him inside. It's perishing out here.'

They made their way into the library, settling Ted in a chair by the fire. He was shaking violently. 'I need a drink,' he gasped.

'I should say you do.' Henry reached for the decanter.

'No alcohol, Henry.' Albert stopped him. 'That's a part of his problem.'

'What?' Henry stared at his brother-in-law in astonishment. 'You mean he's a drunk, and you've brought him here? Are you mad, Albert?'

Albert explained the situation. 'So you see, we couldn't leave him like that.'

'I still say you're crazy.' Henry sighed and turned to his niece. 'Is this your idea? Your father cannot be expected to take care of your other family, you know.'

'But—' Ellie didn't get any further.

'This is not Eleanor's decision. It's mine alone. I don't think she is any happier about this than you, but I want to help him. The rooms over your carriage house would be an ideal place for him to recover, but I'll take him home to our house if you are set against it. Now, are you going to turn him away, Henry?'

'Of course not. He's here now and I wouldn't turn a dog out in this state. Anyway, by the look of him he can't go another step. The poor devil's on his last legs.'

Albert nodded, frowning fiercely as he studied Ted. 'I agree. We must get him into a warm bed as soon as possible. When we first met him I thought he was ill because of too much drink, but it looks more serious than that.'

There was a knock on the door and the butler entered. 'Everything is ready for the gentleman, sir.'

'Good, fetch young Alan, the stable lad, to give us a helping hand. This man is very sick. Ask cook to prepare a hot nourishing meal for him.'

'At once, sir.'

'Queenie?' Ted was staring at her and trying to stand. 'Are you really our little Queenie?'

'Yes, I am.' She was surprised he should ask now, because he had completely ignored her before.

'Oh, God.' Great tears rolled down his cheeks. 'We were so worried about you.'

His reaction made her rush over to him, concerned to see him so upset. Up to now she had been convinced that he didn't care, but he did – too much in fact. It was now becoming clear to her that Ted Bonner was a sensitive man who loved deeply. Losing his wife and child had torn him apart and wrecked his life. She suddenly felt a great tenderness for him.

He ran a finger down the side of her face. 'We always knew you'd be a beauty, and you are. I'm sorry you've had to see me like this.'

'Don't worry about it.' She cradled his hand in both of hers, feeling it tremble. 'You have to concentrate on getting well again.'

He nodded. 'I feel very ill, but it's my own bloody fault. I fell into a pit of depression and couldn't pull myself out again.'

'You will now. We're all here to help you.'

Henry called his butler again. 'Send someone for the doctor and ask him to come as soon as possible. And where's Alan?'

Before the butler had time to answer, a boy of around fifteen rushed in. 'I'm here, sir.'

'Help us to get this man to the carriage house.' Henry glanced at Albert. 'You'll dine here tonight. Eleanor, you look exhausted, rest by the fire until we've made your brother comfortable. Philip will stay with you.'

'Come on, Ted.' Albert took his arm, and with Alan the other side, urged him towards the door.

'Where's my case? Mustn't lose that.'

'It's been taken to your room.' Henry led the way.

Ted stopped suddenly, turned his head and looked at Ellie, a tortured expression in his eyes. 'Oh, dear God, I'm so relieved to see you. I really am.'

She went and slipped her arms around him briefly, then stepped back. 'I know. Get some rest and I'll come and see you in the morning. We can talk then.'

Seeing that Ted was at the end of what little strength he had, Albert made him move forward again.

Fortunately the carriage house was close to the main building, but even so, Ted only made it with the help of all of them. Removing only his shoes and top clothing, they settled him in the bed, propping him up on lots of pillows. His breathing was laboured and sweat was running down his face.

A maid arrived then with a tray of food. 'Cook's prepared a light meal for him, sir.'

'Put it on the table by the fire.'

She did as ordered, and quietly left the room.

Alan picked up a spoon. 'Shall I feed him, sir? I don't think he's able to do it for himself.'

Henry nodded, his expression grim as he studied Ted. 'I hope the doctor comes soon. He's got a high temperature. This man's going to die on us, Albert. We can't leave him here alone all night.'

'I don't mind staying, sir.' Alan was spooning broth into Ted, patiently waiting for him to swallow before giving him more. 'I'll look after him, and let the doctor in when he arrives.'

'That's kind of you.' Albert nodded to the young boy.

'Ain't no problem, sir. I used to do this for my old gran.'

'You come and fetch us if there is a change for the worse.'

'Yes, sir.' Alan continued with his task.

Albert and Henry made their way back to the house and found Eleanor pacing anxiously, with Philip trying to calm her. 'Is he all right? He can't be left alone tonight.' Her eyes were clouded with worry.

'The doctor should be here at any moment, and young Alan has offered to remain with Ted until the morning. There's nothing more we can do now.' Albert held out his arm. 'We've had no time to eat today and I am starving, my dear, so let us enjoy one of Henry's excellent meals.'

During dinner, Henry and Philip had to be told the whole story, and when Henry discovered that Jack, Pearl and her family had been invited to visit next Sunday, he nearly exploded. 'Damn it, Albert, have you taken leave of your senses?'

'I agree that this isn't what we had planned, and I could very well be unwise, but—'

'Unwise!' Henry looked furious. 'It's downright foolhardy. You don't know these people. They could turn up here expecting you to keep them in luxury.'

'They won't do that, Uncle Henry.' Ellie spoke sharply. 'They are good people.'

'Sorry, my dear, I didn't mean to offend you, but you don't know anything about them either.'

Noticing that his daughter was upset about Henry's remarks, Albert stepped in. 'What you say is true, Henry, but before you get on your high horse, remember one thing. You started this fifteen years ago, and now Eleanor wants to meet them. Are we to turn our backs on them if they need help?'

'Damned difficult to do that in the circumstances,' Henry growled.

'Exactly, and I am not a fool, Henry. Have I ever allowed anyone to take advantage of me?'

His brother-in-law smirked. 'Actually, yes.'

'Who?'

'A little girl from the slums by the name of Queenie.'

'Ah.' Albert's expression softened as he gazed at his daughter. 'Well, I couldn't help that, for you see, I fell in love with her.'

Henry laughed then. 'And what a good thing that was for me. I do believe you would have killed me otherwise.'

'I was tempted to.'

The door opened and the butler showed in the doctor. It was the same one who had attended Mary, so Albert knew him well. 'How is he, doctor?'

'He's a very sick man, weak and undernourished, but the thing that concerns me the most is that he has pneumonia.'

'Oh, damn.' Albert held Eleanor's hand to keep her in her seat, as she had been about to leap up in alarm. 'If I'd known that I would never have dragged him down here. I should have taken him to a hospital in London.'

'What are his chances?' Henry signalled to the butler to pour the doctor a cup of coffee.

Taking the cup, he sat down. 'It's hard to say. If he were fit and strong it wouldn't be too much of a problem, but he's in a sorry state. He's quite rational though. He explained that the pain of losing his wife and child in that way was so bad that he'd had a few drinks to dull the senses. After that he couldn't stop. I've told him he must never touch alcohol again.'

'We must get him into hospital now.' Ellie was frantic with worry.

The doctor shook his head. 'He's warm and comfortable where he is, and it would not be wise to move him. Alan is a capable lad, but I shall engage a nurse to take over the care for a couple of days. If the boy could stay as well?'

'Of course.' Henry agreed at once.

Draining his cup, the doctor stood up. 'I'll make the arrangements at once. A nurse will be with him within the hour, and I'll call again in the morning.'

When he'd gone, Ellie bowed her head in sorrow. 'He mustn't die, Father. We shouldn't have moved him.'

Albert was by her side, hating to see his beloved child so

upset. 'No, we shouldn't have, but we all thought his condition was mostly due to drink. But if we had left him there, Eleanor, he would certainly have died. He will receive the best care here.'

She clasped his hand. 'You're right, Father.'

'You go home now and rest.' Henry smiled gently at her. 'Come back in the morning, and I am sure you will find him much improved.'

'You will send someone for us if we are needed in the night?' Albert asked.

'Of course. Now go home, there's nothing more you can do here and Nanny will be worrying about you. Philip, see that the carriage is made ready.'

She wanted to stay, but Ellie had never felt so tired in her life, and knew that she would only be in the way. Everything possible was being done for Ted. She prayed his condition would improve after a good sleep. The day had been a mixture of happiness and horror.

After receiving another assurance from her uncle that he would send someone for them if it became necessary, Ellie reluctantly went out to the waiting carriage.

The night was cold and frosty, making the breath from the horses come out of their nostrils in filmy clouds. As she shivered in the cold night air, she was relieved that Ted was warm and being well looked after. All that could be done for him was being done, and she must be content with that. She couldn't help worrying, though.

As soon as they arrived home, she removed her coat and hat, and went straight to Nanny's room. The elderly woman was in bed, but sitting up, alert, waiting for news.

'There you are at last,' she grumbled. 'Why are you so late?'

'We dined with Uncle Henry. It's been such a day, Nanny.' Tears filled her eyes.

'Now, now, come and sit beside me, and tell me all about it.'

It took nearly an hour to relate everything that had happened, the good and the sad.

Ellie blinked away the tears. 'I'm so ashamed of myself, Nanny. I didn't like him at first. I thought he was some awful drunk, but he isn't really. He's an unhappy man, and so ill. Do you think he will survive?'

Nanny gazed into space for a moment, then nodded. 'Your Uncle Henry is a brusque gentleman, but he has a good heart, and understands the pain of losing a wife, as does your father. With those two looking out for him, he won't dare die on them.'

'Oh, Nanny.' Ellie couldn't help laughing. 'You're a wonder, do you know that?'

'So I've been told – occasionally.' Smoothing a strand of golden hair away from Ellie's face, she said, 'You go and get some sleep. Everything will seem much brighter in the morning.'

She stood up. 'Goodnight, Nanny, sleep well.'

'And you, my little Queenie.' Nanny chuckled. 'I can call you that again now, can't I?'

'Of course you can.' Ellie kissed her leathery cheek. 'See you in the morning.'

Ellie could not sleep; she lay awake listening for the sound of galloping horses coming to bring them bad news. The events of the day ran through her head in vivid colour. She had always believed that she was an only child, and to discover that she wasn't, had come as a tremendous shock. As far as she knew there were seven of her brothers and sisters living – or she hoped so. Jack, Ted and Pearl had been found quickly, but the others were going to be more difficult to trace. She particularly wanted to find out what had happened to Harry. It was alarming to know that he had been out on the streets of London at the age of twelve. All manner of unpleasant things could have happened to him. Her insides churned as she tried to control her imagination. 'Oh, Harry,' she moaned softly, 'please be all right so we can find you.'

A fire had been lit in her bedroom and, fed up with tossing and turning, she slipped out of bed. A quick stir with the poker made it burst into flames, sending fingers of yellow light dancing along the walls. Settling on the carpet in front of the blaze, she gave a ragged sigh, wishing it was morning so she could go to see Ted. Her first impression of him had been totally wrong, and she would make sure she didn't jump to conclusions again. Her father hadn't done that. He had looked beneath the surface and glimpsed a different man. What was it he had said? Oh, yes. 'He is worth saving.'

Resting her head on her knees, she prayed that he would survive the night and she would have the chance to get to know her eldest brother.

Fourteen

The next two days were critical as Ted fought a fever but, much to everyone's relief, on the third day he awoke cool and hungry. Ellie's relief was enormous when the doctor announced that he was out of danger. She had stayed with Ted as much as possible; her father had insisted that she carry on with her lessons, but once they were over he had made no protest about her sitting by her brother's bedside. She had talked to Ted, telling him about her childhood in this beautiful place, though she doubted that he had heard her. Mr Rogers and Philip had also been very kind by visiting, and Ellie was convinced that having people around talking to him had helped with his recovery. Once the fever had broken, her tutor had spent more time with him, and they seemed to be very friendly with each other. Ellie was pleased, for Mr Rogers was a steady, sensible man, and Ted needed a friend to help him through this awful time.

Ellie had ridden over to see Ted on Sunday morning. Ted, knowing his brother and sister were coming, insisted on getting up, although still very weak. With Alan's help he dressed in new clothes her father had ordered for him. She could see from the good bone structure that he was a striking looking man, with dark blonde hair and bright blue eyes. And now the eyes were no longer clouded with drink and sickness there was evidence of a sharp intelligence behind the gaze.

'Ah, good to see you up.' Henry strode in with Philip right behind him. 'Eleanor, I have sent word to your father that he is to bring Ted's family here when they arrive. This young man is still not fit enough to travel, even though the journey to your home is short, so we'll dine here. Philip, help Mr Bonner down the stairs and into the library. It isn't far, do you think you can make it?' he asked Ted.

Ted nodded, holding firmly to Philip for support. 'I will

stay up for as long as possible. I can't thank you enough for your kindness, sir. I will find a way to repay you for your trouble and expense, for I should certainly have died without the care given to me.'

'Think nothing of it.' Henry waved away the expression of gratitude. 'Only too pleased you are still with us. Thought we were going to lose you once or twice.'

'Come on, Mr Bonner.' Philip held Ted as he took a couple of tentative steps forward. 'You lean on me and take your time.'

That made Ellie grin, for Philip was half the size of the man he was supporting. At fourteen he wasn't very tall, but he would probably shoot up all of a sudden. She followed the slow progress down the stairs, across the yard to the main house. Her heart was full of affection for her uncle. Although he had made it clear that he disapproved of her father inviting Jack, Pearl and her family to visit, he had, nevertheless, opened his home to them.

They eventually reached the library, and Ted sat down, giving a ragged sigh of relief.

The maid entered with a tray of tea, placed it on a table, and served each one of them. Her name was Dorothy, and Ellie didn't miss the tender look she gave Ted as she handed him a cup. This girl had been the one to see that Ted had everything he needed, showing the utmost concern for his well-being.

'Thank you, Dorothy.' Ted smiled, and it transformed him.

Ellie caught her breath. Oh, yes, this forgotten brother was special. Uncle Henry was also studying him with a thoughtful expression in his eyes.

'My pleasure, sir.' Dorothy flushed slightly.

'You don't have to call me sir.' Ted grimaced at the unusual deference he was receiving from the staff.

The maid didn't say anything; she busied herself with her job, a little smile still on her face. When they had all been served, she turned to Henry. 'Will that be all, sir?'

'For the moment, but we shall need more refreshments when our other guests arrive.'

'I'll see to it, sir.' With another quick glance at Ted, she left the room.

They had just finished their tea when Philip leapt to his

feet at the sound of the carriage pulling up outside. 'They're here. Uncle Albert's brought Mr Rogers along as well.'

Henry sighed, gazing up at the ceiling in mock despair. 'We might as well have everyone here, I suppose.'

Laughing, Ellie slipped her hand through his arm. 'You do pretend to be such an ogre, Uncle Henry, but you are really so kind and gentle.'

Philip looked at Ellie as if she had gone mad, but wisely said nothing. Shaking his head in disbelief at hearing his father described thus, he helped Ted to his feet ready to greet his family.

Pearl was the first through the door, making straight for her brother. 'Ted, are you all right? Should you be out of bed? Mr Warrender has explained that you have been dreadfully ill.'

'I'm much better now.' He held out his arms to his sister. 'They saved my life, Pearl. I've been a fool, but that's all over now.'

'I'm glad to hear that.' Jack went to him, obviously relieved to see his brother.

Dave followed, carrying the baby. 'Ah, it's good to see you on the road to recovery.'

Ellie hadn't known how she would feel seeing them again, but she was delighted and greeted them with real affection. 'Come and meet my Uncle Henry and his son, Philip.'

When the introductions were over, the maid appeared as if by magic, with refreshments.

Henry studied the baby doubtfully. 'Would you permit my maid to look after the baby for you?' he asked Pearl. 'She's good with children and will see he is fed and entertained.'

Pearl hesitated.

'He'll come to no harm with Dorothy,' Ted assured his sister.

When the maid reached for Jimmy, talking happily to him, he went without protest, and Pearl nodded in agreement.

'Splendid.' Henry couldn't hide his relief. 'You may return him after we have dined. Philip, go with Dorothy and find the baby some toys to play with. The nursery is still full of them, I believe.'

As soon as they left the room, Pearl grinned at Ellie. 'We all went to see Nanny before we came here. I can't believe it. You've lived in that beautiful house, and had a nanny to look after you.'

'What did you think of her?' Ellie was well aware that her world was a very different one from theirs, but she couldn't detect any resentment, only avid interest.

'Oh, she's so sweet.'

That made Ellie laugh. 'I wouldn't call her that. She can be very stern, but I love her dearly.'

Pearl lent close to Ellie's ear. 'And now you've got a private teacher. He's very nice, by the way, and see how he's talking to Ted. They seem to like each other.'

'I think they do. He spent some evenings with Ted as his health improved. I saw them once scribbling all over bits of paper doing sums of some kind. I couldn't understand any of it.'

The girls stopped their conversation at the sound of Jack's voice.

'You have a magnificent house, sir.' Jack was gazing round the comfortable room in appreciation. 'Have you read all these books?'

'Every one. Do you like to read?'

'Very much. I'll read anything and everything.'

'Really.' Henry, whose greatest pleasure in life was books, beamed with pleasure. 'You must have a look and find yourself a couple to take home with you.'

Jack's eyes opened wide in surprise. 'I couldn't do that, sir, they're all leather bound and must be expensive.'

'I insist. I'm sure you'll look after them, and you can always return them after you've read them.' Henry led Jack over to the shelves. 'Tell me what kind of authors you enjoy.'

Dave grinned and said to his wife, 'Jack thinks he's in paradise surrounded by all these books.'

'And our tutor tells me that he considers Ted to be very clever with figures,' Albert said as he joined them. 'He is of the opinion that he should have attended university, and would probably have been a mathematician of note.'

'Oh, sir – ' Pearl shrugged her shoulders – 'the likes of us don't get no chance to go to schools like that. In fact, some don't even go to school. At least our mum was strict about that an' made us all go to school for as long as we could. We

110

know Ted wanted to carry on with his learning, but they chucked us all out at fourteen, some left at twelve.'

'I hope one day that things will change and everyone will have the opportunity for higher education, depending upon their ability and not their circumstances in life.' Albert frowned, looking across at Ted.

'My father was a Member of Parliament and fought hard for the reform of the educational system.' Ellie looked proudly at her father. 'And when our period of mourning is over, I hope he will take up his seat again.'

'It's nice to know someone cares.' Dave slipped an arm around his wife's shoulder. 'The Bonners are a clever lot, but it ain't easy to drag yourself out of the slums. A lot of people think that, just because you're poor, you're daft as well. But we're doing all right for ourselves, aren't we, duckie?'

'You certainly are.' Albert nodded in approval. 'You have your shop, are prepared to work hard, and have a very pleasant home. You have much to be proud of.'

'Thank you, sir.' Pearl glowed at the compliment. 'We was all determined not to live like our mum and dad. That kind of life can make you bitter.'

At that moment the dinner gong sounded and Henry came over with Jack. 'This man knows his books. A pleasure to talk to someone who is so knowledgeable.'

Ted joined them, being helped by Philip and Mr Rogers. 'Jack has had his nose stuck in books from the moment he could toddle.'

'Nothing wrong with that.' Henry clearly approved. 'Now, let us go to the dining room. I'm quite famished.

By three o'clock Ted needed to return to bed. Seeing that he was grey with exhaustion, Jack and Dave hauled him to his feet.

'I'll show you the way.' Philip had become quite eager to help Ellie's brother, and had been bombarding Pearl and Jack with questions about their life.

Taking a couple of deep, steadying breaths, Ted shook hands with Albert and Henry. 'Thank you for allowing my family to come here. It's been good to see them.'

'It has been a pleasure.' Henry really looked as if it had been. 'Now, you must get back to bed. Mustn't overdo it at first.'

111

After saying goodbye to the others, Ted placed an arm around Ellie, then bent to kiss her cheek, too tired to speak any more.

'As soon as they come back, we must leave as well.' Pearl was holding Jimmy on her lap, who was clutching a soft toy rabbit. 'You like that, don't you? But you must be a good boy an' leave it behind, because it belongs to Philip. He's nice, isn't he? You mustn't keep his things.'

'I don't want it. He can keep it.' Philip bounced back into the room.

'We couldn't do that.' Pearl shook her head. 'That's very kind of you, Philip, but it is an expensive toy.'

'I insist.' He sounded very like his father as he sat next to Pearl and tickled Jimmy, making him shriek with glee. 'I'm too old for toys. I'm fifteen.'

'Really, that old?' Pearl teased. 'In that case you might like to keep it for your own children.'

Philip looked horrified. 'I'm not going to marry for ages – if ever – so Jimmy can keep the rabbit.'

'Sir?' Pearl caught Henry's attention. 'I'm sure it isn't right for your son to give this away.' She tried to prise the toy out of her son's hands, only to be greeted with a howl of protest.

'It's quite all right; let your little boy keep it. It's been lying around in the nursery for years now.'

'Well . . . if you're sure.' Pearl had no chance of further protest, as the others returned then.

'He's tucked up nice and comfortable,' Jack told them.

'We must be going, Dave, or we'll miss our train, and Jimmy's had such an exciting day. He's tired out.' The baby was fast asleep, but still had a firm grip on the precious toy.

Henry ordered the carriage to take them to the station, and after fulsome thanks for a wonderful day, and for looking after their brother so well, they left. At Henry's insistence, Jack had three books tucked under his arm. Mr Rogers went with them to see that they caught the train safely.

After waving goodbye, Ellie, Philip, her father and uncle went back to the library.

Ellie was delighted, the day had been a huge success, and she was sure it had done Ted good to see everyone.

'What did you think of them, Henry?' Albert took a glass of brandy from him.

'Surprising.' Henry swished his drink around the glass, thoughtfully. 'They are not at all what I expected. They are polite, but there's a fierce pride about them. They don't want charity. Whatever they manage to accomplish in life, they are going to do it on their own.'

'That was my impression. But they are related to Eleanor, so we shouldn't be surprised. And what is your opinion of Ted?'

'Damned if I can decide. He has the family look, but that is as far as it goes. He's sensitive, thinks deeply, and it's hard to gauge what's going on behind those sharp eyes.' Henry shrugged. 'I'm not sure about him. I'll reserve judgement until I know him better.'

'We should have the opportunity to do that, because he can't leave here for some time.'

'Hmm.' Henry sipped his drink. 'I don't think he should go back to London.'

Ellie listened to them talking, almost holding her breath. Were they thinking of helping Ted once he was fit again? He had nowhere else to go, except to Pearl or Jack, and their houses were hardly big enough to take lodgers.

'I agree. If he stays sober I'll see if I can find a position for him somewhere around here.'

'I think they're all nice.' Philip's face was shining, having thoroughly enjoyed the day with their visitors. 'Do you think the rest of your brothers and sisters will be like that, Ellie?'

'I really don't know. They are all bound to be different. That's if we can find them.'

'I have a man coming to see me tomorrow morning,' her father told her. 'He's highly recommended, and is reputed to be good at finding people.'

'May I meet him as well, Father?' Ellie was pleased her father had arranged this so soon, for she didn't want to waste any time finding the others. Christmas would soon be here and she wanted it over with by then. Because of their loss, the festive season would be sad and very quiet this year, but it would be a comfort to know her family had been found.

'Of course, Eleanor.' Albert finished his drink and stood up. 'I think we should give your uncle some peace and quiet. I have ordered the driver to return Mr Rogers to the gatehouse before coming back here.'

* * *

113

Someone shaking him woke Ted, and feeling drowsy and disorientated for a moment, he gazed up at Alan.

'Mr Bonner, it's eight o'clock and cook has sent you up some dinner.' Alan shrugged apologetically. 'Sorry to disturb you when you was sleeping so peacefully, but cook said you must eat to get back your strength. Here, let me help you.'

Ted struggled out of bed and over to the table set up by the fire. He groaned. 'I'm so weak. Today has taken more out of me than I realized.'

'Bound to.' Alan removed the covers from the plates. 'You eat that lovely bit of beef. It'll make you feel better. Nice to see your family today, was it?'

'Yes, very.' Ted put a forkful of meat in his mouth and felt the beef almost melt it was so tender. 'I'm glad I was well enough to join them.'

Alan busied himself building up the fire, making sure there were enough logs to keep it going through the night, and then folding Ted's clothes neatly. 'Mr Warrender said he was sending you another suit tomorrow, and a warm overcoat.'

Finishing off his meal, Ted sat and stared at the comforting glow of the fire, deep in thought. 'Why are they doing this for me?'

'What?' Alan was loading the empty dishes on a tray.

'Why are these wealthy, influential men treating me with such kindness?'

'You was sick, and they'd do the same for anyone, man or beast.' The stable boy smirked. 'My master, Mr Henry Jenson, can bellow loud enough to frighten the horses, but he's a good man. The same goes for Mr Albert Warrender, but you don't never want to see him in a rage.'

'I believe I already have.' Ted ran a hand over his eyes, grimacing.

'My master runs for cover when that happens.' Alan giggled at the thought. 'There now, that fire should last you through the night, but I'll pop in now and again, just to make sure you don't get cold.'

'You mustn't do that, I can manage, and you need your sleep.'

'Ain't no trouble. We got a sick mare, so I'll be up to check on her a couple of times.' He picked up the tray. 'Now, you just get under the blankets and have a nice sleep.'

The bed was still warm when Ted crawled into it, but he didn't go to sleep immediately. His mind was buzzing with everything that had happened, hardly able to believe that their little Queenie had turned up out of nowhere. He angled his head on the pillow so he could watch the dancing flames. He was lucky to be alive, and he wouldn't have been if Mr Warrender hadn't bullied him and brought him here. Today had been a struggle, not only physically, but mentally as well. There had been decanters full of alcohol in the library, and wine at lunch. God, he wanted a drink. It had taken all of his self control not to beg for one, but the doctor had warned him not to drink again – ever – for it was unlikely that he would be able to control it. That had been hard to believe, but when he looked back he could see something he had never admitted to himself. He'd always liked a drink, stopping at some pub on the way home from work. Just one pint, he had always told himself, but more often than not it had been two or even three. The only thing stopping him had been his eagerness to see Annie. How he'd loved her. Once she had gone his life spiralled out of control. He'd sunk so low. But then a strong, determined man had reached out and pulled him up.

Closing his eyes, he clenched his hands in determination. Strangers had cared enough to try and save him. He mustn't let them, his family, or Queenie down. She was a real lady, and he wouldn't shame her, or himself. It was time to stop using his darling Annie as an excuse. He had a problem and that must be faced. He would *never* again touch alcohol.

Fifteen

Just over four weeks had passed since Mr Steadman had been engaged to find the rest of Eleanor's family. He had warned that it might take time, as there was very little information available for him to work on. Albert knew the waiting was hard on his daughter, but they had to give Mr Steadman a chance to investigate. The problem was that some of the children had just walked out of the house in Whitechapel and not bothered to keep in touch. He thought Maggie might be the easiest to find, so he was concentrating on her first.

Albert walked over to the window, deep in thought, and gazed out. It was a lovely bright day, if a little cold, but just right for a ride. Eleanor and Philip were in the schoolroom, so he might as well go and see Henry. Christmas was nearly here, and he wasn't looking forward to this festive season. Mary had loved it, filling the house with colour and laughter. How he missed her. He still expected her to come and stand beside him, slipping her hand through his arm in her gentle way.

As sorrow gripped him, he spun away from the window, and strode out of the house towards the stables. A good gallop was what he needed. He had never before spent his time in idleness. Henry had been waiting for him to make a decision about buying that extra land, but he just hadn't been able to concentrate on the project.

'Good Lord, that's no way to treat a fine animal.' Henry stormed out of the house as Albert thundered up on a sweating horse.

Albert jumped down, allowing his stallion to be led away. 'Don't fuss, Henry, he enjoyed the ride as much as I.'

His brother-in-law snorted in disgust. 'He told you that, I suppose?'

Feeling more relaxed after his wild ride, Albert grinned. 'What has put you in a bad mood today?'

'Oh, nothing, nothing. Feeling restless, that's all. I'm sure we'll all be relieved when Christmas is over. Going to be damned strange without Mary.'

'I agree, but she wouldn't like it if we were too miserable. You know how she loved this time of the year.'

Henry nodded. 'Must keep up the tradition, I suppose.'

Albert watched Ted walking towards them, now looking fit and healthy. His recovery had been steady.

'I saw you arrive, Mr Warrender, and I wondered if I could have a few minutes of your time.'

'Certainly. Let's go inside.'

Once in the library Albert and Henry sat, but Ted remained standing.

'You have both been generous in caring for me, but I don't feel it would be right for me to impose upon your hospitality any longer. I can never repay you for what you've done for me, but I will try. You saved my life and I'm very grateful to you.'

'Sit down, Ted.' Henry waved him to a chair. 'What are you going to do? Where will you go?'

'I don't know yet, sir. I could stay with Jack for a while until I find a job and somewhere to live.'

'Do you want to return to London?' Albert sat forward, elbows on his knees. 'Have you considered trying to find employment here?'

'I don't want to go back to the city.' Ted pulled a face, showing his distaste at the prospect. 'What could I do here? I'm good at figures and things like that, but I haven't any special qualifications.'

'Don't make any decision at the moment.' Henry smiled. 'You are welcome to stay in the carriage house for as long as you like. It isn't needed for anyone else.'

'That's more than generous of you, sir, but you're feeding me as well, and Mr Warrender has supplied me with new clothes. I can't keep taking from you. It isn't right.'

'We wouldn't be happy if you left without a job or a place of your own to go to.' Albert thought it would be far too easy for him to slip back into his old ways. He liked the man, and he knew Eleanor was happy to be able to see him in her spare time. 'There's no rush for you to leave.'

'I wouldn't be happy staying unless I can pay for my rent

and food.' Ted looked worried. 'Isn't there something I could do on your estates? I don't mind what it is. I'll do anything to pay my way.'

'Let's consider it.' Henry stood up. 'Seeing as you're here, Albert, we should go and have another look at that land before we purchase it.'

'Certainly.' Albert turned to Ted. 'Why don't you come along with us? It's a perfect day for a ride.'

'Erm . . . I would like that, sir, but I have never ridden a horse before.'

Henry laughed. 'Time you did then. Come along, we'll find you a docile animal.'

The ride of some two miles was an experience for Ted, and Albert stayed close by his side as he didn't appear to be too safe in the saddle. But gradually he began to relax and managed to stay seated when Henry urged him to try a trot.

They reached a rise and Albert caught Ted's reins to bring him to a halt. 'There it is.'

Spread out before them was a valley sectioned off into areas of agricultural land and part dense woodland.

'Ah, that's lovely.' Ted stood up in the stirrups to get a better view. 'What section are you thinking of buying?'

'All of it.' Henry dismounted. 'We did originally consider only the wooded area, but the land belongs to Lord Faversham. He died recently and his son has decided to sell off this entire area. They need the money, if you ask me. It's been neglected, but the land is good, just right for orchards.'

'If you're going to plant fruit trees, it will be some time before you show a profit.'

'We realize that, but we could get a good price for the timber.' Albert shaded his eyes against the sun, so low in the sky this time of year.

'You're not going to cut that down, surely? It would be criminal.' Ted looked embarrassed. 'I do beg your pardon, sirs, it is none of my business what you do.'

'Don't apologize.' Albert pursed his lips. 'We are of the same opinion and thought we might replant it after the felling, but we are still trying to decide on the best way to manage it.'

They tied the horses to a tree while they surveyed the area. Albert watched Ted as he moved around, touching one tree after another. Then a small notebook came out of his pocket and he scribbled away, frowning in concentration.

Henry came and stood beside Albert. 'What's he up to?'

'I have a strong feeling that there's a sound business mind at work there.'

'Hmm, that might be useful.'

Ted came back to them, his face glowing, but when he reached them he said nothing, merely stood gazing silently at the trees.

'What do you think, Ted?' Albert prompted.

'Oh I don't know much about this kind of thing. I love the countryside and feel it should be cared for and protected. But my opinions won't be much use to you.'

'We'd still like to hear them,' Albert said.

That was all it took to have his ideas pouring out. 'Selective felling could be the answer. Take out the largest, and that will make room for fresh planting. The area to the left is nothing more than a piece of scrubland, and that could be cleared for planting more trees. If this is husbanded carefully, it could give you a good return on your money while the orchards are coming into fruit. In the end you will have a larger forest than you started with. The landscape will be improved instead of destroyed, as this whole area will eventually be given over to trees of some kind or another.' He took a deep breath, excited with the vision. 'But, of course, doing it that way will cost a great deal of money. It would be a very long term investment.'

'I hadn't considered extending the forest like that. It will be a lot of work, by the sound of it.'

'I'm afraid so, Mr Jenson.'

'It's a sound plan, but Henry and I would not have the time to manage such a project.' Albert pointed out an area by a small stream. 'A house could be built there, don't you think?'

'Perfect.' Ted nodded, puzzled. 'But what for?'

'We'll need an overseer, won't we, Henry? And he'll have to have somewhere to live.'

It took Henry a few moments to realize what Albert was saying. Giving his brother-in-law a nod, he said, 'If we can find a suitable man, then I think we should buy the land and go ahead with Ted's plan.'

'I agree.' Albert walked over to the stream, and then turned back. 'You have vision, Ted, would you be prepared to take on the job of managing this project for us?'

'Me?'

Albert watched him grab hold of a tree for support as the surprise hit him.

'But . . . but, I've never done anything like this before.' He shook his head as if trying to clear his mind. 'I'd love to do it, but you would be taking a great chance on me. Are you sure?'

'We'd appreciate it if you'd give it a try, and we'll give you all the advice you need.' Albert waited as Ted struggled with his emotions. 'We don't want to force you into this. Just say if it doesn't appeal. We shall quite understand.'

'Oh, it does appeal.' Ted gazed around the area with longing. 'I would love to stay here and work for you but, as I've said, this would be something entirely new for me.'

'What do you say about a six month trial? If you don't like the work you can leave, and if we don't think it's working out, we shall have the option of finding someone else to take over.'

The concern cleared from Ted's face, and he reached out to shake hands with them. 'On those terms I would be willing to give it a try.' He grinned. 'Thank you, what a challenge!'

'We wouldn't have asked you unless we thought you could do it.' Albert had seen something special in this brother of Eleanor's, even when he had been in a pitiful condition, and now he was even more convinced.

'That all sounds very satisfactory.' Henry said, pleased. 'That's all settled then. Ted, you can stay in the carriage house until your place is ready.'

The next three hours were spent in hard negotiations. The heir to the property was showing some reluctance to sell as much land as they wanted, and it took all of Albert's skill to finalize a deal.

As they rode away, Henry laughed. 'That was hard going, Albert, but we did well. We've bought prime land for a reasonable price.'

'We did well.' Albert urged his horse into a canter. 'We can begin employing men in the New Year. Then we'll see if Ted can handle the job.'

'Hmm.' Henry looked doubtful. 'I know you want to help the man, and I'm quite willing to go along with that, but I hope we've done the right thing.'

'So do I, but only time will tell, and we can risk six months to see if he can do the job.'

'Yes, that was wise. We should know one way or the other by then.'

On reaching Henry's house, Albert didn't dismount. 'Will you tell Ted that the deal is done?'

'Right away. Come over tomorrow, Albert, for we'll have business to attend to.'

Lifting his hand in a wave, Albert turned for home. It was dark when he arrived and, after giving over his horse to the groom, he strode into the house, well pleased with the day's work.

'Father!' Ellie threw herself at him with such enthusiasm that she nearly knocked him off balance. 'Ted told me you have offered him a job. He's so happy he won't have to go back to London. He loves it here.'

'Don't get too excited, Eleanor.' He sounded a note of caution. 'Ted has six months to prove he can do the job, or decide that it's not what he wants.'

'I know, but you've given him something to strive for. It is more than a job – you have given him hope for the future.' She reached up to kiss his cheek. 'Thank you, Father.'

At lunchtime the next day, Ellie's father sent a message to say that she was to dine with him instead of having her meal in the schoolroom, as she usually did. She hurried downstairs and found him in his study reading a letter.

'Ah, there you are. I have just this moment received a letter from Mr Steadman. He has traced a Margaret Bonner working as a lady's maid to Mrs Montague, and living in Yorkshire.'

Ellie's elation died. 'But that is so far away. How can we go and see if it is my sister?'

'I'll write to Mrs Montague and ask if we may visit her, but it may be some weeks before we can make the journey.' He smiled. 'Don't be disappointed, my dear, Mr Steadman is making every effort to trace the others. If this turns out to be Maggie, then that only leaves Tommy, Bert and Harry. We are making good progress.'

'Yes, of course.' Ellie studied her father, thoughtfully. 'Do you know this lady?'

'No, I've never met her, but I've heard of the family. They have considerable estates in Yorkshire, I believe, and are well regarded.'

The gong sounded. 'I must be patient, but I do keep wondering about the others. I liked Pearl and Jack on sight. And now Ted's recovered and I've been able to spend time with him, I like him very much.' Ellie and her father went through to lunch. 'I wonder if Maggie is anything like Pearl? That is providing it is her,' she added hastily.

'We'll have to wait and see. I will not mention to Mrs Montague the reason for wishing to visit. I will merely say that it is a family matter and we would appreciate her help.'

Ellie giggled. 'That should arouse her curiosity, especially as we've never met her.'

'My very thought' Albert said wryly. 'I hope the lady is approachable.'

'Do you think Mr Steadman will be able to find the others?' Ellie changed the subject, knowing there was nothing more she could do until they heard from Mrs Montague.

'I'm afraid I cannot see the future.'

She slanted him an amused glance. 'I always thought you could. But I do hope Mr Steadman is successful for I would dearly love to meet Harry. I keep wondering all the time what he's like, and why he was so special to me.'

Albert put down his knife and fork. 'I think it highly unlikely that he's still alive, Eleanor. The chances of a twelve-year-old boy surviving on his own is low.'

'That is so sad.' Ellie's mouth thinned, determined not to let this upset her. 'But I am grateful to have found Pearl, Jack and Ted.'

'And there is a chance the lady's maid is Maggie.' Albert continued eating.

'Yes, I do hope she is.'

Sixteen

It was a relief when the New Year of 1906 had been welcomed in. The atmosphere had been subdued with all of them wondering what this coming year would bring. Everyone in the house missed Mary dreadfully, and the festive season had only seemed to highlight the recent loss.

It had been the quietest Christmas Ellie could ever remember. There had been a tree and presents, but it wasn't the same. Her father had been preoccupied and she glimpsed his loneliness. He hid it as best he could, but she knew his every mood.

Mr Rogers spent the holiday with his parents, and Ted with Jack and Pearl. They would be returning today and, weather permitting, Ted would be overseeing the clearing of the land for the orchard.

Her father was already at the breakfast table, with Uncle Henry and Philip, who had been staying with them over the holiday. Ellie had been glad to have her cousin around for company.

'Looks like it might snow.' Philip seemed delighted with the prospect.

'Hope not.' Henry glanced out of the window, frowning. 'The last thing we need is snow. That ground must be cleared by the spring so we can plant fruit trees and, hopefully, get a modest yield from them in about two years time.'

'Sooner than that if we plant mature trees,' Albert commented, then continued reading the letter that had arrived that morning. 'Ah, Eleanor, it seems that Mrs Montague has a house in London. She's staying there now and has asked us to call at our convenience.'

'That's marvellous,' Ellie said excitedly. 'When can we go?'

'Well, Mrs Montague admits to being curious, so I think we had better go tomorrow.'

'Thank you, Father.' Ellie could hardly believe their luck that the lady happened to be visiting London. It would save them a long journey, and her father was already devoting far too much time to this, when he should be attending to his own business. She couldn't help feeling guilty about that.

Albert frowned when he saw his daughter's enthusiasm. 'Don't build up your hopes. It might not be your sister.'

'That's true, but Jack said she went into service so I'm hopeful.'

Philip looked disgruntled. 'I suppose I'll have to spend my day in the school room while you have a trip to London, again.'

'As you are a boy your education is more important than Eleanor's,' Henry reprimanded sternly. 'One day you will have to take over the running of the estate.'

'So will Ellie.' Philip scowled. 'Uncle Albert doesn't have a son.'

'Your cousin will marry one day, and if she is wise will choose a husband capable of the task.'

'Must that be my only criteria for marrying, Uncle Henry?' Ellie's tone was playful. 'Shouldn't I fall in love with him as well?'

'If you must.'

Albert laughed, standing up. 'Stop teasing Eleanor, Henry. She will choose a husband for her own reasons when the time comes. She will only be eighteen this month, so there's plenty of time.'

The next morning Ellie was in a high state of excitement. Would this girl be her sister? Ted had seemed optimistic that it would be. He'd given her all the news from Wandsworth, saying that he'd enjoyed himself, but was happy to be back in the country. He'd said, proudly, that although Jack and Dave had drink in the house, he hadn't touched a drop. It hadn't been easy, but he was much too excited about the challenge of the new job to put it at risk.

'Are you ready, Eleanor?'

'Yes, Father.' She peered in the mirror to adjust her hat.

'A little more to the side, I think.' He laughed as she fussed over her appearance, as this was something she had never taken much interest in. 'You look charming.'

The blue of her dress was the same colour as her eyes, and she gazed at it doubtfully. 'Do you think it proper for me to come out of mourning so soon?'

'Your mother would wish it, for you know how she disliked dark sombre shades. She did choose that outfit for you herself, didn't she?'

Ellie nodded, sadness clouding her eyes. 'I can't get used to her not being here.'

'No, it is hard.' He took her arm and guided her to the waiting carriage. 'But she would want us to get on with our lives. If she's watching from above, then she would approve of what we're doing.'

Mrs Montague's house in Knightsbridge was lovely. The door opened before they could knock, and a butler took Albert's calling card, then showed them into a spacious room just off the hallway. A lot of the furniture was ornate, but the décor was subdued and tasteful.

'This is a lovely house,' Ellie whispered, 'but not as nice as ours. When you look out of the window here you only see more houses, but we have open countryside.'

The butler was back almost immediately to show them to an upstairs drawing room. He opened the door, announced them, and then withdrew.

Ellie had been expecting an older woman, but Mrs Montague was slightly younger than her father, and so elegant. Her smile seemed to light up the room, and the young man standing by her side was obviously her son, for they both had the same golden brown hair.

'It is kind of you to receive us.' Albert said, after a momentary hesitation, for he too was surprised by the lady. 'May I introduce my daughter, Eleanor?'

Ellie found herself being studied intently, and could not believe the colour of the lady's eyes. They were a startling violet colour, and she had never seen anything like them before.

'Your daughter is charming.' She motioned to the young man. 'This is my son, James. You don't mind if he stays while we discuss the reason for your visit?'

'Of course not.'

'Please sit down.' While she was speaking the door opened and a maid came in with tea and cakes. 'You must be in need of refreshments after your journey.'

Once they were all settled, Mrs Montague leaned forward. 'I admit to being rather curious to find out why you wish to see me. You merely said it was a family matter, Mr Warrender, but I don't believe we have met before.'

'That is correct.' Albert didn't waste any time in explaining that Ellie had been adopted, and upon learning that she had come from a large family, wished to trace her other siblings. 'We understand that you have a maid by the name of Margaret Bonner.'

'Yes, she is my personal maid.'

'With your permission, we would like to see her. She may be Eleanor's sister.'

'My goodness!' Mrs Montague rang a bell. 'How very exciting.'

The butler appeared at once, and the lady instructed him to ask Margaret to come at once. When he had closed the door, she said, 'Would you prefer to see her alone?'

'That won't be necessary.' Albert stood as Ellie was already on her feet.

'I am glad you said that, Mr Warrender, for I also am eager to see if my maid is related to your daughter, but I cannot see any resemblance.'

Ellie stood beside her father, disappointed by that announcement, watching the door anxiously. A light tap on the door made her jump in anticipation, she was so nervous.

'You wanted to see me, madam?'

Margaret Bonner was shorter than Ellie, and rather plain, with light brown hair, but her hazel eyes were a redeeming feature. Ellie's heart beat faster; she had a look of Jack about her.

'Mr Warrender and his daughter would like to ask you some questions.'

'Please don't be alarmed, Miss Bonner, but we believe you may be able to help us,' Albert tried to reassure her. 'We are trying to trace all the children of Fred and Hilda Bonner from Whitechapel.'

The maid drew in a deep breath. 'May I ask why, sir?'

'My daughter will explain.' Albert urged Ellie forward.

'Are you Maggie, and do you have brothers by the name of Jack and Ted, and a sister, Pearl?'

'Yes.' She had gone quite pale, gazing suspiciously at Ellie.

126

'Then I am your sister, Queenie.' She waited while Maggie absorbed this; she wanted to reach out to her, but she didn't dare. The girl didn't look pleased to see her.

The silence was enough to take away her breath, as the girl was obviously shaken. Then to Ellie's distress, Maggie turned and fled from the room. She felt her father's hand on her shoulder, steadying her as she fought her bitter disappointment.

There was a sharp exclamation behind her as James spoke. 'What extraordinary conduct, Mother. She has just insulted our guests by leaving the room without permission.'

'Leave it, James, this is not our business. I shall reprimand her later.'

'Oh, you mustn't do that, please.' Ellie was alarmed. 'This has obviously been a great shock for her.'

Albert handed Ellie one of his cards. 'Take this to her, and tell her that she is welcome to call on us if she ever feels like it.'

Taking the card Ellie hurried from the room with James right behind her.

'She will have returned to her room. I'll show you the way.'

It wasn't necessary. Maggie was only next door in the music room. She was holding on to the back of a chair for support, head bowed.

Ellie stood beside her, holding out the card. 'I'm sorry to have upset you. This is where I live in case you ever want to see me. I won't bother you again, the decision will be yours alone.'

Shaking her head, Maggie refused the card. When she spoke her voice was trembling. 'I couldn't wait to get out of that place and away from everyone connected with it. I've made a decent life for myself, put it all behind me, and then you turn up.' She faced Ellie. 'After they'd taken you away, life was hell in that house.'

'That wasn't my fault, Maggie. I was only around two and a half.'

'I know, but I left as soon as I could and I don't want anything, or anyone, to remind me of that time.' Maggie eyed her curiously. 'You're a real posh lady, aren't you? You ain't one of us no more.'

'I may have lived a very different life from yours, but I

127

was born into the same conditions as you. That makes me one of you, and no amount of fine clothes will ever change that fact.' Ellie paused to gain control. 'Again I apologize for upsetting you.' Tossing the card on to the chair, she turned and walked out of the room.

James was waiting outside for her, still annoyed. 'She shouldn't have treated you like that.'

After a mighty struggle Ellie managed to keep her tears at bay, and she looked up at the young man. 'My turning up unannounced must have been a dreadful shock for her. I shouldn't have come, but I don't remember any of my brothers and sisters, and I wanted to meet them.'

'How many did you have?'

'Nine, but two are dead. We've found two brothers and a sister so far, now Maggie, but she doesn't want to know me. The others were pleased to see me – at least two were – the other was ill, but he's better now and happy to know I am all right. They never knew where I went, or who took me. My father warned me that they might not all want to meet me, but I did so hope they would.'

'You have embarked on a very courageous quest, Miss Warrender.'

'Or foolish.' She sighed, feeling she could talk to James. 'But once I was told about my other family, I knew I wouldn't be able to rest until I had found them.' She managed a smile, although she was crying inside. 'It was naive of me to expect them all to accept me. I doubt this will be the last rejection I shall suffer, but I will not stop until all are traced.'

James held out his arm. 'Shall we return to the drawing room, Miss Warrender?'

She nodded. 'I can do no more here, and please call me Ellie.' They walked back together in silence. She couldn't help casting him a quick glance. He was mid-twenties, she guessed, and almost as tall as her father. His eyes were a paler shade than his mother's, but still violet. And although he was now aware of her humble beginnings, he did not seem to be at all bothered by that fact, and continued to treat her with respect. She liked that about him. Her father wasn't ashamed of her background, and neither was she. They would have no time for anyone who thought otherwise.

When they entered the room, Mrs Montague and her father

were in deep conversation, but he stood up as soon as she walked towards him.

'She doesn't want to have anything to do with me, and would not take the card, but I left it for her anyway.'

'I am sorry, my dear.' Albert studied her face carefully, assessing how she had taken the rejection. 'We knew that might happen, didn't we?'

'Yes, we did.' She held her head up high and hoped it was good enough to fool them. She would not show her hurt in front of strangers, pleasant as they appeared to be.

He nodded, touching her hand briefly to let her know he understood how she was feeling. 'Mrs Montague has invited us to stay for lunch.'

Ellie turned to Mrs Montague, all distress wiped from her face, determined not to embarrass anyone by breaking down. 'That is very kind of you, madam. I am rather hungry after all the excitement.'

That light-hearted remark brought a nod of approval from Mrs Montague. 'Your daughter has character, Albert.'

'Indeed she has,' he said, amusement and affection lighting his unusual eyes. 'She has always loved a good scrap, and defends her beliefs rather forcefully, causing two schools to decide they couldn't keep her. She does not tolerate rudeness or snobbery of any kind. And neither do I, Augusta.'

James spluttered on a laugh and winked at Ellie. 'Mother was asked to *leave* her finishing school.'

'Really.' Albert grinned.

Augusta nodded. 'But only one. Eleanor has beaten me on that score. You sound much like myself as a young girl. Ah, there is the luncheon bell, you must tell me all about it while we eat.'

After an excellent meal they retired to the drawing room. James was very interesting to talk to, and had entertained Ellie with tales of his Grand Tour, from which he had recently returned. And she discovered that he was twenty-four, but looked younger.

'Will you be staying in London for a while?' Albert accepted a cup of coffee from his hostess.

'We'll be here until the spring. It can get very cold in Yorkshire during the winter months, but it is marginally warmer down here, and we take this opportunity to visit friends, attend the theatre and social gatherings.'

'It is Eleanor's eighteenth birthday on the sixteenth of this month. We are still in mourning for my wife, but she would not wish us to ignore such an important occasion, so we shall be celebrating in a modest way, and we would be pleased if you could join us. You may stay for a while, if you wish. The countryside around Sevenoaks is very beautiful, even in winter.'

'Thank you, Albert.' She glanced at her son, who nodded in agreement. 'We would be happy to come.'

'Excellent. If you travel down on the fifteenth I'll arrange to have a carriage waiting for you at the station. There is a train that will arrive around midday.'

'We shall look forward to that,' Augusta said, then turned to Ellie. 'Have you had your coming out, or did your mother's ill health make that impossible?'

'I have no wish to go through all that.' Ellie was horrified. She knew it was the normal thing to do and most young ladies looked forward to it, but not her. 'From what I have been told it is all frivolity, and searching for a husband.'

'And you do not wish to marry?'

'One day I expect I will, but I don't want to be forced into it, or put on display for men pretending to like me because of my father's estate.' She shuddered visibly. 'One would be judged on one's wealth, and I would not tolerate that!'

'Quite right.' Augusta approved. 'I felt exactly the same. My husband was the son of a family friend. We fell in love and had a happy marriage. I also refused to be presented at court. It caused quite an uproar. My mother was dismayed, but I would not be moved.'

Ellie studied the woman with renewed interest. She seemed charming and sensible, but she was surprised her father had invited them to stay with them on such a short acquaintance. And a party for her birthday had not been mentioned before. It must be something he had been planning without telling her. She cast him a fond glance. If she was hurting him by insisting that she find her other family, then he had never complained.

They stayed another hour, and then took their leave. It had been a difficult meeting with her sister, and Ellie felt as if all her energy had been drained away. She was longing to get home and talk with Nanny.

Seventeen

James watched the cab till it disappeared, and then turned to his mother. 'What a very interesting visit. Eleanor may not be of Albert Warrender's blood, but he considers her his daughter nonetheless.'

'I liked her, and admire her determination to find her siblings. She is not one to shy away from unpleasant tasks, I think. Once she found out about her parentage, she could not rest until she faced the past. That takes great strength of character, and in that way she is like Albert. When you see them together I would not have doubted that they are father and daughter, although their colouring is quite different they are alike in temperament.'

James nodded. 'She's an intriguing girl.'

'Albert told me that he was frightened to tell her about the adoption in case he lost her.'

'Well, that hasn't happened. I would say they are very close.'

'That was also my impression. He appears to be a kind, understanding man. A rarity these days.'

'Don't be misled by what you saw today. Albert Warrender is a powerful man.' James shook his head, a look of amusement on his face. 'He has been a Member of Parliament for some years, fighting fiercely for the underprivileged. I am informed that you upset him at your peril.'

'Have you been checking up on him, James?'

'Of course, Mother. I wanted to know something about the stranger who was calling on us.' James sat down and crossed his legs. 'But he is highly regarded, and very wealthy, I'm told.'

Augusta gave an inelegant snort. 'Well, he would be highly regarded if he is rich. So are we. Did you find out anything else?'

'Only gossip. It's said that he loved his wife and stayed with her, even though she couldn't have children.' James

131

pursed his lips. 'If he had a mistress, then I couldn't find one.'

'That could only mean he has been discrete.' Augusta studied her son with interest. 'You have been thorough. So, now you've met him, what is your opinion?'

'I would like to know him better before giving an opinion on such a short acquaintance. But he seems an impressive man.'

'Indeed.' Augusta gazed into space. 'He has the most extraordinary eyes, amber, wouldn't you say?'

James laughed. 'I never noticed, Mother.'

A tentative tap on the door stopped their conversation. It opened slightly and a very worried girl looked in.

'Ah, Margaret, I was about to send for you.' Augusta beckoned her to come forward.

She edged into the room, visibly shaking. 'I apologize for leaving the room without permission, madam.' Tears filled her eyes. 'I was so shocked when the girl told me who she was, and I didn't know what I was doing.'

'You need not look so frightened, Margaret,' Augusta said gently to her nervous maid. 'I shall not dispense with your services. You would not be easy to replace.'

'Oh, thank you, madam.' Maggie breathed a huge sigh of relief.

'Your sister is a charming girl, and was dreadfully upset by your rejection, but she understands. But could you not have been a little kinder to her?'

'I know I should have been, but I've always blamed her for the trouble at home, though that was wrong of me. She was just a little thing when she was taken away.'

'Taken away?' James asked, sharply. 'That's a strange way to put it. We understood that she was adopted by Mr Warrender and his wife.'

Maggie shook her head. 'It wasn't him that came for her. There was a woman in the carriage, but we didn't see her. A man got out, picked up Queenie, and shoved her inside, then he handed over some money, and they drove off. My mum and dad sold her.'

'Sold her?' Augusta exclaimed. 'But that is barbaric. And you say it wasn't Mr Warrender?'

'I don't think so. I'd have remembered him. Queenie hung out of the carriage crying for us to help her.' Tears began to trickle down Maggie's face as she remembered. 'I've tried hard to forget that awful day, and her turning up like this has brought it all back. But she's obviously done all right for herself.'

'It has turned out well for her, but it could have been very different.' Augusta turned to her son. 'I don't like the sound of this, James.'

'Neither do I, Mother. It's hard to believe that Mr Warrender sent someone to pluck the child from her family. I would have said he was a man of integrity, but perhaps the façade of a perfect gentleman is not the truth.'

'Well, we shall have the opportunity to find out when we visit him.' She nodded to her maid. 'In two weeks time we shall be going to stay with Mr Warrender. I would like you to accompany me, as always.'

'Of course, madam, you'll need your own staff. There's no telling what the maids are like there.'

Augusta hid her amusement at her maid's possessive attitude. 'I'm sure they are competent, but I would prefer to have you with me.'

The train chugged along, the swaying motion easing some of the tension from Ellie. She gazed at her father who was sitting opposite her, deep in thought. Having the compartment to themselves, they could speak freely. 'Mrs Montague is a handsome lady, do you not think so, Father?'

'Hmm?' He looked up. 'Oh, yes, very charming.'

'We didn't see her husband.'

'She told me she has been a widow this last eighteen months.'

'Oh, in that case then I doubt she will be short of suitors. She will be what they call a good catch.' Ellie's tone was teasing. 'As you will be. By this time next year you will be pursued by many unattached females.'

'I have no intention of being caught.' His mouth twitched.

'Mother always said that she'd had to fight off hoards of women trying to snare you.' Ellie grinned. It was good to talk about the happy times.

He laughed freely for the first time in quite a while. 'It was the other way round. Mary had them queuing at her door. I had to be ruthless to get past them.'

It suddenly occurred to Ellie that her father might remarry one day. Would she find it easy to accept another woman in her mother's place, or her father's affections? Her frown deepened as a vague memory prodded at her of her father bending down and removing her shoes so she could run barefoot through the grass.

'Why the creased brow, Eleanor?'

'Oh, it's nothing. I was trying to remember something, but it's gone now.' She changed the subject. 'I didn't know you were planning a celebration for my birthday.'

'Your mother made me promise that we would mark the occasion of your eighteenth birthday with a celebration.'

Ellie nodded, quite overcome that even in such poor health, her mother had thought about this special birthday. 'We'll make it a happy time.'

'Indeed we shall. You may invite anyone you like.'

'Could we ask Pearl, Dave, Jack and Mr Rogers?'

'I will see that they all receive invitations.'

The next day, Ellie was summoned to her father's study, her excitement rising when she found Mr Steadman there. But apprehension quickly set in when she saw their grave expressions. If one of her family had been found, then it didn't look like good news. She braced herself. 'Which one is it?' she blurted out, unable to control herself.

'I have traced a Thomas Bonner, Miss Warrender, but . . .' Mr Steadman hesitated, glancing at Albert.

'Sit down, Eleanor.' Her father waited until she had done so, hands clasped tightly in her lap.

'Is he dead?' she asked.

'No, he is alive and in Pentonville.'

'Gaol?' She'd heard about that place. 'What has he done?'

'Robbery with violence.' Her father didn't soften the words, knowing she would not want the truth hidden from her. 'It seems he is a persistent offender, and this time a shopkeeper was seriously injured when he tried to stop the robbery.'

She glanced from one man to the other, horrified by this news. 'Is the shopkeeper going to recover?'

'Yes, miss. Tommy Bonner has been lucky. He's serving ten years in gaol, but he could so easily have faced the hangman's noose.'

Ellie shuddered. 'That's horrific. How long ago did this happen?'

'Just a year, Miss.'

'I want to see him, Father.'

'No.' The refusal was firm. 'I will not have my daughter going into such a place.'

'But—'

Her protest was cut off. 'I have been accommodating so far, but this is something I will not agree to. I'll visit him, and this is the only concession I will make. By the sound of him, this is one brother you would do well to cross from your list.'

She knew from his tone and stance – standing straight with feet slightly apart and mouth set in a straight line – that no amount of begging would make him change his mind. He did not often taken such a firm stand against something she wanted to do, but when he did, then she knew better than to pursue the subject.

When she nodded, he softened slightly. 'I'll see him and assess the situation.'

'Will you tell him about me?'

'That will depend on what kind of a man he is. If his character is such that reform seems impossible, then that will be the end of it, Eleanor. I will not allow you anywhere near him. Is that understood? You must trust me.'

'I do, Father,' she said. 'That leaves only Harry and Bert. Is there any news of them?'

'Nothing definite, miss, but I'm still working on it. I have asked Mr Warrender if I can widen the search. He has given me permission to do that, so I'll see what I can find out.'

After Maggie's rejection, and finding out that Tommy was a criminal, Ellie was desperate to trace the remaining brothers.

Watching Eleanor walk from the room, Albert's heart was heavy. There was an air of distraction and confusion about her, almost as if she had lost her way, not knowing who she was any more. This was more than a search for her forgotten family, it was a search for a part of her life.

'Tommy sounds like a bad one, sir. If you like I'll visit him in Pentonville for you.'

Albert shook his head. 'That won't be necessary, Mr

Steadman, thank you all the same, but it won't be the first time I've been inside a gaol. And I've promised my daughter I'll talk to him. I hope we have better luck with the last two. That's if you can find them.'

'I'll do my best, sir, even if it's only a gravestone.'

Eighteen

Three days later Albert was in Pentonville, waiting for Tommy Bonner to be brought to him. He was hoping that this boy was nothing to do with Eleanor, but Mr Steadman was certain that he was her brother. Damn, he'd known this search was going to be fraught, but he couldn't protect Eleanor from every upset in life, and he was certain she would survive this, and emerge a stronger person.

When the door opened he watched with narrowed eyes as Bonner walked towards him. There was no doubt about his parentage. He was the image of his father, Fred Bonner, and full of cocky bravado. It was not a good start.

'Who are you?' Tommy demanded as soon as he sat opposite Albert. 'What you want with me?'

'Who I am can wait for the moment.' Albert held his gaze, trying to see beneath the surface, feeling a jolt as he looked into eyes the same colour as Eleanor's. But these eyes were hooded, wary, and yes, crafty. 'I want you to tell me exactly what happened in the robbery where the man was injured.'

'Why should I tell you? You a lawyer, or something?'

'Something. Now, if you know what's good for you, you'll talk to me. And I want the truth.'

Tommy folded his arms, and glared at Albert. 'I told the truth, but they still put me in here for ten years and bleedin' well threw away the key. I'm a thief, I admit that, but I ain't never hurt no one.'

That remark gave Albert some hope, slim though it was. 'Tell me what happened, and if you're not guilty of a violent crime, then I might be able to help you.'

'Why should you? I don't know you.'

Albert's sigh was one of exasperation. 'You're going to have to trust me. Come on, Tommy, talk to me. What have you got to lose?'

Giving a shrug, Tommy leaned his elbows on the table. 'I was with two others. I shouldn't have got mixed up with them 'cos they're nasty types, but I was broke. They said the shop would be easy as there was only an old bloke on his own. It wasn't my usual caper. I've always worked alone; breaking into houses when I knew everyone was out. You got any fags?'

Expecting this, Albert pushed a packet of cigarettes across the table with matches, and then waited.

Tommy lit one and took a deep drag, then continued. 'Well, I thought we was only going to take things we could sell, but the other two jumped behind the counter and started threatening the old bloke, trying to make him open the safe. I tried to stop them, but they shoved me out of the way. I didn't want to have nothing to do with robbin' the safe.'

When Tommy dropped his gaze and began examining the cigarette packet, Albert's mouth set in an angry line. He knew when someone was lying. 'Start again,' he snapped, 'and I want the truth this time.'

'All right, all right.' Tommy looked up, defiance shining in his eyes. 'I'm good at opening safes. That's why they took me along. I was working on it when the old man tried to stop me, but I didn't hit him. It was the others. When they saw what they'd done they did a runner, and I was the one who got caught. The old man can't remember what happened, so he said it was me.'

That was a more believable tale, though Albert was still not convinced. 'Who were the other two?'

'Oh, no you don't, mate. I ain't no grass. They'd have put me away for robbery anyway.'

'True, but if it could be proved that you didn't hurt that man, then we might be able to get your sentence reduced.'

'The only way you could do that is if the old man remembers who hit him, and from what I've heard, he don't remember a blasted thing.' Tommy eyed the man opposite him with renewed interest. 'All right, I've told you what happened, now it's your turn, mister. Who the bleedin' hell are you, and why are you here?'

Albert didn't like this boy, and he still didn't believe his story. He was very different from Ted and Jack, but he had to do this for Eleanor's sake. If it had been up to him he

138

would have walked away when faced with Tommy's hostility and outright lies. With Ted there had been a spark of something good in him, but he could detect nothing likeable in this Bonner. 'Your sister sent me. She's concerned about you.' Albert sat back watching the boy's expression intently.

Tommy started to stand up. 'You ain't a bad liar yourself, mate. Pearl and Maggie don't know I'm in here.'

'No, but Queenie does.'

It was as if Tommy froze on the spot, taking in deep breaths as he stared at Albert in disbelief. 'Queenie?' The name came out in a growl. 'That poor little bugger? The old man sold her, and we never found out where she'd been taken.'

'I know where she is.'

'It was you! You bought her. A little scrap of a girl, full of laughter and innocence.' Tommy's hands were bunched into tight fists. 'It must have been you, or you wouldn't know about this.' In a rage, Tommy launched himself at Albert. 'You bastard. What kind of a man are you?'

Before Tommy could land a punch, two guards burst into the room, pinning his arms to his side. 'Back to the cells for you.' They started to drag him away.

'Wait!' The authority in Albert's voice stopped them. 'Sit him in the chair. I haven't finished with him yet.'

The guards looked doubtful. 'He's a nasty piece of work, sir.'

'I can look after myself, but if you're that concerned, you can stay in the room.

When the guards moved to the other side of the room, Albert pointed to the chair. 'Sit down, Tommy, and stop acting like a bloody idiot. Do I have to go back to Queenie and tell her you are nothing but a violent criminal?'

The boy slid into the seat, looking thoroughly confused. 'How is she?' he asked, huskily, showing the first sign of gentleness.

'She's very well, and has had a happy life. My wife and I adopted her and brought her up as our own daughter. I've told her how she came to us and she wishes to find all of her siblings.'

Albert then gave him an edited version of what had happened, but mentioned no names. By the time he'd finished talking, Tommy's head was bowed, and when he glanced up, there was a suspicion of tears in his eyes. 'Do you love her?'

'I couldn't love her more if she were my natural daughter.'

Tommy studied Albert with a curious gleam in his eyes. Then he smiled and the tears miraculously vanished. 'You're a posh gent, mate, so how did you manage to tame her. She did love a good scrap.'

'She still does.' Albert's expression remained serious. 'I have had to write numerous letters of apology.'

Slapping the table in glee, Tommy roared. 'You ain't changed her that much, then?'

'We've never tried. Queenie, or Eleanor as we have always called her, is a unique person, loving, loyal, with strong opinions. We have always encouraged her to think for herself, to express her views without fear, and to be the person she was born to be. I could not have wished for a finer daughter.'

'You've done well by her.' Tommy held out the packet of cigarettes. 'Can I keep these?'

Albert nodded. 'I'm afraid I will not allow her to come here, as much as she wants to see you.'

'Oh, no!' Tommy shook his head vigorously. 'You mustn't let her come to a place like this. Can I write to her, though?'

'I'm afraid not. I'm not prepared to give you any further information until I've looked in to your case.' That was crafty of Tommy, but Albert wasn't fooled. By showing concern for his sister, he had tried to get their address.

Tommy gave a resigned shrug. 'I'm sorry I had a go at you.'

'You would do well to hold that temper in check.'

'I know.' Tommy grimaced. 'It keeps getting me into trouble. I always did explode easily.'

Standing up, Albert paused for a moment. 'Will you tell me who the other men were? I promise they will never know the information came from you. I do have connections, but I'm making no promises that I can help you.'

Tommy glanced anxiously at the two guards, and then whispered two names, adding where they lived.

'I'll do what I can for you.' Albert wrote down the names on a piece of paper from his pocket.

Tommy hauled himself out of the chair. 'Tell Queenie that I'm relieved to know she's all right.'

'Of course. Do you happen to know where Bert and Harry might be?'

140

'Bert always said he was going to America, but we all thought it was daft. He was a dreamer, but I hope he made it.' Tommy sighed. 'Harry just seemed to disappear off the face of the earth. He walked out the door and we never saw him again.' Tommy hesitated at the door. 'I really am pleased to know about my little sister.'

Albert watched the door as it closed, hearing the clunk of the locks, then turned, eager to get out of the depressing place. That boy was a fool. He had thrown away ten years of his life. He'd had very little chance in life, by the look of him, but he would have even less now. He would always be labelled a criminal.

Hailing a cab, Albert gave the address of a friend who was a lawyer. He knew he was wasting his time, but he had promised to try. He was not completely convinced that the boy was beyond reform. Or was it just that he didn't want to admit that one of his beloved daughter's brothers was a hardened criminal?

Resting his head against the back of the seat, Albert thought over the meeting, allowing the sway of the cab and clip clop of the horse's hooves to relax him. He must let Mr Steadman know that Tommy mentioned Bert's dream of going to America. It was a hopeful lead, but there would be little chance of finding him in America. It was a big country.

When Eleanor had declared that she wanted to see all of her brothers and sisters, he had never expected his reaction to meeting them. Because they were related to Eleanor, he felt that they were his responsibility, that he owed them something; the same chance in life he and Mary had given that little girl. He swore under his breath. Henry was right, this was crazy, but he couldn't turn back now unless Eleanor decided to stop, and he knew she was never going to do that. Thank God there were only two more, and the chances of tracing them were extremely slim.

The cab stopped outside a fashionable house in Bloomsbury. Albert paid off the driver, and knocked at the door, hoping Joshua Hargreaves was at home. He was lucky, and was quickly shown into the library. As usual, a mountain of papers surrounded his friend.

'Why don't you leave that all at the office?' Albert asked amused.

Josh held out his hand. 'There isn't enough room. The place is full to the ceiling. Good to see you, Albert. What brings you here?'

'I've been visiting a Tommy Bonner in Pentonville prison, and was wondering if you know anything about the case. Robbery with violence.'

'Bonner . . .? The name's familiar.' Josh began to sort through files on his desk, and when that proved fruitless, he started on the heap on the floor. 'What's your interest, Albert?'

'When we adopted Eleanor her name was Bonner, and he's one of her brothers.'

Josh's face appeared from under the desk. 'Ah, you've told her then.'

'Yes, and she wants to trace all her siblings. There were nine, but two are dead. We've found five so far, and that includes Tommy.'

'He must have come as a nasty shock.' Josh heaved himself upright and began on more papers piled high on a chair. 'What are the others like?'

'Decent and hardworking.'

'How did your beautiful girl take the news?'

'She was very upset at first, but she has accepted it. Any hope I had that she would leave things there were soon dashed.' Albert lifted his hands in a resigned gesture. 'But you know Eleanor.'

'Indeed I do.' Josh chuckled. 'A most determined young lady. Pity she wasn't a boy, for she would have made a fine lawyer. Ah –' he held up a file in triumph – 'I thought I knew the name, but I didn't handle the case myself.'

Albert waited while his friend read through the notes, shaking his head from time to time, and muttering under his breath. Then he tossed the file on his desk and sat down, pursing his lips. 'One of our young lawyers took on the defence, but there was little he could do with the evidence against Bonner, even though he was denying he carried out the attack.' He turned a couple of pages. 'He had a fair trial, Albert.'

'He's still saying that he's innocent of the assault.'

'They all say that, but the evidence against him was overwhelming.'

'Tommy told me that there were two other men with him,

142

and they attacked the man while he was trying to open the safe. They fled, leaving Tommy to take the rap.'

'And you believe him?'

'I don't know what to believe, but he did give me two names.'

'Let me see them.' Josh held out his hand.

'Bonner doesn't want it known that he has given these men away.'

'Obviously.' Josh wiggled his fingers. 'I'll be discreet.'

Albert handed over the paper, knowing he could trust Josh not to do anything stupid and get Bonner into even more trouble.

Josh grunted. 'You can safely leave this with me. You have my word that I won't do anything to harm Bonner, or upset Eleanor.'

Albert relaxed, relieved that he'd kept his word and it was now out of his hands. 'We're holding a celebration on Saturday week in honour of Eleanor's eighteenth birthday. We hope you will be able to join us?'

'Wouldn't miss it for anything. Stay for lunch, Albert?'

He readily agreed, looking forward to a relaxing couple of hours with his friend.

Nineteen

The evening of the party arrived. The house was full of guests; some were staying, while others, who lived locally, were returning to their own homes later. They were using the ballroom, which was festooned with flowers. Ellie's dress was the palest of blue, making her eyes shine like sapphires in contrast.

Taking her place beside her father, they gazed at the portrait of her mother, surrounded by garlands of yellow roses, her favourite flowers. She couldn't help wondering where her father had got them at this time of year, but then, he was a man who seemed to be able to manage anything he set out to do. It was only because of him that they had made as much progress as they had in finding her other family.

She tore her eyes away from the portrait, determined not to be sad on this evening, because her mother would not have liked that. Ellie knew that some frowned on the idea of such a celebration so soon after the bereavement, but neither Ellie nor her father cared what people thought, knowing that Mary had insisted they mark this birthday with music and laughter.

Ellie and her father awaited the arrival of their guests. The musicians were already in place, and a sumptuous buffet was laid out at one end of the ballroom.

'It's perfect, Father, thank you.' She stifled a giggle. 'Look at Nanny sitting in state where she can see everything. I'm so pleased she is well enough to attend.'

'Nothing would have kept her away.' Albert laid his hand on top of his daughter's. 'Did you enjoy your ride yesterday afternoon?'

'Yes, James is an excellent horseman, and with Philip, we had a good gallop. James wanted to see as much of the estate as possible.'

'Didn't Ted and Stanley Rogers go with you as well?'

There was a gleeful look in her eyes. 'They are as bad as each other on a horse, so we left them to go at their own pace – very slowly. They can trot along quite happily now, but Ted hasn't the breath to gallop because he's too busy asking Mr Rogers questions. I think he's trying to improve his education.'

'He has a thirst for knowledge, I believe.' Albert changed the subject. 'Have you seen Maggie since she arrived?'

'No.' The animation drained from Ellie's face. 'She has no wish to see me, but I know she's been talking to Ted, so perhaps he can change her mind.'

'You mustn't let it upset you, my dear. It's been a happy outcome with Pearl, Jack and Ted, hasn't it?'

Ellie's smile was back in place. 'It will be lovely to have them all here this evening. Our family is growing, Father.'

'Indeed it is.'

His dry tone made her laugh. Just then the first guests were announced.

'Oh, doesn't Mrs Montague look wonderful,' Ellie whispered. 'That royal blue is perfect for her.' Ellie suddenly looked worried. 'I told Pearl and the others not to be concerned that they can't afford to dress in the latest fashion.'

'I'm sure they won't be.' Albert turned her attention to the door.

She gasped when she saw Pearl glide in wearing a lovely pale gold gown. 'And look at Dave, Jack and Ted. They are as elegant as you.' She looked up at him. 'Or almost. Now, how do you think they managed that, Father?'

He merely smiled.

'You really are a very kind man.' She squeezed his arm. 'You've made sure that they don't feel out of place.'

The first guests had almost reached them, but Ellie's gaze was fixed on her brothers and sister, nearly crying in delight when another girl stepped out from behind them. 'Maggie,' she whispered. 'Why didn't you tell me she was coming?'

'We weren't sure she would. Augusta and I have been trying to persuade her all afternoon. That is one of Augusta's gowns she's wearing.'

Ellie wanted to dance around in joy, but she had to remain composed. However, a gurgle of delight escaped. 'This is rather unconventional, with servants attending the same

145

function as their mistress, and working class children mingling with the titled and wealthy.'

'Yes, isn't it? But you forget that Nanny has always been included in our celebrations, and she is considered a servant by some.'

'I've never thought of her like that.'

'Neither have I. She is one of the family.'

When Maggie reached them, Ellie clasped her hand. 'Thank you for coming. I am so happy to see you here.'

'I shouldn't have come.' Maggie glanced around, anxiously. 'But madam insisted.'

It hurt to know that her sister was only here because Mrs Montague had ordered her to. 'I hope you will enjoy the evening, anyway. But you don't have to stay if you feel uncomfortable. I'll explain to Mrs Montague.'

'Don't be daft, Maggie.' Pearl caught hold of her arm, as her sister made to rush from the room. 'Ellie's our sister, and Mr Warrender wouldn't have invited us if we weren't welcome.'

'That is so,' Albert said. 'And I shall expect you to save me a dance later, Maggie.'

'Erm . . .' Her gaze skittered back and forth between them. 'You can't dance with me, sir. It wouldn't be right.'

'Who says so?'

'Well . . . convention. It's not done, sir. I'm a servant.'

'And this is my house. I can do what I damned well like.'

Maggie laughed then. 'Yes, sir, I guess you can.'

As Ellie watched the change in her sister's expression, she marvelled at the wisdom of her father. Once again, he had known exactly the right thing to say to put Maggie at her ease. She wished she had been able to see him in action in Parliament; it must have been something to behold.

'Please stay,' she urged. 'The others are pleased to see you. Enjoy yourself with them.'

Maggie hesitated. 'I'm glad things turned out well for you.'

'I have been very fortunate.'

When Pearl led Maggie away to join the others, including James and Mr Rogers, Albert signalled to the musicians. 'Time to start the dancing, my dear.'

They moved gracefully to the music, and that was the sign for everyone else to join in the dancing. The celebration was under way.

'Maggie will come around in time.' Albert looked down at his daughter's upturned face. 'Forcing her to come was clever of Augusta, don't you think?'

Ellie nodded. 'Mrs Montague doesn't appear to be at all stuffy.'

'Our situation is unusual, and she understands that. She saw how much it means to you, and she has a kind heart, I believe.'

'I've caused you a great deal of trouble, haven't I, Father?'

'Yes, you have,' he confirmed cheerfully. 'And I've loved every minute of every year since you arrived.' He lowered his head so only she could hear. 'I would have hated a daughter who didn't have an independent spirit.'

'And I've always had that.' Ellie giggled as she remembered the many scrapes she had been in.

The floor was crowded with couples and they stopped to mingle with the guests. Ellie headed towards James, Philip, and her brothers and sisters, who all looked as if they were thoroughly enjoying themselves.

'When do we eat?' Jack grinned at Ellie when she reached them. 'I've never seen so much grub in my life.'

'I believe I have to cut my cake in about an hour, but you can help yourself now if you're hungry.'

'Oh, no, you can't, Jack,' Maggie scolded. 'You must wait for the proper time. Don't encourage him, Queenie.'

Ellie's heart leapt with pleasure at the natural way Maggie had just spoken to her. Ted winked at her and bowed. 'Would you have this dance with me, Eleanor?'

'I would be delighted, sir.' She made a mess of a curtsy, causing them to roar in delight.

'Don't worry about Maggie,' Ted said, when they were dancing. 'We're making it our task to bring her back into the family fold. She always was very proper, and working for a lady like Mrs Montague has made her even more so, but she's always been a kind girl.' He held Ellie away, looking fondly at her. 'Have you noticed that Stan can't keep his eyes off her?'

'Stan?' Ellie frowned.

'Your tutor.'

'Oh.' She peered through the crowd to where they were all sitting. 'Do you think he's taken with Maggie?'

Ted nodded. 'It looks like it, and her with him.'

147

'That's wonderful.' Ellie spun round in delight, and then carried on dancing. 'He's a very nice man.'

'Don't I know it. He's been teaching me all sorts of things I didn't know about the history of this country. He makes it all so interesting.'

'That's how Philip and I feel about him.'

'I'm surprised you're still having lessons. At eighteen most girls have finished their education long ago.'

'I know, but I have a deep curiosity for everything, and I'm keeping Philip company in the schoolroom. And father thinks it will keep me out of trouble.'

'If you're still anything like the little girl I knew, and I think you are, then he has a difficult task on his hands.' Ted chuckled as he remembered.

'I know, but he has infinite patience, and is very forgiving of my misdemeanours.'

'Brothers shouldn't dance with their sisters.' James interrupted them, reaching for Ellie. 'My dance, I believe.'

'All right, James.' Ted stepped away from his sister. 'But I'll expect you to accompany me to the new land tomorrow and give me some helpful tips on management.'

'That's a promise.'

When they were dancing Ellie gave James a curious glance. 'You seem to be very friendly with my brother?'

'He's eager to do a good job for your father.' He tipped his head on one side. 'Stanley told me Ted's a wizard with figures, so we tested him this morning, and do you know, he beat me every time with the calculations. He has a sharp mind.'

'I know, and it's so wonderful to see him happy. He wasn't when we found him.'

'So I believe, but you can rest easy, Eleanor, he's going to be all right from now on. I'm a fairly good judge of character.'

'So is my father,' Ellie told James. 'He saw good in him from the first.'

It made Albert happy to see Eleanor having fun as she danced past with James, waving happily to him. He'd been sick with fear in case she turned away from him in disgust, but that hadn't happened. In fact, if anything, they were closer than ever.

Relaxed now the evening was under way, Albert bowed to Augusta. 'Would you care to dance?'

'I would love to.'

She was an excellent dancer, but that was only to be expected. Augusta Montague was an elegant woman, with many accomplishments, he was sure. As he spun his partner round, he saw Josh arriving, late as usual.

When the dance finished he introduced Augusta to his friend, and when Henry took her off for another dance, he said, 'Any news, Josh?'

'That's why I'm late. Is there somewhere we can talk?'

'The library should be empty, but I'd like Ted to hear what you've got to say. He is the eldest of the Bonners.'

'Do they know about their brother yet?'

'Eleanor is the only one who knows, and I've asked her not to say anything. I'll do that. You know where the library is, Josh, I'll be with you in a moment.'

Albert weaved his way through the crowd to where Ted was. 'I need to take Ted away for a moment,' he told his daughter. 'But I promise not to keep him long.'

When they reached the library, Josh had helped himself to a brandy, and was sitting comfortably in one of the deep, leather armchairs.

'Ted, this is Joshua Hargreaves. He's a lawyer and a good friend of mine.'

They shook hands, but Ted was looking puzzled.

'We've traced Tommy,' Albert explained without wasting any time. 'But I'm afraid the news isn't good. He's in gaol for robbery with violence. A shopkeeper nearly died, and he's been sentenced to ten years.'

'Oh, hell!' Ted exploded. 'He always did have a nasty temper.'

'I saw that for myself when I visited him. Let's all sit down, shall we?' When they were settled, he continued. 'Tommy gave me two names of men he said were with him, saying they were the real culprits. He gave me two different versions of the robbery, so I'm not sure what to believe.'

Ted grimaced. 'He could also spin a good yarn as well. You were right to have doubts.'

'I thought it wise to ask Josh if he could find out anything.' Albert turned his attention to his friend. 'I hope you have good news?'

'I'm afraid not.' Josh shook his head. 'I've had a talk with the man who was in charge of the case, showed him the names Bonner gave you, but he said they had already questioned them, as they were known associates of his. They had unshakable alibis for the time of the robbery. He also told me that this wasn't the first time Tommy Bonner has been accused of a violent attack, but he got off that charge last time.'

'He lied to me.' Albert was furious.

'It looks that way,' Josh said. 'I hope you didn't tell him who you are, or where you live?'

'No, I didn't.' Albert glanced at Ted. 'You know your brother, Ted. If he knew where we were, do you think he would try and cause trouble, even from his cell? I don't want Eleanor upset in any way.'

'He might. He always was a wild one.' Ted stood up and began to pace the room. 'What I don't understand is why he would accuse those other men if they had nothing to do with the robbery?'

'I really have no idea. Perhaps he has a grudge against them, or something like that? Can I leave you to explain to Pearl, Jack and Maggie? Eleanor already knows, of course.'

'I'll do that, but not tonight. We don't want to spoil the party.'

'Certainly not.' Josh got to his feet. 'I'm going to claim a dance with the birthday girl.'

'Ted –' Albert stopped him before he left the room – 'Pearl and Jack are staying overnight at Henry's, and Maggie will still be here in the morning, so I suggest we all meet here around ten o'clock tomorrow. We can explain about Tommy then.'

Nodding, Ted said, 'Mr Warrender, I want you to know that we appreciate your kindness. We're all so happy to have been reunited with our little sister.'

'It's no trouble, Ted, and don't worry, everything will be all right.' Albert patted him on the shoulder, hoping to put his mind at rest. The more he got to know this brother of Eleanor's, the more he liked him. 'If Tommy makes a nuisance of himself, I'll set Eleanor on him. She'll soon deal with him.'

Ted tipped his head back and laughed, the tension leaving his face. 'She's quite a character, isn't she?'

'There's no doubt about that.'

Twenty

On the stroke of ten the next morning they all gathered in the library. Albert nodded to Ted to speak first.

He stood and faced his brothers and sisters. 'Mr Warrender has asked me to tell you what has happened in the search for the missing members of our family. Tommy has been found.'

'Oh, where is he?' Pearl asked. 'We haven't seen him for about four years.'

'Probably in gaol,' Jack remarked dryly.

'Good guess.' Ted then went on to explain what had happened. After he'd finished there was a stunned silence.

'I always knew Tommy was a thief.' Pearl was obviously shocked. 'But I didn't think he was capable of something like this. You saw him, Mr Warrender, do you believe he hurt that poor man?'

'I honestly don't know, Pearl.' Albert glanced at everyone in the room, and then his eyes lingered on his daughter. 'I'm not going to lie to you. He gave me two versions of the robbery and I'm not sure I believe either.'

Ellie gave her father a worried look. 'Perhaps I could write to him?'

'No, Eleanor.' Albert spoke firmly. 'I will not have you communicating with him.'

'Your father's quite right,' Ted said.

'Don't you trust him either, Ted?'

'He's always been the wild one of the family.' Ted frowned. 'I think it would be best if you stayed away from him.'

'But he's in gaol.' Ellie was reluctant to give up. 'He couldn't possibly cause us any trouble.'

'Don't be too sure.' Maggie spoke for the first time. 'Mr Warrender is talking sense. Tommy always did have trouble with the truth.'

There was general agreement, and Ellie had to give way,

although her nature would have been to storm into the gaol and see this wayward brother for herself – make up her own mind.

'Eleanor.' Her father's voice broke through her thoughts. 'There is often one black sheep in a family, and you may have to face the fact that Tommy Bonner is not worth knowing.'

She looked at her other brothers and sisters. They were such nice people. Sighing, she nodded in reluctant agreement.

'Will you excuse me, sir?' Maggie stood up. 'But I must get back to my duties.'

'Of course. There isn't anything else we can do at the moment.'

As Maggie turned to leave the room she stopped next to Ellie. 'It was a lovely party last night, and I'm sorry I was awful to you when we first met. I was wrong.' She touched Ellie's hand. 'I really am very happy to see you, and to know that you've been well looked after.'

'Thank you.' Ellie was taken aback by her sister's show of affection. Now she had two brothers and two sisters, and that was a lot to be grateful for.

By the evening they had the house to themselves again, except for Augusta and James, who they had persuaded to stay for another two days. Ellie and Philip were pleased about this because they found James good company. He could ride as well, if not better than them, and had a quiet sense of humour. He often kept a very straight face, and it wasn't until they saw the glint of amusement in his eyes, that they realized he was making fun of them in a gentle way.

Another person who seemed pleased they were staying was Stanley Rogers. He was taking every opportunity to spend time with Maggie. Also Henry and Albert were enjoying the company of Augusta. For the first time since her mother had died, there was a relaxed air around the house.

After a pleasant couple of days they were all sorry to wave goodbye to their guests. Ellie hadn't seen much of Maggie, but when they did meet it was on friendly terms. On their first meeting, Ellie had thought Maggie cold and hard, but that wasn't the case. She was more like Ted, sensitive and easily hurt, so she had built a wall around her emotions in order to protect herself.

That evening, Ellie studied the list of names. Fred and Hilda had been crossed off, so had the two who had died. There was a tick beside Pearl, Ted and Jack, and now she was able to do the same beside Maggie's name. She put a big question mark beside Tommy. That didn't seem too hopeful. Which left Bert and Harry. If Bert had gone to America, then he might be impossible to find. Ellie chewed the end of her pen, murmuring, 'Where are you Harry? I really have to find you to see what made you so special to me.'

'That was an interesting and entertaining few days, don't you agree?' Augusta and her son were back in London and enjoying coffee after dinner by a roaring log fire. 'You said you would reserve judgement on Albert Warrender until you knew him better. So, what do you think of him now, and Eleanor, of course?' Augusta asked.

Stretching out his long legs, James gazed into space for a moment as he thought about the man they had been staying with. 'The overriding impression is that he thinks everything through carefully before making a decision, and when he does, he will not easily change his mind. He's confident in his own abilities, and with good reason, as far as I could see. He has a fine estate, and it's well managed.' James leant forward. 'He's a strong man, but he does have a softer side. He cares about people, especially those in need, but preferring to give them the means to help themselves rather than hand out money as a temporary relief. Hence the way he's befriending the Bonners.' James frowned fiercely. 'Not that I'm sure he's doing the right thing there. However, it would be foolish to underestimate him. He would be a good man to have as a friend, but a formidable enemy.'

'I agree.' Augusta put her cup back on the table. 'But I believe that the real reason he's helping the Bonners, is for his daughter. He adores her, and makes no effort to hide the fact.'

'And she knows it, not being averse to using that to her advantage when necessary. But she's also wise enough to give way when he refuses her requests. They are very close, Mother. I swear they can read each other's minds.'

'I can understand that. I also found out how they came to adopt her, and he had no hand in buying her.'

'Ah, did he tell you?'

'No, Nanny did.' Augusta looked pleased with herself. 'Always go to the person who sees all.'

'The servants.' James sat back. 'So what did she say?'

Augusta spent the next half an hour relating the story to her son.

When she had finished, James let out a pent up breath. 'He did the only thing he could in the circumstances to protect a vulnerable little girl, and that was adopt her legally. That clears up any doubts we may have had about him.'

Augusta nodded. 'Eleanor may have come from humble stock, and will never be quite tamed, I think, but she's a fine girl.'

'And a fine horsewoman.'

She laughed at her son. 'Ah, well, that says everything about her, doesn't it?'

'Absolutely. She also dances very well, but she cannot curtsy without toppling over.'

'I shall have to see what I can do about that.'

'You've made arrangements to see them again, Mother?'

'Of course. We must return their hospitality.'

February arrived on a bitter cold wind and heavy snow. Ellie was kneeling on the window seat in the library, her nose pressed to the cold glass, watching anxiously for her father. It had begun snowing when he had left this morning, but during the last two hours the weather had turned very nasty. He should have returned as soon as he saw how bad it was becoming. Even Philip hadn't been able to come for his lessons.

Unable to keep still any longer, she jumped up and began exploring the bookshelves, trying to find something to interest her. There were several spaces where Jack had borrowed books. Not only was he working his way through Uncle Henry's library, he had now started on theirs. He came as often as he could to see them, but the first thing he did was head for the library. She wished that she could remember when she had been a little girl and living with them. But try as she might, her first recollections were of living here, safe and secure. How different her life would have been if her mother and Uncle Henry hadn't brought her to this lovely house. Now

154

she had seen Whitechapel, she knew just how lucky she had been.

The light was fading fast. Where was her father? Then a movement caught her eye. There was something out there, and coming closer. She rubbed her hand over the window to clear it where her breath had misted it over. It was a horse . . . a horse without a rider, trailing its reins . . .

With a cry of alarm, she shot out of the room, calling for help. The butler and footman were with her immediately.

'Quickly, please,' she gasped, struggling into her coat and boots. 'Father's horse has come back on its own. If he's out there hurt he'll die in this weather. We've got to find him!'

The footman tried to restrain her, but she fought him off. 'Get all the men.'

Throwing open the door, she stumbled her way over to the horse who was clearly distressed, trembling badly. The snow was almost up to her knees, making it a struggle to move forward, but her mind was crystal clear. She shouted orders to the men already arriving to help. A stable boy took charge of the horse, leading it back to the stables.

'We've got to find my father, so saddle up the horses!'

'We can't take the animals out in this weather, miss.' The head groom was shaking his head. 'The snow's too deep.'

'Then we'll walk. Fetch brandy and blankets. He was going to Lower Farm, so we'll go in that direction.'

'You leave this to us, Miss Warrender.' The footman tried to urge her back indoors. 'Stay inside. We'll find him.'

She shook herself free and glared at the men now assembled. 'Don't you bloody well give me orders!'

'The master will never forgive us if anything happens to you.' The butler, now wrapped from head to toe in clothing, intervened.

Snatching a blanket from one of the men, Ellie wound it round her head and shoulders. 'If we don't find him soon he won't be alive to forgive anyone. Now, move your bloody selves.'

As she stomped off towards Lower Farm, the others followed without further protest. Her outburst had triggered something deep inside her memory, and the picture of a bunch of ragged children had flashed before her eyes with a scruffy urchin crying for 'Arry. It had been so brief that she couldn't hold on to it, and neither did she want to. Her only thought was for her father, maybe injured, snow covering him – maybe already dead.

No, no! She shook herself and pressed on, head bowed against the blinding snow. Please God, lead us to him in time, she prayed, silently. Progress was painfully slow, but Ellie was oblivious to the cold, her eyes scanning the snow for any sign that a horse had come this way. The lanterns the men were carrying shone an eerie light on the glistening snow. They had spread out in a line to cover as much ground as possible, not daring to lose sight of each other in the white wilderness, but there was little hope of finding tracks with the snow falling like a curtain.

Suddenly, there was a shout from the left. Ellie scrambled through the snow, slipping and sliding her way over to the direction of the call. She reached one of the grooms holding a lamp high and pointing in front of him. 'What is it?' she gasped. 'I can't see anything.'

'I saw something move. I'm sure I did.'

They all surged forward, the blizzard so bad it was hard to see anything.

'Father! Father!' Ellie shouted. 'Are you out there? Please answer.'

There was a faint sound, and Ellie strained to hear. Perhaps she was mistaken and it was only the wind howling?

'Father.'

'Someone answered. It came from straight in front, I think.' The butler was already moving forward, with Ellie and the footman trying to run.

A dark figure rose from the ground when they were nearly upon him.

'Father!' She threw herself at him, sobbing in relief, and holding him tightly around the waist. 'Oh, thank God!'

'Are you hurt, sir? Your horse came home without you.' The footman was already supporting Albert.

'I'm glad the animal made it back.' Albert gave a ragged sigh. 'He slipped and threw me. I think I've broken my ankle. I was trying to reach home on my hands and knees.'

Ellie stepped back from her father, taking the blanket from her shoulders to wrap it around him.

'You keep that, miss.' The footman had another one in his

hands and wrapped it round Albert. 'Now, Mr Warrender, let's get you home.'

With one man either side of Albert, they lifted him by putting one hand each under his legs. They had to move slowly to avoid slipping or dropping their burden. Ellie moved out of the way, relieved to have the men helping. Her father was alive, but it was imperative to get him in the warm. From the lantern light she could see that he was in considerable pain by the tight line of his mouth. Catching hold of two of the estate workers, she pushed them forward.

'Go as quickly as you can and warn them back at the house. I want a fire in my father's room, and hot drinks ready for everyone.'

Every step of the way was torture for Ellie. After the joy of finding her father alive, she was anxious to have him home and tended to. It seemed to take an age but, eventually, the welcoming sight of the house was in front of them, candles and lamps blazing from almost every window to guide them home.

Nanny was just inside the entrance, leaning heavily on her cane, a determined look in her eyes. 'Take him straight upstairs,' she ordered, 'and remove those wet clothes. You too, Eleanor. There's plenty of water on the boil, so you can have a hot bath. We'll take care of the master.'

'We must summon the doctor, Nanny. Father thinks he might have broken his ankle.'

'You won't get anyone out here tonight. I've set bones before. Now, go!'

The house was in uproar with servants running around, being directed by a suddenly fierce woman who Ellie had always known for her gentle nature. The man she had looked after from a baby to an adult was hurt, and she was going to see that he was properly taken care of, even if it took every last ounce of her failing strength.

Knowing it was useless to argue, and there was little she could do at the moment, she ran upstairs to do as Nanny had ordered.

Twenty-One

It was three days before the doctor was able to reach them. It had stopped snowing, but the only way he had been able to travel was on a sledge drawn by a farmer's carthorse. After examining Albert he confirmed that the ankle was broken, but Nanny had made a good job of setting the bone, and that Albert did not appear to have suffered anything worse from the experience. He calmly ignored his patient's bad language when he told him that he must stay in bed for a week.

'How long is this bloody thing going to take to mend?'

The doctor pursed his lips. 'You should be walking normally in a couple of months. It's a bad break.'

'And how am I going to run the estate?'

'What about your brother-in-law?'

'He's got enough to do with his own place.' Albert's face was like thunder.

'Losing your temper won't help.' Nanny came into the room, puffing from the exertion of climbing the stairs. 'If it hadn't been for Eleanor shouting at everyone to move themselves, you'd have frozen to death out there.'

'I know.' Albert sighed deeply, resting his head back against the pillows. 'But there's so much to do.'

'You're going to have to find someone to help you over the next few weeks.' Nanny stomped towards the bed. 'What about Ted?'

'I could get him to do some things, but he will have his hands full dealing with the new land. Though this blasted weather will hold up work on clearing the fields. Ted is hiring workman and organizing the building of the house. We want to get it under way as soon as the weather permits.'

Ellie had been listening to this exchange, impatient to speak. Now she could hold back no longer. 'I can help, Father.

You tell me what to do. It's time I learnt more about running the estate.' She sneezed, her nose red from a heavy cold.

Nanny tutted, seeing her for the first time since she arrived. 'What are you doing up, Eleanor?'

'I can't stay in bed any longer, Nanny. I haven't got a fever. It's just a cold.'

'Well, what can you expect going out in that atrocious weather? You were like a block of ice when you arrived back. You're as bad as your father for not allowing other people to do things for you.'

'Father was out longer, but he hasn't caught a cold.'

'Ah, well, that's because he's strong; always has been. And if we don't watch him, he'll be hobbling around the house tomorrow.'

Father and daughter exchanged conspiratorial glances. Nanny, who turned to the doctor, hadn't missed the look. 'I'd better go and see that some sticks are made for the master. We can argue until we're out of breath, but these two are going to do whatever they please.'

'I'm afraid you're right.' Doctor Brewster's expression was resigned. 'I'll warn you one more time, Mr Warrender, keep off that ankle or you could end up with a permanent limp.'

'I won't put it to the ground, but I'm not staying in bed.'

'Always was strong willed,' Nanny muttered as she headed for the door. 'Better get those sticks made.'

When she'd left the room and could be heard tapping her way down the stairs, Albert laughed. 'That's one person who has improved because of this. She's in her element ordering people around again.'

'I'll be leaving then.' The doctor picked up his bag. 'I'll be back in three days, and try to do as you're told – both of you. I came close to losing two of my favourite patients.'

'I was never in danger, doctor.' Ellie sniffed.

'Anyone out on a night like that was in danger.' With a wave, he left.

Albert patted the bed for her to come closer. 'Have I thanked you for saving my life?'

Her chuckle turned into a cough. 'At least twenty times.'

'Now it's twenty-one.'

She tipped her head to one side. 'You haven't answered my request.'

159

'And what was that?' He pretended not to remember.

'Let me help you. I can do it, I know I can.'

He nodded. 'It is time you became more familiar with the workings of the estate. All the books are in my study, so I'll hobble along tomorrow and we'll go through them together. While the weather's bad I will teach you the daily routine, but you will not go out until the snow has cleared.'

Ellie nodded, excited by the prospect of learning about the business side of the estate, and doing something useful.

'I've received a letter this morning from Augusta.' Albert handed it to Ellie to read. 'Though how it was possible to make deliveries in this weather, I really don't know. However, as you can see she has invited us to stay with them in London. We'll have to decline the invitation, and that's a shame, because by the time I am able to travel again, they will be on their way back to Yorkshire.'

'It can't be helped, Father. Mrs Montague will understand.' Ellie hid her disappointment, for she would love to see James again.

'Write and explain, Eleanor.' Albert laid back his head and closed his eyes.

'I'll do the letter today.' Ellie studied her father's drawn face. The ordeal in the snow had taken more out of him than he was admitting. She stood up. 'Sleep now.'

Over the next two weeks, Ellie worked with her father, trying to assimilate all the information he was telling her. She hadn't realized just how large a task it was. Her father had always seemed to deal with everything without rush, or fuss. Whenever he had time, Ted joined them, eager to help in any way he could.

At last the snow began to thaw, but this only seemed to add to her father's frustration. She endured his moods without a word – at least, she only lost her temper once or twice. It was a good thing they loved each other, or they would have come to blows at times. He was not a man who accepted infirmity with good grace, and the household staff was tiptoeing around him in an effort not to incur his wrath.

A sudden shaft of sunlight burst into the study, and Albert hauled himself up, hobbling over to the window on the sticks he had been provided with. Nanny kept a sharp eye on him to see that he didn't try to walk without them.

160

Ellie gave an exasperated sigh. 'Will you please sit down, Father. The doctor said you must stay off that ankle.'

'I'm bloody well off it!' he growled, waving his foot in the air. 'The snow's almost gone. Go and ask them to get the carriage ready and I'll check Lower Farm to see how they're coping.'

'No.' She folded her arms, defiant. 'You can't go bouncing around over ground that is still rock hard.'

He glowered at her. 'You're getting as bossy as Nanny. I'll do what I blasted well like.'

As he started for the door, she beat him to it, blocking his way.

'Move, Eleanor.'

Staying where she was, she shook her head. 'I don't often defy you, but in this case I will. We didn't all risk our lives to find you, only for you to hurt yourself again. For once, you're going to do as you're bleeding well told.' Her accent slipped back fifteen years.

For a long moment he just stared at her, then he began to laugh. 'Your memory is very selective, for you have continually defied me. I've been far too lenient with you. I should take a slipper to your backside for this insubordination.'

Her mouth twitched at the corners, knowing that her little ploy had broken his bad mood. 'I'm stronger than you at the moment, and you've never hit me. You won't start now because you know I'm right. I want to see you striding along in your usual way, not limping like a cripple.'

'I'm a terrible patient, aren't I?'

'I'm not arguing with that.' She held his arm to help him back to the chair. 'I promise I'll go and check on things tomorrow, and take Mr Rogers with me. Now the snow is clearing, Ted will be busy.'

He nodded. 'I'm told the men have made a start on the house at last.'

Ellie could see he was fretting about not being able to get out. 'Uncle Henry and Ted are quite capable of dealing with everything. And the farm manager knows how to look after the stock. He's been doing it for twenty years. You must learn to trust us all, Father.'

'I find that hard. I've always dealt with everything myself. Even when I was in Parliament I still made the rounds to see

161

that everything was all right and give instructions where needed. I can see now that I should have an estate manager like all the other landowners. But you are quite right; until this damned ankle heals I shall have to do as I'm told.'

There was a sharp knock on the door, and they looked at each other, saying, 'Nanny.'

'Come in,' Albert called.

The door swung open and the elderly woman surveyed them with a critical eye. 'Stopped shouting at each other, have you? Could hear you all over the house.'

'Eleanor's becoming a tyrant, just like you.' Albert controlled his smile with difficulty.

'Good.' Nanny nodded in satisfaction. 'You make him keep off that foot.'

'I try, Nanny, but he's very stubborn.'

'Don't I know it.' Nanny pursed her lips. 'The problem is he thinks he's immortal, and after that scare, he ought to know that he isn't.'

Albert sat there, foot resting on a stool, and a glint of amusement in his eyes. There wasn't a sign of the earlier irritation. 'With you two watching my every move I might as well behave myself. It will save a lot of trouble. Eleanor, will you tell cook that we'll eat in here as we still have a lot of work to do. Will you join us, Nanny?'

'I might as well, seeing as I'm here.'

Albert winked at his daughter. 'Make that lunch for three.'

The days flew by as Ellie became her father's eyes, touring the estate and reporting back to him on every small detail. Her daily lessons were suspended, much to Philip's disgust, and he begged to be allowed to go with her. Although he liked Mr Rogers, he didn't like being the only pupil. Ellie, however, was happy with her new role, relishing each new day. She was even more delighted when her father listened to her opinions on how to solve problems as they arose, and with an estate as large as this, it was often. Her father would ask her what she would do in each case, and she almost burst with pride when he agreed with her solution. If he thought she was not right, he would explain why, and suggest another way. Their discussions sometimes became rather heated, for, like her father, she was not one to give way on a point when she felt her idea was the best. Eventually, she would bow to his greater wisdom, and in this way she was learning fast.

After one such exchange, Albert studied her long and hard.

'What have I done?' she asked, knowing that look.

'I've always known that you had a sharp mind, but until recently I hadn't noticed how you have blossomed and grown. Your reasoning is clear. You are becoming wise, Eleanor.'

She smiled, his praise meaning so much to her, and it told her she was doing a good job for him while he was incapacitated. She would miss this when he took over again. 'I love helping you.'

'I can see that.' He gazed into space for a moment, deep in thought, then he turned back to her. 'Would you like to train to be my estate manager?'

'Oh, I would!' She couldn't believe this. 'But I'm a woman and we are not considered suitable for such responsibility.'

'I don't give a damn what the world in general thinks. The only thing that matters to me is if a person, male or female, is capable of doing the work. And I believe you are.'

She gazed at him in astonishment. 'You're serious?'

'I wouldn't have offered you the job if I wasn't. You love the land, and with your natural enthusiasm for everything, you could manage rather well.'

'I accept, I accept!' She cried out in joy. 'I think I should write to Mrs Pankhurst and tell her I'm going to be the first woman estate manager.'

'I'm sure she would be delighted. But don't be too hasty to accept. You will have to serve a rigorous teaching period under my stern tutelage. We'll fight and disagree, for we have differing views on many things.'

She just grinned, relishing the prospect.

'And I may well be wasting my time, for one day you will marry and then your husband will take over when I am no longer capable.'

'He will not!' She was horrified. 'I'll never allow a husband to tell me what I can or cannot do.'

'You are going to have to find a very tolerant husband. You'll have to choose wisely.'

'I shall.' She tipped her head on one side, studying him intently. 'I'll have to find someone like you. Though I doubt

163

that will be possible. The creator threw away the pattern after you were made.'

Albert shook his head ruefully, well aware of his own flaws. 'With relief, I expect, determined not to make the same mistake again.'

When the dinner gong sounded, they were both roaring with laughter.

Twenty-Two

Spring turned to summer, and summer to autumn. They were happy months for Ellie. Her father's recovery had been quite swift, considering the severity of the damage to his ankle. But even when he had regained full mobility, he still included her in the running of the estate. He was a hard taskmaster, watching everything she did, but gradually she was given more and more responsibility. She loved the work and threw herself into it with great enthusiasm. The last few months had also given her the opportunity to get to know her brothers and sisters, and it was hard to imagine what her life had been like without them. They all got on well, and they had quite obviously loved their little sister Queenie. Even Maggie wrote to her from time to time.

She had also been corresponding with James regularly. Their letters were long, telling each other what they were doing, and comparing the work on both estates. Philip was also taking a great interest in management, much to his father's pleasure. He was also eager to start helping, and Mr Rogers was making sure he had a sound education to prepare him for the task. Ellie no longer had lessons so the tutor was able to concentrate on Philip.

Easing her horse into a trot, Ellie lifted her face to the warm sun. September was her favourite time of the year. It had been a good summer and there was going to be an abundant harvest. She was now going to see that the wheat was being safely gathered. Her father had given her this responsibility, telling her that if more workers were needed, she was to employ them. It was imperative that the work was done while the weather was good. She knew James was doing the same thing in Yorkshire, and she smiled to herself as the golden fields came in to sight. It made a glorious picture, as the men were busy cutting the corn and tying it in bundles.

Drawing to a halt, she dismounted and walked over to the farmer. 'Hello Jim.'

'Morning, miss.' He tipped his cap. 'It's going to be a bumper harvest this year. Best we've ever had, by the look of it.'

'Have you got enough men?' She was pleased at the way the workers had accepted her, but she suspected that they were polite and tolerated her because of the high regard they held for her father. That didn't worry her though, as she felt a sense of achievement to be doing what she was.

'Oh, aye, most of them are regulars, but we must move fast before it rains.'

Ellie gazed up at the clear blue sky. 'There isn't a cloud in sight.'

'No.' Jim tipped his head back and sniffed. 'But it's coming. I can smell it.'

He had an uncanny knack for predicting the weather, so Ellie believed him. 'How long have we got?'

'Another two, maybe three days. Time enough. You can tell Mr Warrender that it will all be gathered in time.'

She nodded. 'Is there anything you need?'

'No, thanks, miss.'

'I'll be getting back then.' She remounted and turned her horse for home. Jim had been with them for as long as she could remember, his sole responsibility being the running of the estate farm, and if he said that everything was all right, then that was good enough.

She arrived at the stables the same time as her father. This was a busy month, and they were hot, tired and hungry.

'All well with the harvest, Eleanor?' Albert waited until his daughter had given her horse a carrot as a treat.

'Jim said it will all be gathered in before it rains, and he has enough workers for the job.'

Her father nodded and Ellie fell into step beside him. 'How's the orchard coming along?'

'Taking shape. Ted's doing a good job. They've started felling some of the larger trees. We'll have plenty of wood for the winter.'

'Lovely. Can I see that the estate workers are supplied as well?'

'Of course. Ask Ted and he'll deal with that for you. Oh,

166

and the house is furnished now, so he's moving in at the end of the week.'

'We must throw a party and make it a happy home for Ted.' She was beaming with delight. They'd had great fun choosing pieces of furniture from both houses to make a comfortable home for her brother. It was quite a substantial place, with three bedrooms. Over the last few months she had watched Ted grow in health and confidence, as her father and uncle had shown respect for his judgement in developing the land.

'We're going to, but you mustn't tell him. We're laying on a surprise, and your brothers and sisters are coming, including Maggie.'

'What?' Ellie was surprised. 'But she's still in Yorkshire.'

'They're coming back to London tomorrow.'

Ellie stopped suddenly. 'Mrs Montague and James as well?'

Albert nodded, amused, as he watched his daughter's surprise.

'But I received a letter from James only yesterday, and he didn't think they would be coming back before November. How can he leave the estate when there is so much work to be done over the next month or so?'

'They must have a very good manager, and that is why they can spend so much time away from the estate. They are rather isolated where they are, and Augusta told me that she cannot bear to stay there too long.'

'Does James feel like that?'

'I really don't know, Eleanor. You must ask him.'

She nodded, and then did a little dance, spinning round in excitement. 'This is wonderful news. Ted will be so pleased to have so many of the family around him. And James might have told me he was coming back so soon. Just wait until I see him.'

Keeping arrangements for the party a secret from Ted wasn't easy. Henry devised a plan to keep him out of the way by pretending that he needed advice on a bull he was thinking of buying. When Ellie heard this from Philip she howled with laughter. Although her brother was learning fast, he knew absolutely nothing about livestock.

'He never believed that, surely?'

'Well, he did look rather surprised.' Philip eyed the food being set out in the dining room of the new house.

'I'll bet he did. He must have wondered if Uncle Henry had taken leave of his senses.' She put the finishing touches to a vase of flowers for the centrepiece of the table, and then glanced at the clock. 'I hope they get back in time.'

'Father said he was going to keep him away until everyone else had arrived.' Philip wandered over to the window. 'This is a good house, and in a lovely spot. If you're quiet you can hear the stream running, and when the fruit trees grow they will almost surround the house.'

'Yes, and the smell of the spring blossom will be wonderful.' She sighed. 'But I hope Ted won't find it too lonely.'

'Shouldn't think so. There will be workmen around all day, and he can always come up to the house if he wants to. Father likes him. In fact, everyone likes him, especially our maid, Dorothy.' Philip smirked. 'She can't take her eyes off him when he's around.'

There wasn't time to question Philip further about this, because at that moment, everyone started to arrive. Her father and Mr Rogers were the first, quickly followed by the carriages bearing Augusta, James, Maggie, Pearl, Dave and Jack. Jimmy had been left in the care of Dave's mother for the day.

There was great excitement as they greeted each other, and Ellie couldn't help looking around in wonder. It was almost a year since her mother had died – and what a year it had been. Her life had changed dramatically, and she still found it hard to believe that she had so many brothers and sisters.

'Quiet everyone. They're coming.' Albert held out the keys to Ellie. 'As soon as he comes in you must present him with the keys to the house.'

She took them, and waited by the door while the others kept out of sight. As soon as Ted walked in they all cheered. That was Ellie's signal to curtsy, none too elegantly as usual, and give her brother the keys. 'Mr Ted Bonner, welcome to your new home.'

The scene around him was almost surreal, and James watched in disbelief. This was an extraordinary situation. Ellie had been brought up in luxury, lacking nothing, then she'd been told that she had come from a very different background. If he'd been in her place, he didn't know if he would have had the courage to do what she had, or if he would even have

168

wanted to. He would much rather have left the past alone – undiscovered – where it wouldn't upset his comfortable life. But Ellie wasn't like that. He had begun to understand her a little through her letters, and he guessed that whatever crisis she encountered in life, she would face it head on. That took a special kind of person.

His gaze swept over the people in the room, coming to rest on Albert Warrender. After their first meeting James had thought he understood him, but now he was not so sure. Not only was he helping his daughter to find her siblings, but he had welcomed them, helping where necessary, and making them feel part of the family. Was he merely being kind, or was he a fool? These Bonners had been brought up in a tough world, and could be planning to take advantage of his love for Ellie. But, if that was their intention, then they were hiding it well; he could detect no sign of avarice in them. They just seemed delighted to have found their sister again.

'Eleanor has changed since we were here before.' Augusta spoke quietly to her son, as they stood slightly back.

'She's grown up.'

'It's more than that, James. I agree she has matured, but she's also grown in confidence. When she found out she had been adopted, that must have changed her life completely, but she is handling it well. That points to a sound character.'

'Hmm. And her father has been giving her much more responsibility than is expected of a young woman.'

'From the tone of your voice I detect that you do not approve. I am surprised. I would have expected you to take a more liberal view.'

'I am not Albert Warrender, Mother. He has a reputation for outlandish views.'

'Don't you mean enlightened, James?' There was censure in her voice.

'No, I don't. Look at the way he's welcomed this family into his home, treating them like friends. It doesn't seem to bother him that their speech is common, or that they come from the slums of London.'

'James!' Augusta was taken aback. 'You're a snob, and I haven't noticed that trait in you before. But then I've never seen you with anyone who was not from our class. And you are forgetting one thing.'

'What's that?'

'Eleanor came from there as well. She loves her other family, and is not ashamed of her roots. Neither is Albert.'

'Then he is being most unwise. They will take advantage of his wealth, and he will end up supporting the lot of them.'

'That is his business, and nothing to do with us. I, for one, am honoured to have been invited to this little gathering.' Augusta was angry now. 'And you are underestimating Albert. I don't believe he is the fool you are so rudely suggesting. You have been corresponding with Eleanor all these months, and I thought a friendship was developing between you, so what has brought about this change of attitude? You appeared to be quite happy to mix with them at the birthday party, and I thought you liked them.'

'I do, but—'

Augusta made a quiet sound of impatience, stopping him in mid sentence. 'If you find this happy gathering so distasteful, then I suggest you return to London at once. But before you go I suggest you make yourself agreeable. I shall be most displeased if you embarrass me.'

James watched his mother glide away, elegant as ever, even in her anger. He bit back a groan as her question still ran through his mind. When had his attitude changed, and why? He'd been looking forward to seeing Ellie again. She was an interesting girl, and he had enjoyed receiving her letters. But watching her with her siblings just now had made him uneasy. Why? He'd met them all before and it hadn't bothered him then.

He studied the Bonners, trying to see what was different this time – but there was nothing. Then it hit him with force. It wasn't the Bonners who had changed, it was him! He was frightened of them. But he didn't understand why. Why all of a sudden did he find them a threat? What had happened to him?

'James.' Ellie came towards him, smiling brightly. 'Don't stand in the corner on your own, come and join the party.'

He nodded and allowed her to lead him over to the food, greeting everyone as he went.

'Do you like the house?'

'It's a fine building. Your brother will be very comfortable here. He is lucky to have been so well provided for.' When she looked up sharply, he realized that his tone had been critical.

'You sound as if you don't approve. Father makes sure all his workers are well housed and looked after. If they are happy, then the estate runs smoothly. Don't you do the same for your workers, James, or do you put them in mud huts in Yorkshire?'

His mouth twisted in a wry smile. He had deserved that rebuke. 'No, we're quite civilized up there.'

'I'm glad to hear it. Ted deserves this because he is doing a good job for my father and Uncle Henry. They don't want to lose him now.'

'We most certainly don't.' Albert came and stood beside them. 'Come and have a look at the transformation that Ted has managed to achieve.'

'I'd like that, sir,' James accepted eagerly. He was in such a strange mood that it would be better if he removed himself from here for a while.

Ellie laughed. 'Father, take him for a long walk and see if you can cheer him up. I've been looking forward to seeing him again, but he's in a most disagreeable mood.' Her blue eyes were teasing. 'I'll find myself more convivial company.'

'Is everything all right, James?' Albert asked, as soon as they were away from the house.

'I appear to be upsetting everyone today. My mother left me in disgust, and immediately after that I said something to your daughter and she took exception to my tone.' James gave a resigned shrug. 'I shall have to apologize to both of them.'

'It will save a lot of trouble in the long run.'

'Is that what you would do?' James studied the man beside him, trying to get a clearer picture of his character.

'I would say I was sorry for upsetting them, but I wouldn't apologize for my views if I felt they were right.'

'The problem is I don't think I am right, but I can't help how I feel.'

Albert sat on a felled tree and motioned for James to join him. 'I expect you miss your father.'

James nodded. 'I used to be able to talk everything over with him.'

'Can I help? I'm a good listener.'

'I am going to be very presumptuous, sir.' James had decided to speak freely. He was upsetting everyone today, so why stop now? 'This is none of my business, but would you answer a question for me?'

'If I can.'

'How do you know that the Bonners aren't going to try and get you to support them for the rest of their lives?' James shifted uncomfortably. 'I shouldn't be asking you about your affairs . . .'

'No, you shouldn't, but this is something that is obviously troubling you, so I will tell you. I suppose this doubt has come about because of the way we are providing for Ted.'

'Well, yes.'

'The answer to your questions is that I don't know, but it is a chance I am prepared to take. I would never have given Ted a job and a house if he hadn't proved himself. Pearl, Dave and Jack have their own business and it gives them a decent living. They are happy with that, and have never once indicated that they wanted my financial help. Maggie is happy working for your mother. From what I've seen of them so far, I believe they are all fiercely independent people. The only one I have any qualms about is Tommy, but he's in prison for ten years, and will not be able to cause us any trouble for some time.'

James gasped. 'I didn't know that.'

'A friend of mine investigated the case, but Tommy was proved guilty without a shadow of doubt. He lied to me when I visited him, so I won't try to help him further. I have told him this and he's furious, for he really did think I would be able to get his sentence reduced.' Albert sighed. 'He was wrong. That leaves only two of the children unaccounted for, but we believe one of them may not even be in this country. My daughter wants to find Harry, but all our efforts to trace him have failed.'

'Why don't you put a notice in the London newspapers? Someone might know where he is.'

Albert nodded. 'It might be worth a try. Now, will you answer a question for me?'

'That's the least I can do after you have been so frank with me.'

'Why are you concerned about the Bonners?'

'I'm not sure, but watching the gathering in the house, I

172

suddenly felt uneasy. I was afraid they might try to take advantage of you and Ellie.'

Albert studied James thoughtfully, then said, 'I would *never* allow that to happen.'

A simple statement, but when James looked into Albert Warrender's eyes, he knew it was true.

Twenty-Three

'Did you sleep well, Mrs Montague?' Ellie asked at breakfast.

'Very well, thank you.' Augusta glanced at the clock. 'And so did James by the look of the time. He's usually around long before this. I wonder if he's still sleeping?'

'I am wide-awake, Mother. Good morning, Ellie.' James strode into the room, dressed for riding. 'And I'm very hungry.'

'Have you been out already?' Ellie helped herself to more bacon and eggs, hovered over the mushrooms before deciding against them. 'You should have told me and I'd have come with you.'

'I like to ride on my own in the early morning.' He slanted her a grin. 'I didn't think you would be up at that time.' He sat down at the table, his plate heaped with a little from just about every dish available.

'It's certainly given you an appetite. And, I am always up at dawn.' She was about to take a mouthful of her bacon when she saw a man arriving. Her knife and fork clattered down on the plate, food forgotten, as she leapt to her feet. It was Mr Steadman. She hadn't seen him for months. He must have news. Perhaps he'd found Harry.

'Excuse me, please.' She hurtled from the room, and was in time to see the butler coming out of her father's study.

'Was that Mr Steadman?'

'Yes, miss.'

Knocking on the door, she turned the handle and looked in. 'I saw Mr Steadman arrive, Father. May I come in?'

When he beckoned her forward, she stepped in and closed the door behind her. 'Do you have news, sir?'

'Before you tell us I'll order refreshments. You must be hungry and thirsty, Mr Steadman. Please sit down.' Albert called the butler and gave the instructions.

Ellie waited impatiently until the food arrived, and was relieved when her father asked Mr Steadman to tell them what he had found out.

'I have finally been able to discover what happened to the one called Bert. This happened two years ago, and I'm afraid the news isn't good.' Mr Steadman put down his cup and pulled a small book from his pocket, reading quickly through some notes. Then he cleared his throat. 'He was on a ship bound for America. He worked his passage as a cabin boy, but he never got there.'

'What happened?' Ellie braced herself for the bad news she knew was coming.

'There was a terrible storm, and three men were washed overboard. One was your brother, Miss Warrender. There was no chance of rescuing them from the rough sea.'

'Oh, that's terrible.' Ellie trembled as pain flooded her. She would never know what this brother had been like. Never see him. It surprised her how much the death of an unknown brother could hurt. 'That was an awful way to die. It's dreadfully sad.'

Albert watched his daughter struggle to accept the news. 'I'm so sorry, my dear.'

She straightened up. 'Thank you for finding out for us, Mr Steadman. There is only Harry left now. Have you had any luck with him?'

'No, it's as if he disappeared into thin air.' He turned to Albert. 'I've done all I can, sir. If I didn't know otherwise, I'd say the man doesn't exist.'

'I understand, and there's no point in you pursuing a hopeless task.' Albert stood up. 'Thank you for all your help, Mr Steadman.'

Ellie looked at them in alarm. Her father was giving up the search. 'Oh, we must find Harry,' she pleaded. 'Please, there must be something we can do.'

'Mr Steadman has done everything he can, Eleanor, but I will try one more thing. For the next month we'll put a notice in the London newspapers asking if anyone knows the whereabouts of one Harry Bonner. If that fails, then you will have to accept that he can't be found.'

'Thank you.' Ellie let out a shaky sigh. There was still a glimmer of hope. She stood up. 'I must go and tell Ted the sad news.'

There was no sign of her brother at the house, so Ellie began to walk along the rows of newly planted fruit trees. They were small now, but it would be a beautiful sight when they were larger and in full bloom. She tried to concentrate on her surroundings in an effort to ease her deep disappointment. That must have been a terrible way for a young man to lose his life.

'Ellie!'

She glanced up and saw Ted striding towards her from the wooded area. He had soon dropped the name of Queenie.

'What are you doing here?'

Try as she might, her distress showed as her bottom lip trembled. 'We've had news about Bert.'

He placed an arm around her shoulders, knowing this wasn't going to be a cause for celebration. 'Come back to the house. I'll make us some tea, and you can tell me all about it.'

They said nothing until they were sitting down with cups of steaming tea in front of them. Then Ted asked, 'What's happened to him?'

He listened in silence, and when she had finished talking he slapped the arm of the chair, and swore, 'Poor bugger!'

Ellie wiped a hand over her eyes. 'What makes it worse is that he was so close to realizing his dream. If only he could have made it.'

Ted nodded. 'I'll tell the others.'

'I wish it could have been happier news.' She looked at her eldest brother. 'Tell me what he was like.'

'He was a strange kid. Darker than the rest of us, and we used to joke that Mum must have got too friendly with the barman at the Red Lion.' Ted's smile was strained. 'He was a loner, a dreamer, always yearning for green fields and open spaces. I remember him telling us that in America there was room for everyone.'

'I'm sad I'll never meet him.'

Ted stood up and walked over to the window, gazing out at the young orchard. 'He'd have loved this place. He hated London's crowded streets and the squalid house we lived in.'

'Mr Steadman said this happened two years ago.' She went and stood beside her brother. 'I wonder what he'd been doing before then?'

'No idea.' Ted sighed deeply. 'I wish we'd all kept in touch, but we didn't. Each one of us had only one thought, and that was to get out of Whitechapel.'

From the little she had seen of the place that was understandable. 'There's only Harry to find now. Do you think he's still alive?'

'If he was then we'd have heard from him. I think he must have died or was killed soon after he left us. As I've already told you, he was the best of the bunch, and I don't believe he could have survived out there on his own. He was too young, too trusting, and too gentle.'

Ellie gulped back the tears, lifting her head, refusing to give up hope. She whispered, 'He might still be out there somewhere.'

'If he is then he's hidden himself well.' Ted squeezed her shoulder. 'There isn't much chance. Mr Steadman hasn't found any trace of him, has he?'

'No, and he's done all he can.'

'Then we must face the fact that he's gone.'

Ellie's mouth set in a firm, stubborn line. 'Not yet.'

The sound of approaching horses put a stop to their conversation. They went outside to greet her father, Uncle Henry, Philip and James.

Albert dismounted first, striding towards them. 'I'm sorry about your brother, Ted. If you'd like to go and tell Pearl and Jack now, then Henry and I will take over for you today. Just tell me what needs to be done.'

'Thank you, sir.' Henry joined them and they walked towards the trees with Ted listing the work planned.

'I had better get on, as well.' Ellie unhitched her horse, glancing at her cousin and James. 'I'm going to check on the upper pasture. Do you want to come? Father wants to know if the grass has grown enough to put the sheep there for a while.'

Philip grinned. 'That's why I'm here. I'm your chaperone for the day.'

'I didn't know I needed one.' Ellie mounted.

'Your father's instructions, and I wouldn't dare disobey him.'

'You sound frightened of him.' James laughed at the notion.

'I am.' Philip pretended to shake with fear. 'No one crosses Uncle Albert. His wrath is something to behold.'

'When have you ever seen my father angry?' Ellie glared at her cousin.

'Often, you ought to see him and my father sometimes. And there was that time when one of the workers was caught stealing. Your father picked him up and threw him so hard the man was sprawled out on the ground.'

'He deserved that. He was in the main house where he had no right to be, and father helped him outside. The man was lucky he wasn't handed over to the police.' Ellie looked at Philip in amazement. 'That must have been ten years ago. We were only children.'

'I know, but it made a great impression on me. Your father is very strong and I decided then and there that it would be unwise to make him angry. You're the only one who can get away with that.'

'You do exaggerate, Philip.' Ellie urged her horse into a trot as her cousin came up beside her.

'I'm not.' Philip turned to James, who was now the other side of Ellie. 'And it's not a good idea to upset her, either. She's just like her father. Strong and handy with her fists.'

Ellie leaned across to swipe at him.

'See what I mean.' Philip ducked, and then galloped off, laughing and calling out, 'I'll get to the pasture before you.'

They made a race of it and Ellie beat them by a neck. She dismounted and bent down to pick a handful of grass.

'Looks good.' James did the same, then stood up and swept his gaze around the field, nodding in approval.

'Perfect.' Ellie wandered to the top of the rise, then stopped to take in the view. The countryside was spread out in a patch-work of different shades of green. The trees in the distance marked the boundary of her father's estate, and it never ceased to amaze her just how much land they owned. If only Bert had stayed in this country, they could have given him the open spaces he longed for.

'Your father has a fine estate.' James's voice cut through her thoughts.

'But yours must be just as pleasant,' she said, 'and it's larger, my father told me.'

'Hmm,' was his only comment.

'I don't know how you can leave it for so long each year.'

'It isn't easy, but,' he winked, 'I had to come and see you, didn't I?'

'What nonsense,' she teased, secretly pleased by the thought that he had come just to see her. It wasn't true, of course. He had come to keep his mother company, because she loved London with its shops and theatres. 'Come on, I've got to tell Jim that the pasture is good and he can move the sheep.'

'Shouldn't you report back to your father first?' James frowned.

'She's his estate manager now.' Philip patted his horse before mounting. 'He lets her make decisions. Mind you, I wouldn't trust her.'

He moved away quickly in anticipation of her retaliation.

'But I thought you said in your letters that you were only helping your father until he recovered from his injury.'

'I did such a good job that he's decided to teach me everything about running the estate.' She frowned when she saw James's expression of disapproval. 'If you say it isn't right for a woman to be doing this work, then I'll belt you, James.'

'Oh, oh, watch out,' Philip warned. 'She means it.'

'Then I'd better keep my views to myself.'

'That would be wise.' She couldn't hide her disappointment of his attitude. He clearly disapproved, and that was a surprise because his letters had given no indication that he was prejudiced against women taking on responsible jobs. She decided to test him further. 'What do you think of Mrs Pankhurst and the WSPU?'

'You wouldn't want to know.'

The sharp tone of his voice answered her question. Her eyes were full of devilment. 'James, you are living in the dark ages. I'll have to see if I can change your mind while you are here. I'll ask Father to invite some of the ladies, shall I?'

Philip shrieked in horror. 'Come on, James, it's no good arguing with her on this subject. Let's beat her to the farm.'

Her cousin came first this time, and Ellie slid from her horse, rounding on Philip. 'That's cheating. You had a head start.'

'No, I didn't.' He ducked behind his horse as she advanced on him.

'I'm sure Mr Rogers would be appalled if he could hear you lying.' Ellie stopped, her head on one side, puzzled. 'It's only just occurred to me, but why aren't you in the class-room?'

'I told you; I'm your chaperone for the day. Everyone else was busy, and . . .' He smirked. 'Mr Rogers was happy to let me off because he wanted some time off to take your sister out.'

'Maggie?'

'Oh, Ellie, you ought to see your face. Don't tell me you didn't know? Our tutor has been excited about her coming here again.'

'Excited?' Ellie was bemused. 'That doesn't sound like Mr Rogers.'

'Nevertheless, it's true.'

She turned to James. 'Do you know anything about this?'

'I believe they've been corresponding and have formed an affectionate relationship. Mother is expecting to lose the best personal maid she has ever had.'

This was pleasant news after hearing about the death of her brother Bert. Her face lit up. Mr Rogers and Maggie would suit each other very well.

Twenty-Four

At around nine o'clock the next morning Albert walked into the library, hands lifted in apology. 'Forgive me, Augusta. I have not been a very attentive host.'

She closed the book she had been reading. 'You've been busy. I do understand, so there's no need at apologize.'

'That is gracious of you.' He sat down. 'We shall have coffee, and then I shall devote the entire day to you. What would you like to do?'

After pouring him a cup of coffee from the tray beside her, she gazed out of the window. 'The sun is shining and a guided tour of the estate would be pleasant.'

'That would take more than one day.' He took the cup from her. 'But I could show you some of the beauty spots. Eleanor has gone to see Ted, so do you think James would like to join us?'

'He's already exploring on his own. He has a great love of the land, and admires your estate.' Augusta smiled. 'And the efficient way you handle everything without an estate manager.'

'I have a very good manager. Eleanor is learning fast and already taking some of the burden from me.' Albert drained his cup and stood up. 'Like James, she loves the land. He must find it hard to leave Yorkshire for six months of the year.'

'No, I believe he finds it a relief. As much as he loves the place, he will never own it, and that hurts him.'

Albert stopped in the act of reaching for the bell to order a carriage for them. He turned in astonishment. 'But, surely, he inherited when his father died?'

'James isn't the eldest son. My husband has a son, Giles, from a previous marriage, and he inherited everything in Yorkshire.'

Stunned, Albert sat down again. This was the first mention that James was not the owner of his father's estate, and that revelation made him more than a little uneasy. Why had it not been mentioned before? And he was sure Eleanor didn't know, or she would have told him. He knew she had formed a friendship with him over the last few months, but in light of this news, was James intending to take advantage of his daughter? Did he see her as a way of obtaining land of his own? Many men did marry for that reason. He didn't want that kind of fate for his daughter.

'Your husband must have provided for both of you?'

'The house in London is ours, and we have generous allowances.' Augusta appeared completely unconcerned. 'And we are allowed to stay on the estate for the summer months.'

Albert sat back, frowning. They were *allowed* to stay?

'It is usual for the eldest son to inherit, Albert.' Augusta spoke gently, noting his concern. 'My husband never made a secret of his intentions. Giles has been trained from a child to take over.'

'That doesn't make it right.' He shook his head. 'You shouldn't have been deprived of your home, and James could have been given a small part of the estate as his own. From what you've told me, it is large enough.'

'I agree, and I hope that one day these archaic inheritance practices are changed.' Her face lit up with amusement. 'Perhaps the ladies of the WSPU will manage to convince the men that they are intelligent, worthy citizens.'

Albert laughed, his surprise receding. Augusta probably hadn't mentioned this before because she'd accepted it as the normal state of things. 'Eleanor has strong views about that. Even when she marries she will never hand over the estate to her husband.'

'She may not have a choice. It would be expected.'

'She will have a choice. I've made that clear in my will. The estate will only ever belong to my daughter, and she's strong enough to see that my wishes are carried out.'

Albert stood up, dismissing the subject. 'Let us go and enjoy the good weather.'

While everyone was dressing for dinner that evening, Albert went to visit Nanny. She seldom left her rooms now, and he was worried about her. To him, she was an important member of the family, and he had never considered her a servant. She had been more of a mother to him than his own mother.

'Hello, Nanny.' He walked in, stooping down in front of her. 'How are you?'

'I've had better days.' She pulled a face.

'Shall I send for the doctor?'

'He's already been, but there's nothing he can do. 'It's only old age. Sit down, you look as if you've got something on your mind.'

Giving a short laugh, he sat. He was sure this wise woman could read his mind. Then he told her his fears about James.

'So, the young man will have to marry well if he wants land of his own.' Nanny pursed her lips. 'And you think he might be looking at Eleanor for that reason?'

He nodded. 'He spends a lot of time on his own exploring the estate. I don't want to see her trapped in a marriage of convenience.'

'You can't protect her from every hurt in life, neither should you attempt to.' Nanny spoke firmly. 'She's a sensible girl, and not easily taken in when people are being insincere. She is not a child any longer, and you must trust her to make wise decisions in her life.'

'I know.' He paused in thought. 'I keep thinking she is still a small, vulnerable child. What worries me is that James has kept very quiet about this, allowing us to believe that the estate in Yorkshire was his. Do you think I should alert Eleanor to this fact?'

'No, that is the last thing you should do. Leave it for the time being and see how things go. James might tell her himself, and that would be far the best way for her to find out.' Nanny studied him thoughtfully. 'Has it occurred to you that Mrs Montague may have decided you would make her a fine second husband?'

'Not a chance, Nanny.' Albert stood up. 'She's a charming woman and I enjoy her company, but that's all.'

'Of course it is.' The corners of Nanny's mouth twitched slightly, but she said no more.

'Thank you for your good advice, as usual. It always helps to clear my mind.' Albert left the room, feeling much more at ease. Nanny had always possessed sound common sense.

And his daughter had proved she was able to look after herself on numerous occasions.

During dinner that evening, Albert watched Eleanor, trying to see her not as the little child he had always adored, but as a young girl, growing to womanhood with confidence and a fierce streak of independence. Nanny was right; she must make her own mistakes in life and learn from them. He had been fiercely protective towards her, but it was time to step back, release the reins and let her gallop free. It wasn't going to be an easy thing for him to do, as he had never been able to erase the picture of a small child huddled in the corner of her bedroom, clutching her old frock. Mary hadn't realized what she had done. But his wife had been right about one thing, Eleanor had eventually settled down, bringing them more joy than they could have imagined. Now she was going back to her past again, finding members of her forgotten family, and handling both the pleasure and pain with maturity.

Sipping his wine, he glanced at James as he talked to Eleanor, obviously happy in each other's company. He bit back a deep sigh. All right, he would give them space to develop their friendship, but that didn't mean he wouldn't keep a sharp eye on the young man. And if he hurt his daughter, he would break his bloody neck.

'You look fierce, Albert.' Augusta touched his arm.

He smiled at her, realizing that he was being a bad host again. 'Do I? I'm sorry, my mind was on other things.'

'Father, will you invite Mrs Pankhurst to dine with us one day while James is here? He would like to meet her.'

Albert knew the teasing expression on Eleanor's face so well, and he didn't miss James's look of disgust. 'I've only met her once, but she knows I'm sympathetic to her cause, if not her methods. I shall send an invitation.'

James glared at Eleanor as she enjoyed herself at his expense. 'Your daughter knows very well how I feel about the suffrage movement.'

'Would you share your views with us, James.' Albert wasn't going to miss this opportunity to discover more about the young man's outlook on life.

The lively discussion that followed took them right through to the coffee stage of the meal. James was against equal rights for women, surprising Albert with his vehemence that a woman's place was in the home.

'And do you disapprove of Eleanor being given responsibility and some authority in the running of our estate?'

'As you don't have a son to take over from you, it's understandable that you should want your only child to be familiar with the estate. But I'm sure you cannot mean to make it permanent.'

'I assure you that I have every intention of doing just that.' Albert sat back. 'She is very capable and will have control of the estate for the rest of her life, and then it will be passed on to her children, should she have any.'

'But surely – ' James frowned – 'when she marries her husband will take control?'

'No, he will be expected to help with the running of the estate, but it will always legally be Eleanor's.'

'That is unconventional, sir.' James was clearly shocked.

'Oh, James.' Ellie shook her head. 'You are so old fashioned. Things are changing, and you must change with them.'

His smile was fleeting. 'I have been brought up to hold my father's views.'

'That is true.' Augusta agreed. 'My husband had strong opinions on a woman's place in life.'

'I realized that when we were talking this morning.' Albert glanced across at James. 'My brother-in-law is a lawyer, and between us we have made sure that Eleanor can never be deprived of her inheritance.'

'And what if she never has children?' Augusta asked.

'Then everything will go to Philip and his family. Of course, should a husband outlive Eleanor, he will have a home for the rest of his life.' Albert had made his point, it was now up to any young man Eleanor met to decide if he could marry for love and not gain.

The subject changed to lighter subjects, and if James was troubled by what he had just learned, then he showed no sign of it.

Ellie knew her father was an early riser and would already be in his study. After knocking on the door, she opened it and looked in. 'Good morning, Father. May I come in?'

'Of course, Eleanor. Did you sleep well?'

'Soundly.' She sat in front of the large desk, leaning her elbows on it so she could see what her father was working on. 'They're moving the sheep today.'

'Good, they will be all right there until the cold weather arrives.' Albert sat back, delighted by his daughter's animated expression. 'Do you think it was kind to tease James with a visit by Mrs Pankhurst?'

Ellie gurgled in delight. 'I couldn't resist it. He is rather pompous at times, believing that all women, including me, should sit around the house all day, and not interfere with *men's* work.'

'But you like him?'

'Oh, yes, he can be funny when he relaxes and forgets to be stuffy.'

'He's a rather intense young man, but it's the way he's been brought up. He takes a serious view of life.'

'I expect it's because he has a lot of responsibilities.' Ellie grinned at her father, eyes gleaming with amusement. 'But he's learning to join in with us, and doesn't seem to mind being teased.'

'Ah, that is something he will have to get used to with you and Philip.' Albert closed the account book he had in front of him. 'Now you have turned eighteen, we shall, no doubt, have young men calling to gain your favour. I am surprised there isn't already a line of hopeful suitors knocking on the door.'

Ellie was horrified, then her expression relaxed. 'They will soon leave once they know that they will not gain land by marrying me. That was very clever of you, Father.'

He nodded. 'I wanted to make sure that you were not taken advantage of. When you marry, I want it to be someone of your choosing, and for genuine love and affection.'

'Just like you and mother.' Ellie's expression softened when she thought of the love they had all shared.

'Choose carefully, Eleanor,' he advised.

'I will, but I'm quite happy as I am.' She tipped her head to one side and pursed her lips. 'Anyway, all this talk about someone marrying me for the land is quite unnecessary. You are going to live to a hundred.'

He laughed. 'I'll do my best, but this is something you must consider, Eleanor.'

186

'I know, and I would want a husband and children some time, but not just yet.'

'Your Uncle Henry thinks you should marry Philip—'

Ellie shrieked.

'And then we could join the two estates together.' Albert kept a perfectly straight face.

'He's younger than me, and he's only a child.' She rested her chin in her hands and peered at her father. Was he serious? But as she looked deep into his eyes, she knew. 'You're teasing me. Uncle Henry never said any such thing.'

'Yes, he did, and you must admit that it would solve a lot of problems.' A deep chuckle ran through him. 'You ought to see your face.'

'Well, you would be just as horrified if I suggested that you marry Mrs Dearbourne.'

Albert lifted his hands in horror. 'I see what you mean.'

They were both laughing now. Mrs Dearbourne, a widow, had arrived in the district a year ago, desperate to find herself another husband. She was grossly overweight, rather loud, and pursued every eligible gentleman with determination. They all kept well away from her, and even her obvious wealth had not tempted one man.

Ellie was pleased when the subject of her marrying was dropped. She really didn't want to think about the future at the moment. She was enjoying herself far too much. And she wouldn't be able to rest until they knew what had happened to Harry.

Twenty-Five

October arrived with bright sunshine lighting the country-side in a blaze of red, gold and orange, but for once Ellie was blind to the beauty around her. James had returned to London over a week ago, and she missed him. It was surprising how quickly she had become used to his company. But it was more than that. This month was the anniversary of her mother's death; losing her still hurt so much, and she knew her father was still grieving. Outwardly you would never know, but she only had to look into his eyes to see the pain.

Turning her horse for home, she urged him into a gallop. Even her early morning ride hadn't managed to ease her gloom. It was two weeks since they had put the announcement in the newspapers, but, as far as she knew, no one had come forward with information about Harry. Her father had paid for it to be included every day for a month. In another two weeks the notice would be withdrawn, and that would be the end, unless she could persuade her father to extend the period. He had gone to a lot of trouble and expense, and she would hesitate to ask more of him, but she would if she had to.

'Where are you, Harry?' she cried out as she bent over the horse's neck, her words disappearing on the wind.

Suddenly, the face of a young boy flashed across her memory.

She brought her horse to an abrupt halt, making Silver snort in annoyance at having her gallop interrupted. The picture had been so vivid that tears were streaming down her face. 'He looks like me,' she sobbed, struggling to hold on to the vision. 'He has the same blue eyes and colour hair. He's more like me than any of the others. We've got to find him! I now know how special he was to me.'

Digging in her heels, they started for home again. She had to talk to her father. He was at breakfast when she rushed in, eyes wide and arms outstretched, making him surge to his feet. 'What's the matter, Eleanor?'

'I've remembered Harry!' She gulped, collapsing into a chair, and as her father sat beside her, she clasped his hand. 'I was thinking of him and it was as if some memory buried deep in my mind surfaced. I saw a fleeting image of a young boy, his colouring just like mine, and he was laughing. He was always laughing.' She gazed at her father, pleading, 'I loved him so much. We must find him.'

'I don't know what else we can do.' Albert sighed. 'In a way I'm sorry you have discovered your affection for this brother, because our chances of tracing him are very slim.'

Ellie nodded, knowing this was true. 'Has no one come forward?'

'A few, but . . .' He placed a finger on her lips to stop her saying anything. 'But Joshua has investigated everyone, and they were all people hoping to make some money.'

'Frauds, you mean?'

'Yes, and there will be plenty of them. That's why Josh insisted that the newspaper send everything to him first. Neither of us wanted people turning up here and upsetting you.'

'Uncle Josh will let us know at once if there is even a glimmer of hope, won't he?' She was fond of her father's friend, and had given him the title of uncle many years ago when she had been unable to say Hargreaves.

'He will.' Albert squeezed her hand, and then sat back. 'He has invited us to stay with him in London for a few days. We could do some exploring, go to the theatre, and maybe see an opera. Would you enjoy that?'

'That would be lovely.' Ellie liked the idea. Remembering Harry had shaken her badly, and it would be good to be in bustling London, doing different things. 'Perhaps we could visit James and his mother while we are there?'

'I'm sure that can be arranged,' he said. 'We'll go in two days' time.'

It was four days before they managed to get away, and much to Ellie's delight, her father had left Ted in charge of the estate. Her brother was being given more and more responsibility and he was thriving on it. He was showing a great interest in one of Uncle Henry's maids, Dorothy, and there were signs that he was ready to settle down. They were clearly fond of each other, and it showed that Ted had really put the past behind him. Her thoughts turned to Harry. Even if her father gave up the search, she knew she never would. If it took her the rest of her life, she *would* discover what had happened to him.

'Eleanor!' her father called. 'We are leaving for the opera in fifteen minutes.'

His summons shook her out of her reverie. She had been staring out of the window without seeing a thing, her desire to find the last member of her family wiping everything else from her mind.

'I'll be right down, Father.' Leaping into action she fumbled with the front fastening of her gown, making a mess of it and having to start again. It was time she had a personal maid, as her father suggested, but she had resisted the idea, declaring that she was quite capable of dressing herself.

After a final glance in the mirror to check that the pale blue gown was hanging correctly, she grabbed her purse and hurried for the stairs. Her father and Uncle Joshua were at the bottom waiting for her. Lifting her skirt, she made her way down as quickly as possible. There was only one way to move in clothes like this, and that was with great care. She hated dressing up, and cursed silently under her breath at the restriction.

'You look beautiful, Eleanor.' Joshua turned to Albert. 'We are going to be the envy of all this evening.'

Ellie laughed at the teasing. 'You are quite wrong. It is I who will be looked at with envy for having two such handsome gentlemen as escorts.'

Joshua roared with laughter. 'She's learning how to flatter with style, and is going to be a force to be reckoned with.'

'She always has been.' Albert held out his arm, winking at her. 'I knew that the moment I set eyes on her.'

It was only a short ride to the Royal Opera House at Covent Garden, and Albert took great delight in watching his daughter's animated face as she talked about *La Boheme*. Coming to spend a few days in London had been a good idea. Her distress had concerned him when she'd told him about remembering Harry. He had always known that the boy was special to her, but much to his relief the memories had faded.

The fact that she had recalled him and not any of the others, showed just how close the bond between them had been. His heart ached for her, for he had given up any hope of finding Harry. It was sad he was the only sibling they hadn't been able to trace.

When they arrived at the Opera House, Augusta and James were waiting for them. The sight of Augusta nearly took away Albert's breath. She looked stunning in a gown of palest gold and a diamond necklace gracing her still slender neck. She would, no doubt, marry again, for she would be an asset to any man's household, as well as being a charming and intelligent companion.

As they made their way to Uncle Joshua's box, Ellie couldn't help swivelling her head this way and that in order not to miss a thing.

'Impressive, isn't it?' James said, as she rushed to look over the edge of the box into the main auditorium.

She was speechless, watching as the place filled up rapidly, an excited buzz in the air. The décor was beautiful enough with the ornate carving and sumptuous velvet curtains, but the ladies were outshining their surroundings. Ellie had never seen so many lovely gowns or jewels. She was wearing a sapphire necklace of her mother's, but it was modest compared to some on show tonight.

With a smothered laugh of glee, she turned and pulled her father forward. 'Look at this. There's an absolute fortune out there. Have they come to see the opera, or to be seen?'

'In many cases, the latter.'

'Oh, the lights are dimming.' Ellie sat on the chair between her father and James, eager to enjoy her first opera.

She wasn't disappointed. Every minute had been wonderful, and her father had explained the story so she could follow it. It had been rather sad, but the glorious music was still ringing in her ears as they dined at an exclusive restaurant after the performance. Her father and Joshua were certainly making this an evening to remember. Ellie knew that she could have had many times like this if she had agreed to a season, but, as exciting as it was, she knew that within a couple of days she would be longing for the open spaces and quiet once again. All the opulence she had seen tonight could not compare to home.

* * *

The next morning Ellie's father had left a message to say that they had gone out, but would be back for lunch. So, after breakfast, she wandered into the library to find a book to read. By the window was a huge oak desk completely covered in papers and packages tied up with tape. Right next to it was a waste bin full to the top and spilling some of its contents on to the floor. Uncle Joshua obviously just tossed discarded letters in the general direction of the bin, not caring if they went in or not. Smiling to herself, she set about picking them up, forcing them into the bin. As one piece of paper unfurled she saw the name of Bonner. Smoothing it out, she began to read, her excitement mounting. It was from Fred Bonner saying that they had seen the newspaper and would tell them where Harry was for the sum of ten guineas.

She surged to her feet, furious. Why had this letter been thrown away? Surely every lead was worth following. She wasn't simple, she knew that the Bonners might only be trying to get money out of them, but there was always the chance they did know something. This shouldn't have been tossed away. Her father and Uncle Joshua might not think this important, but she did.

Running up to her room she tipped out her purse. Her father hadn't yet given her the allowance for this month, and all she had was one pound, three shillings and six pence. It would have to do.

Without stopping to think what she was doing, she was running up the road, hailing a cab.

'What's the rush, miss?' a cab driver asked as he clattered to a halt beside her.

'I must get to Whitechapel, please.' She gave him the address.

He looked doubtful. 'That's a rough place. You shouldn't be going there unaccompanied.'

'I'm not. You will stay with me and I'll pay you for your trouble. Now hurry.' She climbed in.

Giving a shrug as if to say that it was none of his business if a young lady wanted to visit such an unsavoury place, he urged the horse forward.

As soon as they arrived, Ellie saw Fred Bonner leaning on the wall outside the house, a cigarette hanging from his lips.

He stood up straight as she alighted and called to his wife. 'Come and see who's calling.'

'Wait right here,' Ellie told the driver, and lifting her skirt she marched over to Fred just as Hilda came out of the front door.

'Where's Harry?' She held out the crumpled letter. 'It says here that you know where he is.'

'Brought the money with you?' Fred smirked. 'If you want to know, then you'll have to pay.'

'No, I won't.' Ellie advanced, fists clenched. 'You'll tell me or you'll be sorry.'

'You can't do nothing to us, girl.'

'Oh, yes I can.' She gestured to the house, furious with Fred's attitude. 'I'll offer your landlord such a high price for this hovel that he won't be able to refuse. And then I'll throw you out.'

'Fred!' Hilda looked alarmed.

'Don't take no notice of her. She couldn't buy the house.'

Ellie wasn't afraid of them. 'I could buy the whole bloody street if I wanted to. Now, where's Harry?'

'Got a sharp tongue on you, ain't you?' Fred edged away from her.

'Of course I have. Look who I had for parents.' She knew they were frightened by her threat. She had to find Harry, and she'd do anything necessary, even sinking to their level. 'I'm waiting.'

'Then you'll wait a long time, girl. I ain't telling you nothing.'

'That's enough, Fred.' Hilda elbowed past her husband to stand in front of Ellie. 'The truth is Queenie; we don't know where he is. He walked out, not understanding or able to forgive us for what we did. Nor did any of the others. They all left as soon as they could.'

'You don't know where he is?' Ellie had known this was a possibility, but hearing it admitted still hurt as her hope crumbled.

Hilda shook her head, then glared at her husband. 'I'm sorry I ever taught him to read and write. I never know what the daft bugger's going to do. Fred's always looking for a chance to make some money, except do an honest day's work.'

'Don't be stupid, woman.' Fred was furious. 'Where can I

get work round here? Go on tell me. More than half the bleedin' street's out of work.'

As Ellie listened to them arguing, it was as if her eyes were opened and she was seeing things clearly for the first time. The slum dwellings, the dirt and poverty came into sharp focus. An overwhelming sense of hopelessness seemed to invade her like a heavy weight. These people were trapped in a squalid life of want and deprivation, with no way of getting out. Each day a constant struggle to keep a roof over their heads and enough food in their bellies. And she had come from here, but had been given a chance of a better life.

Swallowing hard to control her emotions, she watched Fred storm away. Hilda stayed where she was. 'Will you tell me the truth? Why did you sell me?'

'We was in deep trouble. If we hadn't got hold of some money to pay the rent, we'd have ended up in the work-house. They'd have taken all my kids away from me, and I couldn't let that happen. Fred met a man who knew a bloke who was looking for a little one 'cos his wife couldn't have kids of her own. Well, you was the youngest, and –' Hilda's smile was sad – 'and the prettiest little thing. He came and saw you. A real posh gent, he was, and I thought that at least one of my kids would have a better life, so I agreed. I cried for days after you'd gone, but I didn't let no one see, of course. It would have been a sign of weakness, and you don't last long round here if you ain't strong. The money kept us out of the workhouse, and after that I took in extra washing to make sure we didn't end up like that again. Fred ain't a bad man, but this kind of life grinds you down.'

'I understand.' Ellie reached out and touched Hilda's arm. 'I'll get some money to you, but you must keep it for food and rent.'

Hilda nodded. 'I will.'

'Now, I must go, but thank you for talking to me. I'll be back as soon as I can. It might be a few days, though.'

She was about to get into the cab when Hilda called. 'Queenie!'

She turned.

'I did love you – all of you, but I did what I had to. We

was in a terrible mess . . .' Hilda shrugged helplessly. 'How many of them have you found?'

After instructing the driver to wait, she walked back to Hilda. 'Make me a cup of tea and I'll tell you all about them.'

Twenty-Six

'WW here is she?' Albert was storming around the house looking for his daughter.

'Mrs Palmer!' Josh called for his housekeeper, and as soon as she appeared, asked, 'Have you seen Miss Warrender?'

'She went out, sir. I saw her getting into a cab about two hours ago.'

Albert came down the stairs, stopping by the housekeeper, concern on his face. 'Who was she with?'

'She was alone, sir, and she didn't leave a message to say where she was going, or how long she would be.'

'Thank you, Mrs Palmer.' Josh dismissed the housekeeper.

'What the devil does she think she's doing?' Albert was furious – and very worried. 'She shouldn't be wandering around London on her own.'

'Perhaps she became tired of waiting for us and has gone to visit Augusta and James,' Josh suggested.

'I'll go there at once.'

'Ah, there's no need, Albert.' Josh was looking out of the window. 'She's just getting out of a cab.'

Relief swept through Albert as he stood beside his friend, quickly replaced by anger. She looked totally unconcerned. He turned on his heel and strode into the hall. When she entered the house and smiled at him, his fury erupted.

'In the library,' he ordered. 'At once!'

She did as instructed; she faced him, feet slightly apart as she braced herself for the storm she knew was coming. Once again her impulsive nature had got her into trouble. Why didn't she ever stop to think before acting?

'How could you have been so thoughtless? You should not have left this house without saying where you were going, or without a companion. Where have you been?'

She removed the crumpled letter from her purse and held

196

it out to her father. 'I went to see what the Bonners knew about Harry.'

Albert couldn't believe what he was hearing, and speechless for a moment, he took the paper from her. He knew what it was because Joshua had shown it to him yesterday, but they had dismissed it as useless. 'This is disgraceful, Eleanor. You have been going through Joshua's private papers. I'm ashamed that my daughter has acted in such a disrespectful way.'

'But I didn't—'

'Be quiet!' He saw the colour drain from her face, but he was too appalled to let it touch him.

'Let me explain, Father.' Seeing that he was not in any mood to listen, she rushed to Joshua who had just entered the room, eyes wide with distress. 'There were papers on the floor, all screwed up. I was putting them in the waste bin when I saw the name—'

'That's no excuse.' Albert was incandescent with rage, and no excuse would suffice for what she had done. 'We are guests in this house, and you have shamed both of us. You had no right to read it. The Bonners are only after money. They don't know where Harry is, do they?'

'No, but they might have. We can't let any chance slip by. We must follow every lead, even if it does seem unlikely.' Her mouth was set in a determined line now. What she had done was wrong, but nothing would ever stop her from finding Harry. Nothing!

'You will not tell us what we should do.' He looked at her through narrowed eyes. She didn't understand what she had done. Well, he would have to deal very severely with her. It made him go cold when he thought of the danger she had put herself in. 'I have been too lenient with you, Eleanor, but after this act of folly, things will change. Your desire to find your siblings was fraught with danger, but I have helped at every stage. Tracing Harry has become an obsession with you, and I will have no more of it. The newspaper advertisement will be withdrawn immediately.'

She gasped in distress and it went right through him, but he was determined to make her understand that she couldn't do just what came into her head. He continued. 'You must be content with the brothers and sisters we have found. The search ends *now*, and I will not have it mentioned again.'

'Oh, no, Father,' she pleaded. 'I am sorry to have distressed you, but please don't do this.'

'I've said all I am going to on the subject. You obviously cannot be trusted to conduct yourself properly, so we shall return home immediately. Go and pack your things. We will leave within the hour.'

She left the room without a word, closing the door softly behind her.

'There's no need for you to leave, Albert. I'm sure she had no intention of prying into private correspondence,' Joshua said. 'Aren't you being rather harsh?'

'No.' Albert expelled a shaky breath. 'She has no sense of fear or caution, and that is my fault for protecting her too much. But it's a lesson she must learn, and quickly.'

'At least stay for lunch.'

'Thank you, Josh, but we'll leave at once. We were to have dined with Augusta this evening. Please convey my apologies and say that we've had to return home unexpectedly.'

Without calling for a maid to help her, Ellie began stuffing clothes into her cases, hands shaking too badly to bother folding them. Her father's anger had never been directed towards her with such ferocity before. He hadn't given her a chance to explain, and that was unprecedented in her experience. She had always been able to talk freely to him, but not this time. He was absolutely furious. Of course, she had acted without thinking – again. That wasn't unusual though. Her father usually made allowances, accepting her ways with wry humour. He wasn't laughing this time.

She had to sit on the case to close it, crushing the expensive gowns, but she didn't care. The only thing that mattered was that she had made her father so angry that he was giving up the search for Harry. Wiping her hand across her eyes to remove the moisture gathering there, she sat on the edge of the bed, taking deep breaths in an effort to calm herself. She wasn't going to cry, that would only infuriate him more. But she longed to tell him about her talk with Hilda. It had given her a completely different side of the story. The spectre of the workhouse drove those people to desperate actions.

'Eleanor!'

The sound of her father's voice had her leaping off the bed

and dragging her luggage to the door. A footman met her on the landing, taking everything from her.

Holding tightly to the banister in case she tripped, for her legs were none too steady, Ellie made her way down to her father. She was going to have to be careful what she said, because he was still very angry.

When he stepped outside to supervise the loading of the carriage, Ellie gazed at Joshua. When she spoke her voice was husky with distress. 'I apologize for causing this unpleasantness in your house. What I did was wrong, but I did not go through your private papers. I would never do such a thing.' She reached out and touched his arm, silently imploring for understanding. 'I was picking up the papers from the floor when I saw the name Bonner.'

Joshua covered her hand with his own, about to say something when her father returned.

'Come along, Eleanor, or we shall miss the next train. I hope you have had the decency to apologize for your unacceptable conduct?'

'I have, Father.'

'And I have accepted her explanation, Albert. I'm sure Eleanor meant no harm or disrespect.'

Ellie gave him a tremulous smile, grateful for his kindness. Then she hurried out to the waiting carriage. Leaving early in disgrace was not what she had envisioned for this trip, and on the short journey to the station, she began to fret. She had promised to return to Whitechapel with some money. How was she going to do that now?

It was a relief when the dawn arrived the next day, for Ellie had not been able to sleep. She was sure she had heard every tick of the clock on her mantle during the seemingly endless night. She'd had plenty of time to think as she'd stared into the darkness, and she could understand her father's anger. It had been wrong of her to read that letter, and thoughtless to take off without telling anyone where she was going. She was very stupid at times!

She had never been on bad terms with her father, and it was heart-breaking for her. She prayed he was in a better mood this morning, and would allow her to explain, and apologize properly. She would do that before breakfast.

His study door was open, and she tapped on it, waiting for permission to enter. 'Good morning,' she said as soon as he looked up, edging her way into the room and standing just inside the door. She had forgotten to put on her shoes, so she curled her toes into the thick carpet, trying to stop her legs from shaking. 'I apologize for making you angry, Father. I acted without thinking, and I am so very sorry to have caused you distress.'

'I'm glad to hear that you've realized what you have done. I want your promise that you will never do anything like that again.'

'I promise.'

When he merely nodded, she took a deep breath and stepped up to the desk. He still looked very displeased with her. 'I'll work extra hard to make amends. What would you like me to do today?'

'You are confined to the house, so find yourself something useful to do.'

That prospect held no appeal, she would rather clean out the stables. 'But I always have tasks to do around the estate.'

'I will be taking care of everything in the future. This is a large house and you will see that it is run efficiently.'

'But our housekeeper, Mrs Butler, does that already. She would hate me getting under her feet all day. She's excellent at her job.'

'Then she's the right person for you to learn from.'

Ellie could hardly believe her ears. Was her father taking away the job she loved doing? When she spoke, her voice shook. 'Are you saying that I can't help you any more?'

'This episode has made me realize that it is more important for you to learn the responsibilities of a lady than roaming the estate all day.'

The expression on her father's face warned her not to argue, but the disappointment was crushing and she fought for control. This was harsh treatment indeed for her misdemeanour. 'I might as well resume my lessons.'

'Mr Rogers is busy preparing Philip for university. He will not have time to give you separate lessons, Eleanor.'

Her throat clogged with anger now. Even that was being denied her. She had apologized, truly sorry for her conduct, but he was punishing her in the worst possible way. If she stood here much longer she would cry like a baby, and she would *not* allow that to happen. Without saying a word, she turned and ran from the room.

Albert felt as if his heart would shatter as he watched his daughter leave, clearly very upset. He had hurt her so much by denying her the things she loved to do, but he felt it was necessary. She had no fear, no idea what danger she had put herself in. He blamed himself, of course. He should have been firmer with her as she had been growing up, but he had never been able to be angry with her. Until now. Now he had to steel himself to be harsh in order to make her see that she wasn't a child any more. Growing up brought with it responsibilities, and she needed to see that it could be a dangerous world.

He stood up and walked over to the window expecting to see his daughter sitting by the pond, as she always did when she needed quiet, but she wasn't there. Probably hurt too much to even seek out her favourite place. Running a hand over his eyes he realized just how drained he was feeling. He couldn't punish her for long – he wasn't that strong, or that cruel.

Oh, Mary, I miss your gentle presence. You would have known how to deal with this. I'm out of my depth, allowing my emotions to rule me, and I've blown this incident out of all proportion. You would have merely scolded her, telling her not to do it again. Then you would have wanted to know every detail, and ended up laughing with her. I haven't even asked her what happened in Whitechapel. I was very frightened when I discovered that she had left the house on her own. The thought of her wandering round London . . .

He shook his head as if trying to dislodge the memory. I am being unreasonable by hurting her like this, but I don't know how else to handle it. She *must* learn caution.

He strode out of the house, heading for the stables. He'd go and torment Henry. His brother-in-law knew how to tolerate his volcanic moods. He faltered for a moment. He had never thought before that he might be lonely. But with Mary dead this past year, and Eleanor growing more independent, he had to admit that he was.

* * *

At the sound of her father leaving the house, Ellie leapt into action. She was devastated that she had made him so angry with her. This had never happened before, and her actions had been thoughtless many times in the past. She deserved his censure, but a severe telling off would have been sufficient, for she was indeed ashamed of herself. She had caused a great deal of worry, and now she would have to suffer the consequences. But she would not bother their housekeeper. Mrs Butler ran their household with quiet efficiency, and even her mother had never interfered with her routine.

Because of the restrictions now placed upon her, she had a problem. How was she going to get the money to Whitechapel? She had given her word, and it was important to her that her promise was not broken.

Taking a small wooden box from the dressing table drawer, she counted the money. She had four pounds, ten shillings and six pence, money she had saved to buy Christmas gifts, but it would have to be used now. Her father gave her an allowance to spend as she wished, but she doubted very much if he would give her any while she was in disgrace. Four pounds would be a great help to Hilda, and if used carefully, would keep them for quite some time, and give them a better Christmas.

Chewing her lip in concentration she rummaged in a bureau for a small beaded purse. It would be impossible for her to go to London, even if she asked permission to visit Pearl. And, anyway, she couldn't deceive her father like that. But Ted could go. She needed to see him anyway, and tell him what his mother had said. Ellie drew in a sharp breath. After talking to Hilda in that dingy scullery, she began to understand the frightening situation they had been in. It also explained their defensive attitude. Now Hilda had opened up she glimpsed the real woman, but there would never be the same affection in her heart that she held for the mother who had lovingly brought her up. However, she'd accepted that she was Queenie Bonner. And, as such, she must try to do something to ease the abject poverty of their lives. Also, her brothers and sisters must be told the real story of what had happened years ago. If only Harry had known, he might not have run away.

She had been told to remain in the house, but she just couldn't do that, it was asking too much. It would be all right if she stayed on the estate, wouldn't it? And the orchards were part of the estate, weren't they? Yes, of course they were. Her father surely wouldn't object to her visiting Ted.

Having convinced herself that this would be all right, she changed into her riding clothes and hurried to the stables, breathing in the fresh air with relief. She hated staying indoors, always had.

'Will you saddle my horse for me, please.'

The stable lad looked uncomfortable, glancing round anxiously.

The head groom came up to them. 'Where do you wish to go, Miss? Only we have instructions from Mr Warrender that you must be accompanied at all times, and not to pass beyond the estate gates.' He smiled apologetically.

Ellie was mortified, and her hands clenched into tight fists. How could he do this to her? He was treating her like a small child instead of a young woman. Not wishing the servants to witness her mood, she turned and walked back to the house without saying a word, being careful to keep her head up. The realization that her father was *this* angry with her was tearing her apart. She couldn't live like this. She would have to make him listen to her, and she would confront him as soon as he returned. But first, she had to find a way to see Ted.

Returning to her room, she wrote a short note and put it in the purse with the money. Then she made her way up to the schoolroom and waited outside the door for Philip.

It was nearly an hour before he came out. Grabbing his arm she pulled him along the passage to an empty room.

'What are you doing, Ellie?' he protested.

'Shush.' Pushing him in, she closed the door behind them. 'I need you to do something for me, and I don't want anyone to know.'

'What are you up to? You're already in enough trouble, and now you're going to get me into trouble as well, I just know it.' He gave a resigned sigh. 'You'd better tell me quickly, I've only got fifteen minutes.'

Ellie explained about her talk with Hilda, and handed him the purse. 'Give this to Ted on your way home. There's a note inside, but will you ask him to come and see me as soon as possible. Tell him it's urgent.'

Philip put the little purse in his pocket. 'That was a very foolish thing you did, Ellie, and I'm not surprised your father is furious. But I'll see Ted today and give him your message.

'Thanks, Philip.'

Twenty-Seven

'Do stop pacing around, James.' Augusta glanced at her restless son. 'Whatever is the matter with you?'

'Do you think Eleanor's all right?' He sat opposite his mother. 'Joshua never said why they'd had to return home so suddenly.'

'I'm sure he would have told us if she had been unwell. I expect it was a crisis at the estate.'

'Then why didn't Mr Warrender leave Eleanor here? She could have stayed with us for a few days.'

Augusta folded the newspaper she had been attempting to read, placing it on the small table beside her. 'What are your intentions towards Eleanor, James?'

'Pardon?'

'You know what I'm talking about. It's obvious that you like her, but it seems that your feelings may go deeper.'

He stretched his long legs out in front of him, his expression thoughtful. 'She's unconventional, opinionated, speaks her mind without caring what others may think of her, but I do admit to finding her appealing. Under that boisterous, outgoing nature, there is a sharp intellect. But she's hardly good wife material. A man would never know what she was going to do, or say, next.'

Augusta laughed. 'That's true, but she is also a loving and caring girl, and life with her would never be dull.'

'I'm not sure if I could stand the strain.' James pursed his lips. 'Do I take it that you would approve of her as a daughter-in-law, regardless of her background, and the strange family she is gathering around her?'

'She's been brought up as the daughter of Albert Warrender, a part of a highly respected and influential family. The circumstances of her birth are unimportant.'

'That's true, and I'm sure she will have many suitors in the coming months, if they can get past her father.' He laughed. 'I'm not sure how I feel about her, but I am concerned for her welfare as a friend.'

'Of course.' Augusta picked up her newspaper again. 'Why don't you go to Kent tomorrow and see if she's all right?'

James nodded. 'I'll go first thing in the morning.'

It was evening before Ted arrived to see Ellie. She saw him from the window and rushed out to meet him, wanting to talk to her brother in private. She slipped a hand through his arm. 'Let's walk in the garden.'

'It's nearly dark, and there's a cold wind blowing, so wouldn't you prefer to go indoors?'

'Just ten minutes, Ted, then we'll go in.'

He frowned. 'Philip gave me your message and the purse. I haven't opened it, but there seems to be money inside, so what is this all about?'

Ellie then explained about her visit to Whitechapel, and how it had angered her father.

Ted stopped by the pond, shaking his head. 'I'm not surprised. That wasn't a very sensible thing to do, was it?'

'I can see that now, but I just didn't think.' She pulled a face. 'That's a very bad trait of mine, but I want to find Harry so much. However, it wasn't a wasted visit, because I had a long talk with Hilda.'

Ellie then related her conversation in detail. When she'd finished, Ted cursed under his breath. 'Why the hell didn't she tell us at the time? It would have saved a lot of trouble, and Harry might not have walked out.'

'I think she was afraid and didn't want to show that she cared. She told me it would have been a sign of weakness.'

'We had no idea things were so bad.' Ted's expression was sad. 'I know she was terrified of the workhouse – everyone was.'

They began to walk back to the house. 'I promised to take her some money, but I can't do that now. I know it's asking a lot of you, but would you take it for me?'

'I've got a day off tomorrow, so I'll go then.'

'Thank you; there's one more request from your mother. She would like to see you, Jack, Pearl and Maggie. I think she's lonely, Ted.'

'I'll see everyone while I'm in London, and it will be up to them if they want to see Mum and Dad again, but I certainly will.' He slanted his sister a doubtful glance. 'Does your father know what you're doing?'

Ellie shook her head. 'No, he won't even listen to me, and I would appreciate it if you didn't say anything at the moment. This news will have to come from me, and I'm not looking forward to telling him.'

'But you will?'

'Of course, Ted. I've never kept secrets from him, and I don't intend to start now. But I must choose my time with great care.'

It was just the kind of crisp morning Ellie loved. There was frost on the grass, but the sun was rising in a clear sky and would soon melt the sparkling droplets of ice. She gazed out of the bedroom window, drinking in the beauty. Her father would release her from the restrictions today, she was sure. He had never been angry with her for long.

Buoyant with fresh hope, she made for the dining room. Her father was already there, drinking tea and sorting through his correspondence.

He looked up when she entered. 'Good morning, Eleanor, did you sleep well?'

'Yes, thank you, Father.' She smiled as she filled her plate with a little from every dish. She was starving. He *was* in a much better mood, she could tell from the tone of his voice. 'Isn't it a beautiful morning?'

'Is it? I really haven't noticed.'

She nodded, mouth full of creamy scrambled eggs. After swallowing, she decided that this was the right time to talk to him, but she proceeded with care. 'What are you going to do today?'

'I'll be busy checking that we have everything for the animals should we get snowed in at any time.' He drained his cup and stood up.

Ellie put down her knife and fork. 'May I help you? I know what needs doing at this time of the year.'

'I can manage, Eleanor.'

As he left the room, she jumped to her feet and rushed after him, leaving her shoes behind. 'But what am I to do? I am

207

not someone content to sit in idleness. I never have been, Father, you know that. I have no skill with a needle, cannot draw, and have no musical talent. Let me do something. I'll clean the stables, or scrub out the pigsty . . . anything! Please . . . please . . .'

Stopping, he spun round. 'That's enough. Come to my study.'

She padded along after him, feeling utterly wretched. He didn't love her any more, and she couldn't live like this. 'Perhaps Mrs Montague would take me in, or I could go and live with Ted?'

'What are you talking about?'

It was only when she saw her father's puzzled expression that she realized she had spoken her thoughts out loud. 'It seems I am a great disappointment to you, and you no longer care for me. I was wondering who would be prepared to give me a home.'

'Now you're being silly—'

'No, I'm not.' She was, of course. He would never want her to leave, but she was swamped with remorse. 'You are ashamed of me, and I cannot bear that. You were hoping I would grow into a lady, but that hasn't happened. I am impetuous, do not abide by the rules, speak my mind and do things without considering the consequences. That's how I am.' She tapped her chest. 'Deep down inside I am Queenie Bonner, and money, privilege, and some of the best schools have not been able to erase that from me . . .'

'Tell me what happened at Whitechapel.'

'Pardon.' She was so lost in misery that the sudden change of subject threw her for a moment.

They were standing facing each other, too tense to sit down.

'Tell me what happened.'

Relieved that he was going to listen to her at last, the story tumbled out. When she'd finished she dragged in a deep breath. 'I told Ted, and he said they never knew they were in danger of ending up in the workhouse. He's going to tell Pearl, Jack, and Maggie, then go and see his parents.'

'And you believed Hilda Bonner?'

'Yes, I did. I had the impression that she's very lonely now all her children have left home.' She set herself firmly on her two feet, bracing for the onslaught of fury she guessed would come. 'And I've given Ted some money to take to her.'

'How much did you send?'

'Four pounds. It was all I had. No one should have to live like that.'

'I agree. Does Fred Bonner have a job?'

Ellie shook her head.

'Leave it with me, I'll see what I can do.'

Her mouth opened in surprise, then snapped shut again as her father continued speaking. 'What you did, Eleanor, was not only foolhardy, it was highly dangerous.'

'I wasn't in any danger, the cab driver stayed with me all the time.' She could have bitten her tongue off when she saw his eyes blaze. Why couldn't she learn to keep quiet?

'At the first sign of trouble he'd have driven off as fast as he could. He might have called a constable, but it would have been too late then.' Albert held his daughter's gaze. 'Eleanor, it is well known that we are a wealthy family. Someone could have kept you against your will and demanded money for your return.'

'Oh, Father, surely not? You're no longer in parliament.' Ellie was horrified. This kind of thing had never entered her head.

'No, but it's no secret that I have been asked to return. Some don't like my liberal views. But, putting that aside, there are criminals around who, seeing you on your own, could have snatched you, making you tell them your name. In that case I might never have seen you again.'

The colour drained from Ellie's face as the possible consequences of her action dawned on her. 'I have been very foolish, haven't I?'

'I'm relieved you have seen that at last. It is all right to be unaccompanied around the estate, but *never* in London, Eleanor. When I found you were missing I was very frightened for you.'

'I won't ever do that again, I promise. And I won't read anything belonging to someone else, even if it has been thrown away.' How stupid, Ellie silently berated herself. How could she have caused her father such distress? 'I am so sorry,' she whispered.

'Then you are forgiven,' he said gently. 'Don't look so surprised, Eleanor. I do understand. I'm not that much of a monster, am I?'

She shook her head, finding it hard to stand still. He had forgiven her all her misdemeanours, and it sounded as if he was thinking of returning to politics. She was pleased about that.

'Good, and there will be no more foolish talk about leaving home?'

Her head went from side to side again. 'I couldn't have done that anyway; that was my unhappiness talking. How could I leave you and Nanny?'

'I am pleased to hear that. Now, go and change into your riding clothes. We have a lot to do today.'

Ellie was almost bursting with joy, making her cry out with delight. She spun round and ran for the door. Hearing her father's deep chuckle, she hurtled back, threw her arms around his waist and hugged with all her might, then she was off again.'

'Eleanor! Shoes.'

'Whoops.' She looked down at her bare feet, laughing with delight. Everything was back to normal.

Albert was feeling exactly the same. He'd painted an exaggerated picture of what might have happened to her, but he'd needed to frighten her a little in order to make her understand. She was far too trusting, and while that was an appealing trait, she had to learn when to be cautious. That tale about political enemies had been pure fabrication, though. He knew he wasn't liked in some circles for his outspoken views, but that was the game of politics. They all indulged in insults, and the next minute they were sharing a drink. But the point he had been making had got through to her, and that was a relief. He hated being stern with her, but it was something he'd had to do quite often. She had a lovely nature – kind and giving – but it was as if she only saw the best in everyone.

He strode out of the house, his booted heels ringing on the stone path, as he headed for the stables.

The horses were ready when he heard one of the grooms smother a laugh. He looked up to see his daughter running full pelt towards them, a huge smile on her face. A lady she certainly wasn't, but he loved her just the way she was.

She skidded to a halt beside him, not even out of breath. 'Where are we going first?'

He swung himself into the saddle, gazing down at her. 'I think you mentioned a pigsty?'

With a gurgle of amusement, she mounted and they rode out – father and daughter in complete harmony again.

Twenty-Eight

As Ted walked along the street he had grown up in, he saw it with fresh eyes. It was over ten years since he'd been here and the houses looked smaller and more squalid than he remembered. There was an unpleasant smell pervading the dust-laden air. As kids they had accepted this as normal, until they'd been old enough to get out and see how other people lived. Then, each one of them, without exception, had walked away, never returning. A wave of pity swept through him for his mum and dad. They were still trapped in this awful place, and the only one of their kids to show any concern was the girl they had sold.

There was a steady cold drizzle falling, the kind that soaks you, so no one was standing outside, but the front door was open. He knocked and waited. After such a long time he couldn't just walk in.

He hardly recognized the woman when she appeared. Her hair was grey, and she was much too thin, but her carriage was still upright.

'Hello, Mum.'

She stood absolutely still, searching his face as if she couldn't believe her eyes. 'Ted?'

He nodded, his breath catching in his throat when she touched his arm. He hadn't been sure what kind of a reception he would receive. 'Queenie told me what happened all those years ago. You shouldn't have kept it from us.'

'You was only kids and wouldn't have understood. Come in, you're getting drowned out there.'

He followed her into the scullery, removed his coat and sat down at the scrubbed wooden table, marvelling at how empty the house was. When they'd all been here, there hadn't been room for them to sit down at the same time. Meals had been taken in turns.

'We would have understood, Mum.'

She shook her head. 'If I'd told you, you'd have all gone missing school and looking for some way to make money, and I couldn't have that. I was determined that my kids would have a decent education, or as good as you could get from round here. It was the only way you were going to get out of this bloody place.'

Now he understood. She had sacrificed her youngest in order to give the rest of them a chance. What a heart-rending choice that must have been for her to make. Deep sorrow swept through him as he watched his mother lifting the kettle from the top of the old black leaded fire, her hands shaking as she poured water into the teapot.

'Where's Dad?'

'He's heard there might be a job going at Marchants the furniture makers. He's a good carpenter, but will turn his hand to anything.'

'I hope he's lucky.'

'So do I.' She poured them both a cup of tea. 'Would you like a bit of cake?'

His mind went back to this small scullery filled with hungry kids, all eager for a piece of their mum's cake. It wasn't often they'd enough money for her to buy the ingredients for such a treat. 'I'd love some, thanks.'

After giving him the cake, she sat down and warmed her hands around the cup. 'I heard about your wife, Ted. I hoped you would have come home then for a while. I'd have looked after you while you got over it. But you look good, and obviously didn't need my help.'

Ted grimaced. 'Oh, I needed help all right. But how did you find out?'

'You know what it's like round here. Everyone knows everyone else's business, and I tried to keep track of you. When you moved, I lost you, but someone said they'd seen you in Hammersmith, so I guessed you must be living there.' She turned the cup round and round, then gazed at him, eyes worried. 'Queenie told me you was working on the estate, but that was all. Will you tell me how you come to be there?'

He took a deep breath. 'If it wasn't for Mr Warrender and his brother-in-law, I'd be dead now.'

'Who's Mr Warrender?'

'Queenie's dad.' The entire story poured out then, and, much to his relief, he found he could talk about it without wanting to rush for a drink.

Hilda was very quiet when he finished, and she wiped a tear away before it spilled down her face. 'He's a good man, then?'

'Yes, he is, and he loves Queenie very much, and she him.' Ted gave a deep chuckle. 'They renamed her Eleanor, or Ellie to her friends, but she's still our Queenie. Her character and temperament haven't changed.'

'I'm glad about that, but she's grown into a fine young girl. I found that out when we sat down and talked.'

Ted took the purse from his pocket and placed it in front of his mother. 'She's sent you this.'

Hilda tipped out the money. 'Oh, my goodness, that will last us ages if I'm careful. She said she'd come back with this, but I really didn't believe her.'

'She had every intention of doing so, but when Mr Warrender found out she'd come here unaccompanied, he was furious and took her back home. He's got a tight rein on her at the moment, so she asked me to bring it.'

'She always did have a big heart. That was obvious even when she was little.' Hilda pushed the lovely beaded purse back to Ted. 'Tell her I'm right grateful, and give her that back. It's too good for me to keep.'

Slipping the empty purse back in his pocket, he turned slightly in his seat until he was facing his mother. 'I'm going to see Jack, Pearl and Maggie when I leave here. Once they find out why you sold Queenie, I'm sure they'll understand at last, and want to come and see you both. Will that be all right?'

His mother nodded eagerly. 'We'd love that. Thanks, Ted. We was desperate, and only did what we thought was best at the time.'

At that moment his father walked in, stopping suddenly when he saw his eldest son sitting at the table.

'Ted!'

'Hello, Dad.' The smile of pleasure he received from his dad took him by surprise.

He sat beside his son and gripped his arm. 'It's good to see you, son.'

'Did you get the job?' his mother asked, obviously anxious to know.

'I did, but I'll tell you about it later, for now I want to know why Ted's here after all this time, and how he's getting on.'

Ted related the whole story again. When he'd finished talking, Fred was nodding, his expression serious.

'I'm right glad Queenie went to good people. I expect Mum's told you the mess we was in?'

'Yes, and you should have told us. I know we were only kids, but we would have understood.'

'But you wouldn't have agreed, would you?'

Ted shook his head. 'No, never.'

'It was all my fault really, son. I'd lost my job and was drinking too much. Your mum was frantic, and when this bloke said he knew someone who would pay good money for a young kid, I agreed. It near broke your mum's heart but, like me, she was terrified. Another week and we'd have been in the workhouse, and then we'd have lost all of you. When you all left we knew we should have told you at the time, but –' he grimaced in disgust – 'we had our pride, and it was easier to pretend that we didn't want her.'

'I can understand that now.' Ted studied his dad's careworn face. 'Will you tell me why you wrote that letter saying you knew where Harry was?'

'I was angry when the high and mighty girl came round here and said she was Queenie, looking down her nose at us like we was dirt. She obviously had plenty of money, so I thought she could spare us some.' He held up his hand when Hilda would have spoken. 'I'm ashamed of myself. If I ever see her, and that fine gent who's looked after her, then I'll say I'm sorry for causing such trouble. Queenie was that disappointed. I could see it in her eyes, and I walked away, bloody furious with myself.'

'I'll make sure you do apologize, Fred. Now tell us about the job.' Hilda poured him a cup of tea, then sat back and waited.

'I'm only going to be sweeping up, and the pay is bloody awful, but it's a job, and once they see how handy I am with a lathe, it might lead on to better things.'

'Well, it's something.' Hilda looked at the money on the

table. 'Queenie sent this to help us for a while, but now you've got a job, I ought to send it back to her.'

'Don't do that, Mum. You'll be insulting her, and she wants you to have it. Dad won't be paid for a week, so keep it.'

Fred reached out and pushed the money towards Ted. 'Your mum's right. That little girl's been right generous considering what we did to her, and we don't want her to think we're scrounging. Not now we know how nice she's turned out to be. Tell her I've got a job now, and we'll manage. And tell her that I'm bloody sorry about the way I've treated her. I should have been glad she's done so well for herself, and I am, but I didn't dare show it. We gets into the habit of hiding our feelings with anger.'

Ted looked at his father in disbelief. This didn't sound like the man he remembered. 'I'll tell her, but I can't believe you're turning down money?'

'I know just what you're thinking, son, and I admit that I've been a bastard most of my life, but it was always too much drink. I'm not saying I ain't gonna snap and snarl some-times. I'm trying to change, but it ain't easy.'

'I know just what you mean,' Ted said. 'The first time I met Mr Warrender, I tried to hit him.'

'He's the one adopted Queenie,' Hilda told her husband, as Ted hadn't mentioned any names when he'd been talking to his dad.

'Ah, then in that case, Ted, you picked the wrong one. From what I saw of him, he can take care of himself. Tough looking bloke, even if he is posh.'

'I know, but he does have a gentler side. That's obvious when you see him with Queenie, or Eleanor as he calls her. He thinks the world of her.'

'That's good to know.' Fred squeezed his wife's hand. 'Looks like we did right by her after all. Now Ted's come to see us, I'm starting a new job tomorrow, so this'll be a new beginning for us.'

'Yes, perhaps the tide's turning for us at last.'

'It's doing that for all of us.' Ted stood up. 'I'm going to see the others now, and once they know what the trouble really was all those years ago, they'll understand, I'm sure, and want to come and see you. We shouldn't have let this misunderstanding go on for so long. We are a family, and should have stuck together.'

He strode up the street, a smile on his face. The money was still on the table, so they would have to keep it now. He marvelled at the way things were turning out. When their little sister had gone, the family fell apart, but now that same little girl was healing the rift.

When Ellie and her father arrived back at the house for lunch, James was coming out of Nanny's room.

'What are you doing here?' Ellie asked, delighted at this unexpected visit.

'Is your mother with you?' Albert asked, before James had had a chance to answer Ellie's question.

'No, sir. I was concerned when you left London so suddenly, and I've come to see if Ellie's all right.' James studied her beaming face. 'But I can see she's in the best of health.'

'Give us a moment to change and then you must join us for lunch.' Albert headed for the stairs, stopped, and looked back. 'Are you staying overnight, James?'

'No, sir, I'll be returning to London this evening.'

'You must bring your mother back for a visit. I'll give you an invitation before you leave.'

'Thank you, we'd like that.' James watched Ellie's father stride up the stairs, taking them two at a time, then he whispered, 'What have you been up to, Ellie? Nanny said you were in disgrace, but wasn't more forthcoming than that.'

'I was, but Father has forgiven me now.'

James sighed deeply. 'I'm almost afraid to ask, but will you tell me what you did?'

She explained as quickly as she could, anxious to change out of her riding clothes.

'Oh, Ellie!' James exploded. 'Why on earth didn't you come to me? I would have accompanied you. No wonder your father was furious.'

'I just didn't think.'

'You never do. Your father and Mr Hargreaves must have been frantic with worry. I know I would have been.'

Ellie pursed her lips. 'Would you?'

'Of course, I'm just like everyone else who knows you. We care about you.' James reached out and placed his hands on her shoulders. 'I want you to promise that you'll come to me if you have another crazy scheme like that one.'

'I do want to go to Whitechapel again – with my father's permission, of course,' she added quickly. 'But you wouldn't want to come there with me.'

James looked offended. 'What kind of a weakling do you think I am? You make sure you ask me, then you'll see that I'm quite prepared to protect you wherever you go.'

'All right, I will ask you.' She gave him an impish smile, then ran up the stairs, calling out, 'I don't think you're a weakling, just old fashioned in your outlook. Whitechapel will shock you.'

She ran full pelt into Philip, making them grab hold of each other to remain upright.

'Ellie!'

'Sorry, Philip, I'm in a hurry to change for lunch.'

Disentangling himself from her, he groaned, 'Do you ever do anything at a normal pace?'

'This is my normal pace.'

'Of course it is.' He looked down the stairs. 'Did I hear James's voice?'

'Yes, he's joining us for lunch. Are you coming as well?'

'I might as well. Mr Rogers has given me an hour and a half today.'

'Good, I hardly see you these days. Are you really going to university?'

Philip nodded. 'Next year.'

'But you've always hated living away from home.'

'I won't mind so much now.' He stood up straight. 'I've grown up at last, with Mr Rogers' help. He's explained what it will be like, and he's even going to take me to Oxford one day. That's where he went, and it sounds like it might be fun.'

'Eleanor, haven't you changed yet?' Her father came out of his room.

'Sorry, Father, it won't take me long. Philip's going to join us as well.' Then she was off again.

James listened to Ellie's laughing voice and groaned inwardly. What the blazes was he doing? He hadn't missed the gleam of speculation in her expressive eyes when he'd admitted he cared for her. It was true, of course, he had become much too fond of her. That boisterous, outgoing nature attracted and worried him in equal measure. And he had no intention of allowing himself to be drawn into her spell any more than he already was. His life had always been controlled and orderly. The last thing he wanted was to have it turned upside down by Ellie, and she would, she just couldn't help it. His plan had always been to marry well for land, and he wasn't about to change his mind, even though she was the most appealing girl he had ever met.

'Don't look so worried, James.' Mr Warrender's voice brought him out of his musing.

'Not worried, sir, just deep in thought.'

'Hmm, my daughter does that to most people.'

James took a deep breath. 'How do you control her, sir?'

'With great difficulty, but she's easy to forgive because she would never knowingly hurt anyone. She often acts without thinking, and that can get her into trouble, but she has two qualities I noticed in her the moment I saw her.'

'And what are those, sir?'

'Courage, James, and an indomitable spirit.'

What a lovely day it had been so far, Ellie thought. She had been so pleased to see James. He hadn't been able to stay for dinner as he'd had another engagement, but her father had given him an invitation to come and stay, so that was something to look forward to. And now she was waiting anxiously for Ted to return from his visit to Whitechapel. She hoped so much that the family would be reconciled.

Ellie paid her usual visit to Nanny just before dinner.

'Ah, there you are.' Nanny patted the chair next to her. 'Come and tell me about your day.'

'Father has forgiven me.' She sat down.

'I know, he told me.' She gave her former charge a speculative look. 'James spent time with me while he was waiting for you.'

'That was kind of him.' Ellie slipped out of her shoes. 'Do you like him, Nanny?'

'He's a little on the serious side, but he has a good nature. You get on well with him?'

'Oh, yes, he's good company.' Then Ellie changed the subject and began telling her all the things she had done that day. It was a ritual, but she knew Nanny still took a great interest in what she was up to.

They had been talking for about twenty minutes when her father looked in. 'Eleanor, Ted's arrived to see you.'

She was on her feet immediately, eager to speak to her brother. Scrambling back into her shoes she ran after her father.

Her brother was in the library with her father when she arrived. 'How did you get on?' she asked. 'Were they pleased to see you?'

Ted nodded, and when they were all settled he told her about his visit, handing her back the purse. 'Mum wouldn't keep that, but I managed to leave the money.'

'I didn't want the purse back, but thank you, Ted.'

Albert had been listening quietly, but now said, 'You say your father has managed to find work?'

'Yes, sir. It's not much more than sweeping up the factory floor, but he's desperate enough to take anything. He's hoping it will lead on to a better job once he's in.'

'Let's hope so.' The dinner gong sounded, and Albert said, 'You'll stay and eat with us, Ted?'

'Thank you, sir, I'd like that.'

Once they were all seated, Ellie turned to her brother. 'Do you think the others will visit now they know what really happened?'

'They've all said they will go as soon as they can.'

'Oh, that's wonderful!'

'Yes, it is, Ellie, and all because you took the trouble to listen to Mum we are becoming a family again.'

A cloud hovered over Ellie's happiness for a moment as she thought of the brother they hadn't been able to trace, but she pushed it aside. Good had come out of this day, and she wasn't going to allow gloomy thoughts to intrude. This was a time to be hopeful.

Twenty-Nine

Her father was already mounted and ready to ride when Ellie reached the stables the next morning.

'I want you to go and see Jim on Lower Farm, Eleanor. I believe repairs are needed to the roof of one of the farm cottages. Make arrangements for the work to be carried out, and while you're there check to see if anything else needs doing.'

'Yes, Father. What are you going to do?'

'I'm off to the orchards first, then on to see the owner of some land. There is a chance we might be able to purchase the section either side of the orchards.' His mouth turned up in amusement at his daughter's expression of amazement.

Ellie's eyes opened wide at this news. 'But that would join our estate and Uncle Henry's together. It will be enormous.'

'That's right. I think Henry had a sound idea when he suggested that you and Philip should marry. You could manage it together then.'

'Oh, Father.' She laughed. 'We would never stop arguing.'

'Maybe not, but he's growing into a fine young man.'

'I know, and I love him dearly, but as a cousin, not a prospective husband.' She tipped her head to one side. 'I do believe you are determined to marry me off.'

The corners of his mouth twitched. 'Not for a couple of years yet.'

'I'm very pleased to hear that,' she huffed. Marriage wasn't a high priority in her life at the moment.

Her father began to urge his horse forward. 'When you've finished, come to Henry's and we'll lunch there.'

'All right.' They cantered out of the yard together and then went their separate ways.

It took Ellie two hours to see to her allotted task, and by that time she was ravenous. She was just about to leave the estate when a man stepped in front of her, blocking her way.

'What are you doing jumping into my path like that?' Ellie was angry. 'I nearly ran you down.'

He reached out and caught the reins to stop her from going backwards or forwards.

'Let go!' she ordered, her heart pounding, but determined not to show fear. Since her father's warning about kidnapping she was more aware of danger lurking for the unwary. She didn't like the look of this man. He was stocky with brown hair, but it was his pale grey eyes that frightened her. They were so cold and calculating. This was not a man to be trusted.

'My, my, we are the high and mighty lady, aren't we? But just remember that you come from the dirt, just like the rest of us, Queenie.'

Ellie's horse was stamping in agitation, and she was trying hard not to be unseated. There was a certain amount of safety if she were mounted. The use of her other name from this stranger had been a shock. 'Who are you?'

'I'm your brother,' he sneered. 'Don't you recognize me? I knew you as soon as I saw you. The blonde hair and clear blue eyes haven't changed over the years.'

Her brother? But that couldn't be. The only one missing was Harry, and this nasty individual couldn't be him. It just couldn't! Her eyes narrowed in concentration as she studied him. 'You're lying.'

He shook his head in mock dismay. 'I'm hurt you don't remember your brother Tommy.'

She snorted in disgust. 'Now I know you're lying. Tommy's in gaol.'

'I pretended to be ill and escaped when they took me to see the doctor.' He snarled when the horse tried to kick him. 'Keep this damned animal under control, or I'll belt it.'

'She'll keep still if you stop pulling on the bit like that. You're hurting her.'

When he slackened his grip and the horse stilled Ellie breathed out a silent breath of relief, her mind was working frantically. She had to keep him talking in the hope that someone would come along. 'How did you know where to find me?'

'That was easy. The bloke who came to see me is well

known an' one of the guards recognized him. It didn't take much to make the man talk.'

'Well, you're taking a risk coming here.'

'Don't you think I know that? I pinched a change of clothes from someone's washing an' scraped enough together for my train fare. I've had a bloody long walk to get here from the station.'

Ellie fought to remain calm. 'Now you're here, what do you want?'

'Money, of course.' He looked at her as if she ought to know that. 'I tried to get on a boat first, but the crafty captain wanted too much money, knowing I was in trouble. You're the only one I know who's rich, so I came here looking for you. I want enough to get me a long way away from here, an' you're gonna give it to me.'

This was a chance to move back on to the estate and summon help. 'I haven't got any money on me. I'll have to go back to the house to get it. How much do you want?'

'Now, now, Queenie, don't take me for a fool.' He tugged at her foot. 'Get down. I'll bet you're wearing jewels.'

'No, I'm not.' She tried to kick him away, but he was stronger than he looked. With one more tug from him, she was falling to the ground. She landed with a sickening thud, the breath was knocked out of her on impact.

Finding herself free, the horse raced through the gates into the open countryside, and Ellie watched her, praying that she would head for her father or Ted, or anyone who would come to her rescue. There was no doubt in her mind that Tommy was a dangerous man and wouldn't hesitate to hurt anyone to get what he wanted. He was on the run and desperate.

'Stand up.' Tommy dragged her to her feet and began searching her for anything of value.

She struggled. How could this be one of her brothers? He was nothing like any of the others. 'I've told you, I haven't any money or jewellery with me.'

'Then we'll have to go back to the house.' Holding her tightly, he made her walk forward. 'There'll be plenty of good pickings there. You'll smile nicely and do nothing to give me away, because if you do you'll be sorry, and so will anyone who tries to interfere.' He slipped a knife out of his pocket to show her. 'I'm real handy with this.'

She didn't doubt it. Ellie wasn't so eager to get back to the house now and put other people in danger so she walked slowly, pretending to be hurt after the fall from her horse.

'What's the matter with you?'

'I've hurt my leg.'

'Well, get a move on. I don't want to be around here for too long, it's bloody dangerous for me.' He gave her a sharp push.

Ellie threw Tommy a furious look, anger now overriding the fear. 'Don't worry. I'll be only too pleased to give you enough money to enable you to leave this country.'

'That's sensible of you.' The crooked smile didn't reach his eyes. 'Where's your old man?'

'Pardon?'

'Where's that bloke you live with?'

'My father, you mean?'

'If that's what you call him, yes. Where is he?'

'He's right behind you, Tommy.'

Ellie spun round with a cry of relief, which quickly turned to alarm. 'He's got a knife, Father!'

Tommy was also taken by surprise, and before he could do anything, he was being held firmly by her father and Ted.

'Are you unharmed, Eleanor?' Her father looked up from his task of binding Tommy's hands with a length of rope while Ted removed the knife from his brother.

She nodded, so relieved to see them and know that Tommy was now powerless to hurt anyone. 'He pulled me from the saddle, but I'm all right.'

'That's lucky for you, Tommy, because one thing I will not tolerate, is someone hurting my daughter.' He turned to Ellie. 'Your horse is by the gate. Get her and ride for the police. This young man's going back to gaol where he belongs. We'll be at the house.'

It took Ellie less than an hour to alert the constable and return home. There was no sign of them at the stables, so she rushed indoors. Her father and Ted were in the library on their own.

'They are on their way,' she gasped, out of breath from running. 'Where is he?'

'He's in the kitchen being given something to eat,' her father told her.

224

'What? He'll run away again.'

'He's being well guarded by the grooms.' Albert made his daughter sit down, handing her a glass of water, and brushing his hand over her flushed forehead. 'It's all over, you were very brave and handled the situation well. Now, tell me the truth, are you hurt?'

'I was only pretending.' She sipped the cool water in the hope that her heart would stop pounding so erratically. 'I fell heavily, but I'm only bruised, I think. What made you come looking for me?'

'I was still at The Orchards talking to Ted when your horse came thundering up to us, clearly agitated.'

'Our first thought was that you'd had an accident,' Ted said, frowning. 'We set out to find you, and I recognized Tommy at once. We dismounted and crept up behind you. I couldn't believe what I was seeing.'

'Ah, the constables have arrived.' Albert headed for the door.

When Ellie made to follow them out of the room, her father shook his head. 'No, Eleanor, I want you to stay here. It would be better if you didn't see Tommy again.'

She agreed without protest, for she was feeling quite shaken and not eager to see this brother again. However, she did watch from the window as the constables brought out Tommy in handcuffs. Tears of sadness welled up in her eyes. She was brushing them away when her father returned alone.

'Ted's gone back now.' Albert noticed how disturbed she was and placed an arm around her shoulder. 'Don't upset yourself, my dear.'

She sniffed. 'He's only young and is going to spend years in gaol. It's such a waste, Father.'

'Yes, it is. But we are all faced with choices in this life. Tommy grew up in the same environment as the other Bonner children but, as far as we know, he's the only one to go bad. Pearl is a good wife and mother; Jack and Maggie have worked hard to make decent lives for themselves and Ted struggled to get a good education. They made their choices, determined to improve their lives by their own efforts. Tommy thought he could get what he wanted by taking it from other people. He made his choice and now he has to live with the consequences of his violent actions.'

225

'I know, but it's still sad.'

'I agree,' Albert said. 'I want you to know that I'm very proud of you, Eleanor. You handled a potentially dangerous situation with great courage. But you've had a nasty experience and it's unsettled you, so I want you to go and rest for a while. I'll ask cook to bring lunch up to you.'

'I'm quite all right, Father,' she protested.

'Just for an hour to please me.'

She agreed, knowing that his concern was because he loved her very much. 'Very well, just to please you.'

When she entered her room the bed seemed to draw her towards it, and it was at that moment she realized just how exhausted she was. And she was shaking badly. Pausing only to kick off her shoes, she fell on the bed and was instantly asleep.

An hour later, Albert quietly opened the door of his daughter's room and saw her sprawled across the bed, fast asleep. Her shoes were on the floor, one at the side of the bed and the other at the foot. She had always hated wearing shoes, and that hadn't changed over the years.

Closing the door he stood outside deep in thought. He had been talking to her about the choices one was faced with in life. He had married Mary because he'd loved her and had stayed with her through many bitter disappointments. Their love for each other had kept them together, even though they couldn't have the children they had both yearned for. Mary had sacrificed her health for that dream and had died far too young and he missed her – missed the feminine companionship – missed having a woman in his life. He had Eleanor, of course, and she was a great joy to him, but he missed his wife. He'd known that Mary's passing would be painful, but he hadn't realized what a great void it would leave in his life. She had been an intelligent woman, and the only irrational thing she had ever done had been to take a small child out of the slums to be brought up as their daughter. He had been angry at first – but only for a short time. Mary had acted out of desperation and he'd forgiven her shortly after setting eyes on the little girl.

He walked down the stairs, annoyed at the direction of his thoughts. He was getting maudlin, and he blamed the fright he'd had on seeing Tommy with Eleanor, his posture threatening. That was one member of the Bonner family he hoped they never saw again.

'Ah, there you are.' Henry caught up with him in the stables. 'Ted's told me what happened. Is Eleanor all right?'

'She's more shaken by the experience that she is willing to admit. I have managed to persuade her to have a rest and she is now fast asleep.'

'That's the best thing for her, and she'll soon bounce back. Nothing's ever kept her down for long.'

Albert nodded. 'It was a nasty moment though. That boy wouldn't have hesitated to use violence to get what he wanted, even against his own sister. He was desperate to get away before the police caught up with him again.'

'Let's hope the authorities take better care of him this time.' Henry's expression was as grim as his brother-in-law's. 'There was bound to be some unpleasant surprises in tracing this family. I did warn you, Albert.'

'I know you did, but I didn't expect to find one who was capable of murder.'

Henry sucked in a deep breath. 'I know he's a bad lot with a vicious streak, as his conviction shows, but do you believe he is capable of taking the life of one of his own family?'

'Yes, I do.' Albert checked the girth on his horse and then mounted. 'I need a diversion. Let's go and see if we can buy that land, shall we?'

Thirty

The rain was coming down in sheets, making even a ride in one of London's parks out of the question. James gazed out at the grey street, and the grey people hurrying along. He did not relish the winter months here. He was obliged to join in with his mother's social rounds and make polite conversation with the colourless daughters of wealthy families. How he longed for the countryside, always beautiful even in the worst winter. His mind drifted to the Warrender estate. Now there was a lovely place.

'James.' His mother glided into the room, for that was the only way he could describe her elegant movements. 'We have been invited to a musical evening at the Stanhopes.'

'When?' The event did not fill him with any enthusiasm.

'This evening. They have particularly asked that you should accompany me. Their two daughters will be present.'

James tipped back his head and groaned. 'Oh, God.'

His mother ignored the rude remark. 'The eldest is quite presentable, and wealthy in her own right.'

'And dull, Mother. I don't care how wealthy she is. Father provided adequately for me.'

Augusta nodded, her annoyance showing for a moment. 'At least he had the decency to do that, but neither your father nor stepbrother have been fair to you. It wouldn't have hurt Giles to give you a part of the estate. It's large enough.'

'He's never liked me, and he didn't want to split up the estate. As disappointed as I was by his refusal, I can understand that.'

'You're too forgiving, James. From the moment you were born, Giles was afraid you would take part of his inheritance from him. He worked on your father continually to make sure that didn't happen. He took every opportunity to show you in a bad light. You are worth two of him, and you are the more knowledgeable about estate management.'

James chuckled. 'Don't you think that you're somewhat prejudiced, Mother?'

'Of course I am. Come and sit down so we can talk in comfort. I'll order tea.'

When they were settled by the fire with a tray of tea and cakes beside them, Augusta studied her son. 'I've noticed that as soon as you realize a girl has no chance of inheriting land you walk away. You do it very politely, without upsetting anyone, but it has worried me. I've always known that losing the estate was a great blow to you, but is owning land that important to you? Would you sacrifice your happiness for a few acres?'

James leant forward resting his hands on his knees and his expression intense. 'When father died and I had to walk away from the estate I loved with a passion, I determined then that one day I would have a place of my own to rival the one in Yorkshire. Father left me with a steady allowance, but not enough for me to purchase anything of note. As far as I could see there was only one way to achieve my desire, and that would be to marry well. But I'm not so sure I could do that now.'

Relief flooded across Augusta's face. 'What has happened to make you change your mind?'

James shrugged. 'I don't know. Perhaps I've matured enough to let go of my resentment.'

'Or perhaps it has been meeting Eleanor?'

He sat back and pulled a face, making his mother laugh. 'She's enough to shake up any man. Have you ever met anyone like her?'

'No, never.' Augusta was pleased to have prompted her son to talk freely. It was rare he shared his inner thoughts with her.

James put his cup back on the table. 'She's so unpredictable, always rushing into things without giving a thought to the danger. And the relationship between father and daughter is so close. I like Mr Warrender and find him easy to talk to. He's a good listener and a man of high principles.' James hesitated for a moment, and then continued. 'I have grave doubts that he will ever be able to accept any man as a husband for Eleanor.'

'He is protective of her, I agree, but I do believe Eleanor's happiness will be his only concern.' Augusta drew in a silent breath before asking the next question. 'Are you considering offering for her hand in marriage?'

James ignored the question and continued talking in the hope that it would clear his thoughts. 'And look at the strange family she's gathering around her. It does not appear to concern her that they come from the slums.'

'Why would it? She has been brought up in luxury, but she is from the Bonner stock. It cannot be easy for her to come to terms with the fact that she belongs to both those lives.' Augusta's eyes clouded. 'Can you imagine what a shock it must have been to discover that?'

James shook his head.

'No, of course you can't, and neither can I. It's beyond our comprehension, but one thing I do recognize – she has more courage than I would have had if faced with the same situation. I believe she loves the family she has found and is not ashamed of her humble beginnings. Also, Albert is showing the same kind of courage, but he's watching very carefully and will skin alive anyone who dares to hurt her. And that is anyone from both her worlds. Not many of our class could bridge such a wide gap in culture, but father and daughter are doing that. They both have my greatest admiration.'

'That's as may be, Mother, but it's a damned strange family. Being friendly is one thing, but would you be happy if our ties with them were closer?' James watched his mother's expression carefully.

'I would be able to hold my head up high.' There was no doubt about the conviction in her voice, and she repeated her question of earlier. 'Are you thinking of taking such a step?'

James ran his hand through his hair, then said dismissively, 'I am merely speculating.'

'That's as well because I have a feeling that there is a move afoot to marry her to Philip. That would be an ideal solution to both families,' she said. Her son sat in silence digesting that piece of news. 'I think we should accept Albert's invitation to stay with him for a while, and you might be able to decide how you really feel about Eleanor, for she does appear to be occupying your thoughts a great deal.'

James grinned. 'Well, she is quite lovely.'

'I agree.' She changed the subject now knowing her son had said all he was going to on the subject. 'Are you coming with me tonight?'

He sighed deeply. 'I might as well.'

It was dark when Ellie woke up. She felt disorientated, and it took her a few moments to gather her thoughts. The memory of what had happened rushed back and she sat up with a gasp. Tommy was not at all like the rest of the family. That had been apparent as soon as she'd looked into his eyes – this brother had a vicious streak. He had frightened her and that was not a feeling she was used to experiencing.

The fire had been banked high while she had been asleep and the leaping flames gave enough light for her to see by. The clock on the mantelpiece told her that it was six o'clock. She had slept all afternoon. That was unheard of, but it showed that she had been more shaken than she'd realized. Without wasting any more time, she washed and changed for dinner.

As she made her way downstairs, she could hear voices coming from the library, so she went straight there. Ellie was delighted to see Uncle Henry and Philip there, as well as Ted and Nanny.

'Ah, there you are, my dear.' Her father studied her face as she entered the room. 'Are you quite rested after your ordeal?'

Ellie said brightly, 'Yes thank you, Father, I am quite recovered, but I do admit that it was rather unpleasant.'

Ted looked unhappy. 'I am so sorry you had to go through that, Ellie. Tommy had no right to threaten you like that.'

Ellie reached out and grasped her brother's hand, hating him to feel responsible for Tommy's action. 'It wasn't your fault. He must have thought it would be easy to get the money he needed out of me.'

Ted took a deep breath. 'It must have been terrifying for you.'

'I was very frightened.' She gave an embarrassed laugh. Her fear seemed foolish now she was surrounded her loved ones. Tommy wouldn't have hurt her surely?

The dinner gong sounded as she went to Nanny's side. The elderly woman was very frail now and had submitted to using the bath chair with much grumbling and reluctance. Ellie knew how she hated to admit defeat, but it was impossible for her to leave her room unless she had help.

'What do you think about all this excitement, Nanny?' Philip asked as he pushed her into the dining room.

'That boy would have been sorry if I'd been there.' She grunted as the chair was manoeuvred into position at the table, and then she cast Ellie a proud look. 'But our girl is no fool. She knew how to handle him. She's never lacked courage.'

'Thank you, Nanny.' After making sure that Nanny was comfortable, Ellie turned to her cousin who was sitting next to her. They had grown up together and had always been close, but now they hardly saw each other. She was busy around the estate, and Philip was studying hard. 'When are you going to university?'

'Next September, I hope. Mr Rogers thinks I might be ready by then.'

Ellie looked at her father. 'What's going to happen to Mr Rogers then, Father? He does appear to be happy here.'

'There are plenty of good schools in the area who would welcome a teacher of his ability.'

Henry nodded. 'And if he doesn't want to continue teaching, then I'm sure we can find him something else to do. He has a fine mind. Your father and I have bought enough land to join our two estates together. They will still be managed independently for the time being, of course.'

'It will be the best thing to do whilst we are both at the helm,' Albert said. 'Can't have two bosses getting in each other's way. But one day, Eleanor, you and Philip will have to sort it out between you.'

Philip laughed. 'We'll have to put a fence through the middle of the land or we'll never stop arguing.'

Nanny joined in the laughter. 'There is a simple solution. Eleanor and Philip could marry—'

Philip was momentarily speechless with horror as he stared at the elderly woman. Then he cleared his throat. 'She's my cousin, Nanny.'

'Not by blood.'

Ellie leant across and whispered in the elderly woman's ear. 'You know we are most unsuited. You shouldn't tease him so. I value him as a friend, but as a husband and lover it would never work.'

Philip heard and choked on a mouthful of wine. 'Ellie!'

She just smiled as the blush spread across her cousin's face. To save him further discomfort she changed the subject. 'That's wonderful news about the land, Father. Have you told Ted?'

'Yes, and we've given him the task of integrating the land into the estates. He's very excited about the challenge this will give him.'

'Oh, that's marvellous.' Ellie swallowed hard as emotion welled up. 'He's a changed man since we brought him here, sick and with his life in ruins. I don't believe he has ever taken another drink.'

'He won't touch the stuff.' Henry studied his glass as if such a thing was unthinkable. Then he nodded. 'He's right, of course. He's afraid if he lets another drop past his lips again he won't be able to stop. Ted has sound common sense and I've become rather fond of him.'

'I did have some concern that he might find it too lonely living out there, but he seems happy enough and—'

'He'll be even happier soon,' Philip said, not giving Albert a chance to finish his sentence. 'I do believe he's planning to marry our maid, Dorothy.'

Ellie grabbed her cousin's sleeve in excitement. 'Do you think so?' He hasn't said anything to me.'

'Well, he wouldn't. He's been keeping quiet until he was sure Dorothy would marry him.' Philip's expression was smug because he obviously knew something Ellie didn't. 'And that's not all. Mr Rogers is going to marry your sister, Maggie.'

'How do you know all this?' Ellie punched her cousin gently. 'If you're making this up then you'll be sorry, Philip.'

He collapsed into peels of laughter. 'You ought to see your face, Ellie. If you don't believe me then ask them yourself. But I assure you it's true. They probably kept it from you because they knew you'd make a fuss.'

'I would not! I never make a fuss.' There was a look of disbelief on everyone's face at this emphatic declaration. Ellie turned to her father. 'Do you know about this?' When her father nodded, she grinned. 'Did you also know, Nanny?'

The elderly woman gave her a knowing look. 'Of course I did. I might be confined to my room most of the time, but I hear all the gossip.'

Her father rested his hand on Ellie's shoulder to keep her

in her seat. 'They didn't want to raise your hopes until everything was agreed upon. But now Philip has spoilt the surprise we might as well tell you. I've only found out myself today. After Tommy had been taken away, Ted asked if it would be all right if they made The Orchards their home. I told him the house was his and I would be delighted to see him happily married. Henry assures me that Dorothy is a fine, hard-working girl.'

'She certainly is, and I'll be sorry to lose her.' Henry lifted his glass in salute. 'But she'll make Ted a fine wife.'

Ellie leapt to her feet trying to hug everyone at the same time. 'But where are Mr Rogers and Maggie going to live. Will they move away from here?'

Albert tried to make his daughter sit down again but, laughing, he gave up. 'I have given them permission to make the gatehouse their home for as long as they want it. I believe the weddings will be in the spring and early summer of next year.'

'Ooh, that doesn't give us much time.'

'Now, Eleanor.' Her father's tone was stern. 'The couples will make their own arrangements. They won't want you interfering.'

Ellie sat down at last, but still fidgeting. 'I won't interfere. They'll let me help, won't they?'

'I'm sure they will, as long as you don't start trying to take over.'

'I won't do anything they don't want me too. What a wonderful end to a frightening day.'

'Indeed it is,' Albert said and chuckled quietly as Ellie leapt to her feet again to give her cousin a big hug.

'Get off!' Philip complained. 'I don't know what all the excitement's about.'

'You're lucky I'm not hitting you for keeping secrets from me.'

'I haven't had a chance.' Philip pushed her away. 'Mr Rogers only told me after lessons today. But of course, I guessed ages ago. I did mention that I thought there was a romance or two going on, didn't I?'

'So you did.' Ellie sat down again. 'But I thought you might be making it all up. You do let your imagination run wild at times.'

Philip looked offended. 'I don't tell lies, Ellie!'

She reached out to give him another hug, which he dodged expertly. 'I know you don't, but so much has been going on lately it was pushed out of my mind.'

'Our family is growing, Eleanor,' her father said gently.

After Nanny was tucked up in bed and Henry and Philip had left, Ellie approached her father. He had said that he would not discuss Harry again, but she just had to try one more time. Clasping her hands tightly together, she said, 'Father, may I ask if there has been any news at all about Harry?'

'None, Eleanor. I would have told you if there had been.'

Emboldened by his reply, she continued. 'I know you withdrew the newspaper advertisement after my thoughtless visit to Whitechapel, but would you reconsider trying again?' She watched him hopefully, her eyes pleading.

His gaze softened as he studied her troubled face. 'I let the piece run for the allotted time, my dear, but it was to no avail. There isn't a sign of Harry.'

'Oh, thank you, Father. That was more than I deserved,' she said with gratitude. 'Could we try again, please?'

'There's no point.' Albert reached out and took hold of her hands, uncurling the tight fists. 'Everything possible has been done. You must accept that he cannot be found.'

'But how can someone just disappear and never be seen again?'

'It happens many times, Eleanor.'

She nodded, eyes downcast so he couldn't see her pain. Only when she had her emotions in control did she look up again. 'You're right, of course, and we have much to be happy about tonight.'

'A great deal.' Albert stood up. 'Now we must get some rest.'

They walked up the stairs together. Ellie knew her father was right and she should forget about Harry. But it was hard. His laughing face was fixed firmly in her mind and would not go away.

Thirty-One

The next morning Albert caught an early train to London. He was being pressed to return to politics but he knew he wouldn't be able to give the attention and dedication the job demanded at the moment. It would need his full commitment and that was something he couldn't do at this time. His first appointment was lunch with Joshua and two of his parliamentary colleagues. They had been waiting for his answer quite long enough. Today he would refuse their request. It was a dilemma, and he had been beset with indecision, but yesterday's encounter with Tommy had shaken him into making up his mind. There was no way he was going to spend long periods away from home. If anything happened to Eleanor he would never forgive himself. And with the estate expanding he could not afford to spend too much time in London. He'd always thought he would return to politics, but his life had changed so much over the last year. *He* had changed as well. He had different priorities now – and one of those was Augusta. He shook his head in disbelief, not being able to believe he could feel like this about someone again.

Gazing out of the train window he was oblivious to the passing scenery. Last night he had talked this over with Nanny, who had told him straight what she thought. She had stopped short of calling him a fool, but she'd made it clear that it was time he thought about what he wanted out of life. Eleanor was no longer a child; she was grown-up and quite capable of looking after herself. That was true, of course, but until he saw her settled, he would not be able to slacken the reins. Even then it would not be easy. And how was she going to find a suitable husband? She had refused to have a season, and had no desire to attend balls or social gatherings where young men would be in abundance. They kept teasing her about marrying Philip, but anyone with eyes could see that it would never work. He drew in a deep silent breath, his brow furrowed. It would take a special kind of man; one who loved her and her other family, for he was certain that the Bonners would always be a part of her life now. And rightly so, but no matter how much Eleanor wished it were different, there would always be a class divide between them.

A vision of Eleanor's pleading eyes filled his mind when she had asked if they could continue to look for Harry. Finding this brother meant so much to her, but he'd had to be firm. It was only hurting her by keeping the hope alive. He was convinced now that Harry Bonner must have died years ago – unknown and unnamed – or some trace of him would have been found.

Albert arrived in London with a sense of surprise. He had hardly noticed the journey. He hailed a cab, and after directing the driver to Joshua's residence, he sat back and began to plan his day. This afternoon he would call on Augusta and see if he could persuade her and James to join them for the Christmas holiday. He had a desire to have the house full this festive season.

By two thirty, Albert was being shown into Augusta's drawing room by the butler.

'Albert, what a lovely surprise.' Augusta greeted him with real pleasure. 'I was not aware you were in London.'

'I had some business to attend to. I hope you don't mind me calling uninvited?'

'You're always welcome. Please do sit down.' Augusta rang the bell. 'I'll order refreshments.'

'Thank you.' Albert studied the room. It was as he remembered; tastefully furnished, uncluttered and restful. He appreciated the quiet atmosphere after the heated discussions at Joshua's. He was relieved now that he had decided against returning to politics. The more his former colleagues urged him to change his mind, the more he'd resisted. He must be getting old, he thought wryly. There was a time when he had relished the cut and thrust of the political scene.

Albert took the cup of tea being offered, and brought his thoughts back to the present. 'Is James not at home?'

Before Augusta could answer, the door opened and James came in, hand outstretched. 'Mr Warrender, it's good to see you.'

'And you, James.' Albert shook his hand. 'I've called to invite you and your mother to spend Christmas with us. That's if you haven't already made arrangements?'

James glanced hopefully at his mother. 'Nothing we can't change. Is that not so, Mother?'

'We have no firm plans, and would be delighted to come,' Augusta agreed without hesitation.

'Splendid. Eleanor will be pleased. But I must warn you that she will probably enlist your help with decorating the house.'

'That will be a pleasure.' Augusta's face showed that she was telling the truth.

'Is Eleanor well?' James asked.

Albert's frown appeared. 'She is now, thank the Lord.'

'What do you mean?' James leant forward. 'Has she been unwell?'

'No, her health is robust as always, but we had a nasty situation yesterday.' Albert put down his cup and began to tell them about Tommy. By the time he had finished, James was on his feet, very agitated. 'Who is with her now? She shouldn't be alone after that fright.'

Albert was surprised by the degree of concern James was showing. 'She's spending the day with Ted. She is quite safe, James. Tommy is back in gaol where he belongs.'

James didn't appear to be convinced. 'May I have your permission to visit her today, sir?'

'I'm sure she would be delighted to see you. Why don't you both come back with me and stay for a few days?'

'I'm afraid I cannot, Albert, but James hasn't any pressing commitments. I can make his apologies to the Hammonds this evening.'

'Thank you, Mother.' James stood up. 'I would like to go at once, Mr Warrender, if you don't mind? There's a train in half an hour, and I can catch that if I hurry.'

Albert nodded. 'Stay for a few days if you wish, and tell Eleanor I'll be back for dinner.'

After giving his mother a quick kiss on the cheek and a slight bow to Albert, James practically ran out of the room.

Albert stared at the closed door with a puzzled expression on his face.

'He is fond of her,' Augusta said gently.

'Really. I was unsure. Do you know his true feelings for my daughter?'

'No, and he doesn't either. James is confused, Albert. He's never met anyone like Eleanor and, I suspect, he thinks she needs protecting – not only from herself, but also from the other family she is gathering around her.'

Albert's tone was sharper than he intended when he spoke. 'The Bonners are decent people, Augusta. Except for Tommy.'

'I trust your judgement, but James is uneasy about this even though I have had Maggie as my personal maid for the past few years.'

'I don't see that it is any of his business – unless his intentions towards my daughter are of a permanent nature.'

'I doubt that very much,' Augusta assured him. 'He has his life planned, and James will not easily be swayed from his course, even though Eleanor has planted seeds of doubt in his mind.'

Albert couldn't help feeling relieved by Augusta's words. Even if James did decide he wanted Eleanor as his wife, it was most unlikely she would accept him. As far as he had seen, his daughter did not take James seriously. He relaxed, turning the conversation to another matter. 'I expect you will be sorry to lose Maggie in the spring?'

'Indeed I shall, but it was bound to happen one day. Stanley Rogers has visited Maggie here several times, and he seems a fine young man.'

They spent the next hour discussing the upcoming weddings.

The light was fading when Ellie returned to the house. She had spent the day with Ted, and Dorothy had joined them when she'd had an hour off from her work. It had given Ellie a chance to see them together, and it had been obvious that Dorothy and Ted adored each other. She was thrilled that her brother was building a new life for himself.

Before leaving this morning she had nipped up to the schoolroom to congratulate Mr Rogers and let him know how happy she was about his proposed marriage to Maggie.

She was about to go upstairs to her room when she heard

239

laughter coming from Nanny's rooms. Tipping her head to one side she listened to the deep masculine voice. It was familiar so she headed for the door. After tapping, she opened it and looked in. 'James, I thought that was you. What a lovely surprise. When did you arrive?'

He stood up. 'I've only been here about an hour. Your father has given me permission to stay for a couple of days.'

'Is your mother with you?'

'No, but we will be coming to stay over the Christmas holiday.'

Ellie smiled brightly. 'This day is full of good news. Have you told James about Ted and Maggie, Nanny?'

'I have.' Nanny patted the seat beside her. 'Sit for a while. There's fresh tea in the pot. I want to hear about your day.'

After pouring tea for them all, Ellie sat down. 'Dorothy's parents are making the arrangements for the wedding. I would have liked it to be from here, but Ted said it was up to Dorothy and her family.'

'Dorothy is their daughter so it's their duty, Eleanor,' Nanny pointed out gently.

Ellie sighed, not being able to push away the disappointment. 'I know it is, but we could have had such a lovely reception in the ballroom. When I suggested it Ted said that it wouldn't be right. Dorothy is a servant and he an employee of my father's.'

'And he is quite right.' James was watching Ellie intently. 'It would be most inappropriate.'

'Ted's my brother, James, and I don't want us to be divided by class.'

'I'm sure you don't, but that is how it is. You have been brought up a Warrender, and I suspect that you find it easy to bridge the social divide, but they can't. They know their place.' As soon as the words were out of his mouth, James knew he had said the wrong thing.

Ellie glared at James and snorted. 'Their place?'

He hastened to try and put his mistake right. 'I know you don't like it, but there will always be a class barrier between you. Ted and the others love you as their little sister, but they will always be conscious of the difference between you. Ted will never be able to forget that you are his boss's daughter and might one day be his employer.'

240

'Oh, James, do you have to be so sensible?' Ellie scowled.

He lifted his hands in apology. 'That's how I am. I can't change that, any more than you can change your upbringing.'

Nanny nodded in agreement. 'What James says is true. Dorothy's family would be uncomfortable if you interfered in their daughter's wedding Their world is very different from yours, and they will have their own ways.'

'You are right as always, Nanny.' Ellie pulled a face. 'I keep forgetting.'

Nanny patted her hand. 'You will be able to attend the wedding, and perhaps Maggie will need your help.'

That thought cheered Ellie enormously, but she would heed their words of caution and wait for Maggie to approach her. Her sister would have ideas of her own so she would try not to interfere, though it would be hard. Now she had found these siblings, all she wanted for them was to be happy.

'Your father told us what happened yesterday,' James said. 'I came straight away to see how you are.'

Ellie looked at him in surprise. 'That's very kind of you, James. But as you can see, I am all right.'

'This time, but it could have been very different.' James pursed his lips in disapproval. 'Setting out to find the Bonners was not a wise thing to do, Eleanor. And gathering them around you is even more dangerous.'

Leaping to her feet, Ellie bristled with anger. 'They are good people. How dare you judge them all by one who has gone bad.' James stood up, but Ellie pushed him down again. 'You have met Ted, Pearl and Jack, and Maggie has been in your household for years.' She glowered at him. 'Are they dangerous?'

'Of course not! I didn't mean it like that. I was only pointing out—'

'Keep your opinions to yourself. And stop calling me Eleanor. Only my father and Nanny do that.' Ellie laid a hand on Nanny's shoulder. 'I apologize for this scene, Nanny, but I will not have unkind things said about any of them.' With a fulminating glance at James, Ellie stormed out of the room.

'You're lucky you didn't get a black eye.' Nanny was trying hard to keep a straight face. 'If you value your life don't ever criticize anyone Eleanor loves. She will defend them fiercely.'

241

James was speechless. He'd known Eleanor was unpredictable, but he had never guessed she could be so volatile. But the thing that had robbed him of all strength was a realization that had hit him with crippling force. He was in love with Eleanor Warrender . . . and there wasn't a damned thing he could do to change that.

'Oh, dear God, what have I done?' he murmured.

James returned home by lunchtime the next day, much to his mother's surprise. Ellie had quickly recovered, and her usual good humour had been in evidence during dinner that evening. But James had been so shaken by his feelings for her that he'd wanted to get away in order to decide what to do. By the time he walked into their drawing room to greet his mother, he had come to a decision.

'James, I didn't expect you back so soon. Is Eleanor all right?'

He sat opposite his mother and stretched out his legs, giving a deep sigh. 'I've upset her.'

A look of patient resignation crossed Augusta's face. 'And how did you manage that?'

'I was simply pointing out what a dangerous thing she'd done in tracing the Bonners. She erupted like a she-cat defending her young and told me to mind my own business.'

'And quite right too. It isn't any of your business, James.'

'Oh, but it is.' The expression on his face was one of determination. 'It's very much my business because I'm going to marry her.'

There was complete silence while Augusta digested this news. Then she said, 'This is very sudden. Have you spoken to Eleanor or her father?'

James shook his head. 'I only came to that decision on the train. I'll seek Mr Warrender's permission while we're there over Christmas. Then I'll propose to Ellie.' His smile was amused. 'I'm not allowed to call her Eleanor any more.'

'I have my doubts she will accept you.'

'Then I'll keep on proposing until she agrees to become my wife.' James chuckled. 'I might receive a battering in the process. This wasn't what I had planned, or even wanted to happen, but I think I fell in love with her the first time I met her, only I've been reluctant to admit it to myself. However,

242

I now know that she is the only one I will ever want, so she will not be able to get rid of me.'

Augusta couldn't hide her pleasure at this turn of events. 'It's going to be a very interesting Christmas.'

Thirty-Two

'Will this be enough, Ellie?' Ted was hardly visible under the boughs of holly he was carrying.

She jumped down from the chair she had been standing on and laughed in delight. 'Where did you find all that?'

Her brother dropped his burden by the fireplace and plucked off prickly leaves clinging to his jacket. 'There's loads of it in the wood and it's covered with berries.'

'Wonderful, Ted. Are you going to decorate your house as well?'

'I've left that job to Dorothy.' Ted hesitated for a moment, and then said, 'Pearl, Dave, little Jimmy and Jack are staying for Christmas. I've also invited Mum and Dad to join us. I thought this would be a chance for us all to get together and, hopefully, put the past behind us.'

Ellie stopped sorting out the holly and glanced up in surprise. 'Are they coming?'

Ted nodded. 'Jack's bringing them.'

'Oh, I'm so pleased. But where are you going to put everyone?'

'Well, Dorothy's parents are coming as well, so I can put them up and Mum and Dad. Your Uncle Henry said Pearl and Dave can use the room over the stables. You know the one I had when I first arrived here?' He grimaced at the thought of that time. 'God, what a mess I was in.'

'You're fine now, Ted.' Ellie spoke gently, knowing her brother recalled that time with shame.

'Thanks to all of you. Now, where was I? Oh, yes, Jack's staying with Stan at the gatehouse. Maggie will be here, of course, but Stan will bring her to The Orchards on Christmas Day.'

Ellie's smile faded as she realized that her other family were all going to be together for the first time in years, and she would not be a part of that gathering. Her place was with her father as his hostess. 'May I come and see everyone on Boxing Day? I'll have gifts to hand out.'

Her father strode into the room. 'You won't need to go to Ted's, Eleanor. On Boxing Day we'll open the ballroom and give a party for the estate workers and their families. Ted and Stanley can bring all their guests here and we'll make it a celebration to mark their engagements to Dorothy and Maggie.'

'What a wonderful idea!' Ellie was ecstatic. 'This is going to be a lovely Christmas.'

'That's very kind of you, sir.' Ted looked quite overcome by the honour. 'In that case we'll need more holly. I noticed a tree just by the gates.'

As her brother left the room, Ellie glanced up at her mother's portrait. Mary had been gone over a year now, but she still missed her, and so did her father.

He came and stood beside her, draping an arm around her shoulders. 'She would have approved of what we've done, Eleanor.'

'Yes, I do believe she would.' Ellie swallowed to ease the tight constriction in her throat. 'I wish she could see how things are working out.'

Albert's sigh was deep. 'I'm sure she is still watching over you. She loved you so very much.'

'She loved us both, and would only want us to be happy.'

'Then we won't disappoint her. When we set out to find the Bonners it was like dropping a pebble into a pond and watching the ripples spread out in a continually widening circle. So many lives have been touched and changed – and all for the best.'

'And in ways we could never have anticipated.' Ellie's eyes lit up with a glint of devilment. 'We would never have met Mrs Montague and James if we hadn't been searching for Maggie. She's a charming and, I suspect, a very wise woman, isn't she, Father?'

'I agree. I believe Joshua is quite taken with her.'

'Oh, Father.' Ellie laughed at the suggestion. 'Uncle Joshua's a confirmed bachelor and likes it that way. I couldn't imagine him sharing his chaotic life with anyone.'

'Perhaps you're right.' Albert changed the subject. 'Our guests will be arriving soon. Are the rooms ready?'

'Everything has been prepared – except for one thing.'

'And what is that?'

'The Christmas tree.' Ellie shook her head in mock dismay. 'How many times have I asked you to find me one?'

Albert gazed into space for a moment. 'Twice?'

'More than that. I've asked every day for the past week.'

He chuckled. 'Don't worry. Ted has located a fine specimen, but we're waiting for James to arrive. It will take the three of us to cut it down and bring it here.'

Ellie beamed. She knew her father could ask the estate workers to carry out this task, but it was something he had insisted on doing for as long as she could remember.

'Is it big?'

'Huge.' Albert studied the height of the drawing room ceiling just as Ted returned with more holly. 'Do you think we'll get that tree in here, Ted?'

Ted also looked up, assessing the space reserved for the tree. 'Just about, but we could always find a smaller specimen if you're doubtful.'

'Don't you dare!' Ellie ordered. 'I want the biggest one you can squeeze in, and we'll also need another one for the ballroom.'

Albert gave a theatrical groan. 'We'll have to take two large carts and sturdy horses if we are to transport everything Eleanor wants.'

The teasing was interrupted by the sound of approaching carriages. For the next hour Ellie had to leave all thoughts of decorating while she settled their guests in the rooms.

James swung the axe at the base of the tree, relishing the physical labour. While his father had been alive, James had taken an active part in running the estate. He had preferred to pitch in with the work, no matter how hard, rather than stand around issuing orders. He knew the estate workers had respected him for that, and many had been genuinely sorry when Giles relegated him to the sidelines. Still, that was in the past. The future was ahead of him, and it would be what he made of it. As long as Ellie was a part of that future he knew he could face anything. He could even dismiss the dream of owning an estate of his own. He was horrified and rather ashamed at his past plans. By marrying for gain and not love would only have led to a life of misery. No amount of land was worth that.

'Nearly there, James,' Ted called as he tightened his grip on the rope he and Albert were holding to stop the tree crashing to the ground. The last thing they wanted to do was to damage this perfect specimen.

After one more swing of the axe, the tree began to topple. James dropped the axe and caught the rope as well. When the tree had been gently lowered to the ground the three men grunted in satisfaction.

Albert wiped his brow. 'All we have to do now is get it back to the house. While we're here we might as well find smaller ones for Ted, Stanley and the ballroom.'

'Better not make the one for the ballroom too small, sir, or Ellie will never let us hear the last of it.'

Albert raised his eyes to the sky. 'Heaven forbid, Ted.'

As James watched them laugh, he felt excitement race through him. Life with Ellie would never be dull. He would seek her father's permission at the earliest opportunity. James doubted he would get his blessing very easily, but he would just have to convince Mr Warrender of his sincerity. He was pleased that Ellie's father had made it clear that anyone marrying his daughter would never own the estate. There would be no misunderstanding about his motives, or any suspicion that he might be marrying for gain and not love.

James was under no illusions about the task facing him. If he got past her father, he suspected that Ellie would be even more difficult. But he was prepared to fight for what he wanted. And that was Ellie!

The following morning, Ellie and Augusta were busy decorating the trees. When James saw Mr Warrender go into his study, he followed. Bracing himself for what he expected to be a difficult meeting, James knocked on the door and then walked in. 'May I speak with you, sir. It's important.'

'Of course.' Albert indicated a chair. 'Please sit down.'

'I'd rather stand, sir.' James stood in front of the desk, his feet planted slightly apart to steady himself.

Albert studied him through narrowed eyes. 'This sounds serious.'

'Yes, sir.' He grimaced slightly. 'And I would like to be on my feet in case I need to make a hasty retreat.'

'Now I am intrigued.' Albert leant back and crossed his arms. 'What have you done to incur my wrath?'

'Nothing – yet, but I suspect I'm about to.'

'Let's hear it then, shall we?'

'I'm asking for your permission to court your daughter, sir. I want to marry her.' James held his breath and waited for the eruption . . . but it didn't happen. Ellie's father had remained seated, his amber eyes unblinking as they held James's. This he found unnerving. Anger and outright refusal he had expected, not this silent scrutiny.

Finally Albert spoke, his voice quiet, but there was no mistaking the steel in his tone. 'Have you spoken to my daughter about this?'

'No, sir, I've come to you first.'

'Very wise. And what if I won't give my permission?'

'Then I shall keep asking until you change your mind.' James silently prayed that this hadn't sounded too presumptuous. 'I love her, sir, and want to spend the rest of my life looking after her.'

'She isn't easy to look after. Do you believe yourself to be equal to the task?'

James was about to answer in the affirmative, but stopped himself just in time. 'I can't answer that. All I can promise is that I will do my utmost to make her happy.'

'And what is your financial position?'

'My father didn't leave me any property, but I have a substantial income. Enough to keep your daughter in comfort for the rest of her life.' James was beginning to wish for this interview to come to an end. He was not sure of Mr Warrender in this quiet mood, and he couldn't tell which way he was going to go next. It was more than nerve wracking.

The questions continued. 'What makes you think my daughter will accept you?'

'I doubt that she will – at first.' When Ellie's father waved him into a chair he sat down this time with relief.

'You are, of course, aware that this estate will never come to you.'

'I don't care about that, sir.' James had never taken much

notice of the strange colour of Mr Warrender's eyes, but with them fixed firmly on his, he felt as if he was being dissected. He tried not to shift uncomfortably in his seat. His heart was thumping. He hadn't been immediately rejected. Did he have a chance?

'What about the Bonners? They mean a great deal to Eleanor and will always be a part of her life now. Could you accept them into your family? If not, you don't have any place in my daughter's life.' Albert leant forward. 'If you have the slightest unease about Eleanor's humble beginnings then walk away now, James.'

'I can't do that, sir.' James sensed that only the absolute truth would do. 'I admit that I was unsure about the Bonners at first, but I was wrong. They're obviously prepared to work hard and make their own way in life. They love their sister and have shown no thought of personal gain because a wealthy family has brought her up. I respect them. All except the one I haven't met, but he is back in gaol.'

'There is one more we haven't found. What if he should turn up one day and be as bad as Tommy?'

'That is something we'll have to deal with – if it happens.'

Albert nodded, as if satisfied with the answers he had received. 'I will give you permission to see if you can win Eleanor—'

James leapt to his feet, hardly able to believe his ears. 'Oh, thank you, sir!'

'Not so fast.' Albert also stood and came round the desk to James. 'I have conditions. If my daughter refuses you three times then you will give up. Is that understood?'

'Yes, sir.' James wasn't happy with the time limit, but he had gained more than he'd dreamt possible.

'Good.' Albert stepped closer. 'And you will behave yourself, young man. If I discover that you have taken advantage of my daughter's innocence, you will live to regret it.'

James didn't doubt that for one moment. He didn't believe that Ellie's father made idle threats. 'You have my word.'

For the first time since James had entered the room, Albert smiled. 'I don't think you have a chance.'

'What if you're wrong?' James relaxed enough to return the smile. 'Will you accept me as your son-in-law?'

'If that's what my daughter wants, then I will.' Albert

pursed his lip as he looked at James. 'But there's someone else's permission you need to gain.'

'Nanny,' James said.

Albert nodded.

James left the room with a sigh of relief. Mr Warrender had been totally reasonable. Now he had to face the next hurdle.

He knocked on the door, almost as nervous about this interview as he had been with Ellie's father. When he heard her call for him to come in, he opened the door. 'Hello Nanny, can I have a word with you?'

'Of course. Sit down,' she ordered. 'I suppose you want to see how I feel about you asking Eleanor to be your wife?'

'How did you know?' James was amazed.

'Don't look so surprised. I know everything going on concerning my girl – and I've seen the glint in your eyes when you've looked at her just lately.'

James sat down and let out a deep breath. 'Mr Warrender said I must seek your permission as well as his.'

'So you have his permission?' Nanny's gaze was unflinching as she studied James.

'Well, in a way.' James then explained about Mr Warrender's conditions, making Nanny grunt and nod in approval. 'I will abide by his rules, but I also need your approval.'

'You have it. I believe you would make her a suitable husband.'

'Thank you. Do you think she will accept me?'

'Ah, now, that's for you to find out, young man.'

Standing up, James nodded and left the room. If anyone had any idea about how Ellie felt about him, then Nanny would have known, but she wasn't saying anything. He was on his own now, but it was comforting to have the approval of the two most important people in Ellie's life.

Now all he had to do was make Ellie fall in love with him. And he knew this was going to be the most difficult challenge he had ever faced.

Thirty-Three

Christmas Day dawned bright and cold with a heavy frost glistening in the sun. The house was bustling with activity and looking festive. Philip and Uncle Henry were staying with them for the New Year, so was Uncle Joshua, James and his mother. Ellie wished her other family could be here as well, but she understood the need for them to have their reunion with Fred and Hilda at Ted's house. It was neutral ground, so to speak. But they would all be together tomorrow. The ballroom was festooned with holly and her father had engaged musicians to play quietly in the background. Gifts were piled high around the tree. There was something for everyone coming, and they'd all spent yesterday afternoon wrapping the presents. How her mother would have loved it.

Ellie gazed at her mother's portrait. She spoke softly. 'I haven't seen Father this happy for a long time, Mother. He seems to be getting along well with Augusta Montague, and it's lovely to see them laughing together. You don't mind, do you?' She was sure her mother nodded approval. 'I knew you wouldn't. I like her too. I know he said he would never marry again, but if he did change his mind, then I believe she'd make him a good wife.'

She spun round to take in the entire room – and crashed into James.

'Who were you talking to?'

'I was singing to myself.' Ellie cast a guilty look at the portrait.

James followed her gaze and stepped towards the picture. 'That looks perfect there. I wish I'd known her.' He placed his hand through Ellie's arm. 'I've been sent to fetch you. We're about to open our gifts.'

'Before lunch?' She walked beside him, smiling in anticipation. Over the last few days James had become rather

251

attentive and didn't seem quite so stuffy. He really was very nice.

The drawing room was a riot of colour with the enormous tree dominating the room, and a log fire with dancing flames sending fingers of bright warmth around the room.

'There you are, Ellie.' Philip pounced on her immediately. 'We've been waiting for you.'

'I'm sorry to have kept you waiting, but we don't usually do this until after lunch.'

'We're breaking with tradition this year.' Albert chuckled as he watched Philip examining the names on the parcels. 'You and Philip can hand them out now.'

The floor was soon littered with boxes, ribbons and torn paper. Ellie had just opened one box and was staring at the contents in amazement. If this had been a gift from her father she wouldn't have been surprised, but the tag had James's name on it.

'Don't you like it?' James stooped down in front of her, his eyes searching her face.

'It's absolutely beautiful,' she breathed in awe. In her hands was a glorious gold and diamond bracelet. It seemed alive as the stones caught the light and sent out a multitude of dancing colours. 'But . . . but . . .' For once in her life she was lost for words.

He removed it from its black velvet box and fastened it around Ellie's wrist. 'You deserve only the best,' he said softly.

She dragged her eyes away from the jewel and stared at James, stunned. What was going on? When he stood up and bent over to kiss her cheek, she gave her father a questioning look.

Albert held out his hand. 'Come and show us, Eleanor.'

As everyone gathered round exclaiming approval of such a fine gift, Ellie caught Nanny's eye and received a saucy wink from the elderly woman. What on earth did that mean? She wasn't sure it was quite the thing for James to give such an outrageously expensive present to her.

'You have excellent taste, James,' Albert told him.

'Thank you, sir.'

Ellie studied the bracelet again. Her father appeared to approve, so perhaps it was all right for her to accept it. Realizing that she hadn't thanked James properly, she turned to him. 'It's absolutely beautiful, James. I love it, thank you very much.'

'I'm pleased you like it, and it would make me happy if you'd wear it tomorrow for the party.'

There was much to do the next day and Ellie was grateful to have the help of Augusta Montague. She was very organized and obviously used to arranging large functions. Their guests began arriving around one o'clock and Ellie stood with her father to greet them. Nanny was in her element as the young children gathered around her. There was something about Nanny that made children gravitate towards her, just as Ellie herself had done.

The room was filling up rapidly and Ellie waited anxiously to see the arrival of her brothers and sisters. Would Fred and Hilda come? Had the family reunion gone well? She had so wanted to go to Ted's yesterday, but she did understand that her presence might have made it more difficult. After all, it was because of her that the rift had occurred. Not that it had been her fault, of course, but it had been best for her to keep out of the way. Today was different, and she would be upset if they didn't all come.

Her father touched her arm. 'Eleanor, look towards the door.'

She almost cried out with joy, but managed to control herself. She lifted her hand in greeting. Ted was with Dorothy on his arm; Mr Rogers was also there with Maggie. Just behind them were Pearl, Dave and their son, then Jack with Fred and Hilda. They were a family again.

When they reached them, Ellie forgot about decorum, hugging her brothers and sisters in turn. 'I'm so pleased you came,' she said warmly to Fred and Hilda.

Ted got hold of his parents by the arms and urged them forward. 'Sir, may I introduce our mum and dad.'

'We've already met.' Fred spoke gruffly, looking ill at ease in such surroundings. 'Nice place you've got here.'

Albert's mouth twitched at the corners. 'Thank you, we like it.'

Fred hadn't finished. 'Ted said this party was for everyone who works on the estate. These all yours?'

'Some come from my brother-in-law's estate which is next

door. We're delighted you could come. You are welcome in our home.'

Hilda nodded, her eyes misting over. 'Thank you, sir, that's good of you.'

'Not at all.' Albert smiled at Ellie. 'I think everyone has arrived, my dear, and now we have an announcement to make.'

She stood beside him proudly as he told the gathering about the engagements, asking everyone to raise their glasses to toast the happy couples. Her father had such a commanding presence; the way he had welcomed her other family showed him to be a man of great understanding and kindness. But, of course, she had always known that. She glanced across at Fred and Hilda, no longer feeling any animosity towards them, but she would never be able to think of them as her parents. She was sorry for the hard life they had endured, and was happy that they were reconciled with some of their children, but that was all she felt for them.

Next they gave out the presents; the noise was deafening as the children yelled in delight over their toys, with Pearl and Dave's little boy in the thick of the excitement. The servants moved around the room collecting up the paper, serving the food and replenishing drinks.

Only when everyone had eaten did Ellie have a chance to join her brothers and sisters. James and Philip were already with them, and Ellie was pleased to see James laughing with Jack. She had always felt that James viewed her other family with suspicion, but he appeared quite at ease with them. Fred and Hilda also looked as if they were enjoying themselves. Fred was standing with a tankard of beer in his hand as he talked with the head groom. Hilda was with a group of the wives, nodding and smiling as she listened to what was being said. Every so often she glanced across at her children, her face a picture of happiness. It did Ellie good to see it and know that she had been able to help them.

Jack grinned when Ellie reached him. 'This is quite a party. It took a bit of persuading to get Mum and Dad here, but look at them now. They're having the time of their lives.'

'I'm so pleased it's all turned out well.' Ellie stifled a sigh. 'I'm only sorry that there's still one member of the family unaccounted for. Father has given up on the search for Harry. Have you had any luck, Jack?'

'No, sorry. It's as if he walked out and disappeared into thin air. We won't find him now.' Jack gave Ellie a sympathetic look. 'Your dad's right, we've got to accept that we'll never know.'

'Of course.' Ellie pushed the thought away, determined not to let it spoil this happy occasion. 'Come on, I haven't had anything to eat yet and I'm starving.'

The house was quiet when James wandered downstairs the next morning. There had been a light covering of snow during the night and he gazed out of the drawing room window, deep in thought. The party yesterday had been a huge success, and Ellie the perfect hostess. He knew she must have been longing to spend more time with the Bonners, but she had stuck to her duties with cheerful good grace. While she'd been otherwise occupied, he had sought out her other family to try and get to know them better. By the end of the evening all his doubts about them had disappeared. He liked them and had completely revised his earlier view that they would try to take advantage of the situation. They were rough, but they had their own code of conduct in the harsh world of the slums. He'd been wrong to view them with such suspicion.

'Beautiful morning, isn't it?'

The sound of Ellie's voice made him spin round. 'I didn't hear you come in. And, yes, it's a glorious morning.'

Laughing she pointed to her bare feet. 'That's why you didn't know I was here. I love all the seasons, but days like this most of all. Everything is so peaceful.'

James nodded. 'This is a lovely place.'

'I'm very lucky.' Ellie looked up at him. 'It must be hard for you to leave your estate for half of the year.'

'I leave because I have to.' James had never discussed this with Ellie, but it was time he was open and honest with her. 'When my father died he left everything to my stepbrother, Giles, and he doesn't like me being around too much. But he is obliged to allow us to live in the house for six months each year.'

Ellie touched his arm in sympathy. 'I didn't know you had a stepbrother. I just assumed you had inherited the estate.'

'I was unhappy at first that Giles didn't want my help, but if I'd stayed in Yorkshire I would never have met you.'

Ellie pulled a face. 'I wouldn't think that was much of a consolation.'

He turned to face her. 'But it is. I can't imagine my life without you now. Would you marry me?'

For a few seconds she stared at him, stunned, then she laughed. 'Oh, James, you look so serious. Did Philip put you up to this? It's just the sort of daft joke he would think up.'

James hadn't expected Ellie to fall into his arms with rapture at his proposal – and truthfully it had been clumsily done – but he hadn't thought she would take it as a huge joke either. 'I am serious, Ellie. What's your answer?'

She punched his arm, grinning. 'It would serve you right if I accepted, and then you'd regret playing such a silly joke on me. But I won't be that unkind.' She placed a hand over her heart and tried to look suitably impressed. 'I thank you for your kind proposal of marriage, sir, but I'm afraid I cannot accept.'

James decided to join in her fun and make light of it this time. He had two more chances and he'd make a better job of it next time. Taking a small notebook from his pocket he wrote a large figure one in it.

Ellie peered at the page, still laughing. 'What's that for?'

'I'm making a note of how many times I ask you.'

'If it wasn't so early in the day I would believe you'd been drinking Father's best brandy.' She examined him carefully. 'You haven't, have you?'

James shook his head. 'I'm not over fond of strong liqueur.'

'That's true. I've never seen you drink more than one glass. I suggest that you call on Nanny, for you must be sickening for something. She has a remedy for every malady.'

Before James could answer, Philip burst into the room. 'Ellie, have you seen my thick scarf? I had it yesterday, but I can't find it anywhere.'

'It must be in your room.' When her cousin declared that he had searched every inch, Ellie sighed and headed for the door.

James watched them leave, bickering away as usual. Ellie had forgotten about the proposal already. Ah, well, he might as well have breakfast.

The only person in the dining room was Ellie's father helping himself from the many silver dishes. James joined him. 'Good morning, sir.'

'Good morning, James. I hope you slept well?'

'Very soundly.' James contemplated whether to have three or four slices of bacon with his eggs and mushrooms. Ellie's rejection hadn't seemed to blunt his appetite.

'Have you seen my daughter this morning.'

'Philip's taken her off to help him find something he's lost.' With his plate full, James joined Ellie's father at the table. 'I asked her to marry me this morning.'

'And what was her response?'

'She burst out laughing.' James couldn't help chuckling when he saw the amusement on Mr Warrender's face.

'Her refusal doesn't appear to have dented your ego,' Albert said.

'I can't afford to have an ego around your daughter, sir.'

'True. So you have wasted one try.'

'Oh, it wasn't wasted. She'll think it over and wonder if I really was serious. It will make her curious, and the next time she'll know that I mean it.'

Albert laid down his knife and fork. 'And what will you do if she refuses you three times?'

'Then she will have to ask me.' James noticed the gleam of respect in the eyes of the man sitting opposite him and felt a surge of relief when he laughed. He felt sure that he had been accepted. Now all he had to do was make Ellie fall in love with him. He was sure she had some affection for him, but he didn't know how deep her feelings went. He was under no illusion about the difficulty of the task in front of him. Failure was not something he would accept though.

An hour later Albert was sitting in the library reflecting on the changes in his life since Mary had died. He was now at peace with her passing and relieved that her suffering was over. Eleanor had grown up over the last year, and although she was still inclined to be impetuous, she had steadied a little. The party had been a happy affair, and he knew his daughter had been delighted to see the Bonners together again at last. Albert didn't think he would ever like Fred Bonner, but perhaps he wasn't quite as bad as they had first thought. Living with the threat of the workhouse over their heads must have made them very frightened and desperate. Hilda was different and he had warmed to her. He could see that she fought to keep her emotions under control, but she couldn't disguise just how happy she was to be reunited to her children.

'Oh, I do beg your pardon, Albert, I didn't mean to disturb you.'

The sound of Augusta's voice had him surging to his feet. 'You are not disturbing me. Did you sleep well?'

'Yes, thank you. You were deep in thought. I'll find a book to read and then leave you alone again.'

'Please stay. I would welcome your company.' When she was seated he asked, 'Have you had breakfast?'

'Eleanor arranged for me to be served in bed.' Her laugh was soft and musical. 'It was a reward, she said, for helping her yesterday with the party. That was very thoughtful of her. She is a delightful young woman and I would be proud to have her as my daughter-in-law.'

Albert nodded. He had discussed this with Augusta as soon as James had approached him, and they had been in agreement that they would leave their children to make their own decisions. 'James has proposed this morning and didn't seem at all perturbed that Eleanor took it as a joke.'

'And that may well be her only response.' Augusta sighed. 'But I do believe that my son really loves her.'

'Yes, I'm sure he does.' Sitting in the warm room with Augusta, Albert relaxed. It was time to let things take their natural course. Eleanor was quite capable of deciding her own future. It was time he gave some thought to his own.

Thirty-Four

An hour before midnight on New Year's Eve, James managed to spirit Ellie away from the gathering in the drawing room. It wasn't difficult as his mother and Ellie's father were rather occupied with each other – which was an interesting development – and all the Bonners were here again. He now accepted that they were a part of Ellie's life and, truth be told, he had come to like them – or most of them.

'Where are we going, James?' Ellie complained as he towed her along the passage. 'It will be twelve o'clock soon.'

'To the library.' He opened the door, urged her in and closed the door behind him. He spun her round to face him, and then dropped to one knee. 'Would you do me the honour of becoming my wife?'

She didn't laugh this time, but just stared at him. 'Oh, James, do stop messing about and stand up. You're taking this joke too far.'

He rose to his feet, placed his hands on her shoulders and drew her towards him.

'What are you doing?' Ellie made to step away.

James didn't allow her to. The kiss he gave her was long and passionate. He hadn't intended to let his feelings get out of hand, but once she was in his arms he couldn't seem to let go. Her lips were soft and slightly parted – in surprise he guessed – but she didn't push him away. Realizing that she had never been kissed before in this intimate way, made him come to his senses and step back. 'Do you now believe that I love you?' His voice was husky and he swallowed before speaking again. 'Will you give me your answer?'

She appeared to be slightly nonplussed, which was unusual for her. 'You shouldn't have done that. And I'm too young to marry.'

'In a little over two weeks you will be nineteen . . .'

Ellie shook her head firmly, stopping James in mid-sentence. 'We would not suit at all. And does my Father know you have this silly notion in your head?'

'You don't believe I would be foolish enough to ask you without his permission, do you?' James grimaced. 'I'm not that brave.'

Ellie was astonished. 'Are you telling me that my father approves?'

'Well, I wouldn't go as far as that. He gave me permission to approach you, that's all.'

Tipping her head to one side, her composure now fully restored, her eyes gleamed with mischief. 'Did he give you permission to kiss me like that?'

'No, that was my idea. The first time I proposed you laughed in my face so I had to try and convince you that I was serious.' James removed the little book from his pocket and waited, pencil poised. 'You haven't given me your answer.'

Ellie stifled a giggle. 'The answer is still the same – no.'

James wrote the figure two in the book and put it back in his pocket, not allowing his disappointment to show. He only had one more chance. He would wait until her birthday.

The Montagues had stayed for the birthday celebrations, and as Ellie stood with her father and waved them off, she felt sorry to see them go. It had been lovely having them around. Father clearly enjoyed the company of Augusta – as she had insisted Ellie call her – and it had been lovely to have James with her. Philip was so determined to get to university that he was studying every spare moment. Even the holiday hadn't stopped him pouring over his studies whenever he could. She missed him being around, but understood how much this meant to him.

Her party last night had been a great success. Everyone who'd been with them at Christmas had returned, even Fred and Hilda. They had appeared much more relaxed this time and not in such awe of their surroundings, though Hilda had kept a sharp eye on her husband to make sure he didn't do anything to disgrace them.

Ellie pulled her coat around her as a blast of cold wind caught her straight in the face. The carriage was almost at the gates when James leant out and waved madly. She grinned and waved back. He had proposed again last night, but she'd refused, not quite so quickly this time, though.

Her father ushered her indoors and into the warmth of the library. They sat in front of the roaring fire warming their cold hands and feet. The maid immediately appeared with tea and cakes, so they settled down to enjoy a quiet time together.

'How many times has James proposed to you?'

Ellie glanced up from pouring tea. She handed him a cup and sat down, a wry smile on her face. 'Three, and I've refused each time.'

Albert sipped his tea and nodded. 'Ah, that's the end of it then. He won't bother you again.'

'What do you mean, Father?' She frowned.

'I told him he could ask you three times only, and if you refused, he was to give up trying to persuade you to marry him.' He selected a piece of cake from the tray. 'I didn't want you to be pestered, Eleanor. If you refused him that many times it would show you were not interested.'

'I see.' Ellie twisted the bracelet James had given her and wondered why she wasn't feeling happy about this. Now she understood why James had made such a show of writing down each proposal. He'd known he only had three chances. If only he'd told her. But would it have made any difference to her answers? That was something she didn't know, and it would need a lot of thought.

'Why the worried expression,' her father asked. 'If you're having second thoughts then it is too late, for James will not break his promise to me, I'm sure.'

'Oh, no, he wouldn't do that. He has a strong sense of honour . . . and I do believe he's frightened of you.'

'I don't think he is. Cautious, perhaps, but not frightened. So tell me how you really feel about him.'

She gazed at the fire for a moment, and then said, 'I like James and enjoy his company, but that isn't enough to base a lifelong commitment on, is it?'

'No, it isn't,' Albert agreed. 'The foundation of any marriage should be love and mutual respect. There will always be difficult times in any union, but those two qualities will help you to weather any storm. I wouldn't want you to marry unless you truly love someone.'

Ellie knew her father was talking from experience. The deep love her mother and father had shared had been the unshakeable foundation of their marriage. That had been the atmosphere she'd grown up in, and she wouldn't want anything less for any children she might have. 'I wouldn't consider marriage for any other reason.'

'Good.' Albert picked up a book, flicked through a couple of pages, then tossed it down again. 'I'm concerned about Nanny. She was not at all well last night and only stayed at your party from sheer will power, determined not to miss it.'

Ellie nodded. 'I saw her this morning and she told me she was much better, but she is very frail now.'

'We must prepare ourselves to lose her soon, I fear.'

'That will be hard.' Ellie's eyes clouded. 'She has been an important part of my life. I can't imagine what it will be like when she is no longer with us.'

'I know, my dear. It's hard to lose someone we love, but that is all a part of life.' He looked gently at his daughter. 'But we have gained much over the last year, have we not?'

She smiled. 'We have gained a whole new set of family and friends.'

Over the following weeks, Ellie discovered that she missed one of those new friends more than she could ever have believed. James wrote regularly but never mentioned marriage again, or that he loved her. She should have told him that she would think about it, and that would have left the door open. But she hadn't done that, and now regretted her hasty action. The realization that her feelings for him were stronger than friendship, had come as quite a shock in the middle of one sleepless night. She didn't want him to forget the idea of marrying her just because her father had decreed it that way. But what on earth was she going to do about it? Very little, she thought, with him in London and her in Kent.

Walking into her father's study she sat in front of his desk, waiting for him to finish what he was doing. When he looked up, she said, 'Father, spring is just around the corner now, so do you think Augusta and James would like to come and stay before they return to Yorkshire?'

Albert sat back. 'Why don't you write and invite them. I'm sure they will come if they can.'

'Thank you, Father.' Ellie stood up. 'I'll do that straight away.'

Albert watched Eleanor leave the room. Could he have been wrong about her feelings for James? She had certainly seemed restless since he'd returned to London, and he noticed that she wore his bracelet all the time, even when out riding. His own emotions were also in turmoil. He loved Augusta, and was sure that she felt the same about him. She was a charming, intelligent companion – but she was more than that – she was a desirable woman. When Mary had died, he'd believed that he would never love like that again, and it was true, but the feelings he had for Augusta were different. He now knew that it was possible to love more than once, and for each time to be special and unique. If Augusta and James stayed with them again it would give him a chance to try and persuade them not to go to Yorkshire this year. It was almost certain that James would accept the invitation, and he sincerely hoped Augusta would as well.

Seven days later Ellie was agitated and pacing up and down the library, shoes tucked under a chair. 'They're not coming, are they? We'd have heard by now. James is never going to speak to me again.' She headed for the door. 'I'll go to London and see him.'

Albert caught her before she hurtled out of the room. 'Calm down, Eleanor. They might not have received your letter yet. They have other friends and could be staying with them. Be patient.'

Ellie pulled a face. Patience was not a quality she had been endowed with in any measure. 'I never thought of that. You know how I jump at things without giving them proper thought.'

'That's true, hence my restrictions on James.' Albert chuckled as he led her back to the chair. 'Try and sit still for a minute. James told me that he loves you, and I believed him. He won't disappear from your life because you have refused his proposal of marriage.'

'Three times.' Ellie chewed her bottom lip, eyes wide with worry. 'I insulted him, Father. I took it as a joke and laughed at him.'

'That was more or less what he expected you to do.'

'What!' Ellie was on her feet bristling with anger now. 'Was I right? Has he been playing games with me? Am I feeling guilty for nothing?'

'Will you stop jumping to conclusions?' Albert shook his head. 'If he gives up now then he's not the man I believe him to be'

Ellie sighed. 'I didn't realize how much I enjoyed being with him, or how strong my feelings were until he left. He hasn't mentioned marriage again in his letters, so will you remove the restrictions you've placed upon him, please?'

'No, I will not. If he cares enough for you he will find a way round that. It isn't James I'm concerned about, Eleanor. If he's prepared to abandon his dream of owning land to marry you then he loves you. It's you I'm worried about. I don't want you making a hasty decision. You must give this a great deal of thought. It's the rest of your life we're talking about here.'

'I've done nothing but give it thought since he left. And I can't see how he can possibly propose again.'

Sitting back, Albert grinned. 'I'll watch with interest to see what he does, and making you wait for a reply to his letter might be a part of his strategy. Do I understand that you wish to marry him?'

'I haven't decided yet, but I don't want him leaving me until I have sorted out my feelings. And I really ought to apologize for not taking him seriously.' A mischievous grin tipped up the corners of Ellie's mouth. 'I'm having as much trouble making up my mind as you are about Augusta.'

She left the room with her father's laughter echoing in her ears. She'd go and talk to Nanny. The dear woman was feeling much better, much to everyone's relief.

Two days later a letter arrived from Augusta accepting their invitation. Ellie rushed into her father's study, waving the letter. 'They're coming tomorrow. I must see that the rooms are prepared and tell Mr Rogers. He'll be so pleased to see Maggie again.'

'He will, but what about you Eleanor, are you as happy as you look about seeing James again?'

'Of course I am. Will you be pleased to see Augusta again?'

Albert waved her away. 'You just concentrate on sorting out your own romance. That appears to be in quite a mess.

And I don't know where you ever got the idea that I might be looking for another wife. I have no intention of doing any such thing.'

Ellie stifled a laugh. 'No, of course you haven't.' She hadn't missed the looks that passed between Augusta and her father. He might deny it, but it was obvious there was something between them.

Thirty-Five

The Montagues arrived the next day in time for lunch, and for the next few days James was Ellie's constant companion. He was by her side every morning as she rode out to take care of any estate business. She enjoyed his company enormously. He was very knowledgeable, but he never questioned or interfered with her decisions. As the week progressed, she turned to him for advice if she was in any doubt. There was a growing rapport between them.

Spring was almost here now and there were signs that nature was awakening after its dormant time. The year ahead promised to be an exciting one, full of good things. Ted was to marry in April, and Maggie in June. Her sister was giving Augusta plenty of time to replace her with another personal maid before she left. There was only one blot on her horizon, and that was Harry. She now accepted that this special brother would not be found. The picture of him was firmly locked in her mind, and she knew it always would be. But she was grateful for the family she had been able to trace.

She glanced at James as he rode beside her on the way back to the house for lunch. They had fallen into a routine of working during the morning, leaving the afternoons and evenings free to do whatever they pleased. Ellie now knew that she did love James and, although he hadn't said anything, she was sure he still felt the same about her. She was absolutely certain that this was the man she wanted to live with for the rest of her life, and she must have been blind not to see that sooner.

By the time they arrived back the sky had clouded and was sending down sleety rain as if the weather was reminding them that it was too early yet for winter to loosen its grasp. After reporting to her father about the morning's work, it was time for lunch.

Not deterred by the inclement weather, Ellie's father ordered a carriage as soon as the meal was over, and took Augusta off to visit Henry.

'What do you want to do, Ellie?' James asked.

'I want to sit by the fire and talk to you.'

'That's fine by me.' He drew up two of the library chairs to the fire, waited for Ellie to be seated, and then settled down himself. 'What do you want to talk about?'

'Us.' When he merely raised one eyebrow, she knew he wasn't going to make this easy for her. And why should he after the way she had treated him? It had never been in her nature to hedge around a subject, so she pitched straight in. 'First, I must apologize for not taking your proposals seriously. I know my father placed certain restrictions on you, but I've had time to think things over. I would like to know if you still feel the same about me?'

'I don't say things I don't mean, Ellie. You ought to know that by now, and I haven't changed my mind.'

Immensely relieved, Ellie took a deep breath, her sense of devilment returning. 'Did I hurt you when I laughed?'

James shook his head. 'I was disappointed, but I'd known it wouldn't be easy to convince you of my sincerity. I didn't expect you to find it so hilarious though.'

She pulled a face. 'It was all so sudden, and I did find it unbelievable at the time.'

'And now?' James held her gaze.

'I've realized that I do love you. If I look back, it's clear that my feelings for you have been growing all the time. I just wouldn't admit it.' The expression of disbelief on his face made her say quickly, 'I've never been in love before. I love all the members of my family, but I love you in a different way.'

'I'm pleased to hear it.'

Ellie had expected James to show some kind of pleasure, but he remained seated and appeared to be completely unmoved by her declaration. He'd said he still loved her, but had she lost him through her foolish behaviour? That prospect hurt her more than she could have ever believed possible. Now she exploded. 'Is that all you've got to say?'

He lifted his hands. 'What else can I say, Ellie? You know your father told me that if you refused me three times I was to walk away and never bother you again. I am bound by the promise I made him.'

She was on her feet now. 'And that's it, is it? I'm sure my Father wouldn't mind if you proposed one more time. He likes you.'

'And I like him. So much, in fact, that I won't break my promise.' James sat back while Ellie walked up and down.

'You and your sense of honour,' she muttered, removing her shoes and tossing them under a chair.

'Would you expect me to be any other way?'

Ellie stopped in front of his chair and sighed deeply. 'No, of course not. There's only one thing I can do. This is not at all proper, James, but you are forcing me into doing this. And when have I ever been concerned about convention? Will you marry me, James?'

At first she thought he wasn't going to say anything, then he surged to his feet, gathered her into his arms and lifted her off the floor.

'God, Ellie, that took you long enough. Of course I'll marry you, my darling.'

They were both laughing as James spun her round and round.

'What's going on here?'

Ellie disentangled herself from James and ran to her father. 'James didn't break his promise to you, Father. I asked him to marry me and he's accepted.'

'Congratulations.' Albert kissed his daughter and then shook hands with James.

Augusta was clearly delighted and hugged both of them. 'What are your plans?'

James laughed. 'We haven't had time to talk over details yet. You're back so soon.'

'One of the horses went lame and we had to return.' Albert arranged two more chairs so they could all sit down together, and rang the bell. 'We'll have tea while we discuss yet another wedding.'

As soon as the tea arrived, Albert looked at James. 'I'm sure you are impatient to marry, but I'm going to ask you to wait for a year. It will give you a chance to spend time together; get to know each other better. I want you to be absolutely certain that you are meant for each other and will be happy together.'

'I'm already certain, sir.' James couldn't hide his disappointment. 'I was hoping we could marry in the autumn.'

'Albert is right, James,' Augusta told her son. 'How do you feel about waiting a year, Eleanor?'

'Well . . .' Ellie reached out for James's hand. 'We already have two weddings this year, so it would seem wise to leave ours until next year.'

'I suppose you're right.' James agreed reluctantly. 'And we also have to decide where we're going to live.'

'I have a suggestion to make regarding that.' Albert placed his cup on the small table in front of him. 'Henry and I have bought a parcel of land near the orchards. There's a good spot on my section that I think would suit you. Why don't we ride out there tomorrow and you can see what you think of it? If you like it I'll build you a house there.'

James shook his head firmly. 'No, sir.'

'No.' Albert frowned. 'Eleanor has responsibilities here and she must stay on the estate.'

'I realize that, sir, and I'll gladly accept the plot for our house, but I'll pay for the building. I am perfectly capable of providing for my wife.'

'Of course, James,' Albert said. 'I didn't mean to insult you.'

'You haven't, sir, but I insist on building our house. Ellie can tell me what she wants and I'll have an architect draw up plans. If we start at once it might be possible to have the house ready.' James squeezed Ellie's hand. 'Is that all right with you?'

'Oh yes, it will be exciting.' Ellie turned to Augusta. 'Would you advise me on furnishings. You have such excellent taste.'

'I'll be delighted to help in any way I can.'

'That's all settled then,' Albert said.

With the tea and discussion finished, James and Ellie went to break the good news to Nanny.

'About time you two realized how you feel about each other,' she declared. 'And it's right you should have a reasonable length of engagement. You are young, and there's no need to rush into marriage.'

After giving them the benefit of her opinion, she promptly fell asleep with a smile on her face.

Later that evening, when everyone had retired for the night, Albert was still by the fire, deep in thought. He approved of the way James had insisted on meeting the cost of the house. The boy had a sound character, but he was relieved he had persuaded them to wait for a year.

The door opened and Augusta came in. 'Am I disturbing you?'

Albert stood up. 'Not at all. I thought you had retired.'

'I doubt I shall be able to sleep.' Augusta sat down, folded her hands in her lap and bowed her head. Just for a few moments her perfect composure slipped.

Albert sat down again. If there was a problem, then it had to be sorted out now. 'You are not happy about our children marrying?'

She looked up sharply. 'Oh, I couldn't be more pleased that James has fallen in love with Eleanor. They will be good for each other. Eleanor will bring a sense of fun into James's life, and James will be a restraining hand in the union. If they truly love and respect each other – and I believe they do – then the differences in temperament will make for an interesting and happy marriage.'

Albert nodded agreement. 'I believe James is just what Eleanor needs.' He studied Augusta intently. 'So why do you look sad?'

'Our children have grown up, Albert, and ready to make their own way in life. We are losing them.'

'It isn't easy, but we would be more concerned if they did not leave our sides, would we not?'

'You are quite right. How silly of me. I am not losing anything. I am gaining a whole new family.'

Albert chuckled. 'More than you bargained for – more than either of us bargained for. What do you think of the Bonners?'

'I like them. They don't appear to be overawed by the fact that their youngest sister has been brought up in luxury. The elder Bonners are more reticent, but they've had a hard life.'

'Indeed they have.' Albert gazed into the fire, watching the flames dance. 'I was very concerned when Eleanor wanted to trace the family she had no recollection of, but I knew this was something she had to do, or wonder about them for the rest of her life. It's turned out better than I'd dared hope.' He looked up at Augusta, then reached out and took hold of her hand. 'And it brought you into my life.'

Augusta curled her fingers around his hand. 'That is a blessing I shall always be grateful for.'

Albert rose to his feet, pulling Augusta up and slipping his arms around her, lowering his head for a long embrace. He no longer had any doubts. This was what he wanted – what they both wanted.

Thirty-Six

It was nearly the end of March now but the weather was reluctant to loosen its grasp. The cold rain was coming down in torrents. Ellie sighed and returned to her chair, picked up the book she had been attempting to read and flicked through the pages, unable to concentrate. James and Augusta had stayed for two weeks, but had returned to London yesterday. They wouldn't be returning until Ted and Dorothy's wedding in four weeks time. It seemed a long time to wait, for Ellie was missing James already. But they had decided not to spend this summer in Yorkshire, so they wouldn't be far away.

She turned the beautiful diamond and ruby ring round and round her finger. It had belonged to James's grandmother, and she'd been thrilled that it had been given to her. He'd presented her with it just after they'd ridden out to choose a place for their house. They had found the perfect spot. The house would stand on a rise with wonderful views from every window. James would bring some plans with him next time for her to consider.

When she sighed again, Albert laid down his book. 'What is the matter, Eleanor?'

'I wish it would stop raining. I don't like being inactive.' She stood up. 'Perhaps I'll go to the stables and see if there is anything there to do.'

'I doubt there is. And if Silver Princess sees you she'll expect to be taken out. It's a quagmire out there and not safe for either of you at the frantic pace you ride.'

'You're right. I wouldn't want her to slip and hurt herself. Perhaps there is some bookkeeping to do?'

Her father laughed. 'You are desperate. I've never known you to offer to do that. And I've already dealt with it.'

There was a knock on the door and the butler entered.

'There's a young naval gentleman here asking to see you, sir. He says his name is John Fletcher, but he won't state his business.'

'Really?' Albert frowned.

'He insists it's most important, sir.' The butler hesitated. 'Shall I tell him you are not available?'

'No, I'll see what he wants. Send him in please, Dobson.'

'Would you like me to leave, Father?'

Albert shook his head. 'No, I'm sure this won't take long.'

Curious about the unexpected caller, Ellie sat on the window seat. It was a secluded spot and she often sat there out of the way when her father had business to attend to.

The butler soon returned with a man dressed in uniform. Ellie didn't know what the rank was, but it was clear that he wasn't an ordinary seaman. He was quite tall, with a smart military bearing. That was all she could see because he had his back to her as he greeted her father.

'It's good of you to see me, sir. And I apologize for calling without an appointment, but Sir Joshua Hargreaves gave me your address. He would have come with me, but he's embroiled in a difficult case at the moment.'

'You know Joshua?'

'I only met him today.'

'And he sent you here?' Albert was intrigued. 'You had better explain.'

Both men were still standing, and Ellie was sitting on the edge of the window seat, eager to hear what this was all about. She couldn't imagine why Uncle Joshua had sent this man to them.

'I've been at sea for some time, sir, and on my return I happened to see an old newspaper. I understand you are looking for Harry Bonner.'

Ellie shot to her feet, but did not speak or make any other movement. Her heart was pounding. Was there news at last?

Albert nodded. 'My daughter has been trying to trace him. Didn't Josh tell you?'

'All Sir Joshua told me was that you were eager to find the man and, after I'd told him I knew something, he said I was to come here and meet you.'

'Do you know where Harry is?'

'I can't answer that question until I know what this is all

273

about.' The sailor glanced around the elegant room. 'Why would your daughter be looking for someone like Harry Bonner?'

Ellie could stand it no longer. If this man knew something, then he must tell them. Who was he, and why was he so reluctant to say what he knew? And he must have reliable information or Uncle Joshua would never have sent him here. Dreading that the news was going to be bad, she said softly, 'Because he's my brother. Do you know where he is?'

The young man spun round at the sound of her voice, seeing her for the first time. All the breath rushed out of her lungs as she scrutinized his face. Eyes blue, hair fair, and a mouth that was used to smiling . . . But his name was Fletcher . . .? Emotions warred within her as she tried to understand what her eyes and heart were telling her. 'Harry?' she whispered.

The visitor stared, his brow furrowed as he concentrated on the girl in front of him. The only movement he made was to clench and unclench his hands. When he spoke his voice was husky with emotion. 'Hello Queenie.' He held out his arms and she rushed into them. They held each other tightly as their tears mingled in joy.

Harry held her away, unashamed to be showing such emotion. 'Oh, I'm so relieved you're safe. I've never stopped worrying about you. You've grown into a lovely young woman, but I'd have known you anywhere.'

Albert had been standing back as brother and sister greeted each other, but now he intervened. 'If you really are Harry, why are you calling yourself Fletcher?'

Ellie turned to her father, noting the doubt in his voice. 'I know he's Harry. As soon as he faced me I recognized him.'

'I think we *both* have some explaining to do, sir.'

Albert frowned at Harry's abrupt manner, but chose to ignore it. 'You'd better sit down, young man. I'll order refreshments, for we have a lot to talk about.'

Ellie couldn't take her eyes off Harry, hardly being able to believe that this was happening. She sat opposite him where she could study his face. The brother she had loved as a child had turned up when all hope had been abandoned.

'You will dine with us this evening,' Albert wasn't asking a question he was giving an order. 'And stay overnight with us if you don't have to return to your ship immediately.'

'I'm on leave for a few days, but I can find lodgings nearby.'

Ellie gazed from one man to the other. They sounded quite hostile towards each other. That mustn't be so. Not with these two people she loved so much. 'Please stay, Harry.'

Her brother's stern expression softened as he looked at her. 'All right, Queenie.'

'Eleanor, go and see that a room is made ready for our guest. And we'll have afternoon tea in here.'

'Yes, Father.' Ellie hurried out of the room, anxious to deal with this as quickly as possible and return to hear what had happened to Harry over the years. No wonder they hadn't been able to find him; he was using a different name.

As soon as the door closed, Harry turned his gaze to Albert, his eyes frosty. 'Let us deal with whatever is making you angry, young man. I will not have my daughter upset by your obvious dislike of me.'

'How else do you expect me to feel?' Harry's voice was full of fury. 'You took a young child away from her family. You bought her! I'm only staying in your house because my sister asked me to. What you did was despicable.'

'You don't know what really happened.' Albert was determined to clear this up before Eleanor returned. 'You ran away and abandoned the rest of your family.'

Harry leapt to his feet, bristling with indignation. 'Watching Queenie being driven away tore me apart. I couldn't stay in that house. Mum didn't even know where she was going. All they cared about was the money.'

Speaking quietly, Albert said, 'That money kept you all out of the workhouse. Sit down and let me explain.'

As quickly as he could, Albert related the whole story. When he finished the anger had drained away from Harry.

'I didn't know. I should have stayed and tried to help.' Harry hit the arm of the chair in disgust at his action all those years ago.

'There's no point in harbouring regret.' Albert understood just how Harry was feeling at that moment. 'Your parents acted out of desperation, and I gained a much loved daughter.'

Harry's eyes were full of remorse. 'I have misjudged you, sir. I apologize.'

'Apology accepted.'

At that moment Ellie returned, happier once she sensed the hostility had vanished. A maid followed with a trolley laden with tea, bread and butter and cakes. 'The room is being made ready.'

When they were settled, Ellie said eagerly, 'Will you tell us why you are using a different name?'

'Now Mr Warrender has explained what really happened, I feel ashamed of the way I acted. I was devastated when you were taken away. I couldn't understand why.' Harry gazed at Ellie with affection. 'I did try to find you by questioning everyone at the pub Dad went to, but no one knew anything. I was so full of hatred for what they'd done that I never wanted to see or hear from them again. I was so scared about what happened to you, Queenie.'

Ellie reached out and grasped her brother's hand, the action feeling so natural to her. 'I've had a happy life.'

He nodded. 'I can see that now, and it has lifted a great weight from me.'

'Carry on with your story,' Albert urged.

'Well, I had no money or anywhere to go, so after a couple of days sleeping rough, I joined the navy to give me a roof over my head and food. I was so angry that I didn't want the name of Bonner, so I changed it. I discovered I liked the life, and over the years I've worked my way up to Petty Officer.'

'You've done well.' Albert studied the man carefully. That strain of Bonner intelligence was evident with Ted and Jack, but Harry seemed just that little bit sharper than the others.

'Thank you, sir.' Harry acknowledged the compliment. 'You've heard my story and now I would like to know what has happened to Queenie since she was brought here.'

Albert nodded and began to relate in detail about their lives over the years. Harry soon began to laugh when he learned of Ellie's bad language and tendency to fight. He listened intently, never interrupting Albert, eager to hear everything. He looked dismayed when he heard what had happened to some of his siblings.

When the story came to an end, Harry gave Ellie a wry smile. 'You didn't know what you were letting yourself in for by searching for the Bonners, did you little Queenie?'

'I couldn't have done it without my father's help.'

'No, I see that,' Harry said, turning to Albert. 'You've been kind to my sister, sir.'

'I've loved her from the moment she asked me if we eat the fish in the pond.' Albert grinned at Ellie.

Harry watched the affectionate interplay between them and gave a slight nod of satisfaction. 'She always was irresistible. You said Ted was here, sir. I would like to see him.'

'Of course.' Albert stood up and pulled the bell rope. The butler arrived at once. 'Send someone to The Orchards and ask Ted to join us here as soon as he's free. Tell him it's urgent.'

The butler left and Ellie began to ply Harry with questions about his life in the navy, and it seemed no time at all before Ted had arrived.

'I came as soon as I could, Mr Warrender. Was . . .' He stopped mid-sentence when he saw the sailor standing there. For a moment he didn't move, unable to believe his eyes. 'Harry? Harry, you bugger, where have you been?'

Ellie gave her father a watery smile as the brothers launched themselves at each other, hugging and slapping backs in joy. The talking never stopped right through dinner and into the night as they tried to catch up with everything that had happened to each other.

Thirty-Seven

The next morning Ellie took Harry in to see Nanny. The elderly woman now needed constant nursing. The doctor had declared only a week ago that he couldn't understand how she was still alive.

'Nanny, look who arrived yesterday.' She pulled her brother forward.

Nanny subjected him to a thorough scrutiny, then nodded, holding out a shaking hand. 'Ah, you would be Harry. It's about time you turned up, young man.'

'Hello Nanny.' Harry gently took hold of her hand, stooping down in front of her. 'I hear you've taken good care of our Queenie. Thank you for that.'

'She was no trouble at all.' Nanny gave a rattling chuckle. 'Took a time to stop her using bad language though.'

'I'm not surprised,' Harry said. 'She heard that kind of swearing from the moment she was born, and she was a fast learner.'

Nanny still held on to Harry's hand, leaning her head back and closing her eyes. 'I've been waiting for you to show yourself. Our little girl called for you constantly and I knew she would never be completely happy unless she found you again. Now I can go in peace.' She opened her eyes again, smiled at both of them, and promptly fell asleep.

Ellie's father had been standing in the doorway and she turned to him in alarm. 'Father?'

'I'll get someone to sit with her all the time now. We won't leave her alone, Eleanor.'

'Come, Eleanor.' Her father touched her shoulder. 'We have a lot to do today and Nanny would be upset if we didn't carry on with what has to be done.'

Nodding in agreement, Ellie walked out of the room with her father one side of her and Harry the other.

After breakfast, Albert ordered a carriage to take them to the station, collecting Ted on the way. It was time to unite Harry with the rest of his family.

Once in London, Albert ordered them a cab for the day, and another for himself. 'I'll go straight to Augusta's and warn her that you will be arriving sometime this afternoon. You can meet Maggie then, Harry. Visit Jack and Pearl first. After that you can go to Whitechapel.'

When they were on their way, Harry sat back and grimaced. 'I've got some apologizing to do to Mum and Dad.'

'Don't worry, Harry,' Ted said, 'they'll be so relieved to see you're still alive. And you're too big for them to thrash now.'

'That's true.' Harry wiped imaginary sweat from his brow. 'I've never forgotten that last hiding I got from Dad. He damned near killed me. The discipline and tough conditions of the navy were easy after that.'

Ellie could only guess at the harshness of their childhood. She had led such a privileged life. 'I think it's Hilda and Fred who owe you an apology, Harry.'

He shrugged. 'Perhaps it would be better if we forgot the whole episode and just be happy that everything has turned out well in the end?'

'By far the best thing to do,' Ellie agreed. 'I think it's time the past was put behind us.'

When they arrived at Whitechapel, Fred was walking towards the house on his way home for lunch. He stopped, and stared in amazement as two cabs disgorged their passengers. Harry's meeting with Jack and Pearl had been ecstatic, and Dave had insisted on managing the shop on his own while they all went to see Hilda and Fred. They hadn't all been able to squeeze into one cab so they had hired a second one. They were in high spirits at being reunited with Harry.

Ellie could see that Harry was apprehensive about meeting his parents, so she slipped her hand through his arm, and said, 'You're a coward, 'Arry.'

He roared with laughter as he remembered her saying exactly that to him when she'd been a tiny girl. It was enough to break the tension, and Ellie felt him relax.

Hilda had rushed out of the house and stopped dead, staring

at Harry. Her lips began to tremble as she recognized her son. 'Harry,' she gulped. 'Oh, thank God, you're alive.'

'Hello, Mum.' Harry walked towards her and laid his hands on her shoulders.

'Where've you been, Harry? I thought your dad had hurt you bad and you'd died out there somewhere all on your own.' The tears were now running down her face, but she swiped at them hastily, not used to showing her feelings.

'I managed fine, Mum.'

'What the bloody hell—' Fred had reached them. 'Harry? Where have you been? You've caused us all a lot of worry.'

'And whose fault was that?' Harry didn't move to greet his father. Then seeing that his dad was about to open his mouth and argue, Harry held up his hands. 'I'm not going to have another fight with you. That's in the past and all done with, so don't start anything, Dad.'

Fred eyed his son up and down. 'You're right. If you're ready to forget, then I'll do the same. Them was bad times, but we're through them now. You joined the navy then.'

'And real posh he looks too.' Hilda blew her nose and turned to her husband, who was still studying his strong looking son with a wary look in his eyes. 'I think you owe Harry an apology, Fred, no matter what he says about forgetting the past.'

'There's no need, Mum.' Harry held up his hands. 'I know the whole story now and I understand, but you should have told us why you sold Queenie.'

'Wouldn't have made any difference,' Fred said. 'You'd still have been mad. She was your favourite.'

'Agreed.' Harry's smile was wry. 'But if I hadn't walked out I'd never have joined the navy. It's a tough life, but it suits me.'

'Come in, all of you.' Hilda ushered her children into the house. 'I'll make a nice pot of tea and some sandwiches.'

They stayed for nearly two hours. Fred reluctantly returned to work after an hour, but left whistling happily as he walked away.

It was nearly four o'clock when they arrived at Augusta's house, and Ellie smiled proudly as she introduced her brother.

'James, send for Maggie at once,' Augusta said. 'Harry must be anxious to see his sister again.'

'Thank you, madam,' Harry said to their hostess.

Ellie was bursting with happiness. Harry was so polished in his manners and was obviously used to mixing with all classes. Already she could see why they had been so close. He only had to look at her and she could guess what he was thinking. There was a bond between them that the lost years had not diminished. How dreadful it would have been if she'd never found him again.

'You wanted me, madam?' Maggie came into the drawing room and smiled when she saw her brothers and sisters were also there. Then her gaze rested on Harry, puzzled for a brief moment. 'Harry! It's you, isn't it?'

'Hello, Maggie.' He held out his arms and she rushed to him. 'Where on earth have you been? We tried so hard to find you when you left home, but you just disappeared. Queenie's been going frantic trying to trace you.'

'I'm sorry I caused you all such a lot of worry. I've been at sea for most of the time.'

Albert watched the excited scene as the brothers and sisters all tried to speak at the same time, with Eleanor in the thick of things. It was clear that this brother had been greatly loved by all of them, and their joy at being reunited was there for all to see.

James also watched happily, unable to get a word in. Ellie winked at him, leaving her family and going to stand by him. James grabbed his chance during a lull in the chatter, and caught Harry's attention. 'Will you be returning to sea soon?'

'Not for at least six months. I'm waiting for a new ship, but she isn't ready yet.'

'That's wonderful,' Maggie said. 'Does that mean you'll be able to come to our weddings?'

'I'm sure I can arrange that. Queenie has already given me the dates.'

James placed an arm around Ellie. 'As you know, Harry, I'm the happy man who's going to marry your imp of a sister next year. I'd like you to be my best man, if that's possible?'

'Oh, James, that would be lovely.' Ellie was touched by this kind gesture. James had realized just how important it would be to her to have this brother at their wedding.

Harry shook his head. 'I don't know where I'll be once I return to sea.'

'Sir?' James turned to Albert. 'Would you give us permission to bring our wedding forward to August? It would mean a lot to us to have Harry present.'

'Please, Father!' Ellie pleaded.

After only a slight hesitation, Albert nodded. 'Very well.'

Pandemonium erupted as Ellie and James were congratulated. Harry gave Ellie a hug and whispered, 'I'll try not to cry at your wedding.'

Ellie tipped her head back and laughed with happiness. 'You're still daft, do you know that 'Arry?'

Thirty-Eight

The next day Nanny fell into a deep sleep and never woke up. Two days later she passed peacefully from their lives. Ellie and her father grieved for the lovely woman who had been such a large part of their lives, but friends and family surrounded them, and it helped them both. They knew Nanny would disapprove if they changed anything, so they threw themselves into arrangements for the weddings. Now James and Ellie's wedding had been brought forward their house wouldn't be ready in time, so they had decided to make their home temporarily in the west wing of Albert's house.

The months flew by and the weddings of Ted and Dorothy, Maggie and Stanley were lovely occasions. It seemed no time at all before Ellie was dressing for her own wedding. Harry had arrived last night and the entire Bonner family were in various places on the estate or Uncle Henry's. It was going to be a large wedding and Ellie couldn't help feeling nervous.

Augusta, Maggie and Pearl helped Ellie on with her dress, exclaiming approval at the elegant design. Ellie had been worried that it might be too ornate, but now it was finished it looked wonderful. The plain heavy satin skirt flowed from a jewelled bodice, covered in roses embroidered with tiny pearls. Her long veil was held in place by a diamond and pearl tiara. This had been her mother's and she wore it with pride. Pearl and Maggie were maids of honour and looked lovely in dresses of pale lemon.

'Absolutely perfect.' Augusta turned her head towards the door. 'Don't you agree, Albert?'

Ellie hadn't noticed her father come in and she smiled nervously at him. She knew he had wanted the wedding to be a grand affair. 'A day for you to remember,' he had told her.

'You look so beautiful. I am going to be very proud to

escort my daughter to her wedding, and I'm going to be the envy of all to be surrounded by such beautiful ladies.'

Everyone laughed at the compliment as Ellie went and stood beside her father. 'And I'm proud to be on the arm of such a handsome man.'

'That's enough compliments for the time being, don't you think?'

Augusta ushered Pearl and Maggie out of the door, and soon their carriage was leaving for the church.

Father and daughter stood quietly for a moment, remembering the two women who wouldn't be present today – Mary and Nanny – but they were in their thoughts. Albert glanced at the young woman standing beside him, and couldn't help comparing this elegant girl with the little scruff who had come to them all those years ago. He had been afraid that the search for the Bonners would take her away from him. But in actual fact, the bond between them had been strengthened. He had always wanted a large family, and now he had one, and it would get larger now with three weddings this year. The search had also brought James and Augusta into their lives, and that was indeed a great blessing. Not only had Eleanor found a fine husband – and they loved each other deeply, he had discovered over these last months – but against all his declarations that he would never marry again, he had also fallen in love. He and Augusta planned to marry in the spring of next year. He didn't believe it would come as any surprise to anyone, though.

He threaded Eleanor's arm through his. 'It's time we left for the church. We don't want to keep James waiting, do we?'

'Oh, no,' Ellie said, feeling calmer now. 'He'll be racing here to find me.'

The church was packed with family, friends and estate workers. Ellie was pleased to see Fred and Hilda were there, decked out in their finery. Harry was standing beside James, looking splendid in his uniform. When she reached them Harry winked at her and she laughed, turning to James, her eyes shining with happiness. This lovely man was her future, and in that future would be her other family. No longer forgotten, but an important part of her life, as they should be.